THE POEMS
AND FAIRY TALES
OF
OSCAR WILDE

BENNETT A. CERF · DONALD S. KLOPFER

THE MODERN LIBRARY

NEW YORK

New Modern Library Edition
1932

==========

Books by Oscar Wilde
in THE MODERN LIBRARY

THE PICTURE OF DORIAN GRAY   NO.   1
PLAYS   NO.   83
POEMS AND FAIRY TALES   NO.   84
DE PROFUNDIS   NO. 117

Manufactured in the United States of America
Bound for THE MODERN LIBRARY *by* H. Wolff

IN MEMORIAM

C. T. W.

SOMETIME TROOPER OF THE ROYAL HORSE GUARDS
OBIIT H.M. PRISON, READING, BERKSHIRE,
JULY 7, 1896

CONTENTS

	PAGE
THE BALLAD OF READING GAOL	3
Helas!	27
RAVENNA	29
ELEUTHERIA	
SONNET TO LIBERTY	43
AVE IMPERATRIX	44
TO MILTON	49
LOUIS NAPOLEON	50
SONNET	51
QUANTUM MUTATA	52
LIBERTATIS SACRA FAMES	53
THEORETIKOS	54
THE GARDEN OF EROS	57
ROSA MYSTICA	
REQUIESCAT	69
SONNET ON APPROACHING ITALY	70
SAN MINIATO	71
AVE MARIA GRATIA PLENA	72
ITALIA	73
SONNET	74
ROME UNVISITED	75
URBS SACRA ÆTERNA	78
SONNET	79
EASTER DAY	80
E TENEBRIS	81
VITA NUOVA	82
MADONNA MIA	83
THE NEW HELEN	84

PAGE

THE BURDEN OF ITYS 91
WIND FLOWERS
    IMPRESSION DU MATIN 107
    MAGDALEN WALKS 108
    ATHANASIA 110
    SERENADE 113
    ENDYMION 115
    LA BELLA DONNA DELLA MIA MENTE 117
    CHANSON 119
CHARMIDES 123
FLOWERS OF GOLD
    IMPRESSIONS 151
    THE GRAVE OF KEATS 153
    THEOCRITUS 154
    IN THE GOLD ROOM 155
    BALLADE DE MARGUERITE 156
    THE DOLE OF THE KING'S DAUGHTER 159
    AMOR INTELLECTUALIS 161
    SANTA DECCA 162
    A VISION 163
    IMPRESSION DE VOYAGE 164
    THE GRAVE OF SHELLEY 165
    BY THE ARNO 166
IMPRESSIONS DU THEATRE
    FABIEN DEI FRANCHI 169
    PHEDRE 170
    PORTIA 171
    QUEEN HENRIETTA MARIA 172
    CAMMA 173
PANTHEA 177
THE FOURTH MOVEMENT
    IMPRESSION 187
    AT VERONA 188
    APOLOGIA 189
    QUIA MULTUM AMAVI 191
    SILENTIUM AMORIS 192

CONTENTS   vii

                                            PAGE
HER VOICE 193
MY VOICE 195
TÆDIUM VITÆ 196
HUMANITAD 199
FLOWER OF LOVE
ΓΛΥΚΥΠΙΚΡΟΣ ΕΡΩΣ 217
UNCOLLECTED POEMS
    FROM SPRING DAYS TO WINTER 221
    Αἴλινον, αἴλινον εἰπέ, τὸ δ' εὖ νικάτω 222
    THE TRUE KNOWLEDGE 223
    LOTUS LEAVES 224
    WASTED DAYS 227
    IMPRESSIONS 228
    UNDER THE BALCONY 230
    THE HARLOT'S HOUSE 232
    LE JARDIN DES TUILERIES 234
    ON THE SALE BY AUCTION OF KEATS' LOVE LETTERS 235
    THE NEW REMORSE 236
    FANTAISIES DECORATIVES 237
    CANZONET 240
    SYMPHONY IN YELLOW 242
    IN THE FOREST 243
    TO MY WIFE 244
    WITH A COPY OF A "HOUSE OF POMEGRANATES" . . 245
    TO L. L. 246
TRANSLATIONS
    CHORUS OF CLOUD MAIDENS 251
    ΑΝΤΙΣΤΡΟΦΗ 252
    ΘΡΗΝΩΔΙΑ 253
    ΑΝΤΙΣΤΡΟΦΗ 254
    ΣΤΡΟΦΗ Β 255
    ΑΝΤΙΣΤΡΟΦΗ Β 256
    A FRAGMENT FROM THE AGAMEMNON OF ÆSCHYLOS 257
    THE ARTIST'S DREAM 260
THE SPHINX 267

CONTENTS

FAIRY TALES   PAGE

THE YOUNG KING   3
THE BIRTHDAY OF THE INFANTA   24
THE FISHERMAN AND HIS SOUL   53
THE STAR-CHILD   106
THE HAPPY PRINCE   130
THE NIGHTINGALE AND THE ROSE 144
THE SELFISH GIANT   154
THE DEVOTED FRIEND   161
THE REMARKABLE ROCKET   179

POEMS IN PROSE

THE ARTIST   199
THE DOER OF GOOD   200
THE DISCIPLE   202
THE MASTER   203
THE HOUSE OF JUDGMENT   204
THE TEACHER OF WISDOM   207

THE BALLAD OF READING GAOL

THE BALLAD OF READING GAOL

I

He did not wear his scarlet coat,
　For blood and wine are red,
And blood and wine were on his hands
　When they found him with the dead,
The poor dead woman whom he loved,
　And murdered in her bed.

He walked amongst the Trial Men
　In a suit of shabby grey;
A cricket cap was on his head,
　And his step seemed light and gay;
But I never saw a man who looked
　So wistfully at the day.

I never saw a man who looked
　With such a wistful eye
Upon that little tent of blue
　Which prisoners call the sky,
And at every drifting cloud that went
　With sails of silver by.

I walked, with other souls in pain,
　Within another ring,
And was wondering if the man had done
　A great or little thing,
When a voice behind me whispered low,
　"That fellow's got to swing."

3

Dear Christ! the very prison walls
   Suddenly seemed to reel,
And the sky above my head became
   Like a casque of scorching steel;
And, though I was a soul in pain,
   My pain I could not feel.

I only knew what hunted thought
   Quickened his step, and why
He looked upon the garish day
   With such a wistful eye;
The man had killed the thing he loved,
   And so he had to die.

*   *   *   *   *   *

Yet each man kills the thing he loves,
   By each let this be heard,
Some do it with a bitter look,
   Some with a flattering word,
The coward does it with a kiss,
   The brave man with a sword!

Some kill their love when they are young,
   And some when they are old;
Some strangle with the hands of Lust,
   Some with the hands of Gold:
The kindest use a knife, because
   The dead so soon grow cold.

Some love too little, some too long,
   Some sell, and others buy;
Some do the deed with many tears,
   And some without a sigh:
For each man kills the thing he loves,
   Yet each man does not die.

He does not die a death of shame
　　On a day of dark disgrace,
Nor have a noose about his neck,
　　Nor a cloth upon his face,
Nor drop feet foremost through the floor
　　Into an empty space.

　　＊　　＊　　＊　　＊　　＊　　＊

He does not sit with silent men
　　Who watch him night and day;
Who watch him when he tries to weep,
　　And when he tries to pray;
Who watch him lest himself should rob
　　The prison of its prey.

He does not wake at dawn to see
　　Dread figures throng his room,
The shivering Chaplain robed in white,
　　The Sheriff stern with gloom,
And the Governor all in shiny black,
　　With the yellow face of Doom.

He does not rise in piteous haste
　　To put on convict-clothes,
While some coarse-mouthed Doctor gloats, and notes
　　Each new and nerve-twitched pose,
Fingering a watch whose little ticks
　　Are like horrible hammer-blows.

He does not know that sickening thirst
　　That sands one's throat, before
The hangman with his gardener's gloves
　　Slips through the padded door,
And binds one with three leathern thongs,
　　That the throat may thirst no more.

He does not bend his head to hear
    The Burial Office read,
Nor, while the terror of his soul
    Tells him he is not dead,
Cross his own coffin, as he moves
    Into the hideous shed.

He does not stare upon the air
    Through a little roof of glass:
He does not pray with lips of clay
    For his agony to pass;
Nor feel upon his shuddering cheek
    The kiss of Caiaphas.

II

Six weeks our guardsman walked the yard,
    In the suit of shabby grey:
His cricket cap was on his head,
    And his step seemed light and gay,
But I never saw a man who looked
    So wistfully at the day.

I never saw a man who looked
    With such a wistful eye
Upon that little tent of blue
    Which prisoners call the sky,
And at every wandering cloud that trailed
    Its ravelled fleeces by.

He did not wring his hands, as do
    Those witless men who dare
To try to rear the changeling Hope
    In the cave of black Despair:
He only looked upon the sun,
    And drank the morning air.

He did not wring his hands nor weep,
  Nor did he peek or pine,
But he drank the air as though it held
  Some healthful anodyne;
With open mouth he drank the sun
  As though it had been wine!

And I and all the souls in pain,
  Who tramped the other ring,
Forgot if we ourselves had done
  A great or little thing,
And watched with gaze of dull amaze
  The man who had to swing.

And strange it was to see him pass
  With a step so light and gay,
And strange it was to see him look
  So wistfully at the day,
And strange it was to think that he
  Had such a debt to pay.

 * * * * * *

For oak and elm have pleasant leaves
  That in the spring-time shoot:
But grim to see is the gallows-tree,
  With its adder-bitten root,
And, green or dry, a man must die
  Before it bears its fruit!

The loftiest place is that seat of grace
  For which all worldlings try:
But who would stand in hempen band
  Upon a scaffold high,
And through a murderer's collar take
  His last look at the sky?

It is sweet to dance to violins
　　When Love and Life are fair:
To dance to flutes, to dance to lutes
　　Is delicate and rare:
But it is not sweet with nimble feet
　　To dance upon the air!

So with curious eyes and sick surmise
　　We watched him day by day,
And wondered if each one of us
　　Would end the self-same way,
For none can tell to what red Hell
　　His sightless soul may stray.

At last the dead man walked no more
　　Amongst the Trial Men,
And I knew that he was standing up
　　In the black dock's dreadful pen,
And that never would I see his face
　　In God's sweet world again.

Like two doomed ships that pass in storm
　　We had crossed each other's way:
But we made no sign, we said no word,
　　We had no word to say;
For we did not meet in the holy night,
　　But in the shameful day.

A prison wall was round us both,
　　Two outcast men we were:
The world had thrust us from its heart,
　　And God from out His care:
And the iron gin that waits for Sin
　　Had caught us in its snare.

III

In Debtor's Yard the stones are hard,
  And the dripping wall is high,
So it was there he took the air
  Beneath the leaden sky,
And by each side a Warder walked,
  For fear the man might die.

Or else he sat with those who watched
  His anguish night and day;
Who watched him when he rose to weep,
  And when he crouched to pray;
Who watched him lest himself should rob
  Their scaffold of its prey.

The Governor was strong upon
  The Regulations Act:
The Doctor said that Death was but
  A scientific fact:
And twice a day the Chaplain called,
  And left a little tract.

And twice a day he smoked his pipe,
  And drank his quart of beer:
His soul was resolute, and held
  No hiding-place for fear;
He often said that he was glad
  The hangman's hands were near.

But why he said so strange a thing
  No warder dared to ask:
For he to whom a watcher's doom
  Is given as his task,
Must set a lock upon his lips,
  And make his face a mask.

Or else he might be moved, and try
    To comfort or console:
And what should Human Pity do
    Pent up in Murderers' Hole?
What word of grace in such a place
    Could help a brother's soul?

*   *   *   *   *   *

With slouch and swing around the ring
    We trod the Fools' Parade!
We did not care: we knew we were
    The Devil's Own Brigade:
And shaven head and feet of lead
    Make a merry masquerade.

We tore the tarry rope to shreds
    With blunt and bleeding nails;
We rubbed the doors, and scrubbed the floors,
    And cleaned the shining rails:
And, rank by rank, we soaped the plank,
    And clattered with the pails.

We sewed the sacks, we broke the stones,
    We turned the dusty drill:
We banged the tins, and bawled the hymns,
    And sweated on the mill:
But in the heart of every man
    Terror was lying still.

So still it lay that every day
    Crawled like a weed-clogged wave:
And we forgot the bitter lot
    That waits for fool and knave,
Till once, as we trampled in from work,
    We passed an open grave.

With yawning mouth the yellow hole
  Gaped for a living thing;
The very mud cried out for blood
  To the thirsty asphalte ring:
And we knew that ere one dawn grew fair
  Some prisoner had to swing.

Right in we went, with soul intent
  On Death and Dread and Doom:
The hangman, with his little bag,
  Went shuffling through the gloom:
And each man trembled as he crept
  Into his numbered tomb.

*   *   *   *   *   *

That night the empty corridors
  Were full of forms of Fear,
And up and down the iron town
  Stole feet we could not hear,
And through the bars that hide the stars
  White faces seemed to peer.

He lay as one who lies and dreams
  In a pleasant meadow-land,
The watchers watched him as he slept,
  And could not understand
How one could sleep so sweet a sleep
  With a hangman close at hand

But there is no sleep when men must weep
  Who never yet have wept:
So we—the fool, the fraud, the knave—
  That endless vigil kept,
And through each brain on hands of pain
  Another's terror crept.

Alas! it is a fearful thing
  To feel another's guilt!
For, right within, the sword of Sin
  Pierced to its poisoned hilt,
And as molten lead were the tears we shed
  For the blood we had not spilt.

The Warders with their shoes of felt
  Crept by each padlocked door,
And peeped and saw, with eyes of awe,
  Grey figures on the floor,
And wondered why men knelt to pray
  Who never prayed before.

All through the night we knelt and prayed,
  Mad mourners of a corse!
The troubled plumes of midnight were
  The plumes upon a hearse:
And bitter wine upon a sponge
  Was the savour of Remorse.

*   *   *   *   *   *

The grey cock crew, the red cock crew,
  But never came the day:
And crooked shapes of Terror crouched,
  In the corners where we lay:
And each evil sprite that walks by night
  Before us seemed to play.

They glided past, they glided fast,
  Like travellers through a mist:
They mocked the moon in a rigadoon
  Of delicate turn and twist,
And with formal pace and loathsome grace
  The phantoms kept their tryst.

With mop and mow, we saw them go,
    Slim shadows hand in hand:
About, about, in ghostly rout
    They trod a saraband:
And the damned grotesques made arabesques,
    Like the wind upon the sand!

With the pirouettes of marionettes,
    They tripped on pointed tread:
But with flutes of Fear they filled the ear,
    As their grisly masque they led,
And loud they sang, and long they sang,
    For they sang to wake the dead.

"*Oho!*" they cried, "*The world is wide,*
    But fettered limbs go lame!
And once, or twice, to throw the dice
    Is a gentlemanly game,
But he does not win who plays with Sin
    In the secret House of Shame."

No things of air these antics were,
    That frolicked with such glee:
To men whose lives were held in gyves,
    And whose feet might not go free,
Ah! wounds of Christ! they were living things,
    Most terrible to see.

Around, around, they waltzed and wound;
    Some wheeled in smirking pairs;
With the mincing step of a demirep
    Some sidled up the stairs:
And with subtle sneer, and fawning leer,
    Each helped us at our prayers.

The morning wind began to moan,
  But still the night went on:
Through its giant loom the web of gloom
  Crept till each thread was spun:
And, as we prayed, we grew afraid
  Of the Justice of the Sun.

The moaning wind went wandering round
  The weeping prison-wall:
Till like a wheel of turning steel
  We felt the minutes crawl:
O moaning wind! what had we done
  To have such a seneschal?

At last I saw the shadowed bars,
  Like a lattice wrought in lead,
Move right across the whitewashed wall
  That faced my three-plank bed,
And I knew that somewhere in the world
  God's dreadful dawn was red.

At six o'clock we cleaned our cells,
  At seven all was still,
But the sough and swing of a mighty wing
  The prison seemed to fill,
For the Lord of Death with icy breath
  Had entered in to kill.

He did not pass in purple pomp,
  Nor ride a moon-white steed.
Three yards of cord and a sliding board
  Are all the gallows' need:
So with the rope of shame the Herald came
  To do the secret deed.

We were as men who through a fen
   Of filthy darkness grope:
We did not dare to breathe a prayer,
   Or to give our anguish scope:
Something was dead in each of us,
   And what was dead was Hope.

For Man's grim Justice goes its way,
   And will not swerve aside:
It slays the weak, it slays the strong,
   It has a deadly stride:
With iron heel it slays the strong,
   The monstrous parricide!

We waited for the stroke of eight:
   Each tongue was thick with thirst:
For the stroke of eight is the stroke of Fate
   That makes a man accursed,
And Fate will use a running noose
   For the best man and the worst.

We had no other thing to do,
   Save to wait for the sign to come:
So, like things of stone in a valley lone,
   Quiet we sat and dumb:
But each man's heart beat thick and quick,
   Like a madman on a drum!

With sudden shock the prison-clock
   Smote on the shivering air,
And from all the gaol rose up a wail
   Of impotent despair,
Like the sound that frightened marshes hear
   From some leper in his lair.

And as one sees most fearful things
    In the crystal of a dream,
We saw the greasy hempen rope
    Hooked to the blackened beam,
And heard the prayer the hangman's snare
    Strangled into a scream.

And all the woe that moved him so
    That he gave that bitter cry,
And the wild regrets, and the bloody sweats,
    None knew so well as I:
For he who lives more lives than one
    More deaths than one must die.

IV

There is no chapel on the day
    On which they hang a man:
The Chaplain's heart is far too sick,
    Or his face is far too wan,
Or there is that written in his eyes
    Which none should look upon.

So they kept us close till nigh on noon,
    And then they rang the bell,
And the Warders with their jingling keys
    Opened each listening cell,
And down the iron stair we tramped,
    Each from his separate Hell.

Out into God's sweet air we went,
    But not in wonted way,
For this man's face was white with fear,
    And that man's face was grey,
And I never saw sad men who looked
    So wistfully at the day.

I never saw sad men who looked
  With such a wistful eye
Upon that little tent of blue
  We prisoners called the sky,
And at every careless cloud that passed
  In happy freedom by.

But there were those amongst us all
  Who walked with downcast head,
And knew that, had each got his due,
  They should have died instead:
He had but killed a thing that lived,
  Whilst they had killed the dead.

For he who sins a second time
  Wakes a dead soul to pain,
And draws it from its spotted shroud,
  And makes it bleed again,
And makes it bleed great gouts of blood,
  And makes it bleed in vain!

  *   *   *   *   *   *

Like ape or clown, in monstrous garb
  With crooked arrows starred,
Silently we went round and round,
  The slippery asphalte yard;
Silently we went round and round
  And no man spoke a word.

Silently we went round and round,
  And through each hollow mind
The Memory of dreadful things
  Rushed like a dreadful wind,
And Horror stalked before each man,
  And Terror crept behind.

The Warders strutted up and down,
   And kept their herd of brutes,
Their uniforms were spick and span,
   And they wore their Sunday suits,
But we knew the work they had been at,
   By the quicklime on their boots.

For where a grave had opened wide,
   There was no grave at all:
Only a stretch of mud and sand
   By the hideous prison-wall,
And a little heap of burning lime,
   That the man should have his pall.

For he has a pall, this wretched man,
   Such as few men can claim:
Deep down below a prison-yard,
   Naked for greater shame,
He lies, with fetters on each foot,
   Wrapt in a sheet of flame!

And all the while the burning lime
   Eats flesh and bone away,
It eats the brittle bone by night,
   And the soft flesh by day,
It eats the flesh and bone by turns,
   But it eats the heart alway.

*   *   *   *   *   *

For three long years they will not sow
   Or root or seedling there:
For three long years the unblessed spot
   Will sterile be and bare,
And look upon the wondering sky
   With unreproachful stare.

They think a murderer's heart would taint
    Each simple seed they sow.
It is not true! God's kindly earth
    Is kindlier than men know,
And the red rose would but blow more red,
    The white rose whiter blow.

Out of his mouth a red, red rose!
    Out of his heart a white!
For who can say by what strange way,
    Christ brings His will to light,
Since the barren staff the pilgrim bore
    Bloomed in the great Pope's sight?

But neither milk-white rose nor red
    May bloom in prison air;
The shard, the pebble, and the flint,
    Are what they give us there:
For flowers have been known to heal
    A common man's despair.

So never will wine-red rose or white,
    Petal by petal, fall
On that stretch of mud and sand that lies
    By the hideous prison-wall,
To tell the men who tramp the yard
    That God's Son died for all.

*   *   *   *   *   *

Yet though the hideous prison-wall
    Still hems him round and round,
And a spirit may not walk by night
    That is with fetters bound,
And a spirit may but weep that lies
    In such unholy ground,

He is at peace—this wretched man—
    At peace, or will be soon:
There is no thing to make him mad,
    Nor does Terror walk at noon,
For the lampless Earth in which he lies
    Has neither Sun nor Moon.

They hanged him as a beast is hanged:
    They did not even toll
A requiem that might have brought
    Rest to his startled soul,
But hurriedly they took him out,
    And hid him in a hole.

They stripped him of his canvas clothes,
    And gave him to the flies:
They mocked the swollen purple throat,
    And the stark and staring eyes:
And with laughter loud they heaped the shroud
    In which their convict lies.

The Chaplain would not kneel to pray
    By his dishonoured grave:
Nor mark it with that blessed Cross
    That Christ for sinners gave,
Because the man was one of those
    Whom Christ came down to save.

Yet all is well; he has but passed
    To life's appointed bourne:
And alien tears will fill for him
    Pity's long-broken urn,
For his mourners will be outcast men,
    And outcasts always mourn.

V

I know not whether Laws be right,
  Or whether Laws be wrong;
All that we know who lie in gaol
  Is that the wall is strong;
And that each day is like a year,
  A year whose days are long.

But this I know; that every Law
  That men have made for Man,
Since first Man took his brother's life,
  And the sad world began,
But straws the wheat and saves the chaff
  With a most evil fan.

This too I know—and wise it were
  If each could know the same—
That every prison that men build
  Is built with bricks of shame,
And bound with bars lest Christ should see
  How men their brothers maim.

With bars they blur the gracious moon,
  And blind the goodly sun:
And they do well to hide their Hell,
  For in it things are done
That Son of God nor Son of Man
  Ever should look upon!

*   *   *   *   *   *

The vilest deeds like poison weeds,
  Bloom well in prison-air;

It is only what is good in Man
   That wastes and withers there:
Pale Anguish keeps the heavy gate,
   And the Warder is Despair.

For they starve the little frightened child
   Till it weeps both night and day:
And they scourge the weak, and flog the fool,
   And gibe the old and grey,
And some grow mad, and all grow bad,
   And none a word may say.

Each narrow cell in which we dwell
   Is a foul and dark latrine,
And the fetid breath of living Death
   Chokes up each grated screen,
And all, but Lust, is turned to dust
   In Humanity's machine,

The brackish water that we drink
   Creeps with a loathsome slime,
And the bitter bread they weigh in scales
   Is full of chalk and lime,
And Sleep will not lie down, but walks
   Wild-eyed, and cries to Time.

＊   ＊   ＊   ＊   ＊   ＊

But though lean Hunger and green Thirst
   Like asp with adder fight,
We have little care of prison fare,
   For what chills and kills outright
Is that every stone one lifts by day
   Becomes one's heart by night.

With midnight always in one's heart,
  And twilight in one's cell,
We turn the crank, or tear the rope,
  Each in his separate Hell,
And the silence is more awful far
  Than the sound of a brazen bell.

And never a human voice comes near
  To speak a gentle word:
And the eye that watches through the door
  Is pitiless and hard:
And by all forgot, we rot and rot,
  With soul and body marred.

And thus we rust Life's iron chain
  Degraded and alone:
And some men curse, and some men weep,
  And some men make no moan:
But God's eternal Laws are kind
  And break the heart of stone.

*　　*　　*　　*　　*　　*

And every human heart that breaks,
  In prison-cell or yard,
Is as that broken box that gave
  Its treasure to the Lord,
And filled the unclean leper's house
  With the scent of costliest nard.

Ah! happy they whose hearts can break
  And peace of pardon win!
How else may man make straight his plan
  And cleanse his soul from Sin?
How else but through a broken heart
  May Lord Christ enter in?

And he of the swollen purple throat,
    And the stark and staring eyes,
Waits for the holy hands that took
    The Thief to Paradise;
And a broken and a contrite heart
    The Lord will not despise.

The man in red who reads the Law
    Gave him three weeks of life,
Three little weeks in which to heal
    His soul of his soul's strife,
And cleanse from every blot of blood
    The hand that held the knife.

And with tears of blood he cleansed the hand,
    The hand that held the steel:
For only blood can wipe out blood,
    And only tears can heal:
And the crimson stain that was of Cain
    Became Christ's snow-white seal.

VI

In Reading gaol by Reading town
    There is a pit of shame,
And in it lies a wretched man
    Eaten by teeth of flame,
In a burning winding-sheet he lies,
    And his grave has got no name.

And there, till Christ call forth the dead,
    In silence let him lie:
No need to waste the foolish tear,
    Or heave the windy sigh:
The man had killed the thing he loved,
    And so he had to die.

And all men kill the thing they love,
    By all let this be heard,
Some do it with a bitter look,
    Some with a flattering word,
The coward does it with a kiss,
    The brave man with a sword!

HELAS!

To drift with every passion till my soul
Is a stringed lute on which all winds can play,
Is it for this that I have given away
Mine ancient wisdom, and austere control?
Methinks my life is a twice-written scroll
Scrawled over on some boyish holiday
With idle songs for pipe and virelay,
Which do but mar the secret of the whole.
Surely there was a time I might have trod
The sunlit heights, and from life's dissonance
Struck one clear chord to reach the ears of God:
Is that time dead? lo! with a little rod
I did but touch the honey of romance—
And must I lose a soul's inheritance?

RAVENNA

I

A YEAR ago I breathed the Italian air,—
And yet, methinks this northern Spring is fair,—
These fields made golden with the flower of March,
The throstle singing on the feathered larch,
The cawing rooks, the wood-doves fluttering by.
The little clouds that race across the sky;
And fair the violet's gentle drooping head,
The primrose, pale for love uncomforted,
The rose that burgeons on the climbing briar,
The crocus-bed, (that seems a moon of fire
Round-girdled with a purple marriage-ring);
And all the flowers of our English Spring,
Fond snowdrops, and the bright-starred daffodil.
Up starts the lark beside the murmuring mill,
And breaks the gossamer-threads of early dew;
And down the river, like a flame of blue,
Keen as an arrow flies the water-king,
While the brown linnets in the greenwood sing.

A year ago!—it seems a little time
Since last I saw that lordly southern clime,
Where flower and fruit to purple radiance blow,
And like bright lamps the fabled apples glow.
Full Spring it was—and by rich flowering vines,
Dark olive-groves and noble forest-pines,

I rode at will; the moist glad air was sweet,
The white road rang beneath my horse's feet,
And musing on Ravenna's ancient name,
I watched the day till, marked with wounds of flame,
The turquoise sky to burnished gold was turned.

O how my heart with boyish passion burned,
When far away across the sedge and mere
I saw that Holy City rising clear,
Crowned with her crown of towers!—On and on
I galloped, racing with the setting sun,
And ere the crimson after-glow was passed,
I stood within Ravenna's walls at last!

II

How strangely still! no sound of life or joy
Startles the air; no laughing shepherd-boy
Pipes on his reed, nor ever through the day
Comes the glad sound of children at their play:
O sad, and sweet, and silent! surely here
A man might dwell apart from troublous fear,
Watching the tide of seasons as they flow
From amorous Spring to Winter's rain and snow,
And have no thought of sorrow;—here, indeed,
Are Lethe's waters, and that fatal weed
Which makes a man forget his fatherland.

Ay! amid lotus-meadows dost thou stand,
Like Proserpine, with poppy-laden head,
Guarding the holy ashes of the dead.
For though thy brood of warrior sons hath ceased,
Thy noble dead are with thee!—they at least

Are faithful to thine honour:—guard them well,
O childless city! for a mighty spell,
To wake men's hearts to dreams of things sublime,
Are the lone tombs where rest the Great of Time.

III

Yon lonely pillar, rising on the plain,
Marks where the bravest knight of France was slain,—
The Prince of chivalry, the Lord of war,
Gaston de Foix: for some untimely star
Led him against thy city, and he fell,
As falls some forest-lion fighting well.
Taken from life while life and love were new,
He lies beneath God's seamless veil of blue;
Tall lance-like reeds wave sadly o'er his head,
And oleanders bloom to deeper red,
Where his bright youth flowed crimson on the ground.

Look farther north unto that broken mound,—
There, prisoned now within a lordly tomb
Raised by a daughter's hand, in lonely gloom,
Huge-limbed Theodoric, the Gothic king,
Sleeps after all his weary conquering.
Time has not spared his ruin,—wind and rain
Have broken down his stronghold; and again
We see that Death is mighty lord of all,
And king and clown to ashen dust must fall.

Mighty indeed *their* glory! yet to me
Barbaric king, or knight of chivalry,
Or the great queen herself, were poor and vain,
Beside the grave where Dante rests from pain.

His gilded shrine lies open to the air;
And cunning sculptor's hands have carven there
The calm white brow, as calm as earliest morn,
The eyes that flashed with passionate love and scorn,
The lips that sang of Heaven and of Hell,
The almond-face which Giotto drew so well,
The weary face of Dante;—to this day,
Here in his place of resting, far away
From Arno's yellow waters, rushing down
Through the wide bridges of that fairy town,
Where the tall tower of Giotto seems to rise
A marble lily under sapphire skies!
Alas! my Dante! thou hast known the pain
Of meaner lives,—the exile's galling chain,
How steep the stairs within kings' houses are,
And all the petty miseries which mar
Man's nobler nature with the sense of wrong.
Yet this dull world is grateful for thy song;
Our nations do thee homage—even she,
That cruel queen of vine-clad Tuscany,
Who bound with crown of thorns thy living brow,
Hath decked thine empty tomb with laurels now,
And begs in vain the ashes of her son.

O mightiest exile! all thy grief is done:
Thy soul walks now beside thy Beatrice;
Ravenna guards thine ashes: sleep in peace.

IV

How lone this palace is; how grey the walls!
No minstrel now wakes echoes in these halls.
The broken chain lies rusting on the door,
And noisome weeds have split the marble floor:

Here lurks the snake, and here the lizards run
By the stone lions blinking in the sun.
Byron dwelt here in love and revelry
For two long years—a second Anthony,
Who of the world another Actium made!
Yet suffered not his royal soul to fade,
Or lyre to break, or lance to grow less keen,
'Neath any wiles of an Egyptian queen.
For from the East there came a mighty cry,
And Greece stood up to fight for Liberty,
And called him from Ravenna: never knight
Rode forth more nobly to wild scenes of fight!
None fell more bravely on ensanguined field,
Borne like a Spartan back upon his shield!
O Hellas! Hellas! in thine hour of pride,
Thy day of might, remember him who died
To wrest from off thy limbs the trammelling chain;
O Salamis! O lone Platæan plain!
O tossing waves of wild Eubœan sea!
O wind-swept heights of lone Thermopylæ!
He loved you well—ay, not alone in word,
Who freely gave to thee his lyre and sword,
Like Æschylos at well-fought Marathon:

And England, too, shall glory in her son,
Her warrior-poet, first in song and fight.
No longer now shall Slander's venomed spite
Crawl like a snake across his perfect name,
Or mar the lordly scutcheon of his fame.

For as the olive-garland of the race,
Which lights with joy each eager runner's face,

As the red cross which saveth men in war,
As a flame-bearded beacon seen from far
By mariners upon a storm-tossed sea,—
Such was his love for Greece and Liberty!

Byron, thy crowns are ever fresh and green:
Red leaves of rose from Sapphic Pitylene
Shall bind thy brows; the myrtle blooms for thee,
In hidden glades by lonely Castaly;
The laurels wait thy coming: all are thine,
And round thy head one perfect wreath will twine:

V

The pine-tops rocked before the evening breeze
With the hoarse murmur of the wintry seas,
And the tall stems were streaked with amber bright;—
I wandered through the wood in wild delight,
Some startled bird, with fluttering wings and fleet,
Made snow of all the blossoms; at my feet,
Like silver crowns, the pale narcissi lay,
And small birds sang on every twining spray.
O waving trees, O forest liberty!
Within your haunts at least a man is free,
And half forgets the weary world of strife:
The blood flows hotter, and a sense of life
Wakes i' the quickening veins, while once again
The woods are filled with gods we fancied slain.
Long time I watched, and surely hoped to see
Some goat-foot Pan make merry minstrelsy
Amid the reeds! some startled Dryad-maid
In girlish flight! or lurking in the glade,
The soft brown limbs, the wanton treacherous face
Of woodland god! Queen Dian in the chase,

White-limbed and terrible, with look of pride,
And leash of boar-hounds leaping at her side!
Or Hylas mirrored in the perfect stream.

O idle heart! O fond Hellenic dream!
Ere long, with melancholy rise and swell,
The evening chimes, the convent's vesper-bell,
Struck on mine ears amid the amorous flowers.
Alas! alas! these sweet and honied hours
Had whelmed my heart like some encroaching sea,
And drowned all thoughts of black Gethsemane.

VI

O lone Ravenna! many a tale is told
Of thy great glories in the days of old;
Two thousand years have passed since thou didst see
Cæsar ride forth to royal victory.
Mighty thy name when Rome's lean eagles flew
From Britain's isles to far Euphrates blue;
And of the peoples thou wast noble queen,
Till in thy streets the Goth and Hun were seen.
Discrowned by man, deserted by the sea,
Thou sleepest, rocked in lonely misery!
No longer now upon thy swelling tide,
Pine-forest-like, thy myriad galleys ride!
For where the brass-beaked ships were wont to float,
The weary shepherd pipes his mournful note;
And the white sheep are free to come and go
Where Adria's purple waters used to flow.

O fair! O sad! O Queen uncomforted!
In ruined loveliness thou liest dead,
Alone of all thy sisters; for at last
Italia's royal warrior hath passed

Rome's lordliest entrance, and hath worn his crown
In the high temples of the Eternal Town!
The Palatine hath welcomed back her king,
And with his name the seven mountains ring!

And Naples hath outlived her dream of pain,
And mocks her tyrant! Venice lives again,
New risen from the waters! and the cry
Of Light and Truth, of Love and Liberty,
Is heard in lordly Genoa, and where
The marble spires of Milan wound the air,
Rings from the Alps to the Sicilian shore,
And Dante's dream is now a dream no more.

But thou, Ravenna, better loved than all,
Thy ruined palaces are but a pall
That hides thy fallen greatness! and thy name
Burns like a grey and flickering candle-flame,
Beneath the noonday splendour of the sun
Of new Italia! for the night is done,
The night of dark oppression, and the day
Hath dawned in passionate splendour: far away
The Austrian hounds are hunted from the land,
Beyond those ice-crowned citadels which stand
Girdling the plain of royal Lombardy,
From the far West unto the Eastern sea.

I know, indeed, that sons of thine have died
In Lissa's waters, by the mountain-side
Of Aspromonte, on Novara's plain,—
Nor have thy children died for thee in vain:
And yet, methinks, thou hast not drunk this wine
From grapes new-crushed of Liberty divine,

Thou hast not followed that immortal Star
Which leads the people forth to deeds of war.
Weary of life, thou liest in silent sleep,
As one who marks the lengthening shadows creep,
Careless of all the hurrying hours that run,
Mourning some day of glory, for the sun
Of Freedom hath not shewn to thee his face,
And thou hast caught no flambeau in the race.

  Yet wake not from thy slumbers,—rest thee well,
Amidst thy fields of amber asphodel,
Thy lily-sprinkled meadows,—rest thee there,
To mock all human greatness: who would dare
To vent the paltry sorrows of his life
Before thy ruins, or to praise the strife
Of kings' ambition, and the barren pride
Of warring nations! wert not thou the Bride
Of the wild Lord of Adria's stormy sea!
The Queen of double Empires! and to thee
Were not the nations given as thy prey!
And now—thy gates lie open night and day,
The grass grows green on every tower and hall,
The ghastly fig hath cleft thy bastioned wall;
And where thy mailèd warriors stood at rest
The midnight owl hath made her secret nest.
O fallen! fallen! from thy high estate,
O city trammelled in the toils of Fate,
Doth nought remain of all thy glorious days,
But a dull shield, a crown of withered bays!

  Yet who beneath this night of wars and fears,
From tranquil tower can watch the coming years;
Who can foretell what joys the day shall bring,
Or why before the dawn the linnets sing?

Thou, even thou, mayst wake, as wakes the rose
To crimson splendour from its grave of snows;
As the rich corn-fields rise to red and gold
From these brown lands, now stiff with Winter's cold;
As from the storm-rack comes a perfect star!

O much-loved city! I have wandered far
From the wave-circled islands of my home,
Have seen the gloomy mystery of the Dome
Rise slowly from the drear Campagna's way,
Clothed in the royal purple of the day:
I from the city of the violet crown
Have watched the sun by Corinth's hill go down,
And marked the "myriad laughter" of the sea
From starlit hills of flower-starred Arcady;
Yet back to thee returns my perfect love,
As to its forest-nest the evening dove.

O poet's city; one who scarce has seen
Some twenty summers cast their doublets green,
For Autumn's livery, would seek in vain
To wake his lyre to sing a louder strain,
Or tell thy days of glory;—poor indeed
Is the low murmur of the shepherd's reed,
Where the loud clarion's blast should shake the sky,
And flame across the heavens! and to try
Such lofty themes were folly: yet I know
That never felt my heart a nobler glow
Than when I woke the silence of thy street
With clamorous trampling of my horse's feet,
And saw the city which now I try to sing,
After long days of weary travelling.

VII

Adieu, Ravenna; but a year ago,
I stood and watched the crimson sunset glow
From the lone chapel on thy marshy plain:
The sky was as a shield that caught the stain
Of blood and battle from the dying sun,
And in the west the circling clouds had spun
A royal robe, which some great God might wear,
While into ocean-seas of purple air
Sank the gold galley of the Lord of Light.

Yet here the gentle stillness of the night
Brings back the swelling tide of memory,
And wakes again my passionate love for thee:
Now is the Spring of Love, yet soon will come
On meadow and tree the Summer's lordly bloom;
And soon the grass with brighter flowers will blow,
And send up lilies for some boy to mow.
Then before long the Summer's conqueror,
Rich Autumn-time, the season's usurer,
Will lend his hoarded gold to all the trees,
And see it scattered by the spendthrift breeze;
And after that the Winter cold and drear.
So runs the perfect cycle of the year.
And so from youth to manhood do we go,
And fall to weary days and locks of snow.
Love only knows no winter; never dies:
Nor cares for frowning storms or leaden skies.
And mine for thee shall never pass away,
Though my weak lips may falter in my lay.

Adieu! Adieu! yon silent evening star,
The night's ambassador, doth gleam afar,

And bid the shepherd bring his flocks to fold.
Perchance before our inland seas of gold
Are garnered by the reapers into sheaves,
Perchance before I see the Autumn leaves,
I may behold thy city; and lay down
Low at thy feet the poet's laurel crown.

Adieu! Adieu! yon silver lamp, the moon,
Which turns our midnight into perfect noon,
Doth surely light thy towers, guarding well
Where Dante sleeps, where Byron loved to dwell.

ELEUTHERIA

SONNET TO LIBERTY

Nor that I love thy children, whose dull eyes
See nothing save their own unlovely woe,
Whose minds know nothing, nothing care to know.—
But that the roar of thy Democracies,
Thy reigns of Terror, thy great Anarchies,
Mirror my wildest passions like the sea
And give my rage a brother——! Liberty!
For this sake only do thy dissonant cries
Delight my discreet soul, else might all kings
By bloody knout or treacherous cannonades
Rob nations of their rights inviolate
And I remain unmoved—and yet, and yet,
These Christs that die upon the barricades,
God knows it I am with them, in some things.

AVE IMPERATRIX

SET in this stormy Northern sea,
    Queen of these restless fields of tide,
England; what shall men say of thee,
    Before whose feet the worlds divide?

The earth, a brittle globe of glass,
    Lies in the hollow of thy hand,
And through its heart of crystal pass,
    Like shadows through a twilight land,

The spears of crimson-suited war,
    The long white-crested waves of fight,
And all the deadly fires which are
    The torches of the lords of Night.

The yellow leopards, strained and lean,
    The treacherous Russian knows so well,
With gaping blackened jaws are seen
    Leap through the hail of screaming shell.

The strong sea-lion of England's wars
    Hath left his sapphire cave of sea,
To battle with the storm that mars
    The stars of England's chivalry.

The brazen-throated clarion blows
    Across the Pathan's reedy fen,
And the high steeps of Indian snows
    Shake to the tread of armèd men.

And many an Afghan chief, who lies
   Beneath his cool pomegranate-trees,
Clutches his sword in fierce surmise
   When on the mountain-side he sees

The fleet-foot Marri scout, who comes
   To tell how he hath heard afar
The measured roll of English drums
   Beat at the gates of Kandahar.

For southern wind and east wind meet
   Where, girt and crowned by sword and fire,
England with bare and bloody feet
   Climbs the steep road of wide empire.

O lonely Himalayan height,
   Grey pillar of the Indian sky,
Where saw'st thou last in clanging flight
   Our wingèd dogs of Victory?

The almond-groves of Samarcand,
   Bokhara, where red lilies blow,
And Oxus, by whose yellow sand
   The grave white-turbaned merchants go:

And on from thence to Ispahan,
   The gilded garden of the sun,
Whence the long dusty caravan
   Brings cedar wood and vermilion;

And that dread city of Cabool
   Set at the mountain's scarpèd feet,
Whose marble tanks are ever full
   With water for the noonday heat:

Where through the narrow straight Bazaar
    A little maid Circassian
Is led, a present from the Czar
    Unto some old and beared khan,—

Here have our wild war-eagles flown,
    And flapped wide wings in fiery flight;
But the sad dove, that sits alone
    In England—she hath no delight.

In vain the laughing girl will lean
    To greet her love with love-lit eyes:
Down in some treacherous black ravine,
    Clutching his flag, the dead boy lies.

And many a moon and sun will see
    The lingering wistful children wait
To climb upon their father's knee;
    And in each house made desolate

Pale women who have lost their lord
    Will kiss the relics of the slain—
Some tarnished epaulette—some sword—
    Poor toys to soothe such anguished pain.

For not in quiet English fields
    Are these, our brothers, lain to rest,
Where we might deck their broken shields
    With all the flowers the dead love best.

For some are by the Delhi walls,
    And many in the Afghan land,
And many where the Ganges falls
    Through seven mouths of shifting sand.

And some in Russian waters lie,
    And others in the seas which are
The portals to the East, or by
    The wind-swept heights of Trafalgar.

O wandering graves! O restless sleep!
    O silence of the sunless day!
O still ravine! O stormy deep!
    Give up your prey! Give up your prey!

And thou whose wounds are never healed,
    Whose weary race is never won,
O Cromwell's England! must thou yield
    For every inch of ground a son?

Go! crown with thorns thy gold-crowned head,
    Change thy glad song to song of pain;
Wind and wild wave have got thy dead,
    And will not yield them back again.

Wave and wild wind and foreign shore
    Possess the flower of English land—
Lips that thy lips shall kiss no more,
    Hands that shall never clasp thy hand.

What profit now that we have bound
    The whole round world with nets of gold,
If hidden in our heart is found
    The care that groweth never old?

What profit that our galleys ride,
    Pine-forest-like, on every main?
Ruin and wreck are at our side,
    Grim wardens of the House of pain.

Where are the brave, the strong, the fleet?
  Where is our English chivalry?
Wild grasses are their burial-sheet,
  And sobbing waves their threnody

O loved ones lying far away,
  What word of love can dead lips send!
O wasted dust! O senseless clay!
  Is this the end! is this the end!

Peace, peace! we wrong the noble dead
  To vex their solemn slumber so;
Though childless, and with thorn-crowned head,
  Up the steep road must England go,

Yet when this fiery web is spun,
  Her watchmen shall descry from far
The young Republic like a sun
  Rise from these crimson seas of war.

TO MILTON

Milton! I think thy spirit hath passed away
  From these white cliffs and high-embattled towers;
  This gorgeous fiery-coloured world of ours
Seems fallen into ashes dull and grey,
And the age changed unto a mimic play
  Wherein we waste our else too-crowded hours.
  For all our pomp and pageantry and powers
We are but fit to delve the common clay,
Seeing this little isle on which we stand,
  This England, this sea-lion of the sea,
  By ignorant demagogues is held in fee,
Who love her not: Dear God! is this the land
Which bare a triple empire in her hand
  When Cromwell spake the word Democracy!

LOUIS NAPOLEON

EAGLE of Austerlitz! where were thy wings
⠀⠀⠀When far away upon a barbarous strand,
⠀⠀In fight unequaled, by an obscure hand,
Fell the last scion of thy brood of Kings!

Poor boy! thou shalt not flaunt thy cloak of red,
⠀⠀Or ride in state through Paris in the van
⠀⠀Of thy returning legions, but instead
Thy mother France, free and republican,

Shall on thy dead and crownless forehead place
⠀⠀The better laurels of a soldier's crown,
⠀⠀That not dishonoured should thy soul go down
To tell the mighty Sire of thy race

That France hath kissed the mouth of Liberty,
⠀⠀And found it sweeter than his honied bees,
⠀⠀And that the giant wave Democracy
Breaks on the shores where Kings lay crouched at ease.

SONNET

ON THE MASSACRE OF THE CHRISTIANS IN BULGARIA

CHRIST, dost thou live indeed? or are thy bones
Still straitened in their rock-hewn sepulchre?
And was Thy Rising only dreamed by Her
Whose love of thee for all her sin atones?
For here the air is horrid with men's groans,
The priests who call upon thy name are slain,
Dost thou not hear the bitter wail of pain
From those whose children lie upon the stones?
Come down, O Son of God! incestuous gloom
Curtains the land, and through the starless night
Over thy Cross a Crescent moon I see!
If thou in very truth didst burst the tomb
Come down, O Son of Man! and show thy might,
Lest Mahomet be crowned instead of Thee!

QUANTUM MUTATA

THERE was a time in Europe long ago
  When no man died for freedom anywhere,
  But England's lion leaping from its lair
Laid hands on the oppressor! it was so
While England could a great Republic show.
  Witness the men of Piedmont, chiefest care
  Of Cromwell, when with impotent despair
The Pontiff in his painted portico
Trembled before our stern ambassadors.
  How comes it then that from such high estate
  We have thus fallen, save that Luxury
With barren merchandise piles up the gate
Where noble thoughts and deeds should enter by:
  Else might we still be Milton's heritors.

LIBERTATIS SACRA FAMES

Albeit nurtured in democracy,
   And liking best that state republican
   Where every man is Kinglike and no man
Is crowned above his fellows, yet I see,
Spite of this modern fret for Liberty,
   Better the rule of One, whom all obey,
   Than to let clamorous demagogues betray
Our freedom with the kiss of anarchy.
Wherefore I love them not whose hands profane
   Plant the red flag upon the piled-up street
   For no right cause, beneath whose ignorant reign
Arts, Culture, Reverence, Honour, all things fade,
   Save Treason and the dagger of her trade,
   Or Murder with his silent bloody feet.

THEORETIKOS

THIS mighty empire hath but feet of clay:
  Of all its ancient chivalry and might
  Our little island is forsaken quite:
Some enemy hath stolen its crown of bay,
And from its hills that voice hath passed away
  Which spake of Freedom: O come out of it,
  Come out of it, my Soul, thou art not fit
For this vile traffic-house, where day by day
  Wisdom and reverence are sold at mart,
  And the rude people rage with ignorant cries
Against an heritage of centuries.
  It mars my calm: wherefore in dreams of Art
  And loftiest culture I would stand apart,
Neither for God, nor for his enemies.

THE GARDEN OF EROS

THE GARDEN OF EROS

It is full summer now, the heart of June,
  Not yet the sunburnt reapers are astir
Upon the upland meadow where too soon
  Rich autumn time, the season's usurer,
Will lend his hoarded gold to all the trees,
And see his treasure scattered by the wild and spendthrift
    breeze.

Too soon indeed! yet here the daffodil,
  That love-child of the Spring, has lingered on
To vex the rose with jealousy, and still
  The harebell spreads her azure pavilion,
And like a strayed and wandering reveller
Abandoned of its brothers, whom long since June's mes-
    senger

The missel-thrush has frighted from the glade,
  One pale narcissus loiters fearfully
Close to a shadowy nook, where half afraid
  Of their own loveliness some violets lie
That will not look the gold sun in the face
For fear of too much splendour,—ah! methinks it is a place

Which should be trodden by Persephone
  When wearied of the flowerless fields of Dis!
Or danced on by the lads of Arcady!

The hidden secret of eternal bliss
Known to the Grecian here a man might find,
Ah! you and I may find it now if Love and Sleep be kind.

There are the flowers which mourning Herakles
    Strewed on the tomb of Hylas, columbine,
Its white doves all a-flutter where the breeze
    Kissed them too harshly, the small celandine,
That yellow-kirtled chorister of eve,
And lilac lady's-smock,—but let them bloom alone, and
        leave

Yon spirèd hollyhock red-crocketed
    To sway its silent chimes, else must the bee,
Its little bellringer, go seek instead
    Some other pleasaunce; the anemone
That weeps at daybreak, like a silly girl
Before her love, and hardly lets the butterflies unfurl

Their painted wings beside it,—bid it pine
    In pale virginity; the winter snow
Will suit it better than those lips of thine
    Whose fires would but scorch it, rather go.
And pluck that amorous flower which blooms alone,
Fed by the pander wind with dust of kisses not its own.

The trumpet-mouths of red convolvulus
    So dear to maidens, creamy meadow-sweet
Whiter than Juno's throat and odorous
    As all Arabia, hyacinths the feet
Of Huntress Dian would be loth to mar
For any dappled fawn,—pluck these, and those fond flowers
        which are

Fairer than what Queen Venus trod upon
    Beneath the pines of Ida, eucharis,

That morning star which does not dread the sun,
  And budding marjoram which but to kiss
Would sweeten Cytheræa's lips and make
Adonis jealous,—these for thy head,—and for thy girdle take

Yon curving spray of purple clematis
  Whose gorgeous dye outflames the Tyrian King,
And foxgloves with their nodding chalices,
  But that one narciss which the startled Spring
Let from her kirtle fall when first she heard
In her own woods the wild tempestuous song of summer's
    bird,

Ah! leave it for a subtle memory
  Of those sweet tremulous days of rain and sun,
When April laughed between her tears to see
  The early primrose with shy footsteps run
From the gnarled oak-tree roots till all the wold,
Spite of its brown and trampled leaves, grew bright with
    shimmering gold.

Nay, pluck it too, it is not half so sweet
  As thou thyself, my soul's idolatry!
And when thou art a-wearied at thy feet
  Shall ox-slips weave their brightest tapestry,
For thee the woodbine shall forget its pride
And veil its tangled whorls, and thou shalt walk on daisies
    pied.

And I will cut a reed by yonder spring
  And make the wood-gods jealous, and old Pan
Wonder what young intruder dares to sing
  In these still haunts, where never foot of man
Should tread at evening, lest he chance to spy
The marble limbs of Artemis and all her company.

And I will tell thee why the jacinth wears
  Such dread embroidery of dolorous moan,
And why the hapless nightingale forbears
  To sing her song at noon, but weeps alone
When the fleet swallow sleeps, and rich men feast,
And why the laurel trembles when she sees the lightening
    east.

And I will sing how sad Proserpina
  Unto a grave and gloomy Lord was wed,
And lure the silver-breasted Helena
  Back from the lotus meadows of the dead,
So shalt thou see that awful loveliness
For which two mighty Hosts met fearfully in war's abyss.

And then I'll pipe to thee that Grecian tale
  How Cynthia loves the lad Endymion,
And hidden in a grey and misty veil
  Hies to the cliffs of Latmos once the Sun
Leaps from his ocean bed in fruitless chase
Of those pale flying feet which fade away in his embrace.

And if my flute can breathe sweet melody,
  We may behold Her face who long ago
Dwelt among men by the Ægean sea,
  And whose sad house with pillaged portico
And friezeless wall and columns toppled down
Looms o'er the ruins of that fair and violet-cinctured town.

Spirit of Beauty! tarry still awhile,
  They are not dead, thine ancient votaries,
Some few there are to whom thy radiant smile
  Is better than a thousand victories,
Though all the nobly slain of Waterloo
Rise up in wrath against them! tarry still, there are a few

Who for thy sake would give their manlihood
   And consecrate their being, I at least
Have done so, made thy lips my daily food,
   And in thy temples found a goodlier feast
Than this starved age can give me, spite of all
Its new-found creeds so sceptical and so dogmatical.

Here not Cephissos, not Ilissos flows,
   The woods of white Colonos are not here,
On our bleak hills the olive never blows,
   No simple priest conducts his lowing steer
Up the steep marble way, nor through the town
Do laughing maidens bear to thee the crocus-flowered gown.

Yet tarry! for the boy who loved thee best,
   Whose very name should be a memory
To make thee linger, sleeps in silent rest
   Beneath the Roman walls, and melody
Still mourns her sweetest lyre, none can play
The lute of Adonais, with his lips Song passed away.

Nay, when Keats died the Muses still had left
   One silver voice to sing its threnody,
But ah! too soon of it we were bereft
   When on that riven night and stormy sea
Panthea claimed her singer as her own,
And slew the mouth that praised her; since which time we
      walk alone,

Save for that fiery heart, that morning star
   Of re-arisen England, whose clear eye
Saw from our tottering throne and waste of war
   The grand Greek limbs of young Democracy

Rise mightily like Hesperus and bring
The great Republic! him at least thy love hath taught to
    sing,

And he hath been with thee at Thessaly,
    And seen white Atalanta fleet of foot
In passionless and fierce virginity
    Hunting the tuskèd boar, his honied lute
Hath pierced the cavern of the hollow hill,
And Venus laughs to know one knee will bow before her
    still.

And he hath kissed the lips of Proserpine,
    And sung the Galilæan's requiem,
That wounded forehead dashed with blood and wine
    He hath discrowned, the Ancient Gods in him
Have found their last, most ardent worshipper,
And the new Sign grows grey and dim before its conqueror.

Spirit of Beauty! tarry with us still,
    It is not quenched the torch of poesy,
The star that shook above the Eastern hill
    Holds unassailed its argent armoury
From all the gathering gloom and fretful fight,
O tarry with us still! for through the long and common
    night,

Morris, our sweet and simple Chaucer's child,
    Dear heritor of Spenser's tuneful reed,
With soft and sylvan pipe has oft beguiled
    The weary soul of man in troublous need,
And from the far and flowerless fields of ice
Has brought fair flowers to make an earthly paradise.

We know them all, Gudrun the strong men's bride,
  Aslaug and Olafson we know them all,
How giant Grettir fought and Sigurd died,
  And what enchantment held the king in thrall
When lonely Brynhild wrestled with the powers
That war against all passion, ah! how oft through summer
    hours,

Long listless summer hours when the noon
  Being enamoured of a damask rose
Forgets to journey westward, till the moon
  The pale usurper of its tribute grows
From a thin sickle to a silver shield
And chides its loitering car—how oft, in some cool grassy
    field

Far from the cricket-ground and noisy eight,
  At Bagley, where the rustling bluebells come
Almost before the blackbird finds a mate
  And overstay the swallow, and the hum
Of many murmuring bees flits through the leaves,
Have I lain poring on the dreamy tales his fancy weaves,

And through their unreal woes and mimic pain
  Wept for myself, and so was purified,
And in their simple mirth grew glad again;
  For as I sailed upon that pictured tide
The strength and splendour of the storm was mine
Without the storm's red ruin, for the singer is divine,

The little laugh of water falling down
  Is not so musical, the clammy gold
Close hoarded in the tiny waxen town
  Has less of sweetness in it, and the old

Half-withered reeds that waved in Arcady
Touched by his lips break forth again to fresher harmony.

Spirit of Beauty, tarry yet awhile!
  Although the cheating merchants of the mart
With iron roads profane our lovely isle,
  And break on whirling wheels the limbs of Art,
Ay! though the crowded factories beget
The blindworm Ignorance that slays the soul, O tarry yet!

For One at least there is,—he bears his name
  From Dante and the seraph Gabriel,—
Whose double laurels burn with deathless flame
  To light thine altar; He too loves thee well,
Who saw old Merlin lured in Vivien's snare,
And the white feet of angels coming down the golden stair,

Loves thee so well, that all the World for him
  A gorgeous-coloured vestiture must wear,
And Sorrow take a purple diadem,
  Or else be no more Sorrow and Despair,
Gild its own thorns, and Pain, like Adon, he even in
Anguish beautiful;—such is the empery

Which Painters hold, and such the heritage
  This gentle solemn Spirit doth possess,
Being a better mirror of his age
  In all his pity, love, and weariness,
Than those who can but copy common things,
And leave the Soul unpainted with its mighty questionings.

But they are few, and all romance has flown,
  And men can prophesy about the sun,
And lecture on his arrows—how, alone,
  Through a waste void the soulless atoms run,

How from each tree its weeping nymph has fled,
And that no more 'mid English reeds a Naïad shows her
    head.

Methinks these new Actæons boast too soon
    That they have spied on beauty; what if we
Have analysed the rainbow, robbed the moon
    Of her most ancient, chastest mystery,
Shall I, the last Endymion, lose all hope
Because rude eyes peer at my mistress through a telescope!

What profit if this scientific age
    Burst through our gates with all its retinue
Of modern miracles! Can it assuage
    One lover's breaking heart? what can it do
To make one life more beautiful, one day
More godlike in its period? but now the Age of Clay

Returns in horrid cycle, and the earth
    Hath borne again a noisy progeny
Of ignorant Titans, whose ungodly birth
    Hurls them against the august hierarchy
Which sat upon Olympus, to the Dust
They have appealed, and to that barren arbiter they must

Repair for judgment, let them, if they can
    From Natural Warfare and insensate Chance,
Create the new Ideal rule for man!
    Methinks that was not my inheritance;
For I was nurtured otherwise, my soul
Passes from higher heights of life to a more supreme goal.

Lo! while we spake the earth did turn away
    Her visage from the God, and Hecate's boat
Rose silver-laden, till the jealous day
    Blew all its torches out: I did not note

The waning hours, to young Endymions
Time's palsied fingers count in vain his rosary of suns!

Mark how the yellow iris wearily
   Leans back its throat, as though it would be kissed
By its false chamberer, the dragon-fly,
   Who, like a blue vein on a girl's white wrist
Sleeps on that snowy primrose of the night,
Which 'gins to flush with crimson shame, and die beneath
      the light.

Come let us go, against the pallid shield
   Of the wan sky the almond blossoms gleam,
The corncrake nested in the unmown field
   Answers its mate, across the misty stream
On fitful wing the startled curlews fly,
And in his sedgy bed the lark, for joy that Day is nigh,

Scatters the pearlèd drew from off the grass,
   In tremulous ecstasy to greet the sun,
Who soon in gilded panoply will pass
   Forth from yon orange-curtained pavilion
Hung in the burning east, see, the red rim
O'ertops the expectant hills! it is the God! for love of him

Already the shrill lark is out of sight,
   Flooding with waves of song this silent dell,—
Ah! there is something more in that bird's flight
   Than could be tested in a crucible!—
But the air freshens, let us go, why soon
The woodmen will be here; how we have lived this night
      of June!

ROSA MYSTICA

REQUIESCAT

Tread lightly, she is near,
   Under the snow,
Speak gently, she can hear
   The daisies grow.

All her bright golden hair
   Tarnished with rust,
She that was young and fair
   Fallen to dust.

Lily-like, white as snow,
   She hardly knew
She was a woman, so
   Sweetly she grew.

Coffin-board, heavy stone,
   Lie on her breast,
I vex my heart alone,
   She is at rest.

Peace, Peace, she cannot hear
   Lyre or sonnet,
All my life's buried here,
   Heap earth upon it.

Avignon.

SONNET ON APPROACHING ITALY

I REACHED the Alps: the soul within me burned,
  Italia, my Italia, at thy name:
  And when from out the mountain's heart I came
And saw the land for which my life had yearned,
I laughed as one who some great prize had earned:
  And musing on the marvel of thy fame
  I watched the day, till marked with wounds of flame
The turquoise sky to burnished gold was turned.
The pine-trees waved as waves a woman's hair,
  And in the orchards every twining spray
  Was breaking into flakes of blossoming foam:
But when I knew that far away at Rome
  In evil bonds a second Peter lay,
  I wept to see the land so very fair.

TURIN.

SAN MINIATO

See, I have climbed the mountain side
  Up to this holy house of God,
  Where once that Angel-Painter trod
Who saw the heavens opened wide,

And throned upon the crescent moon
  The Virginal white Queen of Grace,—
  Mary! could I but see thy face
Death could not come at all too soon.

O crowned by God with thorns and pain
  Mother of Christ! O mystic wife!
  My heart is weary of this life
And over-sad to sing again.

O crowned by God with love and flame!
  O crowned by Christ the Holy One!
  O listen ere the searching sun
Show to the world my sin and shame.

AVE MARIA GRATIA PLENA

Was this His coming! I had hoped to see
  A scene of wondrous glory, as was told
  Of some great God who in a rain of gold
Broke open bars and fell on Danae:
Or a dread vision as when Semele
    Sickening for love and unappeased desire
    Prayed to see God's clear body, and the fire
Caught her brown limbs and slew her utterly:
With such bad dreams I sought this holy place,
    And now with wondering eyes and heart I stand
    Before this supreme mystery of Love:
Some kneeling girl with passionless pale face,
    An angel with a lily in his hand,
    And over both the white wings of a Dove.

FLORENCE.

ITALIA

ITALIA! thou art fallen, though with sheen
   Of battle-spears thy clamorous armies stride
   From the north Alps to the Sicilian tide!
Ay! fallen, though the nations hail thee Queen
Because rich gold in every town is seen,
   And on thy sapphire-lake in tossing pride
   Of wind-filled vans thy myriad galleys ride
Beneath one flag of red and white and green.
O Fair and Strong! O Strong and Fair in vain!
   Look southward where Rome's desecrated town
   Lies mourning for her God-anointed King!
Look heaven-ward! shall God allow this thing?
   Nay! but some flame-girt Raphael shall come down,
   And smite the Spoiler with the sword of pain.

VENICE.

SONNET

WRITTEN IN HOLY WEEK AT GENOA

I WANDERED through Scoglietto's far retreat,
  The oranges on each o'erhanging spray
  Burned as bright lamps of gold to shame the day;
Some startled bird with fluttering wings and fleet
Made snow of all the blossoms, at my feet
  Like silver moons the pale narcissi lay:
  And the curved waves that streaked the great green bay
Laughed i' the sun, and life seemed very sweet.
Outside the young boy-priest passed singing clear,
  "Jesus the son of Mary has been slain,
  O come and fill his sepulchre with flowers."
Ah, God! Ah, God! those dear Hellenic hours
  Had drowned all memory of Thy bitter pain,
  The Cross, the Crown, the Soldiers and the Spear.

ROME UNVISITED

I

THE corn has turned from grey to red,
  Since first my spirit wandered forth,
  From the dread cities of the north,
And to Italia's mountains fled.

And here I set my face towards home,
  For all my pilgrimage is done,
  Although, methinks, yon blood-red sun
Marshals the way to Holy Rome.

O Blessed Lady, who dost hold
  Upon the seven hills thy reign!
  O Mother without blot or stain,
Crowned with bright crowns of triple gold!

O Roma, Roma, at thy feet
  I lay this barren gift of song!
  For, ah! the way is steep and long
That leads unto thy sacred street.

II

And yet what joy it were for me
  To turn my feet unto the south,
  And journeying towards the Tiber mouth
To kneel again at Fiesole!

And wandering through the tangled pines
   That break the gold of Arno's stream,
   To see the purple mist and gleam
Of morning on the Apennines.

By many a vineyard-hidden home,
   Orchard and olive-garden grey,
   Till from the drear Campagna's way
The seven hills bear up the dome!

III

A pilgrim from the northern seas—
   What joy for me to seek alone
   The wondrous Temple and the throne
Of Him who holds the awful keys!

When, bright with purple and with gold,
   Come priest and holy Cardinal,
   And borne above the heads of all
The gentle Shepherd of the Fold.

O joy to see before I die
   The only God-anointed King,
   And hear the silver trumpets ring
A triumph as He passes by!

Or at the brazen-pillared shrine
   Hold high the mystic sacrifice,
   And shows his God to human eyes
Beneath the veil of bread and wine.

IV

For lo, what changes time can bring!
  The cycles of revolving years
  May free my heart from all its fears,
And teach my lips a song to sing.

Before yon field of trembling gold
  Is garnered into dusty sheaves,
  Or ere the autumn's scarlet leaves
Flutter as birds adown the wold,

I may have run the glorious race,
  And caught the torch while yet aflame,
  And called upon the holy name
Of Him who now doth hide His face.

ARONA.

URBS SACRA ÆTERNA

ROME! what a scroll of History thine has been;
  In the first days thy sword republican
  Ruled the whole world for many an age's span:
Then of the peoples wert thou royal Queen,
Till in thy streets the bearded Goth was seen;
  And now upon thy walls the breezes fan
  (Ah, city crowned by God, discrowned by man!)
The hated flag of red and white and green.
When was thy glory! when in search for power
  Thine eagles flew to greet the double sun,
  And the wild nations shuddered at thy rod?
Nay, but thy glory tarried for this hour,
  When pilgrims kneel before the Holy One,
  The prisoned shepherd of the Church of God.

MONTE MARIO.

SONNET

ON HEARING THE DIES IRÆ SUNG IN THE SISTINE CHAPEL

Nay, Lord, not thus! white lilies in the spring,
  Sad olive-groves, or silver-breasted dove,
  Teach me more clearly of Thy life and love
Than terrors of red flame and thundering.
The hillside vines dear memories of Thee bring:
  A bird at evening flying to its nest
  Tells me of One who had no place of rest:
I think it is of Thee the sparrows sing.
Come rather on some autumn afternoon,
  When red and brown are burnished on the leaves,
  And the fields echo to the gleaner's song,
Come when the splendid fulness of the moon
  Looks down upon the rows of golden sheaves,
  And reap Thy harvest: we have waited long.

EASTER DAY

THE silver trumpets rang across the Dome:
  The people knelt upon the ground with awe:
  And borne upon the necks of men I saw,
Like some great God, the Holy Lord of Rome.
Priest-like, he wore a robe more white than foam,
  And, king-like, swathed himself in royal red,
  Three crowns of gold rose high upon his head:
In splendour and, in light the Pope passed home.
My heart stole back across wide wastes of years
  To one who wandered by a lonely sea,
  And sought in vain for any place of rest:
"Foxes have holes, and every bird its nest.
  I, only I, must wander wearily,
And bruise my feet, and drink wine salt with tears."

E TENEBRIS

COME down, O Christ, and help me! reach thy hand,
    For I am drowning in a stormier sea
    Than Simon on thy lake of Galilee:
The wine of life is spilt upon the sand,
My heart is as some famine-murdered land
    Whence all good things have perished utterly,
    And well I know my soul in Hell must lie
If I this night before God's throne should stand.
"He sleeps perchance, or rideth to the chase,
    Like Baal, when his prophets howled that name
    From morn to noon on Carmel's smitten height."
Nay, peace, I shall behold, before the night,
    The feet of brass, the robe more white than flame,
The wounded hands, the weary human face.

VITA NUOVA

I STOOD by the unvintageable sea
  Till the wet waves drenched face and hair with spray,
  The long red fires of the dying day
Burned in the west; the wind piped drearily;
And to the land the clamorous gulls did flee:
  "Alas!" I cried, "my life is full of pain,
  And who can garner fruit or golden grain
From these waste fields which travail ceaselessly!"
My nets gaped wide with many a break and flaw,
  Nathless I threw them as my final cast
  Into the sea, and waited for the end.
When lo! a sudden glory! and I saw
  From the black waters of my tortured past
  The argent splendour of white limbs ascend!

MADONNA MIA

A LILY-GIRL, not made for this world's pain,
  With brown, soft hair close braided by her ears,
  And longing eyes half veiled by slumberous tears
Like bluest water seen through mists of rain:
Pale cheeks whereon no love hath left its stain,
  Red underlip drawn in for fear of love,
  And white throat, whiter than the silvered dove,
Through whose wan marble creeps one purple vein,
Yet, though my lips shall praise her without cease,
  Even to kiss her feet I am not bold,
  Being o'ershadowed by the wings of awe,
Like Dante, when he stood with Beatrice
  Beneath the flaming Lion's breast, and saw
  The seventh Crystal, and the Stair of Gold.

THE NEW HELEN

Where hast thou been since round the walls of Troy
   The sons of God fought in that great emprise?
   Why dost thou walk our common earth again?
Hast thou forgotten that impassioned boy,
      His purple galley and his Tyrian men
      And treacherous Aphrodite's mocking eyes?
For surely it was thou, who, like a star
   Hung in the silver silence of the night,
   Didst lure the Old World's chivalry and might
Into the clamorous crimson waves of war!

Or didst thou rule the fire-laden moon?
   In amorous Sidon was thy temple built
      Over the light and laughter of the sea?
   Where, behind lattice scarlet-wrought and gilt,
      Some brown-limbed girl did weave thee tapestry,
All through the waste and wearied hours of noon;
Till her wan cheek with flame of passion burned,
   And she rose up the sea-washed lips to kiss
Of some glad Cyprian sailor, safe returned
   From Calpé and the cliffs of Herakles!

No! thou art Helen, and none other one!
   It was for thee that young Sarpedôn died,
      And Memnôn's manhood was untimely spent;
   It was for thee gold-crested Hector tried
With Thetis' child that evil race to run,
      In the last year of thy beleaguerment;

Ay! even now the glory of thy fame
  Burns in those fields of trampled asphodel,
  Where the high lords whom Ilion knew so well
Clash ghostly shields, and call upon thy name.

Where hast thou been? in that enchanted land
  Whose slumbering vales forlorn Calypso knew,
    Where never mower rose at break of day
  But all unswathed the trammelling grasses grew,
And the sad shepherd saw the tall corn stand
    Till summer's red had changed to withered grey?
Didst thou lie there by some Lethæan stream
    Deep brooding on thine ancient memory,
The crash of broken spears, the fiery gleam
    From shivered helm, the Grecian battle-cry?

Nay, thou wert hidden in that hollow hill
  With one who is forgotten utterly,
    That discrowned Queen men call the Erycine;
  Hidden away that never mightst thou see
    The face of Her, before whose mouldering shrine
To-day at Rome the silent nations kneel;
  Who gat from Love no joyous gladdening,
    But only Love's intolerable pain,
    Only a sword to pierce her heart in twain,
  Only the bitterness of child-bearing.

The lotus-leaves which heal the wounds of Death
  Lie in thy hand; O, be thou kind to me,
    While yet I know the summer of my days;
For hardly can my tremulous lips draw breath
    To fill the silver trumpet with thy praise,
  So bowed am I before thy mystery;

So bowed and broken on Love's terrible wheel,
   That I have lost all hope and heart to sing,
   Yet care I not what ruin time may bring
If in thy temple thou wilt let me kneel.

Alas, alas, thou wilt not tarry here,
   But, like that bird, the servant of the sun,
      Who flies before the north wind and the night,
So wilt thou fly our evil land and drear,
      Back to the tower of thine old delight,
   And the red lips of young Euphorion;
Nor shall I ever see thy face again,
   But in this poisonous garden-close must stay,
Crowning my brows with the thorn-crown of pain,
   Till all my loveless life shall pass away.

O Helen! Helen! Helen! yet a while,
   Yet for a little while, O, tarry here,
      Till the dawn cometh and the shadows flee!
For in the gladsome sunlight of thy smile
      Of heaven or hell I have no thought or fear,
   Seeing I know no other god but thee:
No other god save him, before whose feet
   In nets of gold the tired planets move,
   The incarnate spirit of spiritual love
Who in thy body holds his joyous seat.

Thou wert not born as common women are!
   But, girt with silver splendour of the foam,
      Didst from the depths of sapphire seas arise!
And at thy coming some immortal star,
      Bearded with flame, blazed in the Eastern skies,
   And waked the shepherds on thine island home.

Thou shalt not die: no asps of Egypt creep
  Close at thy heels to taint the delicate air;
  No sullen-blooming poppies stain thy hair,
Those scarlet heralds of eternal sleep.

Lily of love, pure and inviolate!
  Tower of ivory! red rose of fire!
    Thou hast come down our darkness to illume:
For we, close-caught in the wide nets of Fate,
  Wearied with waiting for the World's Desire,
    Aimlessly wandered in the House of gloom,
Aimlessly sought some slumberous anodyne
  For wasted lives, for lingering wretchedness,
Till we beheld thy re-arisen shrine,
  And the white glory of thy loveliness.

THE BURDEN OF ITYS

THE BURDEN OF ITYS

THIS English Thames is holier far than Rome,
  Those harebells like a sudden flush of sea
Breaking across the woodland, with the foam
  Of meadow-sweet and white anemone
To fleck their blue waves,—God is likelier there
Than hidden in that crystal-hearted star the pale monks
    bear!

Those violet-gleaming butterflies that take
  Yon creamy lily for their pavilion
Are monsignores, and where the rushes shake
  A lazy pike lies basking in the sun,
His eyes half shut,—He is some mitred old
Bishop *in partibus!* look at those gaudy scales all green and
    gold.

The wind the restless prisoner of the trees
  Does well for Palæstrina, one would say
The mighty master's hands were on the keys
  Of the Maria organ, which they play
When early on some sapphire Easter morn
In a high litter as red as blood or sin the Pope is borne

From his dark House out to the Balcony
  Above the bronze gates and the crowded square,
Whose very fountains seem for ecstasy
  To toss their silver lances in the air,

And stretching out weak hands to East and West
In vain sends peace to peaceless lands, to restless nations rest.

Is not yon lingering orange after-glow
   That stays to vex the moon more fair than all
Rome's lordliest pageants! strange, a year ago
   I knelt before some crimson Cardinal
Who bare the Host across the Esquiline,
And now—those common poppies in the wheat seem twice
     as fine.

The blue-green beanfields yonder, tremulous
   With the last shower, sweeter perfume bring
Through this cool evening than the odorous
   Flame-jewelled censers the young deacons swing,
When the grey priest unlocks the curtained shrine,
And makes God's body from the common fruit corn and
     vine.

Poor Fra Giovanni bawling at the mass
   Were out of tune now, for a small brown bird
Sings overhead, and through the long cool grass
   I see that throbbing throat which once I heard
On starlit hills of flower-starred Arcady,
Once where the white and crescent sand of Salamis meets
     sea.

Sweet is the swallow twittering on the eaves
   At daybreak, when the mower whets his scythe,
And stock-doves murmur, and the milkmaid leaves
   Her little lonely bed, and carols blithe
To see the heavy-lowing cattle wait
Stretching their huge and dripping mouths across the farm-
     yard gate.

And sweet the hops upon the Kentish leas,
  And sweet the wind that lifts the new-mown hay,
And sweet the fretful swarms of grumbling bees
  That round and round the linden blossoms play;
And sweet the heifer breathing in the stall,
And the green bursting figs that hang upon the red-brick
    wall.

And sweet to hear the cuckoo mock the spring
  While the last violet loiters by the well,
And sweet to hear the shepherd Daphnis sing
  The song of Linus through a sunny dell
Of warm Arcadia where the corn is gold
And the slight lithe-limbed reapers dance about the wattled
    fold.

And sweet with young Lycoris to recline
  In some Illyrian valley far away,
Where canopied on herbs amaracine
  We too might waste the summer-trancèd day
Matching our reeds in sportive rivalry,
While far beneath us frets the troubled purple of the sea.

But sweeter far if silver-sandalled foot
  Of some long-hidden God should ever tread
The Nuneham meadows, if with reeded flute
  Pressed to his lips some Faun might raise his head
By the green water-flags, ah! sweet indeed
To see the heavenly herdsman call his white-fleeced flock
    to feed.

Then sing to me thou tuneful chorister,
  Though what thou sing'st be thine own requiem!
Tell me thy tale thou hapless chronicler
  Of thine own tragedies! do not contemn

These unfamiliar haunts, this English field,
For many a lovely coronal our northern isle can yield

Which Grecian meadows know not, many a rose
    Which all day long in vales Æolian
A lad might seek in vain for over-grows
    Our hedges like a wanton courtesan
Unthrifty of its beauty, lilies too
Ilissus never mirrored star our streams, and cockles blue

Dot the green wheat which, though they are the signs
    For swallows going south, would never spread
Their azure tents between the Attic vines;
    Even that little weed of ragged red,
Which bids the robin pipe, in Arcady
Would be a trespasser, and many an unsung elegy

Sleeps in the reeds that fringe our winding Thames
    Which to awake were sweeter ravishment
Than ever Syrinx wept for, diadems
    Of brown bee-studded orchids which were meant
For Cytheræa's brows are hidden here
Unknown to Cytheræa, and by yonder pasturing steer

There is a tiny yellow daffodil,
    The butterfly can see it from afar,
Although one summer evening's dew could fill
    Its little cup twice over ere the star
Had called the lazy shepherd to his fold
And be no prodigal, each leaf is flecked with spotted gold

As if Jove's gorgeous leman Danae
    Hot from his gilded arms had stooped to kiss
The trembling petals, or young Mercury
    Low-lying to the dusky ford of Dis

Had with one feather of his pinions
Just brushed them! the slight stem which bears the burden
 of its suns

Is hardly thicker than the gossamer,
 Or poor Arachne's silver tapestry,—
Men say it bloomed upon the sepulchre
 Of One I sometime worshipped, but to me
It seems to bring diviner memories
Of faun-loved Heliconian glades and blue nymph-haunted
 seas,

Of an untrodden vale at Tempe where
 On the clear river's marge Narcissus lies,
The tangle of the forest in his hair,
 The silence of the woodland in his eyes,
Wooing that drifting imagery which is
No sooner kissed than broken, memories of Salmacis

Who is not boy nor girl and yet is both,
 Fed by two fires and unsatisfied
Through their excess, each passion being loth
 For love's own sake to leave the other's side,
Yet killing love by staying, memories
Of Oreads peeping through the leaves of silent moonlit trees,

Of lonely Ariadne on the wharf
 At Naxos, when she saw the treacherous crew
Far out at sea, and waved her crimson scarf
 And called false Theseus back again nor knew
That Dionysos on an amber pard
Was close behind her, memories of what Mæonia's bard

With sightless eyes beheld, the wall of Troy,
  Queen Helen lying in the ivory room,
And at her side an amorous red-lipped boy
  Trimming with dainty hand his helmet's plume,
And far away the moil, the shout, the groan,
As Hector shielded off the spear and Ajax hurled the stone;

Of wingèd Perseus with his flawless sword
  Cleaving the snaky tresses of the witch,
And all those tales imperishably stored
  In little Grecian urns, freightage more rich
Than any gaudy galleon of Spain
Bare from the Indies ever! these at least bring back again,

For well I know they are not dead at all,
  The ancient Gods of Grecian poesy,
They are asleep, and when they hear thee call
  Will wake and think 'tis very Thessaly,
This Thames the Daulian waters, this cool glade
The yellow-irised mead where once young Itys laughed and
    played.

If it was thou, dear jasmine-cradled bird,
  Who from the leafy stillness of thy throne
Sang to the wondrous boy, until he heard
  The horn of Atalanta faintly blown
Across the Cumnor hills, and wandering
Through Bagley wood at evening found the Attic poet's
    spring,—

Ah! tiny sober-suited advocate
  That pleadest for the moon against the day!
If thou didst make the shepherd seek his mate
  On that sweet questing, when Proserpina

Forgot it was not Sicily and leant
Across the mossy Sandford stile in ravished wonderment,—

Light-winged and bright-eyed miracle of the wood!
    If ever thou didst soothe with melody
One of that little clan, that brotherhood
    Which loved the morning-star of Tuscany
More than the perfect sun of Raphael
And is immortal, sing to me! for I too love thee well,

Sing on! sing on! let the dull world grow young,
    Let elemental things take form again,
And the old shapes of Beauty walk among
    The simple garths and open crofts, as when
The son of Leto bare the willow rod,
And the soft sheep and shaggy goats followed the boyish
        God.

Sing on! sing on! and Bacchus will be here
    Astride upon his gorgeous Indian throne,
And over whimpering tigers shake the spear
    With yellow ivy crowned and gummy cone,
While at his side the wanton Bassarid
Will throw the lion by the mane and catch the mountain
        kid!

Sing on! and I will wear the leopard skin,
    And steal the moonèd wings of Ashtaroth,
Upon whose icy chariot we could win
    Cithæron in an hour ere the froth
Has over-brimmed the wine-vat or the Faun
Ceased from the treading! ay, before the flickering lamp of
        dawn

Has scared the hooting owlet to its nest,
  And warned the bat to close its filmy vans,
Some Mænad girl with vine-leaves on her breast
  Will filch their beech-nuts from the sleeping Pans
So softly that the little nested thrush
Will never wake, and then with shrilly laugh and leap will
    rush

Down the green valley where the fallen dew
  Lies thick beneath the elm and count her store,
Till the brown Satyrs in a jolly crew
  Trample the loosestrife down along the shore,
And where their hornèd master sits in state
Bring strawberries and bloomy plums upon a wicker crate!

Sing on! and soon with passion-wearied face
  Through the cool leaves Apollo's lad will come,
The Tyrian prince his bristled boar will chase
  Adown the chestnut-copses all a-bloom,
And ivory-limbed, grey-eyed, with look of pride,
After yon velvet-coated deer the virgin maid will ride.

Sing on! and I the dying boy will see
  Stain with his purple blood the waxen bell
That overweighs the jacinth, and to me
  The wretched Cyprian her woe will tell,
And I will kiss her mouth and streaming eyes,
And lead her to the myrtle-hidden grove where Adon lies!

Cry out aloud on Itys! memory,
  That foster-brother of remorse and pain,
Drops poison in mine ear,—O to be free,
  To burn one's old ships! and to launch again

Into the white-plumed battle of the waves
And fight old Proteus for the spoil of coral-flowered caves!

O for Medea with her poppied spell!
  O for the secret of the Colchian shrine!
O for one leaf of that pale asphodel
  Which binds the tired brows of Prosperine,
And sheds such wondrous dews at eve that she
Dreams of the fields of Enna, by the far Sicilian sea,

Where oft the golden-girdled bee she chased
  From lily to lily on the level mead,
Ere yet her sombre Lord had bid her taste
  The deadly fruit of that pomegranate seed,
Ere the black steeds had harried her away
Down to the faint and flowerless land, the sick and sunless
    day.

O for one midnight and as paramour
  The Venus of the little Melian farm!
O that some antique statue for one hour
  Might wake to passion, and that I could charm
The Dawn at Florence from its dumb despair,
Mix with those mighty limbs and make that giant breast
    my lair!

Sing on! sing on! I would be drunk with life,
  Drunk with the trampled vintage of my youth,
I would forget the wearying wasted strife,
  The riven veil, the Gorgon eyes of Truth,
The prayerless vigil and the cry for prayer,
The barren gifts, the lifted arms, the dull insensate air!

Sing on! sing on! O feathered Niobe,
    Thou canst make sorrow beautiful, and steal
From joy its sweetest music, not as we
    Who by dead voiceless silence strive to heal
Our too untented wounds, and do but keep
Pain barricaded in our hearts, and murder pillowed sleep.

Sing louder yet, why must I still behold
    The wan white face of that deserted Christ,
Whose bleeding hands my hands did once enfold,
    Whose smitten lips my lips so oft have kissed,
And now in mute and marble misery
Sits in his lone dishonoured House and weeps, perchance for
      me?

O Memory cast down thy wreathèd shell!
    Break thy hoarse lute O sad Melpomene!
O Sorrow, Sorrow keep thy cloistered cell
    Nor dim with tears this limpid Castaly!
Cease, Philomel, thou dost the forest wrong
To vex its sylvan quiet with such wild impassioned song!

Cease, cease, or if 'tis anguish to be dumb
    Take from the pastoral thrush her simpler air,
Whose jocund carelessness doth more become
    This English woodland than thy keen despair,
Ah! cease and let the north wind bear thy lay
Back to the rocky hills of Thrace, the stormy Daulain bay.

A moment more, the startled leaves had stirred,
    Endymion would have passed across the mead
Moonstruck with love, and this still Thames had heard
    Pan plash and paddle groping for some reed

To lure from her blue cave that Naiad maid
Who for such piping listens half in joy and half afraid.

A moment more, the waking dove had cooed,
   The silver daughter of the silver sea
With the fond gyves of clinging hands had wooed
   Her wanton from the chase, and Dryope
Had thrust aside the branches of her oak
To see the lusty gold-haired lad rein in his snorting yoke.

A moment more, the trees had stooped to kiss
   Pale Daphne just awakening from the swoon
Of tremulous laurels, lonely Salmacis
   Had bared his barren beauty to the moon,
And through the vale with sad voluptuous smile
Antinous had wandered, the red lotus of the Nile

Down leaning from his black and clustering hair,
   To shade those slumberous eyelids' caverned bliss,
Or else on yonder grassy slope with bare
   High-tuniced limbs unravished Artemis
Had bade her hounds give tongue, and roused the deer
From his green ambuscade with shrill halloo and pricking
    spear.

Lie still, lie still, O passionate heart, lie still!
   O Melancholy, fold thy raven wing!
O sobbing Dryad, from thy hollow hill
   Come not with such despondent answering!
No more thou wingèd Marsyas complain,
Apollo loveth not to hear such troubled songs of pain!

It was a dream, the glade is tenantless,
    No soft Ionian laughter moves the air,
The Thames creeps on in sluggish leadenness,
    And from the copse left desolate and bare
Fled is young Bacchus with his revelry,
Yet still from Nuneham wood there comes that thrilling
      melody

So sad, that one might think a human heart
    Brake in each separate note, a quality
Which music sometimes has, being the Art
    Which is most nigh to tears and memory,
Poor mourning Philomel, what dost thou fear?
Thy sister doth not haunt these fields, Pandion is not here.

Here is no cruel Lord with murderous blade,
    No woven web of bloody heraldries,
But mossy dells for roving comrades made,
    Warm valleys where the tired student lies
With half-shut book, and many a winding walk
Where rustic lovers stray at eve in happy simple talk.

The harmless rabbit gambols with its young
    Across the trampled towing-path, where late
A troop of laughing boys in jostling throng
    Cheered with their noisy cries the racing eight;
The gossamer, with ravelled silver threads,
Works at its little loom, and from the dusky red-eaved sheds

Of the lone Farm a flickering light shines out
    Where the swinked shepherd drives his bleating flock
Back to their wattled sheep-cotes, a faint shout
    Comes from some Oxford boat at Sandford lock,

And starts the moor-hen from the sedgy rill,
And the dim lengthening shadows flit like swallows up the
    hill.

The heron passes homeward to the mere,
   The blue mist creeps among the shivering trees,
Gold world by world the silent stars appear,
   And like a blossom blown before the breeze
A white moon drifts across the shimmering sky,
Mute arbitress of all thy sad, thy rapturous threnody.

She does not heed thee, wherefore should she heed,
   She knows Endymion is not far away,
'Tis I, 'tis I, whose soul is as the reed
   Which has no message of its own to play,
So pipes another's bidding, it is I,
Drifting with every wind on the wide sea of misery.

Ah! the brown bird has ceased: one exquisite trill
   About the sombre woodland seems to cling
Dying in music, else the air is still,
   So still that one might hear the bat's small wing.
Wander and wheel above the pines, or tell
Each tiny dew-drop dripping from the bluebell's brimming
    cell.

And far away across the lengthening wold,
   Across the willowy flats and thickets brown,
Magdalen's tall tower tipped with tremulous gold
   Marks the long High Street of the little town,
And warns me to return; I must not wait,
Hark! 'tis the curfew booming from the bell at Christ
    Church gate.

WIND FLOWERS

IMPRESSION DU MATIN

The Thames nocturne of blue and gold
  Changed to a Harmony in grey:
  A barge with ochre-coloured hay
Dropt from the wharf: and chill and cold

The yellow fog came creeping down
  The bridges, till the houses' walls
  Seemed changed to shadows and St. Paul's
Loomed like a bubble o'er the town.

Then suddenly arose the clang
  Of waking life; the streets were stirred
  With country wagons: and a bird
Flew to the glistening roofs and sang.

But one pale woman all alone,
  The daylight kissing her wan hair,
  Loitered beneath the gas lamps' flare,
With lips of flame and heart of stone.

MAGDALEN WALKS

THE little white clouds are racing over the sky,
And the fields are strewn with the gold of the flower of
March,
The daffodil breaks under foot, and the tasselled larch
Sways and swings as the thrush goes hurrying by.

A delicate odour is borne on the wings of the morning
breeze,
The odour of deep wet grass, and of brown new-furrowed
earth,
The birds are singing for joy of the Spring's glad birth,
Hopping from branch to branch on the rocking trees.

And all the woods are alive with the murmur and sound of
Spring.
And the rose-bud breaks into pink on the climbing briar,
And the crocus-bed is a quivering moon of fire
Girdled round with the belt of an amethyst ring.

And the plane of the pine-tree is whispering some tale of
love
Till it rustles with laughter and tosses its mantle of green,
And the gloom of the wych-elm's hollow is lit with the
iris sheen
Of the burnished rainbow throat and the silver breast of a
dove.

See! the lark starts up from his bed in the meadow there,
  Breaking the gossamer threads and the nets of dew,
  And flashing adown the river, a flame of blue!
The kingfisher flies like an arrow, and wounds the air.

And the sense of my life is sweet! though I know that the
      end is nigh:
  For the ruin and rain of winter will shortly come,
  The lily will lose its gold, and the chestnut-bloom
In billows of red and white on the grass will lie.

And even the light of the sun will fade at the last,
  And the leaves will fall, and the birds will hasten away,
  And I will be left in the snow of a flowerless day
To think on the glories of Spring, and the joys of a youth
      long past.

Yet be silent, my heart! do not count it a profitless thing
  To have seen the splendour of the sun, and of grass, and of
      flower!
  To have lived and loved! for I hold that to love for an
      hour
Is better for man and woman than cycles of blossoming
      Spring.

ATHANASIA

To that gaunt House of Art which lacks for naught
  Of all the great things men have saved from Time,
The withered body of a girl was brought
  Dead ere the world's glad youth had touched its prime,
And seen by lonely Arabs lying hid
In the dim womb of some black pyramid.

But when they had unloosed the linen band
  Which swathed the Egyptian's body,—lo! was found
Closed in the wasted hollow of her hand
  A little seed, which sown in English ground
Did wondrous snow of starry blossoms bear
And spread rich odours through our spring-time air.

With such strange arts this flower did allure
  That all forgotten was the asphodel,
And the brown bee, the lily's paramour,
  Forsook the cup where he was wont to dwell,
For not a thing of earth it seemed to be,
But stolen from some heavenly Arcady.

In vain the sad narcissus, wan and white
  As its own beauty, hung across the stream,
The purple dragon-fly had no delight
  With its gold dust to make his wings a-gleam,
Ah! no delight the jasmine-bloom to kiss,
Or brush the rain-pearls from the eucharis.

For love of it the passionate nightingale
　　Forgot the hills of Thrace, the cruel king,
And the pale dove no longer cared to sail
　　Through the wet woods at time of blossoming,
But round this flower of Egypt sought to float,
With silvered wing and amethystine throat.

While the hot sun blazed in his tower of blue
　　A cooling wind crept from the land of snows,
And the warm south with tender tears of dew
　　Drenched its white leaves when Hesperos up-rose
Amid those sea-green meadows of the sky
On which the scarlet bars of sunset lie.

But when o'er wastes of lily-haunted field
　　The tired birds had stayed their amorous tune,
And broad and glittering like an argent shield
　　High in the sapphire heavens hung the moon,
Did no strange dream or evil memory make
Each tremulous petal of its blossoms shake?

Ah no! to this bright flower a thousand years
　　Seemed but the lingering of a summer's day,
It never knew the tide of cankering fears
　　Which turn a boy's gold hair to withered grey,
The dread desire of death it never knew,
Or how all folk that they were born must rue.

For we to death with pipe and dancing go,
　　Nor would we pass the ivory gate again,
As some sad river wearied of its flow
　　Through the dull plains, the haunts of common men,
Leaps lover-like into the terrible sea!
And counts it gain to die so gloriously.

We mar our lordly strength in barren strife
 With the world's legions led by clamorous care,
It never feels decay but gathers life
 From the pure sunlight and the supreme air,
We live beneath Time's wasting sovereignty,
It is the child of all eternity.

The woes of man may serve an idle lay,
 Nor were it hard fond hearers to enthral,
Telling how Egypt's glory passed away,
 How London from its pinnacle must fall;
But this white flower, the conqueror of time,
Seems all too great for any boyish rhyme.

SERENADE

(FOR MUSIC)

THE western wind is blowing fair
  Across the dark Ægean sea,
And at the secret marble stair
  My Tyrian galley waits for thee.
Come down! the purple sail is spread,
  The watchman sleeps within the town.
O leave thy lily-flowered bed,
  O Lady mine, come down, come down!

She will not come, I know her well,
  Of lover's vows she hath no care,
And little good a man can tell
  Of one so cruel and so fair.
True love is but a woman's toy,
  They never know the lover's pain,
And I who loved as loves a boy
  Must love in vain, must love in vain.

O noble pilot, tell me true,
  Is that the sheen of golden hair?
Or is it but the tangled dew
  That blinds the passion-flower there?
Good sailor, come and tell me now
  Is that my Lady's lily hand?
Or is it but the gleaming prow,
  Or is it but the silver sand?

No! no! 'tis not the tangled dew,
   'Tis not the silver-fretted sand,
It is my own dear Lady true
   With golden hair and lily hand!
O noble pilot, steer for Troy,
   Good sailor, ply the labouring oar,
This is the Queen of life and joy
   Whom we must bear from Grecian shore!

The waning sky grows faint and blue,
   It wants an hour still of day,
Aboard! aboard! my gallant crew,
   O Lady mine, away! away!
O noble pilot, steer for Troy,
   Good sailor, ply the labouring oar,
O loved as only loves a boy!
   O loved for ever evermore!

ENDYMION

(FOR MUSIC)

THE apple trees are hung with gold,
  And birds are loud in Arcady,
The sheep lie bleating in the fold,
The wild goat runs across the wold,
But yesterday his love he told,
  I know he will come back to me.
O rising moon! O lady moon!
  Be you my lover's sentinel,
  You cannot choose but know him well,
For he is shod with purple shoon,
You cannot choose but know my love,
  For he a shepherd's crook doth bear,
And he is soft as any dove,
  And brown and curly is his hair.

The turtle now has ceased to call
  Upon her crimson-footed groom,
The grey wolf prowls about the stall,
The lily's singing seneschal
Sleeps in the lily-bell, and all
  The violet hills are lost in gloom.
O risen moon! O holy moon!
  Stand on the top of Helice,
  And if my own true love you see,
Ah! if you see the purple shoon,

The hazel crook, the lad's brown hair,
  . The goat-skin wrapped about his arm,
Tell him that I am waiting where
    The rushlight glimmers in the Farm.

The falling dew is cold and chill,
    And no bird sings in Arcady,
The little fauns have left the hill,
Even the tired daffodil
Has closed its gilded doors, and still
    My lover comes not back to me.
False moon! False moon! O waning moon!
    Where is my own true lover gone,
    Where are the lips vermilion,
The shepherd's crook, the purple shoon?
Why spread that silver pavilion,
    Why wear that veil of drifting mist?
Ah! thou hast young Endymion,
    Thou hast the lips that should be kissed!

LA BELLA DONNA DELLA MIA MENTE

My limbs are wasted with a flame,
　My feet are sore with travelling,
For, calling on my Lady's name,
　My lips have now forgot to sing.

O Linnet in the wild-rose brake
　Strain for my Love thy melody,
O Lark sing louder for love's sake,
　My gentle Lady passeth by.

O almond-blossoms bend adown
　Until ye reach her drooping head;
O twining branches weave a crown
　Of apple-blossoms white and red.

She is too fair for any man
　To see or hold his heart's delight,
Fairer than Queen or courtesan
　Or moon-lit water in the night.

Her hair is bound with myrtle leaves,
　(Green leaves upon her golden hair!)
Green grasses through the yellow sheaves
　Of autumn corn are not more fair.

Her little lips, more made to kiss
　Than to cry bitterly for pain,
Are tremulous as brook-water is,
　Or roses after evening rain.

Her neck is like white melilote
  Flushing for pleasure of the sun,
The throbbing of the linnet's throat
  Is not so sweet to look upon.

As a pomegranate, cut in twain,
  White-seeded, is her crimson mouth,
Her cheeks are as the fading stain
  Where the peach reddens to the south.

O twining hands! O delicate
  White body made for love and pain!
O House of Love! O desolate
  Pale flower beaten by the rain!

God can bring Winter unto May,
  And change the sky to flame and blue,
Or summer corn to gold from grey:
  One thing alone He cannot do.

He cannot change my love to hate,
  Or make thy face less fair to see,
Though now He knocketh at the gate
  With life and death—for you and me.

CHANSON

A RING of gold and a milk-white dove
  Are goodly gifts for thee,
And a hempen rope for your own love
  To hang upon a tree.

For you a House of Ivory,
  (Roses are white in the rose-bower)!
A narrow bed for me to lie,
  (White, O white, is the hemlock flower)'

Myrtle and jessamine for you,
  (O the red rose is fair to see)!
For me the cypress and the rue,
  (Fairest of all is rosemary)!

For you three lovers of your hand,
  (Green grass where a man lies dead)!
For me three paces on the sand,
  (Plant lilies at my head)!

CHARMIDES

CHARMIDES

I

He was a Grecian lad, who coming home
  With pulpy figs and wine from Sicily
Stood at his galley's prow, and let the foam
  Blow through his crisp brown curls unconsciously,
And holding wave and wind in boy's despite
Peered from his dripping seat across the wet and stormy
    night

Till with the dawn he saw a burnished spear
  Like a thin thread of gold against the sky,
And hoisted sail, and strained the creaking gear,
  And bade the pilot head her lustily
Against a nor'west gale, and all day long
Held on his way, and marked the rower's time with meas-
    ured song,

And when the faint Corinthian hills were red
  Dropped anchor in a little sandy bay,
And with fresh boughs of olive crowned his head,
  And brushed from cheek and throat the hoary spray,
And washed his limbs with oil, and from the hold
Brought out his linen tunic and his sandals brazen-soled,

And a rich robe stained with the fishes' juice
  Which of some swarthy trader he had bought
Upon the sunny quay at Syracuse,
  And was with Tyrian broideries inwrought,

And by the questioning merchants made his way
Up through the soft and silver woods, and when the labour-
    ing day

Had spun its tangled web of crimson cloud,
  Clomb the high hill, and with swift silent feet
Crept to the fane unnoticed by the crowd
  Of busy priests, and from some dark retreat
Watched the young swains his frolic playmates bring
The firstling of their little flock, and the shy shepherd fling

The crackling salt upon the flame, or hang
  His studded crook against the temple wall
To Her who keeps away the ravenous fang
  Of the base wolf from homestead and from stall,
And then the clear-voiced maidens 'gan to sing,
And to the altar each man brought some goodly offering,

A beechen cup brimming with milky foam,
  A fair cloth wrought with cunning imagery
Of hounds in chase, a waxen honey-comb
  Dripping with oozy gold which scarce the bee
Had ceased from building, a black skin of oil
Meet for the wrestlers, a great boar the fierce white-tusked
    spoil

Stolen from Artemis that jealous maid
  To please Athena, and the dappled hide
Of a tall stag who in some mountain glade
  Had met the shaft; and then the herald cried,
And from the pillared precinct one by one
Went the glad Greeks well pleased that they their simple
    vows had done.

And the old priest put out the waning fires
  Save that one lamp whose restless ruby glowed
For ever in the cell, and the shrill lyres
  Came fainter on the wind, as down the road
In joyous dance these country folk did pass,
And with stout hands the warder closed the gates of polished
    brass.

Long time he lay and hardly dared to breathe,
  And heard the cadenced drip of spilt-out wine,
And the rose-petals falling from the wreath
  As the night breezes wandered through the shrine,
And seemed to be in some entrancèd swoon
Till through the open roof above the full and brimming
    moon

Flooded with sheeny waves the marble floor,
  When from his nook up leapt the venturous lad,
And flinging wide the cedar-carven door
  Beheld an awful image saffron-clad
And armed for battle! the gaunt Griffin glared
From the huge helm, and the long lance of wreck and ruin
    flared

Like a red rod of flame, stony and steeled
  The Gorgon's head its leaden eyeballs rolled,
And writhed its snaky horrors through the shield,
  And gaped aghast with bloodless lips and cold
In passion impotent, while the blind gaze
The blinking owl between the feet hooted in shrill amaze.

The lonely fisher as he trimmed his lamp
  Far out at sea off Sunium, or cast
The net for tunnies, heard a brazen tramp
  Of horses smite the waves, and a wild blast

Divide the folded curtains of the night,
And knelt upon the little poop, and prayed in holy fright.

And guilty lovers in their venery
   Forgat a little while their stolen sweets,
Deeming they heard dread Diana's bitter cry;
   And the grim watchman on their lofty seats
Ran to their shields in haste precipitate,
Or strained black-bearded throats across the dusky parapet.

For round the temple rolled the clang of arms,
   And the twelve Gods leapt up in marble fear,
And the air quaked with dissonant alarums
   Till huge Poseidon shook his mighty spear,
And on the frieze the prancing horses neighed,
And the low tread of hurrying feet rang from the cavalcade.

Ready for death with parted lips he stood,
   And well content at such a price to see
That calm wide brow, that terrible maidenhood,
   The marvel of that pitiless chastity,
Ah! well content indeed, for never wight
Since Troy's young shepherd prince had seen so wonderful
    a sight.

Ready for death he stood, but lo! the air
   Grew silent, and the horses ceased to neigh,
And off his brow he tossed the clustering hair,
   And from his limbs he threw the cloak away,
For whom would not such love make desperate,
And nigher came, and touched her throat, and with hands
    violate

Undid the cuirass, and the crocus gown,
  And bared the breasts of polished ivory,
Till from the waist the peplos falling down
  Left visible the secret mystery
Which to no lover will Athena show,
The grand cool flanks, the crescent thighs, the bossy hills of
    snow.

Those who have never known a lover's sin
  Let them not read my ditty, it will be
To their dull ears so musicless and thin
  That they will have no joy in it, but ye
To whose wan cheeks now creeps the lingering smile,
Ye who have learned who Eros is,—O listen yet awhile.

A little space he let his greedy eyes
  Rest on the burnished image, till mere sight
Half swooned for surfeit of such luxuries,
  And then his lips in hungering delight
Fed on her lips, and round the towered neck
He flung his arms, nor cared at all his passion's will to check.

Never I ween did lover hold such tryst,
  For all night long he murmured honeyed word,
And saw her sweet unravished limbs, and kissed
  Her pale and argent body undisturbed,
And paddled with the polished throat, and pressed
His hot and beating heart upon her chill and icy breast.

It was as if Numidian javelins
  Pierced through and through his wild and whirling brain,
And his nerves thrilled like throbbing violins
  In exquisite pulsation, and the pain

Was such sweet anguish that he never drew
His lips from hers till overhead the lark of warning flew.

They who have never seen the daylight peer
   Into a darkened room, and drawn the curtain,
And with dull eyes and wearied from some dear
   And worshipped body risen, they for certain
Will never know of what I try to sing,
How long the last kiss was, how fond and late his lingering.

The moon was girdled with a crystal rim,
   The sign which shipmen say is ominous
Of wrath in heaven, the wan stars were dim,
   And the low lightening east was tremulous
With the faint fluttering wings of flying dawn,
Ere from the silent sombre shrine this lover had withdrawn.

Down the steep rock with hurried feet and fast
   Clomb the brave lad, and reached the cave of Pan,
And heard the goat-foot snoring as he passed,
   And leapt upon a grassy knoll and ran
Like a young fawn unto an olive wood
Which in a shady valley by the well-built city stood.

And sought a little stream, which well he knew
   For oftentimes with boyish careless shout
The green and crested grebe he would pursue,
   Or snare in woven net the silver trout,
And down amid the startled reeds he lay
Panting in breathless sweet affright, and waited for the day.

On the green bank he lay, and let one hand
   Dip in the cool dark eddies listlessly,
And soon the breath of morning came and fanned
   His hot flushed cheeks, or lifted wantonly

The tangled curls from off his forehead, while
He on the running water gazed with strange and secret
   smile.

And soon the shepherd in rough woolen cloak
   With his long crook undid the wattled cotes,
And from the stack a thin blue wreath of smoke
   Curled through the air across the ripening oats,
And on the hill the yellow house-dog bayed
As through the crisp and rustling fern the heavy cattle
   strayed.

And when the light-foot mower went afield
   Across the meadows laced with threaded dew,
And the sheep bleated on the misty weald,
   And from its nest the waking corncrake flew,
Some woodmen saw him lying by the stream
And marvelled much that any lad so beautiful could seem

Nor deemed him born of mortals, and one said,
   "It is young Hylas, that false runaway
Who with a Naiad now would make his bed,
   Forgetting Herakles," but others, "Nay,
It is Narcissus, his own paramour,
Those are the fond and crimson lips no woman can allure."

And when they nearer came a third one cried,
   "It is young Dionysos who has hid
His spear and fawnskin by the river side
   Weary of hunting with the Bassarid,
And wise indeed were we away to fly,
They live not long who on the gods immortal come to spy."

So turned they back, and feared to look behind,
  And told the timid swain how they had seen
Amid the reeds some woodland God reclined,
  And no man dared to cross the open green,
And on that day no olive-tree was slain,
No rushes cut, but all deserted was the fair domain,

Save when the neat-herd's lad, his empty pail
  Well slung upon his back, with leap and bound
Raced on the other side, and stopped to hail,
  Hoping that he some comrade new had found,
And gat no answer, and then half afraid
Passed on his simple way, or down the still and silent glade

A little girl ran laughing from the farm,
  Not thinking of love's secret mysteries,
And when she saw the white and gleaming arm
  And all his manlihood, with longing eyes
Whose passion mocked her sweet virginity
Watched him awhile, and then stole back sadly and wearily.

Far off he heard the city's hum and noise,
  And now and then the shriller laughter where
The passionate purity of brown-limbed boys
  Wrestled or raced in the clear healthful air,
And now and then a little tinkling bell
As the shorn wether led the sheep down to the mossy well.

Through the grey willows danced the fretful gnat,
  The grasshopper chirped idly from the tree,
In sleek and oily coat the water-rat
  Breasting the little ripples manfully
Made for the wild duck's nest, from bough to bough
Hopped the shy finch, and the huge tortoise crept across the
    slough.

On the faint wind floated the silky seeds
  As the bright scythe swept through the waving grass,
The ousel-cock splashed circles in the reeds
  And flecked with silver whorls the forest's glass,
Which scarce had caught again its imagery
Ere from its bed the dusky trench leapt at the dragon-fly.

But little care he had for anything
  Though up and down the beech the squirrel played,
And from the copse the linnet 'gan to sing
  To her brown mate her sweetest serenade;
Ah! little care indeed, for he had seen
The breasts of Pallas and the naked wonder of the Queen.

But when the herdsman called his straggling goats
  With whistling pipe across the rocky road,
And the shard-beetle with its trumpet-notes
  Boomed through the darkening woods, and seemed to
    bode
Of coming storm, and the belated crane
Passed homeward like a shadow, and the dull big drops of
  rain

Fell on the pattering fig-leaves, up he rose,
  And from the gloomy forest went his way
Past sombre homestead and wet orchard-close
  And came at last unto a little quay,
And called his mates aboard, and took his seat
On the high poop, and pushed from land, and loosed the
    dripping sheet,

And steered across the bay, and when nine suns
  Passed down the long and laddered way of gold,
And nine pale moons had breathed their orisons
  To the chaste stars their confessors, or told

Their dearest secret to the downy moth
That will not fly at noonday, through the foam and surging
     froth

Came a great owl with yellow sulphurous eyes
     And lit upon the ship, whose timbers creaked
As though the lading of three argosies
     Were in the hold, and flapped its wings and shrieked,
And darkness straightway stole across the deep,
Sheathed was Orion's sword, dread Mars himself fled down
     the steep,

And the moon hid behind a tawny mask
     Of drifting cloud, and from the ocean's marge
Rose the red plume, the huge and hornèd casque,
     The seven-cubit spear, the brazen targe!
And clad in bright and burnished panoply
Athena strode across the stretch of sick and shivering sea!

To the dull sailors' sight her loosened locks
     Seemed like the jagged storm-rack, and her feet
Only the spume that floats on hidden rocks,
     And, marking how the rising waters beat
Against a rolling ship, the pilot cried
To the young helmsman at the stern to luff to windward
     side.

But he, the overbold adulterer,
     A dear profaner of great mysteries,
An ardent amorous idolater,
     When he beheld those grand relentless eyes
Laughed loud for joy, and crying out "I come"
Leapt from the lofty poop into the chill and churning foam,

Then fell from the high heaven one bright star,
   One dancer left the circling galaxy,
And back to Athens on her clattering car
   In all the pride of venged divinity
Pale Pallas swept with shrill and steely clank,
And a few gurgling bubbles rose where her boy lover sank.

And the mast shuddered as the gaunt owl flew
   With mocking hoots after the wrathful Queen,
And the old pilot bade the trembling crew
   Hoist the big sail, and told how he had seen
Close to the stern a dim and giant form,
And like a dippling swallow the stout ship dashed through
      the storm.

And no man dared to speak of Charmides
   Deeming that he some evil thing had wrought,
And when they reached the strait Symplegades
   They beached their galley on the shore, and sought
The toll-gate of the city hastily,
And in the market showed their brown and pictured pottery.

II

But some good Triton-god had ruth, and bare
   The boy's drowned body back to Grecian land,
And mermaids combed his dank and dripping hair
   And smoothed his brow, and loosed his clenching hand,
Some brought sweet spices from far Araby,
And others bade the halcyon sing her softest lullaby.

And when he neared his old Athenian home,
   A mighty billow rose up suddenly
Upon whose oily back the clotted foam
   Lay diapered in some strange fantasy,

And clasping him unto its glassy breast
Swept landward, like a white-maned steed upon a venturous
      quest!

Now where Colonos leans unto the sea
   There lies a long and level stretch of lawn,
The rabbit knows it, and the mountain bee
   For it deserts Hymettus, and the Faun
Is not afraid, for never through the day
Comes a cry ruder than the shout of shepherd lads at play.

But often from the thorny labyrinth
   And tangled branches of the circling wood
The stealthy hunter sees young Hyacinth
   Hurling the polished disk, and draws his hood
Over his guilty gaze, and creeps away,
Nor dares to wind his horn, or—else at the first break of day

The Dryads come and throw the leathern ball
   Along the reedy shore, and circumvent
Some goat-eared Pan to be their seneschal
   For fear of bold Poseidon's ravishment,
And loose their girdles, with shy timorous eyes,
Lest from the surf his azure arms and purple beard should
      rise

On this side and on that a rocky cave,
   Hung with the yellow-belled laburnum, stands,
Smooth is the beach, save where some ebbing wave
   Leaves its faint outline etched upon the sands,
As though it feared to be too soon forgot
By the green rush, its playfellow,—and yet, it is a spot

So small, that the inconstant butterfly
  Could steal the hoarded honey from each flower
Ere it was noon, and still not satisfy
  Its over-greedy love,—within an hour
A sailor boy, were he but rude enow
To land and pluck a garland for his galley's painted prow,

Would almost leave the little meadow bare,
  For it knows nothing of great pageantry,
Only a few narcissi here and there
  Stand separate in sweet austerity,
Dotting the un-mown grass with silver stars,
And here and there a daffodil waves tiny scimitars.

Hither the billow brought him, and was glad
  Of such dear servitude, and where the land
Was virgin of all waters laid the lad
  Upon the golden margent of the strand,
And like a lingering lover oft returned
To kiss those pallid limbs which once with intense fire
    burned,

Ere the wet seas had quenched that holocaust,
  That self-fed flame, that passionate lustihead,
Ere grisly death with chill and nipping frost
  Had withered up those lilies white and red
Which, while the boy would through the forest range,
Answered each other in a sweet antiphonal counter-change.

And when at dawn the wood-nymphs, hand-in-hand,
  Threaded the bosky dell, their satyr spied
The boy's pale body stretched upon the sand,
  And feared Poseidon's treachery, and cried,
And like bright sunbeams flitting through a glade
Each startled Dryad sought some safe and leafy ambuscade,

Save one white girl, who deemed it would not be
  So dread a thing to feel a sea-god's arms
Crushing her breasts in amorous tyranny,
  And longed to listen to those subtle charms
Insidious lovers weave when they would win
Some fencèd fortress, and stole back again, nor thought it
    sin

To yield her treasure unto one so fair,
  And lay beside him, thirsty with love's drouth,
Called him soft names, played with his tangled hair,
  And with hot lips made havoc of his mouth
Afraid he might not wake, and then afraid
Lest he might wake too soon, fled back, and then, fond
    renegade,

Returned to fresh assault, and all day long
  Sat at his side, and laughed at her new toy,
And held his hand, and sang her sweetest song,
  Then frowned to see how froward was the boy
Who would not with her maidenhood entwine,
Nor knew that three days since his eyes had looked on Pros-
    erpine,

Nor knew what sacrilege his lips had done,
  But said, "He will awake, I know him well,
He will awake at evening when the sun
  Hangs his red shield on Corinth's citadel,
This sleep is but a cruel treachery
To make me love him more, and in some cavern of the sea

Deeper than ever falls the fisher's line,
  Already a huge Triton blows his horn,
And weaves a garland from the crystalline
  And drifting ocean-tendrils to adorn

The emerald pillars of our bridal bed,
For sphered in foaming silver, and with coral-crownèd head,

We two will sit upon a throne of pearl,
  · And a blue wave will be our canopy,
And at our feet water-snakes will curl
    In all their amethystine panoply
Of diamonded mail, and we will mark
The mullets swimming by the mast of some storm-foundered
    bark,

Vermilion-finned with eyes of bossy gold
    Like flakes of crimson light, and the great deep
His glassy-portaled chamber will unfold,
    And we will see the painted dolphins sleep
Cradled by murmuring halcyons on the rocks
Where Proteus in quaint suit of green pastures his monstrous
    flocks.

And tremulous opal-hued anemones
    Will wave their purple fringes where we tread
Upon the mirrored floor, and argosies
    Of fishes flecked with tawny scales will thread
The drifting cordage of the shattered wreck,
And honey-coloured amber beads our twining limbs will
    deck."

But when that baffled Lord of War the Sun
    With gaudy pennon flying passed away
Into his brazen House, and one by one
    The little yellow stars began to stray
Across the field of heaven, ah! then indeed
She feared his lips upon her lips would never care to feed,

And cried, "Awake, already the pale moon
    Washes the trees with silver, and the wave
Creeps grey and chilly up this sandy dune,
    The croaking frogs are out, and from the cave
The night-jar shrieks, the fluttering bats repass,
And the brown stoat with hollow flanks creeps through the
    dusky grass.

Nay, though thou art a God, be not so coy,
    For in yon stream there is a little reed
That often whispers how a lovely boy
    Lay with her once upon a grassy mead,
Who when his cruel pleasure he had done
Spread wings of rustling gold and soared aloft into the sun.

Be no so coy, the laurel trembles still
    With great Apollo's kisses, and the fir
Whose clustering sisters fringe the seaward hill
    Hath many a tale of that bold ravisher
Whom men call Boreas, and I have seen
The mocking eyes of Hermes through the poplar's silvery
    sheen.

Even the jealous Naiads call me fair,
    And every morn a young and ruddy swain
Woos me with apples and with locks of hair,
    And seeks to soothe my virginal disdain
By all the gifts the gentle wood-nymphs love;
But yesterday he brought to me an iris-plumaged dove

With little crimson feet, which with its store
    Of seven spotted eggs the cruel lad
Had stolen from the lofty sycamore
    At daybreak, when her amorous comrade had

Flown off in search of berried juniper
Which most they love; the fretful wasp, that earliest vintager

Of the blue grapes, hath not persistency
   So constant as this simple shepherd-boy
For my poor lips, his joyous purity
   And laughing sunny eyes might well decoy
A Dryad from her oath to Artemis;
For very beautiful is he, his mouth was made to kiss,

His argent forehead, like a rising moon
   Over the dusky hills of meeting brows,
Is crescent shaped, the hot and Tyrian noon
   Leads from the myrtle-grove no goodlier spouse
For Cytheræa, the first silky down
Fringes his blushing cheeks, and his young limbs are strong
      and brown:

And he is rich, and fat and fleecy herds
   Of bleating sheep upon his meadows lie,
And many an earthen bowl of yellow curds
   Is in his homestead for the thievish fly
To swim and drown in, the pink clover mead
Keeps its sweet store for him, and he can pipe on oaten reed.

And yet I love him not, for it was for thee
   I kept my love, I knew that thou would'st come
To rid me of this pallid chastity;
   Thou fairest flower of the flowerless foam
Of all the wide Ægean, brightest star
Of ocean's azure heavens where the mirrored planets are!

I knew that thou would'st come, for when at first
   The dry wood burgeoned, and the sap of Spring
Swelled in my green and tender bark or burst
   To myriad multitudinous blossoming
Which mocked the midnight with its mimic moons
That did not dread the dawn, and first the thrushes' rap-
     turous tunes

Startled the squirrel from its granary,
   And cuckoo flowers fringed the narrow lane,
Through my young leaves a sensuous ecstasy
   Crept like new wine, and every mossy vein
Throbbed with the fitful pulse of amorous blood,
And the wild winds of passion shook my slim stem's maiden-
     hood.

The trooping fawns at evening came and laid
   Their cool black noses on my lowest boughs,
And on my topmost branch the blackbird made
   A little nest of grasses for his spouse,
And now and then a twittering wren would light
On a thin twig which hardly bare the weight of such delight.

I was the Attic shepherd's trysting place,
   Beneath my shadow Amaryllis lay,
And round my trunk would laughing Daphnis chase
   The timorous girl, till tired out with play
She felt his hot breath stir her tangled hair,
And turned, and looked, and fled no more from such de-
     lightful snare.

Then come away unto my ambuscade
   Where clustering woodbine weaves a canopy
For amorous pleasaunce, and the rustling shade
   Of Paphian myrtles seems to sanctify

The dearest rites of love, there in the cool
And green recesses of its farthest depth there is a pool,

The ouzel's haunt, the wild bee's pasturage,
    For round its rim great creamy lilies float
Through their flat leaves in verdant anchorage,
    Each cup a white-sailed golden-laden boat
Steered by a dragon-fly,—be not afraid
To leave this wan and wave-kissed shore, surely the piace
        was made

For lovers such as we; the Cyprian Queen,
    One arm around her boyish paramour,
Strays often there at eve, and I have seen
    The moon strip off her misty vestiture
For young Endymion's eyes; be not afraid,
The panther feet of Dian never tread that secret glade.

Nay, if thou will'st, back to the beating brine,
    Back to the boisterous billow let us go,
And walk all day beneath the hyaline
    Huge vault of Neptune's watery portico,
And watch the purple monsters of the deep
Sport in ungainly play, and from his lair keen Xiphias leap.

For if my mistress find me lying here
    She will not ruth or gentle pity show,
But lay her boar-spear down, and with austere
    Relentless fingers string the cornel bow,
And draw the feathered notch against her breast,
And loose the archèd cord, ay, even now upon the quest

I hear her hurrying feet,—awake, awake,
    Thou laggard in love's battle! once at least
Let me drink deep of passion's wine, and slake
    My parchèd being with the nectarous feast

Which even Gods affect! O come, Love, come,
Still we have time to reach the cavern of thine azure home."

Scarce had she spoken when the shuddering trees
    Shook, and the leaves divided, and the air
Grew conscious of a God, and the grey seas
    Crawled backward, and a long and dismal blare
Blew from some tasselled horn, a sleuth-hound bayed,
And like a flame a barbèd reed flew whizzing down the
    glade.

And where the little flowers of her breast
    Just brake into their milky blossoming,
This murderous paramour, this unbidden guest,
    Pierced and struck deep in horrid chambering,
And ploughed a bloody furrow with its dart,
And dug a long red road, and cleft with wingèd death her
    heart.

Sobbing her life out with a bitter cry
    On the boy's body fell the Dryad maid,
Sobbing for incomplete virginity,
    And raptures unenjoyed, and pleasures dead,
And all the pain of things unsatisfied,
And the bright drops of crimson youth crept down her
    throbbing side.

Ah! pitiful it was to hear her moan,
    And very pitiful to see her die
Ere she had yielded up her sweets, or known
    The joy of passion, that dread mystery
Which not to know is not to live at all,
And yet to know is to be held in death's most deadly thrall.

But as it hapt the Queen of Cythere,
  Who with Adonis all night long had lain
Within some shepherd's hut in Arcady,
  On team of silver doves and gilded wain
Was journeying Paphos-ward, high up afar
From mortal ken between the mountains and the morning
    star,

And when low down she spied the hapless pair,
  And heard the Oread's faint despairing cry,
Whose cadence seemed to play upon the air
  As though it were a viol, hastily
She bade her pigeons fold each straining plume,
And dropt to earth, and reached the strand, and saw their
    dolorous doom.

For as a gardener turning back his head
  To catch the last notes of the linnet, mows
With careless scythe too near some flower bed,
  And cuts the thorny pillar of the rose,
And with the flower's loosened loveliness
Strews the brown mould, or as some shepherd lad in wan-
    tonness

Driving his little flock along the mead
  Treads down two daffodils which side by side
Have lured the lady-bird with yellow brede
  And made the gaudy moth forget its pride,
Treads down their brimming golden chalices
Under light feet which were not made for such rude ravages,

Or as a schoolboy tired of his book
  Flings himself down upon the reedy grass
And plucks two water-lilies from the brook,
  And for a time forgets the hour glass,

Then wearies of their sweets, and goes his way,
And lets the hot sun kill them, even so these lovers lay.

And Venus cried, "It is dread Artemis
    Whose bitter hand hath wrought this cruelty,
Or else that mightier maid whose care it is
    To guard her strong and stainless majesty
Upon the hill Athenian,—alas!
That they who loved so well unloved into death's house
    should pass."

So with soft hands she laid the boy and girl
    In the great golden waggon tenderly,
Her white throat whiter than a moony pearl
    Just threaded with a blue vein's tapestry
Had not yet ceased to throb, and still her breast
Swayed like a wind-stirred lily in ambiguous unrest.

And then each pigeon spread its milky van,
    The bright car soared into the dawning sky,
And like a cloud the aerial caravan
    Passed over the Ægean silently,
Till the faint air was troubled with the song
From the wan mouths that call on bleeding Thammuz all
    night long.

But when the doves had reached their wonted goal
    Where the wide star of orbèd marble dips
Its snows into the sea, her fluttering soul
    Just shook the trembling petals of her lips
And passed into the void, and Venus knew
That one fair maid the less would walk amid her retinue,

And bade her servants carve a cedar chest
   With all the wonder of this history,
Within whose scented womb their limbs should rest
   Where olive-trees make tender the blue sky
On the low hills of Paphos, and the faun
Pipes in the noonday, and the nightingale sings on till dawn

Nor failed they to obey her hest, and ere
   The morning bee had stung the daffodil
With tiny fretful spear, or from its lair
   The waking stag had leapt across the rill
And roused the ouzel, or the lizard crept
Athwart the sunny rock, beneath the grass their bodies slept.

And when day brake, within that silver shrine
   Fed by the flames of cressets tremulous,
Queen Venus knelt and prayed to Proserpine
   That she whose beauty made Death amorous
Should beg a guerdon from her pallid Lord,
And let Desire pass across dread Charon's icy ford.

III

In melancholy moonless Acheron,
   Far from the goodly earth and joyous day,
Where no spring ever buds, nor ripening sun
   Weighs down the apple trees, nor flowery May
Chequers with chestnut blooms the grassy floor,
Where thrushes never sing, and piping linnets mate no more,

There by a dim and dark Lethæan well
   Young Charmides was lying, wearily
He plucked the blossoms from the asphodel,
   And with its little rifled treasury

Strewed the dull waters of the dusky stream,
And watched the white stars founder, and the land was like
a dream,

When as he gazed into the watery glass
  And through his brown hair's curly tangles scanned
His own wan face, a shadow seemed to pass
  Across the mirror, and a little hand
Stole into his, and warm lips timidly
Brushed his pale cheeks, and breathed their secret forth into
a sigh.

Then turned he round his weary eyes and saw,
  And ever nigher still their faces came,
And nigher ever did their young mouths draw
  Until they seemed one perfect rose of flame,
And longing arms around her neck he cast,
And felt her throbbing bosom, and his breath came hot and
fast,

And all his hoarded sweets were hers to kiss,
  And all her maidenhood was his to slay,
And limb to limb in long and rapturous bliss
  Their passion waxed and waned,—O why essay
To pipe again of love, too venturous reed!
Enough, enough that Erôs laughed upon that flowerless
mead.

Too venturous poesy, O why essay
  To pipe again of passion! fold thy wings
O'er daring Icarus and bid thy lay
  Sleep hidden in the lyre's silent strings
Till thou hast found the old Castalian rill,
Or from the Lesbian waters plucked drowned Sappho's
golden quill!

Enough, enough that he whose life had been
  A fiery pulse of sin, a splendid shame,
Could in the loveless land of Hades glean
  One scorching harvest from those fields of flame
Where passion walks with naked unshod feet
And is not wounded,—ah! enough that once their lips could
    meet

In that wild throb when all existences
  Seemed narrowed to one single ecstasy
Which dies through its own sweetness and the stress
  Of too much pleasure, ere Persephone
Had bade them serve her by the ebon throne
Of the pale God who in the fields of Enna loosed her zone.

FLOWERS OF GOLD

IMPRESSIONS

I

LES SILHOUETTES

THE sea is flecked with bars of grey,
The dull dead wind is out of tune,
And like a withered leaf the moon
Is blown across the stormy bay.

Etched clear upon the pallid sand
Lies the black boat: a sailor boy
Clambers aboard in careless joy
With laughing face and gleaming hand.

And overhead the curlews cry,
Where through the dusky upland grass
The young brown-throated reapers pass,
Like silhouettes against the sky.

II

LA FUITE DE LA LUNE

To outer senses there is peace,
A dreamy peace on either hand,
Deep silence in the shadowy land,
Deep silence where the shadows cease.

Save for a cry that echoes shrill
From some lone bird disconsolate;
A corncrake calling to its mate;
The answer from the misty hill.

And suddenly the moon withdraws
Her sickle from the lightening skies,
And to her sombre cavern flies,
Wrapped in a veil of yellow gauze.

THE GRAVE OF KEATS

RID of the world's injustice, and his pain,
  He rests at last beneath God's veil of blue:
  Taken from life when life and love were new
The youngest of the martyrs here is lain,
Fair as Sebastian, and as early slain.
  No cypress shades his grave, no funeral yew,
  But gentle violets weeping with the dew
Weave on his bones an ever-blossoming chain.
O proudest heart that broke for misery!
  O sweetest lips since those of Mitylene!
  O poet-painter of our English Land!
Thy name was writ in water—it shall stand:
  And tears like mine will keep thy memory green,
  As Isabella did her Basil-tree.

ROME.

THEOCRITUS

A VILLANNELLE

O SINGER of Persephone!
  In the dim meadows desolate
Dost thou remember Sicily?

Still through the ivy flits the bee
  Where Amaryllis lies in state;
O Singer of Persephone!

Simætha calls on Hecate
  And hears the wild dogs at the gate:
Dost thou remember Sicily?

Still by the light and laughing sea
  Poor Polypheme bemoans his fate;
O Singer of Persephone!

And still in boyish rivalry
  Young Daphnis challenges his mate;
Dost thou remember Sicily?

Slim Lacon keeps a goat for thee,
  For thee the jocund shepherds wait;
O Singer of Persephone!
Dost thou remember Sicily?

IN THE GOLD ROOM

A HARMONY

HER ivory hands on the ivory keys
   Strayed in a fitful fantasy,
Like the silver gleam when the poplar trees
   Rustle their pale leaves listlessly,
   Or the drifting foam of a restless sea
When the waves show their teeth in the flying breeze.

Her gold hair fell on the wall of gold
   Like the delicate gossamer tangles spun
On the burnished disk of the marigold,
   Or the sunflower turning to meet the sun
   When the gloom of the dark blue night is done,
And the spear of the lily is aureoled.

And her sweet red lips on these lips of mine
   Burned like the ruby fire set
In the swinging lamp of a crimson shrine,
   Or the bleeding wounds of the pomegranate,
   Or the heart of the lotus drenched and wet
With the spilt-out blood of the rose-red wine.

BALLADE DE MARGUERITE

(NORMANDE)

I AM weary of lying within the chase
When the knights are meeting in market-place.

Nay, go not thou to the red-roofed town
Lest the hoofs of the war-horse tread thee down.

But I would not go where the Squires ride,
I would only walk by my Lady's side.

Alack! and alack! thou art overbold,
A Forester's son may not eat off gold.

Will she love me the less that my Father is seen
Each Martinmas day in a doublet green?

Perchance she is sewing at tapestrie,
Spindle and loom are not meet for thee.

Ah, if she is working the arras bright
I might ravel the threads by the fire-light.

Perchance she is hunting of the deer,
How could you follow o'er hill and mere?

Ah, if she is riding with the court,
I might run beside her and wind the morte.

Perchance she is kneeling in St. Denys,
(On her soul may our Lady have gramercy!)

Ah, if she is praying in lone chapelle,
I might swing the censer and ring the bell.

Come in, my son, for you look sae pale,
The father shall fill thee a stoup of ale.

But who are these knights in bright array?
Is it a pageant the rich folks play?

'Tis the King of England from over sea,
Who has come unto visit our fair countrie.

But why does the curfew toll sae low?
And why do the mourners walk a-row?

O 'tis Hugh of Amiens my sister's son
Who is lying stark, for his day is done.

Nay, nay, for I see white lilies clear,
It is no strong man who lies on the bier.

O 'tis old Dame Jeannette that kept the hall,
I knew she would die at the autumn fall.

Dame Jeanette has not that gold-brown hair,
Old Jeannette was not a maiden fair.

O 'tis none of our kith and none of our kin,
(Her soul may our Lady assoil from sin!)

But I hear the boy's voice chaunting sweet,
"*Elle est morte, la Marquerite.*"

Come in, my son, and lie on the bed,
And let the dead folk bury their dead.

O mother, you know I loved her true:
O mother, hath one grave room for two?

THE DOLE OF THE KING'S DAUGHTER

(BRETON)

SEVEN stars in the still water,
    And seven in the sky;
Seven sins on the King's daughter,
    Deep in her soul to lie.

Red roses are at her feet,
    (Roses are red in her red-gold hair)
And O where her bosom and girdle meet
    Red roses are hidden there.

Fair is the knight who lieth slain
    Amid the rush and reed,
See the lean fishes that are fain
    Upon dead men to feed.

Sweet is the page that lieth there,
    (Cloth of gold is goodly prey,)
See the black ravens in the air,
    Black, O black as the night are they.

What do they there so stark and dead?
    (There is blood upon her hand)
Why are the lilies flecked with red?
    (There is blood on the river sand.)

There are two that ride from the south and east,
 And two from the north and west,
For the black raven a goodly feast,
 For the King's daughter rest.

There is one man who loves her true,
 (Red, O red, is the stain of gore!)
He hath duggen a grave by the darksome yew,
 (One grave will do for four.)

No moon in the still heaven,
 In the black water none,
The sins on her soul are seven.
 The sin upon his is one.

AMOR INTELLECTUALIS

Oft have we trod the vales of Castaly
  And heard sweet notes of sylvan music blown
  From antique reeds to common folk unknown:
And often launched our bark upon that sea
Which the nine Muses hold in empery,
  And ploughed free furrows through the wave and foam,
  Nor spread reluctant sail for more safe home
Till we had freighted well our argosy.
Of which despoilèd treasures these remain,
  Sordello's passion, and the honeyed line
Of young Endymion, lordly Tamburlaine
  Driving his pampered jades, and, more than these,
The seven-fold vision of the Florentine,
  And grave-browed Milton's solemn harmonies.

SANTA DECCA

THE Gods are dead: no longer do we bring
  To grey-eyed Pallas crowns of olive-leaves!
  Demeter's child no more hath tithe of sheaves,
And in the noon the careless shepherds sing,
For Pan is dead, and all the wantoning
  By secret glade and devious haunt is o'er:
  Young Hylas seeks the water-springs no more;
Great Pan is dead, and Mary's son is King.

And yet—perchance in this sea-trancèd isle,
  Chewing the bitter fruit of memory,
  Some God lies hidden in the asphodel.
Ah Love! if such there be, then it were well
  For us to fly his anger: nay, but see,
  The leaves are stirring: let us watch awhile.

CORFU.

A VISION

Two crownèd Kings, and One that stood alone   2
    With no green weight of laurels round his head,
    But with sad eyes as one uncomforted,
And wearied with man's never-ceasing moan
For sins no bleating victim can atone,
    And sweet long lips with tears and kisses fed.
    Girt was he in a garment black and red,
And at his feet I marked a broken stone
    Which sent up lilies, dove-like, to his knees.
Now at their sight, my heart being lit with flame
    I cried to Beatricé, "Who are these?"
And she made answer, knowing well each name,
    "Æschylos first, the second Sophokles,
    And last (wide stream of tears!) Euripides."

IMPRESSION DE VOYAGE

THE sea was sapphire coloured, and the sky
 Burned like a heated opal through the air;
 We hoisted sail; the wind was blowing fair
For the blue lands that to the eastward lie.
From the steep prow I marked with quickening eye
 Zakynthos, every olive grove and creek,
 Ithaca's cliff, Lycaon's snowy peak,
And all the flower-strewn hills of Arcady.
The flapping of the sail against the mast,
 The ripple of the water on the side,
 The ripple of girls' laughter at the stern,
The only sounds:—when 'gan the West to burn
 And a red sun upon the seas to ride,
 I stood upon the soil of Greece at last!

KATAKOLS.

THE GRAVE OF SHELLEY

LIKE burnt-out torches by a sick man's bed
  Gaunt cypress-trees stand round the sun-bleached stone;
  Here doth the little night-owl make her throne,
And the slight lizard show his jewelled head.
And, where the chaliced poppies flame to red,
  In the still chamber of yon pyramid
  Surely some Old-World Sphinx lurks darkly hid,
Grim warder of this pleasaunce of the dead.

Ah! sweet indeed to rest within the womb
  Of Earth, great mother of eternal sleep,
But sweeter far for thee a restless tomb
  In the blue cavern of an echoing deep,
Or where the tall ships founder in the gloom
  Against the rocks of some wave-shattered steep.

ROME.

BY THE ARNO

THE oleander on the wall
Grows crimson in the dawning light,
Though the grey shadows of the night
Lie yet on Florence like a pall.

The dew is bright upon the hill,
And bright the blossoms overhead,
But ah! the grasshoppers have fled,
The little Attic song is still.

Only the leaves are gently stirred
By the soft breathing of the gale,
And in the almond-scented vale
The lonely nightingale is heard.

The day will make thee silent soon,
O nightingale sing on for love!
While yet upon the shadowy grove
Splinter the arrows of the moon.

Before across the silent lawn
In sea-green vest the morning steals,
And to love's frightened eyes reveals
The long white fingers of the dawn

Fast climbing up the eastern sky
To grasp and slay the shuddering night
All careless of my heart's delight,
Or if the nightingale should die.

IMPRESSIONS DU THÉÂTRE

FABIEN DEI FRANCHI

To My Friend HENRY IRVING

THE silent room, the heavy creeping shade,
  The dead that travel fast, the opening door,
  The murdered brother rising through the floor,
The ghost's white fingers on thy shoulders laid,
And then the lonely duel in the glade,
  The broken swords, the stifled scream, the gore,
  Thy grand revengeful eyes when all is o'er,—
These things are well enough,—but thou wert made
  For more august creation! frenzied Lear
  Should at thy bidding wander on the heath
  With the shrill fool to mock him, Romeo
For thee should lure his love, and desperate fear
Pluck Richard's recreant dagger from its sheath—
  Thou trumpet set for Shakespeare's lips to blow!

PHEDRE

To SARAH BERNHARDT

How vain and dull this common world must seem
  To such a One as thou, who should'st have talked
  At Florence with Mirandola, or walked
Through the cool olives of the Academe:
Thou should'st have gathered reeds from a green stream
  For Goat-foot Pan's shrill piping, and have played
  With the white girls in that Phæacian glade
Where grave Odysseus wakened from his dream.

Ah! surely once some urn of Attic clay
  Held thy wan dust, and thou hast come again
  Back to this common world so dull and vain,
For thou wert weary of the sunless day,
  The heavy fields of scentless asphodel,
  The loveless lips with which men kiss in Hell.

WRITTEN AT THE LYCEUM THEATRE

I

PORTIA

To ELLEN TERRY

I MARVEL not Bassanio was so bold
To peril all he had upon the lead,
Or that proud Aragon bent low his head
Or that Morocco's fiery heart grew cold:
For in that gorgeous dress of beaten gold
    Which is more golden than the golden sun
    No woman Veronesé looked upon
Was half so fair as thou whom I behold.
Yet fairer when with wisdom as your shield
    The sober-suited lawyer's gown you donned,
And would not let the laws of Venice yield
    Antonio's heart to that accursèd Jew—
O Portia! take my heart: it is thy due:
I think I will not quarrel with the Bond.

II

QUEEN HENRIETTA MARIA

To ELLEN TERRY

In the lone tent, waiting for victory,
   She stands with eyes marred by the mists of pain,
   Like some wan lily overdrenched with rain:
The clamorous clang of arms, the ensanguined sky,
War's ruin, and the wreck of chivalry
   To her proud soul no common fear can bring:
   Bravely she tarrieth for her Lord the King,
Her soul a-flame with passionate ecstasy.
O Hair of God! O Crimson Lips! O Face
   Made for the luring and the love of man!
   With thee I do forget the toil and stress,
The loveless road that knows no resting place,
   Time's straitened pulse, the soul's dread weariness,
   My freedom, and my life republican!

CAMMA

As one who poring on a Grecian urn
  Scans the fair shapes some Attic hand hath made,
  God with slim goddess, goodly man with maid,
And for their beauty's sake is loth to turn
And face the obvious day, must I not yearn
  For many a secret moon of indolent bliss,
  When in the midmost shrine of Artemis
I see thee standing, antique-limbed, and stern?

And yet—methinks I'd rather see thee play
  That serpent of old Nile, whose witchery
Made Emperors drunken,—come, great Egypt, shake
  Our stage with all thy mimic pageants! Nay,
  I am grown sick of unreal passions, make
The world thine Actium, me thine Anthony!

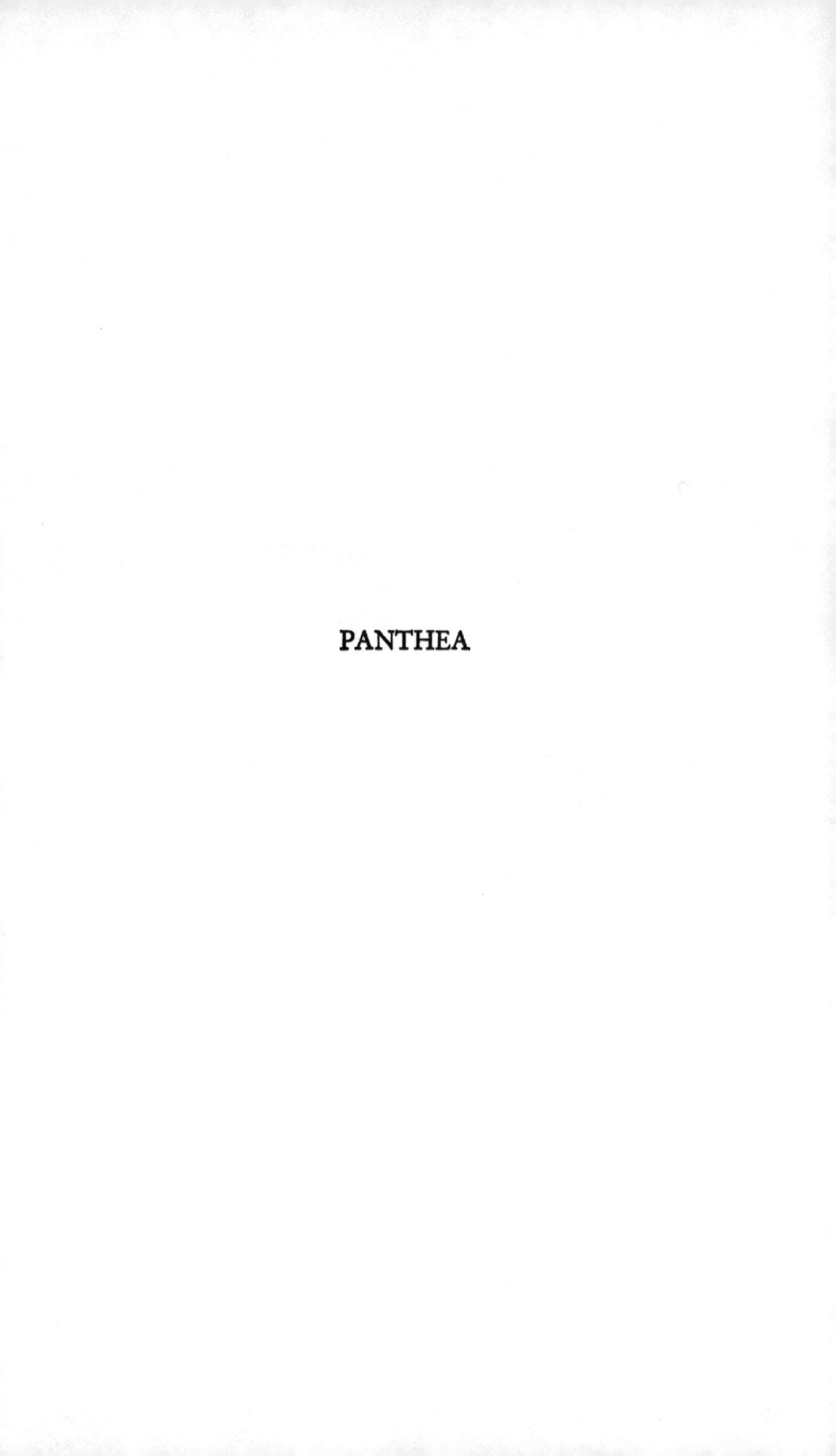

PANTHEA

PANTHEA

Nay, let us walk from fire unto fire,
  From passionate pain to deadlier delight,—
I am too young to live without desire,
  Too young art thou to waste this summer night
Asking those idle questions which of old
Man sought of seer and oracle, and no reply was told.

For, sweet, to feel is better than to know,
  And wisdom is a childless heritage,
One pulse of passion—youth's first fiery glow,—
  Are worth the hoarded proverbs of the sage:
Vex not thy soul with dead philosophy,
  Have we not lips to kiss with, hearts to love and eyes to
    see!

Dost thou not hear the murmuring nightingale,
  Like water bubbling from a silver jar,
So soft she sings the envious moon is pale,
  That high in heaven she is hung so far
She cannot hear that love-enraptured tune,—
Mark how she wreathes each horn with mist, yon late and
  labouring moon.

White lilies, in whose cups the gold bees dream,
  The fallen snow of petals where the breeze
Scatters the chestnut blossom, or the gleam
  Of boyish limbs in water,—are not these

Enough for thee, dost thou desire more?
Alas! the Gods will give nought else from their eternal store.

For our high Gods have sick and weary grown
  Of all endless sins, our vain endeavour
For wasted days of youth to make atone
  By pain or prayer or priest, and never, never,
Hearken they now to either good or ill,
But send their rain upon the just and the unjust at will.

They sit at ease, our Gods they sit at ease,
  Strewing with leaves of rose their scented wine,
They sleep, they sleep, beneath the rocking trees
  Where asphodel and yellow lotus twine,
Mourning the old glad days before they knew
What evil things the heart of man could dream, and dream-
  ing do.

And far beneath the brazen floor they see
  Like swarming flies the crowd of little men,
The bustle of small lives, then wearily
  Back to their lotus-haunts they turn again
Kissing each others' mouths, and mix more deep
The poppy-seeded draught which brings soft purple-lidded
  sleep.

There all day long the golden-vestured sun,
  Their torch-bearer, stands with his torch ablaze,
And, when the gaudy web of noon is spun
  By its twelve maidens, through the crimson haze
Fresh from Endymion's arms comes forth the moon,
And the immortal Gods in toils of mortal passions swoon.

There walks Queen Juno through some dewy mead,
  Her grand white feet flecked with the saffron dust

Of wind-stirred lilies, while young Ganymede
  Leaps in the hot and amber-foaming must,
His curls all tossed, as when the eagle bare
The frightened boy from Ida through the blue Ionian air.

There in the green heart of some garden close
  Queen Venus with the shepherd at her side,
Her warm soft body like the briar rose
  Which would be white yet blushes at its pride,
Laughs low for love, till jealous Salmacis
Peers through the myrtle-leaves and sighs for pain of lonely
    bliss.

There never does that dreary north-wind blow
  Which leaves our English forests bleak and bare,
Nor ever falls the swift white-feathered snow,
  Nor ever doth the red-toothed lightning dare
To wake them in the silver-fretted night
When we lie weeping for some sweet sad sin, some dead
    delight.

Alas! they know the far Lethæan spring,
  The violet-hidden waters well they know,
Where one whose feet with tired wandering
  Are faint and broken may take heart and go,
And from those dark depths cool and crystalline
Drink, and draw balm, and sleep for sleepless souls, and
    anodyne.

But we oppress our natures, God or Fate
  Is our enemy, we starve and feed
On vain repentance—O we are born too late!
  What balm for us in bruisèd poppy seed
Who crowd into one finite pulse of time
The joy of infinite love and the fierce pain of infinite crime.

O we are wearied of this sense of guilt,
  Wearied of pleasure's paramour despair,
Wearied of every temple we have built,
  Wearied of every right, unanswered prayer,
For man is weak; God sleeps: and heaven is high:
One fiery-coloured moment: one great love; and lo! we die.

Ah! but no ferry-man with labouring pole
  Nears his black shallop to the flowerless strand,
No little coin of bronze can bring the soul
  Over Death's river to the sunless land,
Victim and wine and vow are all in vain,
The tomb is sealed; the soldiers watch; the dead rise not
    again.

We are resolved into the supreme air,
  We are made one with what we touch and see
With our heart's blood each crimson sun is fair,
  With our young lives each spring-impassioned tree
Flames into green, the wildest beasts that range
The moor our kinsmen are, all life is one, and all is change.

With beat of systole and of diastole
  One grand great life throbs through earth's giant heart,
And mighty waves of single Being roll
  From nerveless germ to man, for we are part
Of every rock and bird and beast and hill,
One with the things that prey on us, and one with what we
    kill.

From lower cells of waking life we pass
  To full perfection; thus the world grows old:
We who are godlike now were once a mass
  Of quivering purple flecked with bars of gold,

Unsentient or of joy or misery,
And tossed in terrible tangles of some wild and wind-swept
    sea.

This hot hard flame with which our bodies burn
    Will make some meadow blaze with daffodil,
Ay! and those argent breasts of thine will turn
    To water-lilies; the brown fields men till
Will be more fruitful for our love to-night,
Nothing is lost in nature, all things live in Death's despite.

The boy's first kiss, the hyacinth's first bell,
    The man's last passion, and the last red spear
That from the lily leaps, the asphodel
    Which will not let its blossoms blow for fear
Of too much beauty, and the timed shame
Of the young bridegroom at his lover's eyes,—these with
    the same

One sacrament are consecrate, the earth
    Not we alone hath passions hymeneal,
The yellow buttercups that shake for mirth
    At daybreak know a pleasure not less real
Than we do, when in some fresh-blossoming wood,
We draw the spring into our hearts, and feel that life is
    good.

So when men bury us beneath the yew
    Thy crimson-stainèd mouth a rose will be,
And thy soft eyes lush bluebells dimmed with dew,
    And when the white narcissus wantonly
Kisses the wind its playmate some faint joy
Will thrill our dust, and we will be again fond maid and boy.

And thus without life's conscious torturing pain
  In some sweet flower we will feel the sun,
And from the linnet's throat will sing again,
  And as two gorgeous-mailèd snakes will run
Over our graves, or as two tigers creep
Through the hot jungle where the yellow-eyed huge lions
    sleep

And give them battle! How my heart leaps up
  To think of that grand living after death
In beast and bird and flower, when this cup,
  Being filled too full of spirit, bursts for breath,
And with the pale leaves of some autumn day
The soul earth's earliest conqueror becomes earth's last great
    prey.

O think of it! We shall inform ourselves
  Into all sensuous life, the goat-foot Faun,
The Centaur, or the merry bright-eyed Elves
  That leave their dancing rings to spite the dawn
Upon the meadows, shall not be more near
Than you and I to nature's mysteries, for we shall hear

The thrush's heart beat, and the daisies grow,
  And the wan snowdrop sighing for the sun
On sunless days in winter, we shall know
  By whom the silver gossamer is spun,
Who paints the diapered fritillaries,
On what wide wings from shivering pine to pine the eagle
    flies.

Ay! had we never loved at all, who knows
  If yonder daffodil had lured the bee
Into its gilded womb, or any rose
  Had hung with crimson lamps its little tree!

Methinks no leaf would ever bud in spring,
But for the lovers' lips that kiss, the poets' lips that sing.

Is the light vanished from our golden sun,
   Or is this dædal-fashioned earth less fair,
That we are nature's heritors, and one
   With every pulse of life that beats the air?
Rather new suns across the sky shall pass,
New splendour come unto the flower, new glory to the
      grass.

And we two lovers shall not sit afar,
   Critics of nature, but the joyous sea
Shall be our raiment, and the bearded star
   Shoot arrows at our pleasure! We shall be
Part of the mighty universal whole,
And through all æons mix and mingle with the Kosmic
      Soul!

We shall be notes in that great Symphony
   Whose cadence circles through the rhythmic spheres,
And all the live World's throbbing heart shall be
   One with our heart, the stealthy creeping years
Have lost their terrors now, we shall not die,
The Universe itself shall be our Immortality!

THE FOURTH MOVEMENT

IMPRESSION

LE REVEILLON

THE sky is laced with fitful red,
The circling mists and shadows flee,
The dawn is rising from the sea,
Like a white lady from her bed.

And jagged brazen arrows fall
Athwart the feathers of the night,
And a long wave of yellow light
Breaks silently on tower and hall,

And spreading wide across the wold
Wakes into flight some fluttering bird,
And all the chestnut tops are stirred,
And all the branches streaked with gold.

AT VERONA

How steep the stairs within Kings' houses are
For exile-wearied feet as mine to tread,
And O how salt and bitter is the bread
Which falls from his Hound's table,—better far
That I had died in the red ways of war,
  Or that the gate of Florence bare my head,
  Than to live thus, by all things comraded
Which seek the essence of my soul to mar.

"Curse God and die: what better hope than this?
  He hath forgotten thee in all the bliss
  Of his gold city, and eternal day"—
Nay peace: behind my prison's blinded bars
  I do possess what none can take away,
  My love, and all the glory of the stars.

APOLOGIA

Is it thy will that I should wax and wane,
  Barter my cloth of gold for hodden grey,
And at thy pleasure weave that web of pain
  Whose brightest threads are each a wasted day?

Is it thy will—Love that I love so well—
  That my Soul's House should be a tortured spot
Wherein, like evil paramours, must dwell
  The quenchless flame, the worm that dieth not?

Nay, if it be thy will I shall endure,
  And sell ambition at the common mart,
And let dull failure be my vestiture,
  And sorrow dig its grave within my heart.

Perchance it may be better so—at least
  I have not made my heart a heart of stone,
Nor starved my boyhood of its goodly feast,
  Nor walked where Beauty is a thing unknown.

Many a man hath done so sought to fence
  In straitened bonds the soul that should be free,
Trodden the dusty road of common sense,
  While all the forest sang of liberty,

Not marking how the spotted hawk in flight
  Passed on wide pinion through the lofty air,
To where some steep untrodden mountain height
  Caught the last tresses of the Sun God's hair.

Or how the little flower he trod upon,
   The daisy, that white-feathered shield of gold,
Followed with wistful eyes the wandering sun
   Content if once its leaves were aureoled.

But surely it is something to have been
   The best belovèd for a little while,
To have walked hand in hand with Love, and seen
   His purple wings flit once across thy smile.

Ay! though the gorgèd asp of passion feed
   On my boy's heart, yet have I burst the bars,
Stood face to face with Beauty, known indeed
   The Love which moves the Sun and all the stars!

QUIA MULTUM AMAVI

DEAR Heart, I think the young impassioned priest
    When first he takes from out the hidden shrine
His God imprisoned in the Eucharist,
    And eats the bread, and drinks the dreadful wine.

Feels not such awful wonder as I felt
    When first my smitten eyes beat full on thee,
And all night long before thy feet I knelt
    Till thou wert wearied of Idolatry.

Ah! hadst thou liked me less and loved me more,
    Through all those summer days of joy and rain,
I had not now been sorrow's heritor,
    Or stood a lackey in the House of Pain.

Yet, though remorse, youth's white-faced seneschal,
    Tread on my heels with all his retinue,
I am most glad I loved thee—think of all
    The suns that go to make one speedwell blue!

SILENTIUM AMORIS

As often-times the too resplendent sun
  Hurries the pallid and reluctant moon
Back to her sombre cave, ere she hath won
  A single ballad from the nightingale,
  So doth thy Beauty make my lips to fail,
And all my sweetest singing out of tune.

And as at dawn across the level mead
  On wings impetuous some wind will come,
And with its too harsh kisses break the reed
  Which was its only instrument of song,
  So my too stormy passions work me wrong,
And for excess of Love my Love is dumb.

But surely unto thee mine eyes did show
  Why I am silent, and my lute unstrung;
Else it were better we should part, and go,
  Thou to some lips of sweeter melody,
  And I to nurse the barren memory
Of unkissed kisses, and songs never sung.

HER VOICE

THE wild bee reels from bough to bough
　With his furry coat and his gauzy wing,
Now in a lily-cup, and now
　Setting a jacinth bell a-swing,
　　In his wandering;
Sit closer to love: it was here I trow
　　I made that vow,

Swore that two lives should be like one
　As long as the sea-gull loved the sea,
As long as the sunflower sought the sun,—
　It shall be, I said, for eternity
　　'Twixt you and me!
Dear friend, those times are over and done,
　　Love's web is spun,

Look upward where the poplar trees
　Sway and sway in the summer air,
Here in the valley never a breeze
　Scatters the thistledown, but there
　　Great winds blow fair
From the mighty murmuring mystical seas,
　　And the wave-lashed leas.

Look upward where the white gull screams,
　What does it see that we do not see?
Is that a star? or the lamp that gleams

On some outward voyaging argosy,—
   Ah, can it be
We have lived our lives in a land of dreams!
   How sad it seems.

Sweet, there is nothing left to say
   But this, that love is never lost,
Keen winter stabs the breasts of May
   Whose crimson roses burst his frost,
      Ships tempest-tossed
Will find a harbour in some bay,
   And so we may.

And there is nothing left to do
   But to kiss once again, and part,
Nay, there is nothing we should rue,
   I have my beauty,—you your Art,
      Nay, do not start,
One world was not enough for two
   Like me and you.

MY VOICE

WITHIN this restless, hurried, modern world
  We took our hearts' full pleasure—You and I,
And now the white sails of our ship furled,
  And spent the lading of our argosy.

Wherefore my cheeks before their time are wan,
  For very weeping is my gladness fled,
Sorrow has paled my young mouth's vermilion,
  And Ruin draws the curtains of mv bed.

But all this crowded life has been to thee
  No more than lyre, or lute, or subtle spell
Of viols, or the music of the sea
  That sleeps, a mimic echo, in the shell.

TÆDIUM VITÆ

To stab my youth with desperate knives, to wear
This paltry age's gaudy livery,
To let each base hand filch my treasury,
To mesh my soul within a woman's hair,
And by mere Fortune's lackeyed groom,—I swear
I love it not! these things are less to me
Than the thin foam that frets upon the sea,
Less than the thistledown of summer air
Which hath no seed: better to stand aloof
Far from these slanderous fools who mock my life
Knowing me not, better the lowliest roof
Fit for the meanest hind to sojourn in,
Than to go back to that hoarse cave of strife
Where my white soul first kissed the mouth of sin.

HUMANITAD

HUMANITAD

It is full winter now: the trees bare,
  Save where the cattle huddle from the cold
Beneath the pine, for it doth never wear
  The Autumn's gaudy livery whose gold
Her jealous brother pilfers, but is true
To the green doublet; bitter is the wind, as though it blew

From Saturn's cave; a few thin wisps of hay
  Lie on the sharp black hedges, where the wain
Dragged the sweet pillage of a summer's day
  From the low meadows up the narrow lane;
Upon the half-thawed snow the bleating sheep
Press close against the hurdles, and the shivering house-dogs
    creep

From the shut stable to the frozen stream
  And back again disconsolate, and miss
The bawling shepherds and the noisy team;
  And overhead in circling littleness
The cawing rooks whirl round the frosted stack,
Or crowd the dripping boughs; and in the fen the ice-pools
    crack

Where the gaunt bittern stalks among the reeds
  And flaps his wings, and stretches back his neck,
And hoots to see the moon; across the meads
  Limps the poor frightened hare, a little speck;

And a stray seamew with its fretful cry
Flits like a sudden drift of snow against the dull grey sky

Full winter: and the lusty goodman brings
    His load of faggots from the chilly byre,
And stamps his feet upon the hearth, and flings
    The sappy billets on the waning fire,
And laughs to see the sudden lightning scare
His children at their play; and yet,—the Spring is in the
        air,

Already the slim crocus stirs the snow,
    And soon yon blanchèd fields will bloom again
With nodding cowslips for some lad to mow,
    For with the first warm kisses of the rain
The winter's icy sorrow breaks to tears,
And the brown thrushes mate, and with bright eye the
        rabbit peers

From the dark warren where the fir-cones lie,
    And treads one snowdrop under foot, and runs
Over the mossy knoll, and blackbirds fly
    Across our path at evening, and the suns
Stay longer with us; ah! how good to see
Grass-girdled Spring in all her joy of laughing greenery

Dance through the hedges till the early rose,
    (That sweet repentance of the thorny briar!)
Burst from its sheathèd emerald and disclose
    The little quivering disk of golden fire
Which the bees know so well, for with it come
Pale boy's-love, sops-in-wine, and daffodillies all in bloom.

Then up and down the field the sower goes,
    While close behind the laughing younker scares
With shrilly whoop the black and thievish crows,

And then the chestnut-tree its glory wears,
And on the grass the creamy blossom falls
In odorous excess, and faint half-whispered madrigals

Steal from the bluebells' nodding carillons
  Each breezy morn, and then white jessamine,
That star of its own heaven, snap-dragons
  With lolling crimson tongues, and eglantine
In dusty velvets clad usurp the bed
And woodland empery, and when the lingering rose hath
    shed

Red leaf by leaf its folded panoply,
  And pansies closed their purple-lidded eyes,
Chrysanthemums from gilded argosy
  Unload their gaudy scentless merchandise,
And violets getting overbold withdraw
From their sky nooks, and scarlet berries dot the leafless
    haw.

O happy field! and O thrice happy tree!
  Soon will your queen in daisy-flowered smock
And crown of flower-de-luce trip down the lea,
  Soon will the lazy shepherds drive their flock
Back to the pasture by the pool, and soon
Through the green leaves will float the hum of murmuring
    bees at noon.

Soon will the glade be bright with bellamour,
  The flower which wantons love, and those sweet nuns
Vale-lilies in their snowy vestiture
  Will tell their beaded pearls, and carnations
With mitred dusky leaves will scent the wind,
And straggling traveller's-joy each hedge with yellow stars
    will bind.

Dear Bride of Nature and most bounteous Spring!
  That canst give increase to the sweet-breath'd kine,
And to the kid its little horns, and bring
  The soft and silky blossoms to the vine,
Where is that old nepenthe which of yore
Man got from poppy root and glossy-berried mandragore!

There was a time when any common bird
  Could make me sing in unison, a time
When all the strings of boyish life were stirred
  To quick response or more melodious rhyme
By every forest idyll;—do I change?
Or rather doth some evil thing through thy fair pleasaunce
    range?

Nay, nay, thou art the same: 'tis I who seek
  To vex with sighs thy simple solitude,
And because fruitless tears bedew my cheek
  Would have thee weep with me in brotherhood;
Fool! shall each wronged and restless spirit dare
To taint such wine with the salt poison of his own despair!

Thou art the same: 'tis I whose wretched soul
  Takes discontent to be its paramour,
And gives its kingdom to the rude control
  Of what should be its servitor,—for sure
Wisdom is somewhere, though the stormy sea
Contain it not, and the huge deep answer " 'Tis not in me."

To burn with one clear flame, to stand erect
  In natural honour, not to bend the knee
In profitless prostrations whose effect
  Is by itself condemned, what alchemy
Can teach me this? what herb Medea brewed
Will bring the unexultant peace of essence not subdued?

The minor chord which ends the harmony,
  And for its answering brother waits in vain
Sobbing for incompleted melody,
  Dies a Swan's death; but I the heir of pain,
A silent Memnon with blank lid-less eyes,
Wait for the light and music of those suns which never rise.

The quenched-out torch, the lonely cypress-gloom,
  The little dust stored in the narrow urn,
The gentle XAIPE of the Attic tomb,—
  Were not these better far than to return
To my old fitful restless malady,
Or spend my days within the voiceless cave of misery?

Nay! for perchance that poppy-crownèd God
  Is like the watcher by a sick man's bed
Who talks of sleep but gives it not; his rod
  Hast lost its virtue, and, when all is said,
Death is too rude, too obvious a key
To solve one single secret in a life's philosophy.

And Love! that noble madness, whose august
  And inextinguishable might can slay
The soul with honeyed drugs,—alas! I must
  From such sweet ruin play the runaway,
Although too constant memory never can
Forget the archèd splendour of those brows Olympian

Which for a little season made my youth
  So soft a swoon of exquisite indolence
That all the chiding of more prudent Truth
  Seemed the thin voice of jealousy,—O Hence
Thou huntress deadlier than Artemis!
Go seek some other quarry! for of thy too perilous bliss

My lips have drunk enough,—no more, no more,—
  Though Love himself should turn his gilded prow
Back to the troubled waters of this shore
  Where I am wrecked and stranded, even now
The chariot wheels of passion sweep too near,
Hence! Hence! I pass unto a life more barren, more austere

More barren—ay, those arms will never lean
  Down through the trellised vines and draw my soul
In sweet reluctance through the tangled green;
  Some other head must wear that aureole,
For I am Hers who loves not any man
Whose white and stainless bosom bears the sign Gorgonian.

Let Venus go and chuck her dainty page,
  And kiss his mouth, and toss his curly hair,
With net and spear and hunting equipage
  Let young Adonis to his tryst repair,
But me her fond and subtle-fashioned spell
Delights no more, though I could win her dearest citadel.

Ay, though I were that laughing shepherd boy
  Who from Mount Ida saw the little cloud
Pass over Tenedos and lofty Troy
  And knew the coming of the Queen, and bowed
In wonder at her feet, not for the sake
Of a new Helen would I bid her hand the apple take.

Then rise supreme Athena argent-limbed!
  And, if my lips be music-less, inspire
At least my life: was not thy glory hymned
  By One who gave to thee his sword and lyre
Like Æschylos at well-fought Marathon,
And died to show that Milton's England still could bear a
    son!

And yet I cannot tread the Portico
  And live without desire, fear and pain,
Or nurture that wise calm which long ago
  The grave Athenian master taught to men,
Self-poised, self-centred, and self-comforted,
To watch the world's vain phantasies go by with un-bowed
    head.

Alas! that serene brow, those eloquent lips,
  Those eyes that mirrored all eternity,
Rest in their own Colonos, an eclipse
  Hath come on Wisdom, and Mnemosyne
Is childless; in the night which she had made
For lofty secure flight Athena's owl itself hath strayed.

Nor much with Science do I care to climb,
  Although by strange and subtle witchery
She draw the moon from heaven: the Muse of Time
  Unrolls her gorgeous-coloured tapestry
To no less eager eyes; often indeed
In the great epic of Polymnia's scroll I love to read

How Asia sent her myriad hosts to war
  Against a little town, and panoplied
In gilded mail with jewelled scimitar,
  White-shielded, purple-crested, rode the Mede
Between the waving poplars and the sea
Which men call Artemisium, till he saw Thermopylæ

Its steep ravine spanned by a narrow wall,
  And on the nearer side a little brood
Of careless lions holding festival!
  And stood amazèd at such hardihood,
And pitched his tent upon the reedy shore,
And stayed two days to wonder, and then crept at mid·
    night o'er

Some unfrequented height, and coming down
  The autumn forests treacherously slew
What Sparta held most dear and was the crown
  Of far Eurotas, and passed on, now knew
How God had staked an evil net for him
In the small bay at Salamis,—and yet, the page grows dim,

Its cadenced Greek delights me not, I feel
  With such a goodly time too out of tune
To love it much: for like the Dial's wheel
  That from its blinded darkness strikes the noon
Yet never sees the sun, so do my eyes
Restlessly follow that which from my cheated vision flies.

O for one grand unselfish simple life
  To teach us what is Wisdom! speak ye hills
Of lone Helvellyn, for this note of strife
  Shunned your untroubled crags and crystal rills,
Where is that Spirit which living blamelessly
Yet dared to kiss the smitten mouth of his own century!

Speak ye Rydalian laurels! where is He
  Whose gentle head ye sheltered, that pure soul
Whose gracious days of uncrowned majesty
  Through lowliest conduct touched the lofty goal
Where Love and Duty mingle! Him at least
The most high Laws were glad of, He had sat at Wisdom's
        feast,

But we are Learning's changelings, know by rote
  The clarion watchword of each Grecian school
And follow none, the flawless sword which smote
  The pagan Hydra is an effete tool

Which we ourselves have blunted, what man now
Shall scale the august ancient heights and to old Reverence
    bow?

One such indeed I saw, but, Ichabod!
   Gone is that last dear son of Italy,
Who being man died for the sake of God,
   And whose un-risen bones sleep peacefully,
O guard him, guard him well, my Giotto's tower,
Thou marble lily of the lily town! let not the lour

Of the rude tempest vex his slumber, or
   The Arno with its tawny troubled gold
O'er-leap its marge, no mightier conqueror
   Clomb the high Capitol in the days of old
When Rome was indeed Rome, for Liberty
Walked like a Bride beside him, at which sight pale Mystery

Fled shrieking to her farthest sombrest cell
   With an old man who grabbled rusty keys,
Fled shuddering, for that immemorial knell
   With which oblivion buries dynasties
Swept like a wounded eagle on the blast,
As to the holy heart of Rome the great triumvir passed.

He knew the holiest heart and heights of Rome,
   He drave the base wolf from the lion's lair,
And now lies dead by that empyreal dome
   Which overtops Valdaro hung in air
By Brunelleschi—O Melpomene
Breathe through thy melancholy pipe thy sweetest threnody!

Breathe through the tragic stops such melodies
   That Joy's self may grow jealous, and the Nine
Forget awhile their discreet emperies,
   Mourning for him who on Rome's lordliest shrine

Lit for men's lives the light of Marathon,
And bare to sun-forgotten fields the fire of the sun!

O guard him, guard him well, my Giotto's tower,
    Let some young Florentine each eventide
Bring coronals of that enchanted flower
    Which the dim woods of Vallombrosa hide,
And deck the marble tomb wherein he lies
Whose soul is as some mighty orb unseen of mortal eyes.

Some mighty orb whose cycled wanderings,
    Being tempest-driven to the farthest rim
Where Chaos meets Creation and the wings
    Of the eternal chanting Cherubim
Are pavilioned on Nothing, passed away
Into a moonless void,—and yet—though he is dust and clay,

He is not dead, the immemorial Fates
    Forbid it, and the closing shears refrain,
Lift up your heads, ye everlasting gates!
    Ye argent clarions, sound a loftier strain!
For the vile thing he hated lurks within
Its sombre house, alone with God and memories of sin.

Still what avails it that she sought her cave
    That murderous mother of red harlotries?
At Munich on the marble architrave
    The Grecian boys die smiling, but the seas
Which wash Ægina fret in loneliness
Not mirroring their beauty, so our lives grow colourless

For lack of our ideals, if one star
    Flame torch-like in the heavens the unjust
Swift daylight kills it, and no trump of war
    Can wake to passionate voice the silent dust

Which was Mazzini once! rich Niobe
For all her stony sorrows hath her sons, but Italy!

What Easter Day shall make her children rise,
    Who were not Gods yet suffered? what sure feet
Shall find their grave-clothes folded? what clear eyes
    Shall see them bodily? O it were meet
To roll the stone from off the sepulchre
And kiss the bleeding roses of their wounds, in love of Her

Our Italy! our mother visible!
    Most blessed among nations and most sad,
For whose dear sake the young Calabrian fell
    That day at Aspromonte and was glad
That in an age when God was bought and sold
One man could die for Liberty! but we, burnt out and cold,

See Honour smitten on the cheek and gyves
    Bind the sweet feet of Mercy: Poverty
Creeps through our sunless lanes and with sharp knives
    Cuts the warm throats of children stealthily,
And no word said:—O we are wretched men
Unworthy of our great inheritance! where is the pen

Of austere Milton? where the mighty sword
    Which slew its master righteously? the years
Have lost their ancient leader, and no word
    Breaks from the voiceless tripod on our ears:
While as a ruined mother in some spasm
Bears a base child and loathes it, so our best enthusiasm

Genders unlawful children, Anarchy
    Freedom's own Judas, the vile prodigal
Licence who steals the gold of Liberty
    And yet has nothing, Ignorance the real

One Fratricide since Cain, Envy the asp
That stings itself to anguish, Avarice whose palsied grasp

Is in its extent stiffened, moneyed Greed
  For whose dull appetite men waste away
Amid the whirr of wheels and are the seed
  Of things which slay their sower, these each day
Sees rife in England, and the gentle feet
Of Beauty tread no more the stones of each unlovely street.

What even Cromwell spared is desecrated
  By weed and worm, left to the stormy play
Of wind and beating snow, or renovated
  By more destructful hands: Time's worst decay
Will wreathe its ruins with some loveliness,
But these new Vandals can but make a rain-proof bar-
    renness.

Where is that Art which bade the Angels sing
  Through Lincoln's lofty choir, till the air
Seems from such marble harmonies to ring
  With sweeter song than common lips can dare
To draw from actual reed? ah! where is now
The cunning hand which made the flowering hawthorn
    branches bow

For Southwell's arch, and carved the House of One
  Who loved the lilies of the field with all
Our dearest English flowers? the same sun
  Rises for us: the seasons natural
Weave the same tapestry of green and grey:
The unchanged hills are with us: but that Spirit hath
    passed away.

And yet perchance it may be better so,
   · For Tyranny is an incestuous Queen,
Murder her brother is her bedfellow,
   And the Plague chambers with her: in obscene
And bloody paths her treacherous feet are set;
Better the empty desert and a soul inviolate!

For gentle brotherhood, the harmony
   Of living in the healthful air, the swift
Clean beauty of strong limbs when men are free
   And women chaste, these are the things which lift
Our souls up more than even Agnolo's
Gaunt blinded Sibyl poring o'er the scroll of human woes,

Or Titian's little maiden on the stair
   White as her own sweet lily and as tall,
Or Mona Lisa smiling through her hair,—
   Ah! somehow life is bigger after all
Than any painted Angel, could we see
The God that is within us! The old Greek serenity

Which curbs the passion of that level line
   Of marble youths, who with untroubled eyes
And chastened limbs ride round Athena's shrine
   And mirror her divine economies,
And balanced symmetry of what in man
Would else wage ceaseless warfare,—this at least within the
      span

Between our mother's kisses and the grave
   Might so inform our lives, that we could win
Such mighty empires that from her cave
   Temptation would grow hoarse, and pallid Sin

Would walk ashamed of his adulteries,
And Passion creep from out the House of Lust with startled
    eyes.

To make the Body and the Spirit one
    With all right things, till no thing live in vain
From morn to noon, but in sweet unison
    With every pulse of flesh and throb of brain
The Soul in flawless essence high enthroned,
Against all outer vain attack invincibly bastioned,

Mark with serene impartiality
    The strife of things, and yet be comforted,
Knowing that by the chain causality
    All separate existences are wed
Into one supreme whole, whose utterance
Is joy, or holier praise! ah! surely this were governance

Of Life in most august omnipresence,
    Through which the rational intellect would find
In passion its expression, and mere sense,
    Ignoble else, lend fire to the mind,
And being joined with it in harmony
More mystical than that which binds the stars planetary,

Strike from their several tones one octave chord
    Whose cadence being measureless would fly
Through all the circling spheres, then to its Lord
    Return refreshed with its new empery
And more exultant power,—this indeed
Could we but reach it were to find the last, the perfect
    creed.

Ah! it was easy when the world was young
   To keep one's life free and inviolate,
From our sad lips another song is rung,
   By our own hands our heads are desecrate,
Wanderers in drear exile, and dispossessed
Of what should be our own, we can but feed on wild unrest.

Somehow the grace, the bloom of things has flown,
   And of all men we are most wretched who
Must live each other's lives and not our own
   For very pity's sake and then undo
All that we lived for—it was otherwise
When soul and body seemed to blend in mystic symphonies.

But we have left those gentle haunts to pass
   With weary feet to the new Calvary,
Where we behold, as one who in a glass
   Sees his own face, self-slain Humanity,
And in the dumb reproach of that sad gaze
Learn what an awful phantom the red hand of man can
   raise.

O smitten mouth! O forehead crowned with thorn!
   O chalice of all common miseries!
Thou for our sakes that loved thee not hast borne
   An agony of endless centuries,
And we were vain and ignorant nor knew
That when we stabbed thy heart it was our own real hearts
   we slew.

Being ourselves the sowers and the seeds,
   The night that covers and the lights that fade,
The spear that pierces and the side that bleeds,
   The lips betraying and the life betrayed;

The deep hath calm: the moon hath rest: but we
Lords of the natural world are yet our own dread enemy.

Is this the end of all that primal force
   Which, in its changes being still the same,
From eyeless Chaos cleft its upward course,
   Through ravenous seas and whirling rocks and flame,
Till the suns met in heaven and began
Their cycles, and the morning stars sang, and the Word
    was Man!

Nay, nay, we are but crucified, and though
   The bloody sweat falls from our brows like rain,
Loosen the nails—we shall come down I know,
   Staunch the red wounds—we shall be whole again,
No need have we of hyssop-laden rod,
That which is purely human, that is Godlike, that is God.

FLOWER OF LOVE

ΓΛΥΚΥΠΙΚΡΟΣ ΕΡΩΣ

Sweet, I blame you not, for mine the fault was, had I not
been made of common clay
I had climbed the higher heights unclimbed yet, seen the
fuller air, the larger day.

From the wildness of my wasted passion I had struck a
better, clearer song,
Lit some lighter light of freer freedom, battled with some
Hydraheaded wrong.

Had my lips been smitten into music by the kisses that made
them bleed,
You had walked with Bice and the angels on that verdant
and enamelled mead.

I had trod the road which Dante treading saw the sun of
seven circles shine,
Ay! Perchance had seen the heavens opening, as they opened
to the Florentine.

And the mighty nations would have crowned me, who am
crownless now and without name,
And some orient dawn had found me kneeling on the
threshold of the House of Fame.

I had sat within that marble circle where the oldest bard
is as the young,
And the pipe is ever dropping honey, and the lyre's strings
are ever strung.

Keats had lifted up his hymeneal curls from out the poppy-
seeded wine,
With ambrosial mouth had kissed my forehead, clasped the
hand of noble love in mine.

And at springtide, when the apple-blossoms brush the burnished bosom of the dove,
Two young lovers lying in an orchard would have read the
story of our love.

Would have read the legend of my passion, known the
bitter secret of my heart,
Kissed as we have kissed, but never parted as we two are
fated now to part.

For the crimson flower of our life is eaten by the canker-
worm of truth,
And no hand can gather up the fallen withered petals of the
rose of youth.

Yet I am not sorry that I loved you—ah! what else had I
a boy to do,—
For the hungry teeth of time devour, and the silent-footed
years pursue.

Rudderless, we drift athwart a tempest, and when once the
storm of youth is past,
Without lyre, without lute or chorus, Death the silent pilot
comes at last.

And within the grave there is no pleasure, for the blindworm
battens on the root,
And Desire shudders into ashes, and the tree of Passion
bears no fruit.

Ah! what else had I to do but love you, God's own mother
was less dear to me,
And less dear the Cytheræan rising like an argent lily from
the sea.

I have made my choice, have lived my poems, and, though
youth is gone in wasted days,
I have found the lover's crown of myrtle better than the

UNCOLLECTED POEMS

FROM SPRING DAYS TO WINTER

(FOR MUSIC)

IN the glad spring time when leaves were green,
  O merrily the throstle sings!
I sought, amid the tangled sheen,
Love whom mine eyes had never seen,
  O the glad dove has golden wings!

Between the blossoms red and white,
  O merrily the throstle sings!
My love first came into my sight,
O perfect vision of delight,
  O the glad dove has golden wings!

The yellow apples glowed like fire,
  O merrily the throstle sings!
O Love too great for lip or lyre,
Blown rose of love and of desire,
  O the glad dove has golden wings!

But now with snow the tree is grey,
  Ah, sadly now the throstle sings!
My love is dead: ah! well-a-day,
See at her silent feet I lay
  A dove with broken wings!
  Ah, Love! ah, Love! that thou wert slain—
Fond Dove, fond Dove return again!

Αἴλινον, αἴλινον εἰπέ, τὸ δ' εὖ νικάτω.

O WELL for him who lives at ease
  With garnered gold in wide domain,
  Nor heeds the splashing of the rain,
The crashing down of forest trees.

O well for him who ne'er hath known
  The travail of the hungry years,
  A father grey with grief and tears,
A mother weeping all alone.

But well for him whose foot hath trod
  The weary road of toil and strife,
  Yet from the sorrows of his life
Builds ladders to be nearer God.

THE TRUE KNOWLEDGE

. . . ἀναγκαίως δ' ἔχει
βίον θερίζειν ὥστε χάρπιμον στάχυν,
καὶ τὸν μὲν εἶναι τὸν δὲ μή.

THOU knowest all; I seek in vain
  What lands to till or sow with seed—
  The land is black with briar and weed,
Nor cares for falling tears or rain.

Thou knowest all; I sit and wait
  With blinded eyes and hands that fail,
  Till the last lifting of the veil
And the first opening of the gate.

Thou knowest all; I cannot see.
  I trust I shall not live in vain,
  I know that we shall meet again
In some divine eternity.

LOTUS LEAVES

νεμεσσῶαί γε μὲν οὐδὲν
κλαίειν ὅζ κε θάνῃσι βροτῶν καὶ πότμον ἐπίσπῃ,
τουτό νυ καὶ γέραζ οἶον ὀϊζυροῖσι βροτῖσι
κείρασθαί τε κόμην βαλέειν τ' ἀπὸ δάκρυ παρειῶν.

THERE is no peace beneath the noon.
Ah! in those meadows is there peace
Where, girdled with a silver fleece,
As a bright shepherd, strays the moon?

Queen of the gardens of the sky,
Where stars like lilies, white and fair,
Shine through the mists of frosty air,
Oh, tarry, for the dawn is nigh!

Oh, tarry, for the envious day
Stretches long hands to catch thy feet,
Alas! but thou art over-fleet,
Alas! I know thou wilt not stay.

Up sprang the sun to run his race,
The breeze blew fair on meadow and lea;
But in the west I seemed to see
The likeness of a human face.

A linnet on the hawthorn spray
  Sang of the glories of the spring,
  And made the flow'ring copses ring
With gladness for the new-born day.

A lark from out the grass I trod
  Flew wildly, and was lost to view
  In the great seamless veil of blue
That hangs before the face of God.

The willow whispered overhead
  That death is but a newer life,
  And that with idle words of strife
We bring dishonour on the dead.

I took a branch from off the tree,
  And hawthorn-blossoms drenched with dew,
  I bound them with a sprig of yew,
And made a garland fair to see.

I laid the flowers where He lies,
  (Warm leaves and flowers on the stone);
  What joy I had to sit alone
Till evening broke on tired eyes:

Till all the shifting clouds had spun
  A robe of gold for God to wear,
  And into seas of purple air
Sank the bright galley of the sun.

*   *   *   *   *   *

Shall I be gladdened for the day,
  And let my inner heart be stirred
  By murmuring tree or song of bird,
And sorrow at the wild wind's play?

Not so: such idle dreams belong
   To souls of lesser depth than mine;
   I feel that I am half divine;
I know that I am great and strong.

I know that every forest tree
   By labour rises from the root;
   I know that none shall gather fruit
By sailing on the barren sea.

WASTED DAYS

(FROM A PICTURE PAINTED BY MISS V. T.)

A FAIR slim boy not made for this world's pain,
  With hair of gold thick clustering round his ears,
  And longing eyes half veiled by foolish tears
Like bluest water seen through mists of rain;
Pale cheeks whereon no kiss hath left its stain,
  Red under-lip drawn in for fear of Love,
  And white throat whiter than the breast of dove—
Alas! alas! if all should be in vain.

Corn-fields behind, and reapers all a-row
In weariest labour toiling wearily,
To no sweet sound of laughter or of lute.

And careless of the crimson sunset glow,
The boy still dreams; nor knows that night is night,
And in the night-time no man gathers fruit.

IMPRESSIONS

I

LE JARDIN

THE lily's withered chalice falls
　Around its rod of dusty gold,
　And from the beech-trees on the wold
The last wood-pigeon coos and calls.

The gaudy leonine sunflower
　Hangs black and barren on its stalk,
　And down the windy garden walk
The dead leaves scatter,—hour by hour.

Pale privet-petals white as milk
　Are blown into a snowy mass:
　The roses lie upon the grass
Like little shreds of crimson silk.

II

LA MER

A WHITE mist drifts across the shrouds,
  A wild moon in this wintry sky
  Gleams like an angry lion's eye
Out of a mane of tawny clouds.

The muffled steersman at the wheel
  Is but a shadow in the gloom;—
  And in the throbbing engine room
Leap the long rods of polished steel.

The shattered storm has left its trace
  Upon this huge and heaving dome,
  For the thin threads of yellow foam
Float on the waves like ravelled lace.

UNDER THE BALCONY

O BEAUTIFUL star with the crimson mouth!
    O moon with the brows of gold!
Rise up, rise up, from the odorous south!
      And light for my love her way,
      Lest her little feet should stray
    On the windy hill and the wold!
O beautiful star with the crimson mouth!
    O moon with the brows of gold!

O ship that shakes on the desolate sea!
    O ship with the wet, white sail!
Put in, put in, to the port to me!
      For my love and I would go
      To the land where the daffodils blow
    In the heart of a violet dale!
O ship that shakes on the desolate sea!
    O ship with the wet, white sail!

O rapturous bird with the low, sweet note!
    O bird that sings on the spray!
Sing on, sing on, from your soft brown throat!
      And my love in her little bed
      Will listen, and lift her head
    From the pillow, and come my way!
O rapturous bird with the low, sweet note!
    O bird that sits on the spray!

O blossom that hangs in the tremulous air!
  O blossom with lips of snow!
Come down, come down, for my love to wear!
    You will die on her head in a crown,
    You will die in a fold of her gown,
   To her little light heart you will go!
O blossom that hangs in the tremulous air!
  O blossom with lips of snow!

THE HARLOT'S HOUSE

WE caught the tread of dancing feet,
We loitered down the moonlit street,
And stopped beneath the harlot's house.

Inside, above the din and fray,
We heard the loud musicians play
The "Treues Liebes Herz" of Strauss.

Like strange mechanical grotesques,
Making fantastic arabesques,
The shadows raced across the blind.

We watched the ghostly dancers spin
To sound of horn and violin,
Like black leaves wheeling in the wind.

Like wire-pulled automatons,
Slim silhouetted skeletons
Went sidling through the slow quadrille.

They took each other by the hand,
And danced a stately saraband;
Their laughter echoed thin and shrill.

Sometimes a clockwork puppet pressed
A phantom lover to her breast,
Sometimes they seemed to try to sing.

Sometimes a horrible marionette
Came out, and smoked its cigarette
Upon the steps like a live thing.

Then, turning to my love, I said,
"The dead are dancing with the dead,
The dust is whirling with the dust."

But she—she heard the violin,
And left my side and entered in:
Love passed into the house of lust.

Then suddenly the tune went false,
The dancers wearied of the waltz,
The shadows ceased to wheel and whirl.

And down the long and silent street,
The dawn, with silver-sandalled feet,
Crept like a frightened girl.

LE JARDIN DES TUILERIES

THIS winter air is keen and cold,
   And keen and cold this winter sun,
   But round my chair the children run
Like little things of dancing gold.

Sometimes about the painted kiosk
   The mimic soldiers strut and stride,
   Sometimes the blue-eyed brigands hide
In the bleak tangles of the bosk.

And sometimes, while the old nurse cons
   Her book, they steal across the square,
   And launch their paper navies where
Huge Triton writhes in greenish bronze.

And now in mimic flight they flee,
   And now they rush, a boisterous band—
   And, tiny hand on tiny hand,
Climb up the black and leafless tree.

Ah! cruel tree! if I were you,
   And children climbed me, for their sake
   Though it be winter I would break
Into spring blossoms white and blue!

ON THE SALE BY AUCTION OF KEATS' LOVE LETTERS

THESE are the letters which Endymion wrote
To one he loved in secret, and apart.
And now the brawlers of the auction mart
Bargain and bid for each poor blotted note,
Ay! for each separate pulse of passion quote
  The merchant's price. I think they love not art
  Who break the crystal of a poet's heart
That small and sickly eyes may glare and gloat.

Is it not said that many years ago,
  In a far Eastern town, some soldiers ran
  With torches through the midnight, and began
To wrangle for mean raiment, and to throw
  Dice for the garments of a wretched man,
Not knowing the God's wonder, or His woe?

THE NEW REMORSE

THE sin was mine; I did not understand.
  So now is music prisoned in her cave,
  Save where some ebbing desultory wave
Frets with its restless whirls this meagre strand.
And in the withered hollow of this land
  Hath Summer dug herself so deep a grave,
  That hardly can the leaden willow crave
One silver blossom from keen Winter's hand.
But who is this who cometh by the shore?
(Nay, love, look up and wonder!) Who is this
  Who cometh in dyed garments from the South?
It is thy new-found Lord, and he shall kiss
  The yet unravished roses of thy mouth,
And I shall weep and worship, as before.

FANTAISIES DECORATIVES

I

LE PANNEAU

UNDER the rose-tree's dancing shade
There stands a little ivory girl,
Pulling the leaves of pink and pearl
With pale green nails of polished jade.

The red leaves fall upon the mould,
The white leaves flutter, one by one,
Down to a blue bowl where the sun,
Like a great dragon, writhes in gold.

The white leaves float upon the air,
The red leaves flutter idly down,
Some fall upon her yellow gown,
And some upon her raven hair.

She takes an amber lute and sings,
And as she sings a silver crane
Begins his scarlet neck to strain,
And flap his burnished metal wings.

She takes a lute of amber bright,
  And from the thicket where he lies
  Her lover, with his almond eyes,
Watches her movements in delight.

And now she gives a cry of fear,
  And tiny tears begin to start:
  A thorn has wounded with its dart
The pink-veined sea-shell of her ear.

And now she laughs a merry note:
  There has fallen a petal of the rose
  Just where the yellow satin shows
The blue-veined flower of her throat.

With pale green nails of polished jade,
  Pulling the leaves of pink and pearl,
  There stands a little ivory girl
Under the rose-tree's dancing shade.

II

LES BALLONS

AGAINST these turbid turquoise skies
  The light and luminous balloons
  Dip and drift like satin moons,
Drift like silken butterflies;

Reel with every windy gust,
  Rise and reel like dancing girls,
  Float like strange transparent pearls,
Fall and float like silver dust.

Now to the low leaves they cling,
  Each with coy fantastic pose,
  Each a petal of a rose
Straining at a gossamer string.

Then to the tall trees they climb,
  Like thin globes of amethyst,
  Wandering opals keeping tryst
With the rubies of the lime.

CANZONET

I HAVE no store
Of gryphon-guarded gold;
 Now, as before,
Bare is the shepherd's fold.
 Rubies, nor pearls,
Have I to gem thy throat;
 Yet woodland girls
Have loved the shepherd's note.

Then, pluck a reed
And bid me sing to thee,
 For I would feed
Thine ears with melody,
 Who art more fair
Than fairest fleur-de-lys,
 More sweet and rare
Than sweetest ambergris.

What dost thou fear?
Young Hyacinth is slain,
 Pan is not here,
And will not come again.
 No hornèd Faun
Treads down the yellow leas,
 No god at dawn
Steals through the olive trees.

Hylas is dead,
Nor will he e'er divine
Those little red
Rose-petalled lips of thine.
On the high hill
No ivory dryads play,
Silver and still
Sinks the sad autumn day.

SYMPHONY IN YELLOW

An omnibus across the bridge
  Crawls like a yellow butterfly,
   And, here and there, a passer-by
Shows like a little restless midge.

Big barges full of yellow hay
  Are moved against the shadowy wharf,
   And, like a yellow silken scarf,
The thick fog hangs along the quay.

The yellow leaves begin to fade
  And flutter from the Temple elms,
   And at my feet the pale green Thames
Lies like a rod of rippled jade.

IN THE FOREST

Out of the mid-wood's twilight
　　Into the meadow's dawn,
Ivory limbed and brown-eyed,
　　Flashes my Faun!

He skips through the copses singing,
　　And his shadow dances along,
And I know not which I should follow,
　　Shadow or song!

O Hunter, snare me his shadow!
　　O Nightingale, catch me his strain!
Else moonstruck with music and madness
　　I track him in vain!

TO MY WIFE

WITH A COPY OF MY POEMS

I can write no stately proem
  As a prelude to my lay;
From a poet to a poem
  I would dare to say.

For if of these fallen petals
  One to you seem fair,
Love will waft it till it settles
  On your hair.

And when wind and winter harden
  All the loveless land,
It will whisper of the garden,
  You will understand.

WITH A COPY OF "A HOUSE
OF POMEGRANATES"

Go, little book,
To him who, on a lute with horns of pearl,
Sang of the white feet of the Golden Girl:
And bid him look
Into thy pages: it may hap that he
May find that golden maidens dance through thee.

TO L. L.

COULD we dig up this long-buried treasure,
  Were it worth pleasure,
We never could learn love's song,
  We are parted too long.

Could the passionate past that is fled
  Call back its dead,
Could we live it all over again,
  Were it worth the pain!

I remember we used to meet
  By an ivied seat,
And you warbled each pretty word
  With the air of a bird;

And your voice had a quaver in it,
  Just like a linnet,
And shook, as the blackbird's throat
  With its last big note;

And your eyes, they were green and grey
  Like an April day,
But lit into amethyst
  When I stooped and kissed;

And your mouth, it would never smile
  For a long, long while,
Then it rippled all over with laughter
  Five minutes after.

You were always afraid of a shower,
    Just like a flower:
I remember you started and ran
    When the rain began.

I remember I never could catch you,
    For no one could match you,
You had wonderful, luminous, fleet,
    Little wings to your feet.

I remember your hair—did I tie it?
    For it always ran riot—
Like a tangled sunbeam of gold:
    These things are old.

I remember so well the room,
    And the lilac bloom
That beat at the dripping pane
    In the warm June rain;

And the colour of your gown,
    It was amber-brown,
And two yellow satin bows
    From your shoulders rose.

And the handkerchief of French lace
    Which you held to your face—
Had a small tear left a stain?
    Or was it the rain?

On your hand as it waved adieu
    There were veins of blue;
In your voice as it said good-bye
    Was a petulant cry,

"You have only wasted your life."
  (Ah, that was the knife!)
When I rushed through the garden gate
  It was all too late.

Could we live it over again,
  Were it worth the pain,
Could the passionate past that is fled
  Call back its dead!

Well, if my heart must break,
  Dear love, for your sake,
It will break in music, I know,
  Poets' hearts break so.

But strange that I was not told
  That the brain can hold
In a tiny ivory cell
  God's heaven and hell.

TRANSLATIONS

CHORUS OF CLOUD MAIDENS

('Αριστοφάνους Νεφέλαι, 275-290, 298-313.)

ΣΤΡΟΦΗ

CLOUD-MAIDENS that float on for ever,
 Dew-sprinkled, fleet bodies, and fair,
Let us rise from our Sire's loud river,
 Great Ocean, and soar through the air
To the peaks of the pine-covered mountains where the
 pines hang as tresses of hair.
Let us seek the watch-towers undaunted,
 Where the well-watered corn-fields abound,
And through murmurs of rivers nymph-haunted
 The songs of the sea-waves resound;
And the sun in the sky never wearies of spreading his radi-
 ance around.
 Let us cast off the haze
 Of the mists from our band,
 Till with far-seeing gaze
 We may look on the land.

·   ·   ·   ·   ·   ·   ·   ·   ·

ΑΝΤΙΣΤΡΟΦΗ

Cloud maidens that bring the rain-shower,
   To the Pallas-loved land let us wing,
To the land of stout heroes and Power,
   Where Kekrops was hero and king,
Where honour and silence is given
   To the mysteries that none may declare,
Where are gifts to the high gods in heaven
   When the house of the gods is laid bare,
Where are lofty roofed temples, and statues well
      carven and fair;
   Where are feasts to the happy immortals
When the sacred procession draws near,
   Where garlands make bright the bright portals
At all seasons and months in the year;
   And when spring days are here,
Then we tread to the wine-god a measure,
   In Bacchanal dance and in pleasure,
'Mid the contests of sweet singing choirs,
   And the crash of loud lyres.

ΘΡΗΝΩΔΙΑ

(Eur. *Hec.*, 444-483)

Song sung by captive women of Troy on the sea beach at Aulis,
while the Achæans were there storm-bound through the wrath of
dishonoured Achilles, and waiting for a fair wind to bring them home.

ΣΤΡΟΦΗ

O FAIR wind blowing from the sea!
    Who through the dark and mist dost guide
    The ships that on the billows ride,
Unto what land, ah, misery!
Shall I be borne, across what stormy wave
Or to whose house a purchased slave?

O sea-wind blowing fair and fast
    Is it unto the Dorian strand,
      Or to those far and fabled shores,
      Where great Apidanus outpours
    His streams upon the fertile land,
    Or shall I tread the Phthian sand,
Borne by the swift breath of the blast?

ΑΝΤΙΣΤΡΟΦΗ

O blowing wind! you bring my sorrow near,
  For surely borne with splashing of the oar,
And hidden in some galley-prison drear
  I shall be led unto that distant shore
    Where the tall palm-tree first took root, and
      made,
    With clustering laurel leaves, a pleasant shade
For Leto when with travail great she bore
A god and goddess in Love's bitter fight,
Her body's anguish, and her soul's delight.

      It may be in Delos,
        Encircled of seas,
      I shall sing with some maids
        From the Cyclades,
      Of Artemis goddess
        And queen and maiden,
      Sing of the gold
        In her hair heavy-laden.
      Sing of her hunting,
        Her arrows and bow,
      And in singing find solace
        From weeping and woe.

ΣΤΡΟΦΗ Β

Or it may be my bitter doom
To stand a handmaid at the loom,
In distant Athens of supreme renown;
   And weave some wondrous tapestry,
   Or work in bright embroidery,
Upon the crocus-flowered robe and saffron-coloured
       gown,
   The flying horses wrought in gold,
   The silver chariot onward rolled
That bears Athena through the Town;
  Or the warring giants that strove to climb
   From earth to heaven to reign as kings,
  And Zeus the conquering son of Time
   Borne on the hurricane's eagle wings;
And the lightning flame and the bolts that fell
   From the risen cloud at the god's behest,
And hurled the rebels to darkness of hell,
   To a sleep without slumber or waking or rest.

ΑΝΤΙΣΤΡΟΦΗ B

Alas! our children's sorrow, and their pain
        In slavery.
Alas! our warrior sires nobly slain
        For liberty.
Alas! our country's glory, and the name
        Of Troy's fair town;
By the lances and the fighting and the flame
        Tall Troy is down.

I shall pass with my soul over-laden,
        To a land far away and unseen,
For Asia is slave and handmaiden,
        Europa is Mistress and Queen.
Without love, or love's holiest treasure,
I shall pass into Hades abhorred,
To the grave as my chamber of pleasure,
        To death as my Lover and Lord.

A FRAGMENT FROM THE AGAMEMNON OF ÆSCHYLOS

(Lines 1140-1173)

[The scene is the court-yard of the Palace at Argos. Agamemnon has already entered the House of Doom, and Clytemnestra has followed close on his heels. Cassandra is left alone upon the stage. The conscious terror of death and the burden of prophecy lie heavy upon her; terrible signs and visions greet her approach. She sees blood upon the lintel, and the smell of blood scares her, as some bird, from the door. The ghosts of the murdered children come to mourn with her. Her second sight pierces the Palace walls; she sees the fatal bath, the trammeling net, and the axe sharpened for her own ruin and her lord's.

But not even in the hour of her last anguish is Apollo merciful; her warnings are unheeded, her prophetic utterances made mock of.

The orchestra is filled with a chorus of old men weak, foolish, irresolute. They do not believe the weird woman of mystery till the hour for help is past, and the cry of Agamemnon echoes from the house, "Oh me! I am stricken with a stroke of death."]

CHORUS

THY prophecies are but a lying tale,
   For cruel gods have brought thee to this state,
   And of thyself and thine own wretched fate
Sing you this song and these unhallowed lays,
   Like the brown bird of grief insatiate
Crying for sorrow of its dreary days;
     Crying for Itys, Itys, in the vale—
     The nightingale! The nightingale!

CASSANDRA

Yet I would that to me they had given
  The fate of that singer so clear,
Fleet wings to fly up into heaven,
  Away from all mourning and fear;
  For ruin and slaughter await me—the cleaving with
    sword and the spear.

CHORUS

  Whence come these crowding fancies on thy brain,
    Sent by some god it may be, yet for naught?
  Why dost thou sing with evil-tongued refrain,
  Moulding thy terrors to this hideous strain
    With shrill, sad cries, as if by death distraught?
  Why dost thou tread that path of prophecy,
        Where, upon either hand,
        Landmarks for ever stand
  With horrid legend for all men to see?

CASSANDRA

  O bitter bridegroom who didst bear
    Ruin to those that loved thee true!
  O holy stream Scamander, where
    With gentle nurturement I grew
    In the first days, when life and love were new.
  And now—and now—it seems that I must lie
    In the dark land that never sees the sun;
  Sing my sad songs of fruitless prophecy
    By the black stream Cokytos that doth run
    Through long, low hills of dreary Acheron.

CHORUS

Ah, but thy word is clear!
Even a child among men,
Even a child might see
What is lying hidden here.
Ah! I am smitten deep
To the heart with a deadly blow
At the evil fate of the maid,
At the cry of her song of woe!
Sorrows for her to bear!
Wonders for me to hear!

CASSANDRA

O my poor land laid waste with flame and fire!
  O ruined city overthrown by fate!
Ah, what availed the offerings of my Sire
  To keep the foreign foemen from the gate!
Ah, what availed the herds of pasturing kine
To save my country from the wrath divine!

Ah, neither prayer nor priest availèd aught,
Nor the strong captains that so stoutly fought,
  For the tall town lies desolate and low.
  And I, the singer of this song of woe,
Know, by the fires burning in my brain,
That Death, the healer of all earthly pain,
  Is close at hand! I will not shirk the blow.

THE ARTIST'S DREAM
OR
SAN ARTYSTY

TRANSLATED FROM THE POLISH OF MADAME
HELENA MODJESKA

I too have had my dreams: ay, known indeed
The crowded visions of a fiery youth
Which haunt me still.

*   *   *   *   *   *   *

                Methought that once I lay
Within some garden close, what time the Spring
Breaks like a bird from Winter, and the sky
Is sapphire-vaulted. The pure air was soft,
And the deep grass I lay on soft as air.
The strange and secret life of the young trees
Swelled in the green and tender bark, or burst
To buds of sheathèd emerald; violets
Peered from their nooks of hiding, half afraid
Of their own loveliness; the vermeil rose
Opened its heart, and the bright star-flower
Shone like a star of morning. Butterflies,
In painted liveries of brown and gold,
Took the shy bluebells as their pavilions
And seats of pleasaunce; overhead a bird
Made show of all the blossoms as it flew
To charm the woods with singing: the whole world
Seemed waking to delight!

And yet—and yet—
My soul was filled with leaden heaviness:
I had no joy in Nature; what to me,
Ambition's slave, was crimson-stainèd rose
Or the gold-sceptred crocus? The bright bird
Sang out of tune for me, and the sweet flowers
Seemed but a pageant, and an unreal show
That mocked my heart; for, like the fabled snake
That stings itself to anguish, so I lay
Self-tortured, self-tormented.
                                   The day crept
Unheeded on the dial, till the sun
Dropt, purple-sailed, into the gorgeous East,
When, from the fiery heart of that great orb,
Came One whose shape of beauty far outshone
The most bright vision of this common earth.
Girt was she in a robe more white than flame
Or furnace-heated brass; upon her head
She bare a laurel crown, and, like a star
That falls from the high heaven suddenly,
Passed to my side.
                        Then kneeling low, I cried
"O much-desired! O long-waited for!
Immortal Glory! Great world-conqueror!
Oh, let me not die crownless; once, at least,
Let thine imperial laurels bind my brows,
Ignoble else. Once let the clarion note
And trump of loud ambition sound my name
And for the rest I care not."
                                   Then to me,
In gentle voice, the angel made reply:
"Child, ignorant of the true happiness,
Nor knowing life's best wisdom, thou wert made

For light and love and laughter, not to waste
Thy youth in shooting arrows at the sun,
Or nurturing that ambition in thy soul
Whose deadly poison will infect thy heart,
Marring all joy and gladness! Tarry here
In the sweet confines of this garden-close
Whose level meads and glades delectable
Invite for pleasure; the wild bird that wakes
These silent dells with sudden melody
Shall be thy playmate; and each flower that blows
Shall twine itself unbidden in thy hair—
Garland more meet for thee than the dread weight
Of Glory's laurel wreath."
                          "Ah! fruitless gifts,"
I cried, unheeding of her prudent word,
"Are all such mortal flowers, whose brief lives
Are bounded by the dawn and setting sun.
The anger of the noon can wound the rose,
And the rain robs the crocus of its gold;
But thine immortal coronal of Fame,
Thy crown of deathless laurel, this alone
Age cannot harm, nor winter's icy tooth
Pierce to its hurt, nor common things profane."
No answer made the angel but her face
Dimmed with the mists of pity.
                          Then methought
That from thine eyes, wherein ambition's torch
Burned with its latest and most ardent flame,
Flashed forth two level beams of straitened light,
Beneath whose fulgent fires the laurel crown
Twisted and curled, as when the Sirian star
Withers the ripening corn, and one pale leaf
Fell on my brow; and I leapt up and felt

The mighty pulse of Fame, and heard far off
The sound of many nations praising me!

     *   *   *   *   *   *   *

One fiery-coloured moment of great life!
And then—how barren was the nations' praise!
How vain the trump of Glory! Bitter thorns
Were in that laurel leaf, whose toothèd barbs
Burned and bit deep till fire and red flame
Seemed to feed full upon my brain, and make
The garden a bare desert.
                       With wild hands
I strove to tear it from my bleeding brow,
But all in vain; and with a dolorous cry
That paled the lingering stars before their time,
I waked at last, and saw the timorous dawn
Peer with grey face into my darkened room,
And would have deemed it a mere idle dream
But for this restless pain that gnaws my heart,
And the red wounds of thorns upon my brow.

THE SPHINX

THE SPHINX

In a dim corner of my room for longer than my fancy
    thinks
A beautiful and silent Sphinx has watched me through the
    shifting gloom.

Inviolate and immobile she does not rise, she does not stir
For silver moons are naught to her and naught to her the
    suns that reel.

Red follows grey across the air, the waves of moonlight
    ebb and flow
But with the Dawn she does not go and in the night-time
    she is there.

Dawn follows Dawn and Nights grow old and all the while
    this curious cat
Lies crouching on the Chinese mat with eyes of satin
    rimmed with gold.

Upon the mat she lies and leers and on the tawny throat
    of her
Flutters the soft and silky fur or ripples to her pointed ears.

Come forth, my lovely seneschal! so somnolent, so statu-
    esque!
Come forth you exquisite grotesque! half woman and half
    animal!

Come forth my lovely languorous Sphinx! and put your
    head upon my knee!
And let me stroke your throat and see your body spotted
    like the Lynx!

And let me touch those curving claws of yellow ivorv and
    grasp
The tail that like a monstrous Asp coils round your heavy
    velvet paws!

A THOUSAND weary centuries are thine while I have hardly
    seen
Some twenty summers cast their green for Autumn's gaudy
    liveries.

But you can read the Hieroglyphs on the great sandstone
    obelisks,
And you have talked with Basilisks, and you have looked
    on Hippogriffs.

O tell me, were you standing by when Isis to Osiris knelt?
And did you watch the Egyptian melt her union for Antony

And drink the jewel-drunken wine and bend her head in
    mimic awe
To see the huge proconsul draw the salted tunny from the
    brine?

And did you mark the Cyprian kiss white Adon on his
    catafalque?
And did you follow Amenalk, the God of Héliopolis?

And did you talk with Thoth, and did you hear the moon-
    horned Io weep?
And know the painted kings who sleep beneath the wedge-
    shaped Pyramid?

———————

Lift up your large black satin eyes which are like cushions
    where one sinks!
Fawn at my feet, fantastic Sphinx! and sing me all your
    memories!

Sing to me of the Jewish maid who wandered with the
    Holy Child,
And how you led them through the wild, and how they slept
    beneath your shade.

Sing to me of that odorous green eve when couching by
    the marge
You heard from Adrian's gilded barge the laughter of
    Antinous

And lapped the stream and fed your drouth and watched
    with hot and hungry stare
The ivory body of that rare young slave with his pome-
    granate mouth!

Sing to me of the Labyrinth in which the twy-formed bull
    was stalled!
Sing to me of the night you crawled across the temple's
    granite plinth

When through the purple corridors the screaming scarlet
    Ibis flew
In terror, and a horrid dew dripped from the moaning
    Mandragores,

And the great torpid crocodile within the tank shed slimy
    tears,
And tare the jewels from his ears and staggered back into
    the Nile,

And the priests cursed you with shrill psalms as in your
    claws you seized their snake
And crept away with it to slake your passion by the shud-
    dering palms.

———

Who were your lovers? who were they who wrestled for
    you in the dust?
Which was the vessel of your lust? What Leman had you,
    every day?

Did giant Lizards come and crouch before you on the reedy
    banks?
Did Gryphons with great metal flanks leap on you in your
    trampled couch?

Did monstrous hippotami come sidling toward you in the
    mist?
Did gilt-scaled dragons writhe and twist with passion as you
    passed them by?

And from the brick-built Lycian tomb what horrible Chimera
    came
With fearful heads and fearful flame to breed new wonders
    from your womb?

OR HAD you shameful secret quests and did you hurry to
your home
Some Nereid coiled in amber foam with curious rock crystal
breasts?

Or did you treading through the froth call to the brown
Sidonian
For tidings of Leviathan, Leviathan or Behemoth?

Or did you when the sun was set climb up the cactus-
covered slope
To meet your swarthy Ethiop whose body was of polished jet?

Or did you while the earthen skiffs dropped down the grey
Nilotic flats
At twilight and the flickering bats flew round the temple's
triple glyphs

Steal to the border of the bar and swim across the silent
lake
And slink into the vault and make the Pyramid your
lúpanar

Till from each black sarcophagus rose up the painted
swathèd dead?
Or did you lure unto your bed the ivory-horned Tragela-
phos?

Or did you love the god of flies who plagued the Hebrews
and was splashed
With wine unto the waist? or Pasht, who had green beryls
for her eyes?

Or that young god, the Tyrian, who was more amorous
    than the dove
Of Ashtaroth? or did you love the god of the Assyrian

Whose wings, like strange transparent talc, rose high above
    his hawk-faced head,
Painted with silver and with red and ribbed with rods of
    Oreichalch?

Or did huge Apis from his car leap down and lay before
    your feet
Big blossoms of the honey-sweet and honey-coloured nenu-
    phar?

How subtle-secret is your smile! Did you love none then?
    Nay, I know
Great Ammon was your bedfellow! He lay with you beside
    the Nile!

The river-horses in the slime trumpeted when they saw him
    come
Odorous with Syrian galbanum and smeared with spikenard
    and with thyme.

He came along the river bank like some tall galley argent-
    sailed,
He strode across the waters, mailed in beauty, and the
    waters sank.

He strode across the desert sand: he reached the valley
    where you lay:
He waited till the dawn of day: then touched your black
    breasts with his hand.

You kissed his mouth with mouths of flame: you made the
    hornèd god your own:
You stood behind him on his throne: you called him by his
    secret name.

You whispered monstrous oracles into the caverns of his
    ears:
With blood of goats and blood of steers you taught him mon-
    strous miracles.

White Ammon was your bedfellow! Your chamber was the
    steaming Nile!
And with your curved archaic smile you watched his pas-
    sion come and go.

WITH Syrian oils his brows were bright: and widespread
    as a tent at noon
His marble limbs made pale the moon and lent the day a
    larger light.

His long hair was nine cubits' span and coloured like that
    yellow gem
Which hidden in their garment's hem the merchants bring
    from Kurdistan.

His face was as the must that lies upon a vat of new-made
    wine:
The seas could not insapphirine the perfect azure of his
    eyes.

His thick soft throat was white as milk and threaded with
the veins of blue:
And curious pearls like frozen dew were broidered on his
flowing silk.

On pearl and porphyry pedestalled he was too bright to
look upon:
For on his ivory breast there shone the wondrous ocean-
emerald,

That mystic moonlit jewel which some diver of the Colchian caves
Had found beneath the blackening waves and carried to
the Colchian witch.

Before his gilded galiot ran naked vine-wreathed cory-
bants,
And lines of swaying elephants knelt down to draw his
chariot,

And lines of swarthy Nubians bare up his litter as he rode
Down the great granite-paven road between the nodding
peacock-fans.

The merchants brought him steatite from Sidon in their
painted ships:
The meanest cup that touched his lips was fashioned from
a chrysolite.

The merchants brought him cedar chests of rich apparel
bound with cords:
His train was borne by Memphian lords: young kings were
glad to be his guests.

Ten hundred shaven priests did bow to Ammon's altar day
and night,
Ten hundred lamps did wave their light through Ammon's
carven house—and now

Foul snake and speckled adder with their young ones crawl
from stone to stone
For ruined is the house and prone the great rose-marble
monolith!

Wild ass or trotting jackal comes and couches in the mouldering gates:
Wild satyrs call unto their mates across the fallen fluted
drums.

And on the summit of the pile the blue-faced ape of Horus
sits
And gibbers while the fig-tree splits the pillars of the per-
istyle.

———

THE GOD is scattered here and there: deep hidden in the
windy sand
I saw his giant granite hand still clenched in impotent despair.

And many a wandering caravan of stately negroes silken-
shawled,
Crossing the desert halts appalled before the neck that none
can span.

And many a bearded Bedouin draws back his yellow-striped
burnous
To gaze upon the Titan thews of him who was thy paladin.

Go, seek his fragments on the moor and wash them in the
evening dew,
And from their pieces make anew thy mutilated paramour!

Go, seek them where they lie alone and from their broken
pieces make
Thy bruisèd bedfellow! And wake mad passions in the
senseless stone!

Charm his dull ear with Syrian hymns! he loved your body!
oh, be kind,
Pour spikenard on his hair, and wind soft rolls of linen
round his limbs!

Wind round his head the figured coins! stain with red fruits
those pallid lips!
Weave purple for his shrunken hips! and purple for his
barren loins!

———

Away to Egypt! Have no fear. Only one God has ever
died.
Only one God has let His side be wounded by a soldier's
spear.

But these, thy lovers, are not dead. Still by the hundred-
cubit gate
Dog-faced Anubis sits in state with lotus-lilies for thy
head.

Still from his chair of porphyry gaunt Memnon strains his
lidless eyes
Across the empty land, and cries each yellow morning unto
thee.

And Nilus with his broken horn lies in his black and oozy
bed
And till thy coming will not spread his waters on the with-
ering corn.

Your lovers are not dead, I know. They will rise up and
hear your voice
And clash their cymbals and rejoice and run to kiss your
mouth! And so,

Set wings upon your argosies! Set horses to your ebon
car!
Back to your Nile! Or if you are grown sick of dead di-
vinities

Follow some roving lion's spoor across the copper-coloured
plain,
Reach out and hale him by the mame and bid him be your
paramour!

Couch by his side upon the grass and set your white teeth
in his throat
And when you hear his dying note lash your long flanks of
polished brass

And take a tiger for your mate, whose amber sides are
flecked with black,
And ride upon his gilded back in triumph through the
Theban gate,

And toy with him in amorous jests, and when he turns, and
snarls, and gnaws,
O smite him with your jasper claws! and bruise him with
your agate breasts!

WHY are you tarrying? Get hence! I weary of your sullen
    ways,
I weary of your steadfast gaze, your somnolent magnifi-
    cence.

Your horrible and heavy breath makes the light flicker in
    the lamp,
And on my brow I feel the damp and dreadful dews of
    night and death.

Your eyes are like fantastic moons that shiver in some stag-
    nant lake,
Your tongue is like a scarlet snake that dances to fantastic
    tunes,

Your pulse makes poisonous melodies, and your black throat
    is like the hole
Left by some torch or burning coal on Saracenic tapestries.

Away! The sulphur-coloured stars are hurrying through the
    Western gate!
Away! Or it may be too late to climb their silent silver
    cars!

See, the dawn shivers round the grey gilt-dialled towers, and
    the rain
Streams down each diamonded pane and blurs with tears
    the wannish day.

What snake-tressed fury fresh from Hell, with uncouth
    gestures and unclean,
Stole from the poppy-drowsy queen and led you to a stu-
    dent's cell?

WHAT songless tongueless ghost of sin crept through the curtains of the night,
And saw my taper burning bright, and knocked, and bade you enter in.

Are there not others more accursed, whiter with leprosies than I?
Are Abana and Pharphar dry that you come here to slake your thirst?

Get hence, you loathsome mystery! Hideous animal, get hence!
You wake in me each bestial sense, you make me what I would not be.

You make my creed a barren sham, you wake foul dreams of sensual life,
And Atys with his blood-stained knife were better than the thing I am.

False Sphinx! False Sphinx! By reedy Styx old Charon, leaning on his oar,
Waits for my coin. Go thou before, and leave me to my crucifix,

Whose pallid burden, sick with pain, watches the world with wearied eyes,
And weeps for every soul that dies, and weeps for every soul in vain.

FAIRY TALES

THE YOUNG KING.

It was the night before the day fixed for his coronation, and the young King was sitting alone in his beautiful chamber. His courtiers had all taken their leave of him, bowing their heads to the ground, according to the ceremonious usage of the day, and had retired to the Great Hall of the Palace, to receive a few last lessons from the Professor of Etiquette; there being some of them who had still quite natural manners, which in a courtier is, I need hardly say, a very grave offense.

The lad—for he was only a lad, being but sixteen years of age—was not sorry at their departure, and had flung himself back with a deep sigh of relief on the soft cushions of his embroidered couch, lying there, wild-eyed and open-mouthed, like a brown woodland Faun, or some young animal of the forest newly snared by the hunters.

And, indeed, it was the hunters who had found him, coming upon him almost by chance as, bare-limbed and pipe in hand, he was following the flock of the poor goatherd who had brought him up, and whose son he had always fancied himself to be. The

3

child of the old King's only daughter by a secret
marriage with one much beneath her in station—a
stranger, some said, who, by the wonderful magic
of his lute-playing, had made the young Princess
love him; while others spoke of an artist from
Rimini, to whom the Princess had shown much, perhaps too much honour, and who had suddenly disappeared from the city, leaving his work in the
Cathedral unfinished—he had been, when but a
week old, stolen away from his mother's side, as she
slept, and given into the charge of a common peas-
ant and his wife, who were without children of their
own, and lived in a remote part of the forest, more
than a day's ride from the town. Grief, or the
plague, as the court physician stated, or, as some
suggested, a swift Italian poison administered in a
cup of spiced wine, slew, within an hour of her
wakening, the white girl who had given him birth,
and as the trusty messenger who bare the child
across his saddle-bow, stooped from his weary horse
and knocked at the rude door of the goatherd's hut,
the body of the Princess was being lowered into an
open grave that had been dug in a deserted church-
yard, beyond the city gates, a grave where, it was
said, that another body was also lying, that of a
young man of marvellous and foreign beauty, whose
hands were tied behind him with a knotted cord,
and whose breast was stabbed with many red
wounds.

Such, at least, was the story that men whispered

to each other. Certain it was that the old King, when on his death-bed, whether moved by remorse for his great sin, or merely desiring that the kingdom should not pass away from his line, had had the lad sent for, and, in the presence of the Council, had acknowledged him as his heir.

And it seems that from the very first moment of his recognition he had shown signs of that strange passion for beauty that was destined to have so great an influence over his life. Those who accompanied him to the suite of rooms set apart for his service, often spoke of the cry of pleasure that broke from his lips when he saw the delicate raiment and rich jewels that had been prepared for him, and of the almost fierce joy with which he flung aside his rough leathern tunic and coarse sheepskin cloak. He missed, indeed, at times the fine freedom of his forest life, and was always apt to chafe at the tedious Court ceremonies that occupied so much of each day, but the wonderful palace—*Joyeuse,* as they called it—of which he now found himself lord, seemed to him to be á new world fresh-fashioned for his delight; and as soon as he could escape from the council-board or audience-chamber, he would run down the great staircase, with its lions of gilt bronze and its steps of bright porphyry, and wander from room to room, and from corridor to corridor, like one who was seeking to find in beauty an anodyne from pain, a sort of restoration from sickness.

Upon these journeys of discovery, as he would

call them—and, indeed, they were to him real voyages through a marvellous land, he would sometimes be accompanied by the slim, fair-haired Court pages, with their floating mantles, and gay fluttering ribands; but more often he would be alone, feeling through a certain quick instinct, which was almost a divination, that the secrets of art are best learned in secret, and that Beauty, like Wisdom, loves the lonely worshipper.

Many curious stories were related about him at this period. It was said that a stout Burgomaster, who had come to deliver a florid oratorical address on behalf of the citizens of the town, had caught sight of him kneeling in real adoration before a great picture that had just been brought from Venice, and that seemed to herald the worship of some new gods. On another occasion he had been missed for several hours, and after a lengthened search had been discovered in a little chamber in one of the northern turrets of the palace gazing, as one in a trance, at a Greek gem carved with the figure of Adonis. He had been seen, so the tale ran, pressing his warm lips to the marble brow of an antique statue that had been discovered in the bed of the river on the occasion of the building of the stone bridge, and was inscribed with the name of the Bithynian slave of Hadrian. He had passed a whole night in noting the effect of the moonlight on a silver image of Endymion.

All rare and costly materials had certainly a

great fascination for him, and in his eagerness to
procure them he had sent away many merchants,
some to traffic for amber with the rough fisher-folk
of the north seas, some to Egypt to look for that
curious green turquoise which is found only in the
tombs of kings, and is said to possess magical prop-
erties, some to Persia for silken carpets and painted
pottery, and others to India to buy gauze and stained
ivory, moonstones and bracelets of jade, sandal-
wood and blue enamel and shawls of fine wool.

But what had occupied him most was the robe
he was to wear at his coronation, the robe of tissued
gold, and the ruby-studded crown, and the sceptre
with its rows and rings of pearls.   Indeed, it was
of this that he was thinking to-night, as he lay back
on his luxurious couch, watching the great pinewood log that was burning itself out on the open
hearth.   The designs, which were from the hands
of the most famous artists of the time, had been
submitted to him many months before, and he had
given orders that the artificers were to toil night
and day to carry them out, and that the whole world
was to be searched for jewels that would be worthy
of their work.   He saw himself in fancy standing
at the high altar of the cathedral in the fair raiment
of a King, and a smile played and lingered about
his boyish lips, and lit up with a bright lustre his
dark woodland eyes.

After some time he rose from his seat, and leaning against the carved penthouse of the chimney,

looked round at the dimly-lit room. The walls were
hung with rich tapestries representing the Triumph
of Beauty. A large press, inlaid with agate and
lapis-lazuli, filled one corner, and facing the window
stood a curiously wrought cabinet with lacquer pan-
els of powdered and mosaiced gold, on which were
placed some delicate goblets of Venetian glass, and
a cup of dark-veined onyx. Pale poppies were embroidered on the silk coverlet of the bed, as though
they had fallen from the tired hands of sleep, and
tall reeds of fluted ivory bare up the velvet canopy,
from which great tufts of ostrich plumes sprang,
like white foam, to the pallid silver of the fretted
ceiling. A laughing Narcissus in green bronze held
a polished mirror above its head. On the table stood
a flat bowl of amethyst.

Outside he could see the huge dome of the cathedral, looming like a bubble over the shadowy houses,
and the weary sentinels pacing up and down on the
misty terrace by the river. Far away, in an orchard,
a nightingale was singing. A faint perfume of jas-
mine came through the open window. He brushed
his brown curls back from his forehead, and, taking
up a lute, let his fingers stray across the cords. His
heavy eyelids drooped, and a strange languor came
over him. Never before had he felt so keenly, or
with such exquisite joy, the magic and the mystery
of beautiful things.

When midnight sounded from the clock-tower he
touched a bell, and his pages entered and disrobed

him with much ceremony, pouring rose-water over
his hands, and strewing flowers on his pillow. A
few moments after that they had left the room, he
fell asleep.

And as he slept he dreamed a dream, and this
was his dream.

He thought that he was standing in a long, low
attic, amidst the whirr and clatter of many looms.
The meagre daylight peered in through the grated
windows, and showed him the gaunt figures of the
weavers bending over their cases. Pale, sickly-
looking children were crouched on the huge cross-
beams. As the shuttles dashed through the warp
they lifted up the heavy battens, and when the shuttles stopped they let the battens fall and pressed the
threads together. Their faces were pinched with
famine, and their thin hands shook and trembled.
Some haggard women were seated at a table sewing. A horrible odour filled the place. The air was
foul and heavy, and the walls dripped and streamed
with damp.

The young King went over to one of the weavers,
and stood by him and watched him.

And the weaver looked at him angrily, and said,
"Why art thou watching me? Art thou a spy set
on us by our master?"

"Who is thy master?" asked the young King.

"Our master!" cried the weaver, bitterly. "He
is a man like myself. Indeed, there is but this dif-

ference between us—that he wears fine clothes while
I go in rags, and that while I am weak from hunger
he suffers not a little from overfeeding."

"The land is free," said the young King, "and
thou art no man's slave."

"In war," answered the weaver, "the strong make
slaves of the weak and in peace the rich make slaves
of the poor. We must work to live, and they give
us such mean wages that we die. We toil for them
all day long, and they heap up gold in their coffers,
and our children fade away before their time, and
the faces of those we love become hard and evil.
We tread out the grapes, and another drinks the
wine. We sow the corn, and our own board is
empty. We have chains, though no eye beholds
them; and are slaves, though men call us free."

"Is it so with all?" he asked.

"It is so with all," answered the weaver, "with
the young as well as with the old, and the women
as well as with the men, with the little children as
well as with those who are stricken in years. The
merchants grind us down, and we must needs do
their bidding. The priest rides by and tells his
beads, and no man has care of us. Through our
sunless lanes creeps Poverty with her hungry eyes,
and Sin with his sodden face follows close behind
her. Misery wakes us in the morning, and Shame
sits with us at night. But what are these things to
thee? Thou art not one of us. Thy face is too
happy." And he turned away scowling, and threw

the shuttle across the loom, and the young King saw
that it was threaded with a thread of gold.

And a great terror seized upon him, and he said
to the weaver, "What robe is this that thou art
weaving?"

"It is the robe for the coronation of the young
King," he answered; "what is that to thee?"

And the young King gave a loud cry and woke,
and lo! he was in his own chamber, and through the
window he saw the great honey-coloured moon
hanging in the dusky air.

And he fell asleep again and dreamed, and this
was his dream:

He thought that he was lying on the deck of a
huge galley that was being rowed by a hundred
slaves. On a carpet by his side the master of the
galley was seated. He was black as ebony, and
his turban was of crimson silk. Great ear-rings of
silver dragged down the thick lobes of his ears, and
in his hands he had a pair of ivory scales.

The slaves were naked, but for a ragged loin-
cloth, and each man was chained to his neighbour.
The hot sun beat brightly upon them, and the negroes ran up and down the gangway and lashed
them with whips of hide. They stretched out their
lean arms and pulled the heavy oars through the
water. The salt spray flew from the blades.

At last they reached a little bay, and began to take
soundings. A light wind blew from the shore, and

covered the deck and the great lateen sail with a fine red dust. Three Arabs mounted on wild asses rode out and threw spears at them. The master of the galley took a painted bow in his hand and shot one of them in the throat. He fell heavily into the surf, and his companions galloped away. A woman wrapped in a yellow veil followed slowly on a camel, looking back now and then at the dead body.

As soon as they had cast anchor and hauled down the sail, the negroes went into the hold and brought up a long rope-ladder, heavily weighted with lead. The master of the galley threw it over the side, making the ends fast to two iron stanchions. Then the negroes seized the youngest of the slaves, and knocked his gyves off, and filled his nostrils and his ears with wax, and tied a big stone round his waist. He crept wearily down the ladder, and disappeared into the sea. A few bubbles rose where he sank. Some of the other slaves peered curiously over the side. At the prow of the galley sat a shark-charmer, beating monotonously upon a drum.

After some time the diver rose up out of the water, and clung panting to the ladder with a pearl in his right hand. The negroes seized it from him, and thrust him back. The slaves fell asleep over their oars.

Again and again he came up, and each time that he did so he brought with him a beautiful pearl. The master of the galley weighed them, and put them into a little bag of green leather.

The young King tried to speak, but his tongue seemed to cleave to the roof of his mouth, and his lips refused to move. The negroes chattered to each other, and began to quarrel over a string of bright beads. Two cranes flew round and round the vessel.

Then the diver came up for the last time, and the pearl that he brought with him was fairer than all the pearls of Ormuz, for it was shaped like the full moon, and whiter than the morning star. But his face was strangely pale, and as he fell upon the deck the blood gushed from his ears and nostrils. He quivered for a little, and then he was still. The negroes shrugged their shoulders and threw the body overboard.

And the master of the galley laughed, and, reaching out, he took the pearl, and when he saw it he pressed it to his forehead and bowed. "It shall be," he said, "for the sceptre of the young King," and he made a sign to the negroes to draw up the anchor.

And when the young King heard this he gave a great cry, and woke, and through the window he saw the long grey fingers of the dawn clutching at the fading stars.

And he fell asleep again, and dreamed, and this was his dream:

He thought that he was wandering through a dim wood, hung with strange fruits and with beautiful poisonous flowers. The adders hissed at him

as he went by, and the bright parrots flew screaming from branch to branch. Huge tortoises lay
asleep upon the hot mud. The trees were full of
apes and peacocks.

On and on he went, till he reached the outskirts
of the wood, and there he saw an immense multitude of men toiling in the bed of a dried-up river.
They swarmed up the crag like ants. They dug deep
pits in the ground and went down into them. Some
of them cleft the rocks with great axes; others
grabbled in the sand. They tore up the cactus by
its roots, and trampled on the scarlet blossoms.
They hurried about, calling to each other, and no
man was idle.

From the darkness of a cavern Death and Avarice
watched them, and Death said, "I am weary; give
me a third of them and let me go."

But Avarice shook her head. "They are my servants," she answered.

And Death said to her, "What hast thou in thy
hand?"

"I have three grains of corn," she answered;
"what is that to thee?"

"Give me one of them," cried Death, "to plant
in my garden; only one of them, and I will go
away."

"I will not give thee anything," said Avarice, and
she hid her hand in the fold of her raiment.

And Death laughed, and took a cup, and dipped
it into a pool of water, and out of the cup rose

Ague. She passed through the great multitude, and a third of them lay dead. A cold mist followed her, and the water-snakes ran by her side.

And when Avarice saw that a third of the multitude was dead she beat her breast and wept. She beat her barren bosom, and cried aloud. "Thou hast slain a third of my servants," she cried, "get thee gone. There is war in the mountains of Tartary, and the kings of each side are calling to thee. The Afghans have slain the black ox, and are marching to battle. They have beaten upon their shields with their spears, and have put on their helmets of iron. What is my valley to thee, that thou should'st tarry in it? Get thee gone, and come here no more."

"Nay," answered Death, "but till thou hast given me a grain of corn I will not go."

But Avarice shut her hand and clenched her teeth. "I will not give thee anything," she muttered.

And Death laughed, and took a cup, and stone, and threw it into the forest, and out of a thicket of wild hemlock came Fever in a robe of flame. She passed through the multitude, and touched them, and each man that she touched died. The grass withered beneath her feet as she walked.

And Avarice shuddered, and put ashes on her head. "Thou art cruel," she cried; "thou art cruel. There is famine in the walled cities of India, and the cisterns of Samarcand have run dry. There is famine in the walled cities of Egypt, and the locusts

have come up from the desert. The Nile has not
overflowed its banks, and the priests have cursed
Isis and Osiris. Get thee gone to those who need
thee, and leave me my servants."

"Nay," answered Death, "but till thou hast given
me a grain of corn, I will not go."

"I will not give thee anything," said Avarice.

And Death laughed again, and he' whistled
through his fingers, and a woman came flying
through the air. Plague was written upon her forehead, and a crowd of lean vultures wheeled round
her. She covered the valley with her wings, and
no man was left alive.

And Avarice fled shrieking through the forest,
and Death leaped upon his red horse and galloped
away, and his galloping was faster than the wind.

And out of the slime at the bottom of the valley
crept dragons and horrible things with scales, and
the jackals came trotting along the sand, sniffing up
the air with their nostrils.

And the young King wept, and said: "Who
were these men, and for what were they seeking?"

"For rubies for a king's crown," answered one
who stood behind him.

And the young King started, and, turning round,
he saw a man habited as a pilgrim and holding in
his hand a mirror of silver.

And he grew pale, and said: "For what king?"

And the pilgrim answered: "Look in this mirror,
and thou shalt see him."

And he looked in the mirror, and, seeing his own face, he gave a great cry and woke, and the bright sunlight was streaming into the room, and from the trees of the garden and pleasaunce the birds were singing.

And the Chamberlain and the high officers of State came in and made obeisance to him, and the pages brought him the robe of tissued gold, and set the crown and the sceptre before him.

And the young King looked at them, and they were beautiful. More beautiful were they than aught that he had ever seen. But he remembered his dreams, and he said to his lords: "Take these things away, for I will not wear them."

And the courtiers were amazed, and some of them laughed, for they thought that he was jesting.

But he spake sternly to them again, and said: "Take these things away, and hide them from me. Though it be the day of my coronation, I will not wear them. For on the loom of Sorrow, and by the white hands of Pain, has this my robe been woven. There is Blood in the heart of the ruby, and Death in the heart of the pearl." And he told them his three dreams.

And when the courtiers heard them they looked at each other and whispered, saying: "Surely he is mad; for what is a dream but a dream, and a vision but a vision? They are not real things that one should heed them. And what have we to do with the lives of those who toil for us? Shall a man not eat bread till he has seen the sower, nor drink wine till he has talked with the vinedresser?"

And the Chamberlain spake to the young King, and said, "My lord, I pray thee set aside these black thoughts of thine, and put on this fair robe, and set this crown upon thy head. For how shall the people know that thou art a king, if thou hast not a king's raiment?"

And the young King looked at him. "Is it so, indeed?" he questioned. "Will they not know me for a king if I have not a king's raiment?"

"They will not know thee, my lord," cried the Chamberlain.

"I had thought that there had been men who were kinglike," he answered, "but it may be as thou sayest. And yet I will not wear this robe, nor will I be crowned with this crown, but even as I came to the palace so will I go forth from it."

And he bade them all leave him, save one page whom he kept as his companion, a lad a year younger than himself. Him he kept for his service, and when he had bathed himself in clear water, he opened a great painted chest, and from it he took the leathern tunic and rough sheepskin cloak that he had worn when he had watched on the hillside the shaggy goats of the goatherd. These he put on, and in his hand he took his rude shepherd's staff.

And the little page opened his big blue eyes in wonder, and said smiling to him, "My lord, I see thy robe and thy sceptre, but where is thy crown?"

And the young King plucked a spray of wild briar that was climbing over the balcony, and bent it, and made a circlet of it, and set it on his own head.

"This shall be my crown," he answered.

And thus attired he passed out of his chamber into the Great Hall where the nobles were waiting for him.

And the nobles made merry, and some of them cried out to him, "My lord, the people wait for their king, and thou showest them a beggar," and others were wrath and said, "He brings shame upon our state, and is unworthy to be our master." But he answered them not a word, but passed on, and went down the bright porphyry staircase, and out through the gates of bronze, and mounted upon his horse, and rode towards the cathedral, the little page running beside him.

And the people laughed and said, "It is the King's fool who is riding by," and they mocked him.

And he drew rein and said, "Nay, but I am the King." And he told them his three dreams.

And a man came out of the crowd, and spake bitterly to him, and said, "Sir, knowest thou not that out of the luxury of the rich cometh the life of the poor? By your pomp we are nurtured, and your vices give us bread. To toil for a hard master is bitter, but to have no master to toil for is more bitter still. Thinkest thou that the ravens will feed us? And what cure hast thou for these things? Wilt thou say to the buyer, 'Thou shalt buy for so much,' and to the seller, 'Thou shalt sell at this price?' I trow not. Therefore go back to thy Palace and put on thy purple and fine linen. What hast thou to do with us, and what we suffer?"

"Are not the rich and the poor brothers?" asked the young King.

"Aye," answered the man, "and the name of the rich brother is Cain."

And the young King's eyes filled with tears, and he rode on through the murmurs of the people, and the little page grew afraid and left him.

And when he reached the great portal of the cathedral, the soldiers thrust their halberts out and said, "What dost thou seek here? None enters by this door but the King."

And his face flushed with anger, and he said to them, "I am the King," and waved their halberts aside and passed in.

And when the old Bishop saw him coming in his goatherd's dress, he rose up in wonder from his throne, and went to meet him, and said to him, "My son, is this a king's apparel? And with what crown shall I crown thee, and what sceptre shall I place in thy hand? Surely this should be to thee a day of joy, and not a day of abasement."

"Shall Joy wear what Grief has fashioned?" said the young King. And he told him his three dreams.

And when the Bishop had heard them he knit his brows, and said, "My son, I am an old man, and in the winter of my days, and I know that many evil things are done in the wide world. The fierce robbers come down from the mountains and carry off the little children, and sell them to the Moors. The lions lie in wait for the caravans, and leap upon the camels. The wild boar roots up the corn in the valley, and the foxes gnaw the vines upon the hill. The pirates lay waste the sea-coast and burn the ships of the fishermen, and take their nets from them. In the salt-marshes live the lepers; they have houses of wattled reeds, and none may come nigh them. The beggars wander through the cities, and eat their food with the dogs. Canst thou make these things not to be? Wilt thou take the leper for thy bedfellow, and set the beggar at thy board? Shall the lion do thy bidding, and the wild boar obey thee? Is not He who made misery wiser than thou art? Wherefore I praise thee not for this that thou hast done, but I bid thee ride back to the Palace and make thy face glad, and put on the raiment that beseemeth a king, and with the crown of gold I will crown thee, and the sceptre of pearl will I place in thy hand. And as for thy dreams, think no more of them. The burden of this world is too great for one man to bear, and the world's sorrow too heavy for one heart to suffer."

"Sayest thou that in this house?" said the young King, and he strode past the Bishop, and climbed up the steps of the altar, and stood before the image of Christ.

He stood before the image of Christ, and on his right hand and on his left were the marvellous vessels of gold, the chalice with the yellow wine, and the vial with the holy oil. He knelt before the image of Christ, and the candles burned brightly by the jewelled shrine, and the smoke of the incense curled in thin blue wreaths through the dome. He bowed his head in prayer and the priests in their stiff copes crept away from the altar.

And suddenly a wild tumult came from the street outside, and in entered the nobles with drawn swords and nodding plumes, and shields of polished steel. "Where is this dreamer of dreams?" they cried. "Where is this King, who is apparelled like a beggar—this boy who brings shame upon our State? Surely we will slay him, for he is unworthy to rule over us."

And the young King bowed his head again, and prayed, and when he had finished his prayer he rose up, and turning round he looked at them sadly.

And lo! through the painted windows came the sunlight streaming upon him, and the sunbeams wove round him a tissued robe that was fairer than the robe that had been fashioned for his pleasure. The dead staff blossomed, and bare lilies that were whiter than pearls. The dry thorn blossomed, and bare roses that were redder than rubies. Whiter than fine pearls were the lilies, and their stems were of bright silver. Redder than male rubies were the roses, and their leaves were of beaten gold.

He stood there in the raiment of a king, and the gates of the jewelled shrine flew open, and from the crystal of the many-rayed monstrance shone a marvellous and mystical light. He stood there in a king's raiment, and the Glory of God filled the place, and the saints in their carven niches seemed to move. In the fair raiment of a king he stood before them, and the organ pealed out its music, and the trumpeters blew upon their trumpets, and the singing boys sang.

And the people fell upon their knees in awe, and the nobles sheathed their swords and did homage, and the Bishop's face grew pale, and his hands trembled. "A greater than I hath crowned thee," he cried, and he knelt before him.

And the young King came down from the high altar, and passed home through the midst of the people. But no man dared look upon his face, for it was like the face of an angel.

THE BIRTHDAY OF THE INFANTA

It was the birthday of the Infanta. She was just twelve years of age, and the sun was shining brightly in the gardens of the palace.

Although she was a real Princess and the Infanta of Spain, she had only one birthday every year, just like the children of quite poor people, so it was naturally a matter of great importance to the whole country that she should have a really fine day for the occasion. And a really fine day it certainly was. The tall striped tulips stood straight up upon their stalks, like long rows of soldiers, and looked defiantly across the grass at the roses, and said: "We are quite as splendid as you are now." The purple butterflies fluttered about with gold dust on their wings, visiting each flower in turn; the little lizards crept out of the crevices of the wall, and lay basking in the white glare; and the pomegranates split and cracked with the heat, and showed their bleeding red hearts. Even the pale yellow lemons, that hung in such profusion from the mouldering trellis and along the dim arcades, seemed to have caught a richer colour from the wonderful sunlight, and the magnolia trees opened their great globe-like blossoms of folded ivory, and filled the air with a sweet heavy perfume.

The little Princess herself walked up and down the terrace with her companions, and played at hide and seek round the stone vases and the old moss-grown statues. On ordinary days she was only allowed to play with children of her own rank, so she had always to play alone, but her birthday was an exception, and the King had given orders that she was to invite any of her young friends whom she liked to come and amuse themselves with her. There was a stately grace about these slim Spanish children as they glided about, the boys with their large-plumed hats and short fluttering cloaks, the girls holding up the trains of their long brocaded gowns, and shielding the sun from their eyes with huge fans of black and silver. But the Infanta was the most graceful of all, and the most tastefully attired, after the somewhat cumbrous fashion of the day. Her robe was of grey satin, the skirt and the wide puffed sleeves heavily embroidered with silver, and the stiff corset studded with rows of fine pearls. Two tiny slippers with big pink rosettes peeped out beneath her dress as she walked. Pink and pearl was her great gauze fan, and in her hair, which like an aureole of faded gold stood out stiffly round her pale little face, she had a beautiful white rose.

From a window in the palace the sad melancholy

King watched them. Behind him stood his brother, Don Pedro of Aragon, whom he hated, and his confessor, the Grand Inquisitor of Granada, sat by his side. Sadder even than usual was the King, for as he looked at the Infanta bowing with childish gravity to the assembling courtiers, or laughing behind her fan at the grim Duchess of Albuquerque who always accompanied her, he thought of the young Queen, her mother, who but a short time before—so it seemed to him—had come from the gay country of France, and had withered away in the sombre splendour of the Spanish court, dying just six months after the birth of her child, and before she had seen the almonds blossom twice in the orchard, or plucked the second year's fruit from the old gnarled fig-tree that stood in the centre of the now grass-grown courtyard. So great had been his love for her that he had not suffered even the grave to hide her from him. She had been embalmed by a Moorish physician, who in return for this service had been granted his life, which for heresy and suspicion of magical practices had been already forfeited, men said, to the Holy Office, and her body was still lying on its tapestried bier in the black marble chapel of the Palace, just as the monks had borne her in on that windy March day nearly twelve years before. Once every month the King, wrapped in a dark cloak and with a muffled lantern in his hand, went in and knelt by her side, calling out, *"Mi reina! Mi reina!"* and sometimes break-

ing through the formal etiquette that in Spain gov-
erns every separate action of life, and sets limits
even to the sorrow of a King, he would clutch at the
pale jewelled hands in a wild agony of grief, and try
to wake by his mad kisses the cold painted face.

To-day he seemed to see her again, as he had seen
her first at the Castle of Fontainebleau, when he was
but fifteen years of age, and she still younger. They
had been formally betrothed on that occasion by
the Papal Nuncio in the presence of the French
King and all the Court, and he had returned to the
Escurial bearing with him a little ringlet of yellow
hair, and the memory of two childish lips bending
down to kiss his hand as he stepped into his carriage.
Later on had followed the marriage, hastily performed at Burgos, a small town on the frontier between the two countries, and the grand public entry
into Madrid with the customary celebration of high
mass at the Church of La Atocha, and a more than
usually solemn *auto-da-fé,* in which nearly three
hundred heretics, amongst whom were many Eng-
lishmen, had been delivered over to the secular arm
to be burned.

Certainly he had loved her madly, and to the ruin,
many thought, of his country, then at war with England for the possession of the empire of the New
World. He had hardly ever permitted her to be out
of his sight; for her, he had forgotten, or seemed
to have forgotten, all grave affairs of State; and,
with that terrible blindness that passion brings upon

its servants, he had failed to notice that the elaborate ceremonies by which he sought to please her
did but aggravate the strange malady from which
she suffered. When she died he was, for a time,
like one bereft of reason. Indeed, there is no doubt
but that he would have formally abdicated and retired to the great Trappist monastery at Granada, of
which he was already titular Prior, had he not been
afraid to leave the little Infanta at the mercy of his
brother, whose cruelty, even in Spain, was notorious,
and who was suspected by many of having caused
the Queen's death by means of a pair of poisoned
gloves that he had presented to her on the occasion
of her visiting his castle in Aragon. Even after
the expiration of the three years of public mourning
that he had ordained throughout his whole dominions by royal edict, he would never suffer his ministers to speak about any new alliance, and when the
Emperor himself sent to him, and offered him the
hand of the lovely Archduchess of Bohemia, his
niece, in marriage, he bade the ambassadors tell
their master that the King of Spain was already
wedded to Sorrow, and that though she was but a
barren bride he loved her better than Beauty; an
answer that cost his crown the rich provinces of the
Netherlands, which soon after, at the Emperor's
instigation, revolted against him under the leader-
ship of some fanatics of the Reformed Church.

His whole married life, with its fierce, fiery-
coloured joys and the terrible agony of its sudden

ending, seemed to come back to him to-day as he watched the Infanta playing on the terrace. She had all the Queen's pretty petulance of manner, the same wilful way of tossing her head, the same proud, curved beautiful mouth, the same wonderful smile—*vrai sourire de France* indeed—as she glanced up now and then at the window, or stretched out her little hand for the stately Spanish gentleman to kiss. But the shrill laughter of the children grated on his ears, and the bright, pitiless sunlight mocked his sorrow, and a dull odour of strange spices, spices such as embalmers use, seemed to taint —or was it fancy?—the clear morning air. He buried his face in his hands, and when the Infanta looked up again the curtains had been drawn, and the King had retired.

She made a little *moue* of disappointment, and shrugged her shoulders. Surely he might have stayed with her on her birthday. What did the stupid State-affairs matter? Or had he gone to that gloomy chapel, where the candles were always burning, and where she was never allowed to enter? How silly of him, when the sun was shining so brightly, and everybody was so happy! Besides, he would miss the sham bull-fight for which the trumpet was already sounding, to say nothing of the puppet show and the other wonderful things. Her uncle and the Grand Inquisitor were much more sensible. They had come out on the terrace, and paid her nice compliments. So she tossed her pretty head,

and taking Don Pedro by the hand, she walked
slowly down the steps towards a long pavilion of
purple silk that had been erected at the end of the
garden, the other children following in strict order
of precedence, those who had the longest names going first.

A procession of noble boys, fantastically dressed
as *toreadors,* came out to meet her, and the young
Count of Tierra-Nueva, a wonderfully handsome lad
of about fourteen years of age, uncovering his head
with all the grace of a born hidalgo and grandee of
Spain, led her solemnly in to a little gilt and ivory
chair that was placed on a raised daïs above the
arena. The children grouped themselves all around,
fluttering their big fans and whispering to each
other, and Don Pedro and the Grand Inquisitor
stood laughing at the entrance. Even the Duchess
—the Camerera-Mayor as she was called—a thin,
hard-featured woman with a yellow ruff, did not
look quite so bad-tempered as usual, and something
like a chill smile flitted across her wrinkled face and
twitched her thin, bloodless lips.

It certainly was a marvelous bull-fight, and much
nicer, the Infanta thought, than the real bull-fight
that she had been brought to see at Seville, on the
occasion of the visit of the Duke of Parma to her
father. Some of the boys pranced about on richly-
caparisoned hobby-horses brandishing long javelins
with gay streamers of bright ribands attached to

them; others went on foot waving their scarlet cloaks before the bull, and vaulting lightly over the barrier when he charged them; and as for the bull himself he was just like a live bull, though he was only made of wicker-work and stretched hide, and sometimes insisted on running round the arena on his hind legs, which no live bull ever dreams of doing. He made a splendid fight of it, too, and the children got so excited that they stood up upon the benches, and waved their lace handkerchiefs and cried out: *Bravo toro! Bravo toro!* just as sensibly as if they had been grown-up people. At last, however, after a prolonged combat, during which several of the hobby-horses were gored through and through, and their riders dismounted, the young Count of Tierra-Nueva brought the bull to his knees, and having obtained permission from the Infanta to give the *coup de grâce,* he plunged his wooden sword into the neck of the animal with such violence that the head came right off, and disclosed the laughing face of little Monsieur de Lorraine, the son of the French Ambassador at Madrid.

The arena was then cleared amidst much applause, and the dead hobby-horses dragged solemnly away by two Moorish pages in yellow and black liveries, and after a short interlude, during which a French posture-master performed upon the tight rope, some Italian puppets appeared in the semi-classical tragedy of *Sophonisba* on the stage of a small theatre that had been built up for the purpose. They acted so

well, and their gestures were so extremely natural,
that at the close of the play the eyes of the Infanta
were quite dim with tears. Indeed some of the
children really cried, and had to be comforted with
sweetmeats, and the Grand Inquisitor himself was
so affected that he could not help saying to Don
Pedro that it seemed to him intolerable that things
made simply out of wood and coloured wax, and
worked mechanically by wires, should be so unhappy
and meet with such terrible misfortunes.

An African juggler followed, who brought in a
large flat basket covered with a red cloth, and having
placed it in the centre of the arena, he took from his
turban a curious reed pipe, and blew through it.
In a few moments the cloth began to move, and as
the pipe grew shriller and shriller two green and
gold snakes put out their strange wedge-shaped
heads and rose slowly up, swaying to and fro with
the music as a plant sways in the water. The children,
however, were rather frightened at their spotted
hoods and quick darting tongues, and were much
more pleased when the juggler made a tiny orange-
tree grow out of the sand and bear pretty white blossoms and clusters of real fruit; and when he took the
fan of the little daughter of the Marquess de Las-
Torres, and changed it into a blue bird that flew all
round the pavilion and sang, their delight and
amazement knew no bounds. The solemn minuet,
too, performed by the dancing boys from the church
of Neustra Señora Del Pilar, was charming. The

Infanta had never before seen this wonderful ceremony which takes place every year at May-time in
front of the high altar of the Virgin, and in her
honour; and, indeed, none of the royal family of
Spain had entered the great cathedral of Saragossa
since a mad priest, supposed by many to have been
in the pay of Elizabeth of England, had tried to
administer a poisoned wafer to the Prince of the
Asturias. So she had known only by hearsay of
"Our Lady's Dance," as it was called, and it certainly was a beautiful sight. The boys wore old-
fashioned court dresses of white velvet, and their
curious three-cornered hats were fringed with silver
and surmounted with huge plumes of ostrich feathers, the dazzling whiteness of their costumes, as they
moved about in the sunlight, being still more ac-
centuated by their swarthy faces and long black
hair. Everybody was fascinated by the grave dignity with which they moved through the intricate
figures of the dance, and by the elaborate grace of
their slow gestures, and stately bows, and when they
had finished their performance and doffed their
great plumed hats to the Infanta, she acknowledged
their reverence with much courtesy, and made a vow
that she would send a large wax candle to the shrine
of Our Lady of Pilar in return for the pleasure that
she had given her.

A troop of handsome Egyptians—as the gipsies
were termed in those days—then advanced into the
arena, and sitting down cross-legs, in a circle, began

to play softly upon their zithers, moving their bodies
to the tune, and humming, almost below their breath,
a low, dreamy air. When they caught sight of Don
Pedro they scowled at him, and some of them looked
terrified, for only a few weeks before he had had
two of their tribe hanged for sorcery in the market-
place at Seville, but the pretty Infanta charmed them
as she leaned back peeping over her fan with her
great blue eyes, and they felt sure that one so lovely
as she was could never be cruel to anybody. So they
played on very gently and just touching the cords
of the zithers with their long pointed nails, and
their heads began to nod as though they were falling
asleep. Suddenly, with a cry so shrill that all the
children were startled and Don Pedro's hand
clutched at the agate pommel of his dagger, they
leapt to their feet and whirled madly round the en-
closure beating their tambourines, and chanting
some wild love-song in their strange guttural lan-
guage. Then at another signal they all flung themselves again to the ground and lay there quite still,
the dull strumming of the zithers being the only
sound that broke the silence. After they had done
this several times, they disappeared for a moment and came back leading a brown shaggy bear
by a chain, and carrying on their shoulders some little Barbary apes. The bear stood upon his head with
the utmost gravity, and the wizened apes played all
kinds of amusing tricks with two gipsy boys who
seemed to be their masters, and fought with tiny

swords, and fired off guns, and went through a regular soldier's drill just like the King's own bodyguard. In fact the gipsies were a great success.

But the funniest part of the whole morning's entertainment was undoubtedly the dancing of the little Dwarf. When he stumbled into the arena, waddling on his crooked legs and wagging his huge, misshapen head from side to side, the children went off into a loud shout of delight, and the Infanta herself laughed so much that the Camerera was obliged to remind her that although there were many precedents in Spain for a King's daughter weeping before her equals, there were none for a Princess of the blood royal making so merry before those who were her inferiors in birth. The Dwarf, however, was really quite irresistible, and even at the Spanish Court, always noted for its cultivated passion for the horrible, so fantastic a little monster had never been seen. It was his first appearance, too. He had been discovered only the day before, running wild through the forest, by two of the nobles who happened to have been hunting in a remote part of the great cork-wood that surrounded the town, and had been carried off by them to the Palace as a surprise for the Infanta; his father, who was a poor charcoal-burner, being but too well pleased to get rid of so ugly and useless a child. Perhaps the most amusing thing about him was his complete unconsciousness of his own grotesque appearance. Indeed, he seemed quite happy and full of the highest spirits.

When the children laughed, he laughed as freely and as joyously as any of them, and at the close of each dance he made them each the funniest of bows, smiling and nodding at them just as if he was really one of themselves, and not a little misshapen thing that Nature, in some humorous mood, had fashioned for others to mock at. As for the Infanta, she absolutely fascinated him. He could not keep his eyes off her, and seemed to dance for her alone, and when at the close of the performance, remembering how she had seen the great ladies of the Court throw bouquets to Caffarelli the famous Italian treble, whom the Pope had sent from his own chapel to Madrid that he might cure the King's melancholy by the sweetness of his voice, she took out of her hair the beautiful white rose, and partly for a jest and partly to tease the Camerera, threw it to him across the arena with her sweetest smile; he took the whole matter quite seriously, and pressing the flower to his rough, coarse lips he put his hand upon his heart, and sank on one knee before her, grinning from ear to ear, and with his little bright eyes sparkling with pleasure.

This so upset the gravity of the Infanta that she kept on laughing long after the little Dwarf had run out of the arena, and expressed a desire to her uncle that the dance should be immediately repeated. The Camerera, however, on the plea that the sun was too hot, decided that it would be better that her Highness should return without delay to the Palace, where a wonderful feast had been already prepared for her, including a real birthday cake with her own initials worked all over it in painted sugar and a lovely silver flag waving from the top. The Infanta accordingly rose up with much dignity, and having given orders that the little Dwarf was to dance again for her after the hour of siesta, and conveyed her thanks to the young Count of Tierra-Nueva for his charming reception, she went back to her apartments, the children following in the same order in which they had entered.

Now when the little Dwarf heard that he was to dance a second time before the Infanta, and by her own express command, he was so proud that he ran out into the garden, kissing the white rose in an absurd ecstasy of pleasure, and making the most uncouth and clumsy gestures of delight.

The Flowers were quite indignant at his daring to intrude into their beautiful home, and when they saw him capering up and down the walks, and waving his arms above his head in such a ridiculous manner, they could not restrain their feelings any longer.

"He is really far too ugly to be allowed to play in any place where we are," cried the Tulips.

"He should drink poppy-juice, and go to sleep for a thousand years," said the great scarlet Lilies, and they grew quite hot and angry.

"He is a perfect horror!" screamed the Cactus. "Why, he is twisted and stumpy, and his head is

completely out of proportion with his legs. Really
he makes me feel prickly all over, and if he comes
near me I will sting him with my thorns."

"And he has actually got one of my best blooms!"
exclaimed the White Rose-Tree. "I gave it to the
Infanta this morning myself, as a birthday present,
and he has stolen it from her." And she called out:
"Thief, thief, thief!" at the top of her voice.

Even the red Geraniums, who did not usually give
themselves airs, and were known to have a great
many poor relations themselves, curled up in disgust
when they saw him, and when the Violets meekly remarked that though he was certainly extremely
plain, still he could not help it, they retorted with a
good deal of justice that that was his chief defect,
and that there was no reason why one should admire
a person because he was incurable; and, indeed, some
of the Violets themselves felt that the ugliness of
the little Dwarf was almost ostentatious, and that
he would have shown much better taste if he had
looked sad, or at least pensive, instead of jumping
about merrily, and throwing himself into such
grotesque and silly attitudes.

As for the old Sundial, who was an extremely
remarkable individual, and had once told the time
of day to no less a person than the Emperor Charles
V. himself, he was so taken aback by the little
Dwarf's appearance, that he almost forgot to mark
two whole minutes with his long shadowy finger,
and could not help saying to the great milk-white

Peacock, who was sunning herself on the balustrade, that everyone knew that the children of Kings were Kings, and that the children of charcoal-burners were charcoal-burners, and that it was absurd to pretend that it wasn't so; a statement with which the Peacock entirely agreed, and indeed screamed out, "Certainly, certainly," in such a loud, harsh voice, that the gold-fish who lived in the basin of the cool splashing fountain put their heads out of the water and asked the huge stone Tritons what on earth was the matter.

But somehow the Birds liked him. They had seen him often in the forest, dancing about like an elf after the eddying leaves, or crouched up in the hollow of some old oak-tree, sharing his nuts with the squirrels. They did not mind his being ugly, a bit. Why, even the nightingale herself, who sang so sweetly in the orange groves at night that sometimes the Moon leaned down to listen, was not much to look at after all; and, besides, he had been kind to them, and during that terribly bitter winter, when there were no berries on the trees, and the ground was as hard as iron, and the wolves had come down to the very gates of the city to look for food, he had never forgotten them, but had always given them crumbs out of his little hunch of black bread, and divided with them whatever poor breakfast he had.

So they flew round and round him, just touching his cheek with their wings as they passed, and chat-

tered to each other, and the little Dwarf was so
pleased that he could not help showing them the
beautiful white rose, and telling them that the Infanta herself had given it to him because she loved
him.

They did not understand a single word of what
he was saying, but that made no matter, for they
put their heads on one side, and looked wise, which
is quite as good as understanding a thing, and very
much easier.

The Lizards also took an immense fancy to him,
and when he grew tired of running about and flung
himself down on the grass to rest, they played and
romped all over him, and tried to amuse him in the
best way they could. "Every one cannot be as
beautiful as a lizard," they cried; "that would be too
much to expect. And, though it sounds absurd to
say so, he is really not so ugly after all, provided,
of course, that one shuts one's eyes, and does not
look at him." The Lizards were extremely philo-
sophical by nature, and often sat thinking for hours
and hours together, when there was nothing else to
do, or when the weather was too rainy for them to
go out.

The flowers, however, were excessively annoyed
at their behaviour, and at the behaviour of the birds.
"It only shows," they said, "what a vulgarising effect this incessant rushing and flying about has.
Well-bred people always stay exactly in the same
place, as we do. No one ever saw us hopping up

and down the walks, or galloping madly through the grass after dragonflies. When we do want change of air, we send for the gardener, and he carries us to another bed. This is dignified, and as it should be. But birds and lizards have no sense of repose, and, indeed, birds have not even a permanent address. They are mere vagrants like the gipsies, and should be treated in exactly the same manner." So they put their noses in the air, and looked very haughty, and were quite delighted when after some time they saw the little Dwarf scramble up from the grass, and make his way across the terrace to the palace.

"He should certainly be kept indoors for the rest of his natural life," they said. "Look at his hunched back, and his crooked legs," and they began to titter.

But the little Dwarf knew nothing of all this. He liked the birds and the lizards immensely, and thought that the flowers were the most marvellous things in the whole world, except, of course, the Infanta, but then she had given him the beautiful white rose, and she loved him, and that made a great difference. How he wished that he had gone back with her! She would have put him on her right hand, and smiled at him, and he would have never left her side, but would have made her his playmate, and taught her all kinds of delightful tricks. For though he had never been in a palace before, he knew a great many wonderful things. He could make little cages out of rushes for the grasshoppers

to sing in, and fashion the long-jointed bamboo into
the pipe that Pan loves to hĕar. He knew the cry
of every bird, and could call the starlings from the
tree-top, or the heron from the mere. He knew the
trail of every animal, and could track the hare by
its delicate footprints, and the boar by the trampled
leaves. All the wind-dances he knew, the mad dance
in red raiment with the autumn, the light dance in
blue sandals over the corn, the dance with white
snow-wreaths in winter, and the blossom-dance
through the orchards in spring. He knew where the
wood-pigeons built their nests, and once when a
fowler had snared the parent birds, he had brought
up the young ones himself, and had built a little
dovecot for them in the cleft of a pollard elm. They
were quite tame, and used to feed out of his hands
every morning. She would like them, and the rabbits that scurried about in the long fern, and the
jays with their steely feathers and black bills, and
the hedgehogs that could curl themselves up into
prickly balls, and the great wise tortoises that
crawled slowly about, shaking their heads and nib-
bling at the young leaves. Yes, she must certainly
come to the forest and play with him. He would
give her his own little bed, and would watch outside
the window till dawn, to see that the wild horned
cattle did not harm her, nor the gaunt wolves creep
too near the hut. And at dawn he would tap at the
shutters and wake her, and they would go out and
dance together all the day long. It was really not

a bit lonely in the forest.   Sometimes a Bishop rode
through on his white mule, reading out of a painted
book.   Sometimes in their green velvet caps, and
their jerkins of tanned deerskin, the falconers passed
by, with hooded hawks on their wrists.   At vintage
time came the grape-treaders, with purple hands and
feet, wreathed with glossy ivy and carrying dripping skins of wine; and the charcoal-burners sat
round their huge braziers at night, watching the dry
logs charring slowly in the fire, and roasting chest-
nuts in the ashes, and the robbers came out of their
caves and made merry with them.   Once, too, he
had seen a beautiful procession winding up the long
dusty road to Toledo.   The monks went in front
singing sweetly, and carrying bright banners and
crosses of gold, and then, in silver armour, with
match-locks and pikes came the soldiers, and in their
midst walked three barefooted men, in strange yellow dresses painted all over with wonderful figures,
and carrying lighted candles in their hands.   Certainly there was a great deal to look at in the forest,
and when she was tired he would find a soft bank
of moss for her, or carry her in his arms, for he
was very strong, though he knew that he was not
tall.   He would make her a necklace of red bryony
berries, that would be quite as pretty as the white
berries that she wore on her dress, and when she
was tired of them, she could throw them away, and
he would find her others.   He would bring her
acorn-cups and dew-drenched anemones, and tiny

glow-worms to be stars in the pale gold of her hair. But where was she? He asked the white rose, and it made him no answer. The whole palace seemed asleep, and even where the shutters had not been closed, heavy curtains had been drawn across the windows to keep out the glare. He wandered all round looking for some place through which he might gain an entrance, and at last he caught sight of a little private door that was lying open. He slipped through, and found himself in a splendid hall, far more splendid, he feared, than the forest, there was so much gilding everywhere, and even the floor was made of great coloured stones, fitted together into a sort of geometrical pattern. But the little Infanta was not there, only some wonderful white statues that looked down on him from their jasper pedestals, with sad blank eyes and strangely smiling lips.

At the end of the hall hung a richly embroidered curtain of black velvet, powdered with suns and stars, the King's favourite devices, and broidered on the colour he loved best. Perhaps she was hiding behind that? He would try at any rate.

So he stole quietly across, and drew it aside. No; there was only another room, though a prettier room, he thought, than the one he had just left. The walls were hung with a many-figured green arras of needle-wrought tapestry representing a hunt, the work of some Flemish artists who had spent more than seven years in its composition. It had once been the chamber of *Jean le Fou*, as he was called, that mad King who was so enamoured of the chase, that he had often tried in his delirium to mount the huge rearing horses, and to drag down the stag on which the great hounds were leaping, sounding his hunting horn, and stabbing with his dagger at the pale flying deer. It was now used as the council-room, and on the centre table were lying the red portfolios of the ministers, stamped with the gold tulips of Spain, and with the arms and emblems of the house of Hapsburg.

The little Dwarf looked in wonder all round him, and was half-afraid to go on. The strange silent horsemen that galloped so swiftly through the long glades without making any noise, seemed to him like those terrible phantoms of whom he had heard the charcoal burners speaking—the Comprachos, who hunt only at night, and if they meet a man, turn him into a hind, and chase him. But he thought of the pretty Infanta, and took courage. He wanted to find her alone, and to tell her that he, too, loved her. Perhaps she was in the room beyond.

He ran across the soft Moorish carpets, and opened the door. No! She was not here either. The room was quite empty.

It was a throne-room, used for the reception of foreign ambassadors, when the King, which of late had not been often, consented to give them a personal audience; the same room in which, many years before, envoys had appeared from England to make arrangements for the marriage of their Queen, then one of the Catholic sovereigns of Europe, with the Emperor's eldest son. The hangings were of gilt Cordovan leather, and a heavy gilt chandelier with branches for three hundred wax lights hung down from the black and white ceiling. Underneath a great canopy of gold cloth, on which the lions and towers of Castile were broidered in seed pearls, stood the throne itself, covered with a rich pall of black velvet studded with silver tulips and elaborately fringed with silver and pearls. On the second step of the throne was placed the kneeling-stool of the Infanta, with its cushion of cloth of silver tissue, and below that again, and beyond the limit of the canopy, stood the chair for the Papal Nuncio, who alone had the right to be seated in the King's presence on the occasion of any public ceremonial, and whose Cardinal's hat, with its tangled scarlet tassels, lay on a purple *tabouret* in front. On the wall, facing the throne, hung a life-sized portrait of Charles V. in hunting dress, with a great mastiff by his side, and a picture of Philip II. receiving the homage of the Netherlands occupied the centre of the other wall. Between the windows stood a black ebony cabinet, inlaid with plates of ivory, on which the figures from Holbein's Dance of Death had been graved—by the hand, some said, of that famous master himself.

But the little Dwarf cared nothing for all this magnificence. He would not have given his rose

for all the pearls on the canopy, nor one white petal
of his rose for the throne itself. What he wanted
was to see the Infanta before she went down to the
pavilion, and to ask her to come away with him when
he had finished his dance. Here, in the Palace, the
air was close and heavy, but in the forest the wind
blew free, and the sunlight with wandering hands of
gold moved the tremulous leaves aside. There were
flowers, too, in the forest, not so splendid, perhaps,
as the flowers in the garden, but more sweetly
scented for all that; hyacinths in early spring that
flooded with waving purple the cool glens, and
grassy knolls; yellow primroses that nestled in little
clumps round the gnarled roots of the oak-trees;
bright celandine, and blue speedwell, and irises lilac
and gold. There were grey catkins on the hazels,
and the fox-gloves drooped with the weight of their
dappled bee-haunted cells. The chestnut had its
spires of white stars, and the hawthorn its pallid
moons of beauty. Yes: surely she would come if
he could only find her! She would come with him
to the fair forest, and all day long he would dance
for her delight. A smile lit up his eyes at the
thought, and he passed into the next room.

Of all the rooms this was the brightest and the
most beautiful. The walls were covered with a
pink-flowered Lucca damask, patterned with birds
and dotted with dainty blossoms of silver; the fur-
niture was of massive silver, festooned with florid
wreaths, and swinging Cupids; in front of the two

large fire-places stood great screens broidered with
parrots and peacocks, and the floor, which was of
sea-green onyx, seemed to stretch far away into the
distance. Nor was he alone. Standing under the
shadow of the doorway, at the extreme end of the
room, he saw a little figure watching him. His heart
trembled, a cry of joy broke from his lips, and he
moved out into the sunlight. As he did so, the
figure moved out also, and he saw it plainly.

The Infanta! It was a monster, the most grotesque monster he had ever beheld. Not properly
shaped, as all other people were, but hunchbacked,
and crooked-limbed, with huge lolling head and
mane of black hair. The little Dwarf frowned, and
the monster frowned also. He laughed, and it
laughed with him, and held its hands to its sides, just
as he himself was doing. He made it a mocking
bow, and it returned him a low reverence. He went
towards it, and it came to meet him, copying each
step that he made, and stopping when he stopped
himself. He shouted with amusement, and ran forward, and reached out his hand, and the hand of
the monster touched his, and it was as cold as ice.
He grew afraid, and moved his hand across, and
the monster's hand followed it quickly. He tried
to press on, but something smooth and hard stopped
him. The face of the monster was now close to his
own, and seemed full of terror. He brushed his hair
off his eyes. It imitated him. He struck at it, and
it returned blow for blow. He loathed it, and it

made hideous faces at him. He drew back, and it retreated.

What is it? He thought for a moment, and looked round at the rest of the room. It was strange, but everything seemed to have its double in this invisible wall of clear water. Yes, picture for picture was repeated, and couch for couch. The sleeping Faun that lay in the alcove by the doorway had its twin brother that slumbered, and the silver Venus that stood in the sunlight held out her arms to a Venus as lovely as herself.

Was it Echo? He had called to her once in the valley, and she had answered him word for word. Could she mock the eye, as she mocked the voice? Could she make a mimic world just like the real world? Could the shadows of things have colour and life and movement? Could it be that—?

He started, and taking from his breast the beautiful white rose, he turned round, and kissed it. The monster had a rose of its own, petal for petal the same! It kissed it with like kisses, and pressed it to its heart with horrible gestures.

When the truth dawned upon him, he gave a wild cry of despair, and fell sobbing to the ground. So it was he who was misshapen and hunchbacked, foul to look at and grotesque. He himself was the monster, and it was at him that all the children had been laughing, and the little Princess who he thought loved him—she, too, had been merely mocking at his ugliness, and making merry over his twisted limbs.

Why had they not left him in the forest, where there was no mirror to tell him how loathsome he was? Why had his father not killed him, rather than sell him to his shame? The hot tears poured down his cheeks, and he tore the white rose to pieces. The sprawling monster did the same, and scattered the faint petals in the air. It grovelled on the ground, and, when he looked at it, it watched him with a face drawn with pain. He crept away, lest he should see it, and covered his eyes with his hands. He crawled, like some wounded thing, into the shadow, and lay there moaning.

And at that moment the Infanta herself came in with her companions through the open window and, when they saw the ugly little dwarf lying on the ground and beating the floor with his clenched hands, in the most fantastic and exaggerated manner, they went off into shouts of happy laughter, and stood all round him and watched him.

"His dancing was funny," said the Infanta; "but his acting is funnier still. Indeed he is almost as good as the puppets, only, of course, not quite so natural." And she fluttered her big fan, and applauded.

But the little Dwarf never looked up, and his sobs grew fainter and fainter, and suddenly he gave a curious gasp, and clutched his side. And then he fell back again, and lay quite still.

"That is capital," said the Infanta, after a pause; "but now you must dance for me."

"Yes," cried all the children, "you must get up and dance, for you are as clever as the Barbary apes, and much more ridiculous."

But the little Dwarf made no answer.

And the Infanta stamped her foot, and called out to her uncle, who was walking on the terrace with the Chamberlain, reading some despatches that had just arrived from Mexico where the Holy Office had recently been established. "My funny little dwarf is sulking," she cried, "you must wake him up, and tell him to dance for me."

They smiled at each other, and sauntered in, and Don Pedro stooped down, and slapped the Dwarf on the cheek with his embroidered glove. "You must dance," he said, "*petit monstre*. You must dance. The Infanta of Spain and the Indies wishes to be amused."

But the little Dwarf never moved.

"A whipping master should be sent for," said Don Pedro wearily, and he went back to the terrace. But the Chamberlain looked grave, and he knelt beside the little dwarf, and put his hand upon his heart. And after a few moments he shrugged his shoulders, and rose up, and having made a low bow to the Infanta, he said:

"*Mi bella Princesa*, your funny little dwarf will never dance again. It is a pity, for he is so ugly that he might have made the King smile."

"But why will he not dance again?" asked the Infanta, laughing.

"Because his heart is broken," answered the Chamberlain.

And the Infanta frowned, and her dainty rose-leaf lips curled in pretty disdain. "For the future let those who come to play with me have no hearts," she cried, and she ran out into the garden.

THE FISHERMAN AND HIS SOUL

EVERY evening the young Fisherman went out upon the sea, and threw his nets into the water.

When the wind blew from the land he caught nothing, or but little at best, for it was a bitter and black-winged wind, and rough waves rose up to meet it. But when the wind blew to the shore, the fish came in from the deep, and swam into the meshes of his nets, and he took them to the market-place and sold them.

Every evening he went out upon the sea, and one evening the net was so heavy that hardly could he draw it into the boat. And he laughed, and said to himself, "Surely I have caught all the fish that swim, or snared some dull monster that will be a marvel to men, or some thing of horror that the great Queen will desire," and putting forth all his strength, he tugged at the coarse ropes till, like lines of blue enamel round a vase of bronze, the long veins rose up on his arms. He tugged at the thin ropes, and nearer and nearer came the circle of flat corks, and the net rose at last to the top of the water.

But no fish at all was in it, nor any monster or
thing of horror, but only a little Mermaid lying fast
asleep.

Her hair was as a wet fleece of gold, and each
separate hair as a thread of fine gold in a cup of
glass. Her body was as white ivory, and her tail
was of silver and pearl. Silver and pearl was her
tail, and the green weeds of the sea coiled round it;
and like sea-shells were her ears, and her lips were
like sea-coral. The cold waves dashed over her
cold breasts, and the salt glistened upon her eyelids.

So beautiful was she that when the young Fisherman saw her he was filled with wonder, and he put
out his hand and drew the net close to him, and
leaning over the side he clasped her in his arms.
And when he touched her, she gave a cry like a
startled sea-gull and woke, and looked at him in terror with her mauve-amethyst eyes, and struggled
that she might escape. But he held her tightly to
him, and would not suffer her to depart.

And when she saw that she could in no way escape
from him, she began to weep, and said, "I pray thee
let me go, for I am the only daughter of a King,
and my father is aged and alone."

But the young Fisherman answered, "I will not
let thee go save thou makest me a promise that
whenever I call thee, thou wilt come and sing to me,
for the fish delight to listen to the song of the Sea-
folk, and so shall my nets be full."

"Wilt thou in very truth let me go, if I promise thee this?" cried the Mermaid.

"In very truth I will let thee go," said the young Fisherman.

So she made him the promise he desired, and sware it by the oath of the Sea-folk. And he loosened his arms from about her, and she sank down into the water, trembling with a strange fear.

Every evening the young Fisherman went out upon the sea, and called to the Mermaid, and she rose out of the water and sang to him. Round and round her swam the dolphins, and the wild gulls wheeled above her head.

And she sang a marvellous song. For she sang of the Sea-folk who drive their flocks from cave to cave, and carry the little calves on their shoulders; of the Tritons who have long green beards, and hairy breasts, and blow through twisted conchs when the King passes by; of the palace of the King which is all of amber, with a roof of clear emerald, and a pavement of bright pearl; and of the gardens of the sea where the great filigrane fans of coral wave all day long, and the fish dart about like silver birds, and the anemones cling to the rocks, and the pinks bourgeon in the ribbed yellow sand. She sang of the big whales that come down from the north seas and have sharp icicles hanging to their fins; of the Sirens who tell of such wonderful things that the merchants have to stop their ears with wax lest they

should hear them, and leap into the water and be
drowned; of the sunken galleys with their tall masts,
and the frozen sailors clinging to the rigging, and
the mackerel swimming in and out of the open port-
holes; of the little barnacles who are great travellers,
and cling to the keels of the ships and go round and
round the world; and of the cuttle-fish who live in
the sides of the cliffs and stretch out their long black
arms, and can make night come when they will it.
She sang of the nautilus who has a boat of her own
that is carved out of an opal and steered with a
silken sail; of the happy Mermen who play upon
harps and can charm the great Kraken to sleep; of
the little children who catch hold of the slippery
porpoises and ride laughing upon their backs; of the
Mermaids who lie in the white foam and hold out
their arms to the mariners; and of the sea-lions with
their curved tusks, and the sea-horses with their
floating manes.

And as she sang, all the tunny-fish came in from
the deep to listen to her, and the young Fisherman
threw his nets round them and caught them, and
others he took with a spear. And when his boat
was well-laden, the Mermaid would sink down into
the sea, smiling at him.

Yet would she never come near him that he might
touch her. Oftentimes he called to her and prayed
of her, but she would not; and when he sought to
seize her she dived into the water as a seal might
dive, nor did he see her again that day. And each

day the sound of her voice became sweeter to his ears. So sweet was her voice that he forgot his nets and his cunning, and had no care of his craft. Vermilion-finned and with eyes of bossy gold, the tunnies went by in shoals, but he heeded them not. His spear lay by his side unused, and his baskets of plaited osier were empty. With lips parted, and eyes dim with wonder, he sat idle in his boat and listened, listening till the sea-mists crept round him, and the wandering moon stained his brown limbs with silver.

And one evening he called to her, and said: "Little Mermaid, little Mermaid, I love thee. Take me for thy bridegroom, for I love thee."

But the Mermaid shook her head. "Thou hast a human soul," she answered. "If only thou would'st send away thy soul, then could I love thee."

And the young Fisherman said to himself, "Of what use is my soul to me? I cannot see it. I may not touch it. I do not know it. Surely I will send it away from me, and much gladness shall be mine." And a cry of joy broke from his lips, and standing up in the painted boat, he held out his arms to the Mermaid. "I will send my soul away," he cried, "and you shall be my bride, and I will be thy bridegroom, and in the depth of the sea we will dwell together, and all that thou hast sung of thou shalt show me, and all that thou desirest I will do, nor shall our lives be divided."

And the little Mermaid laughed for pleasure, and hid her face in her hands.

"But how shall I send my soul from me?" cried the young Fisherman. "Tell me how I may do it, and lo! it shall be done."

"Alas! I know not," said the little Mermaid: "the Sea-folk have no souls." And she sank down into the deep, looking wistfully at him.

Now early on the next morning, before the sun was the span of a man's hand above the hill, the young Fisherman went to the house of the Priest and knocked three times at the door.

The novice looked out through the wicket, and when he saw who it was, he drew back the latch and said to him, "Enter."

And the young Fisherman passed in, and knelt down on the sweet-smelling rushes of the floor, and cried to the Priest who was reading out of the Holy Book and said to him, "Father, I am in love with one of the Sea-folk, and my soul hindereth me from having my desire. Tell me how I can send my soul away from me, for in truth I have no need of it. Of what value is my soul to me? I cannot see it. I may not touch it. I do not know it."

And the Priest beat his breast, and answered, "Alack, Alack, thou art mad, or hast eaten of some poisonous herb, for the soul is the noblest part of man, and was given to us by God that we should nobly use it. There is no thing more precious than a human soul, nor any earthly thing that can be weighed with it. It is worth all the gold that is in the world, and is more precious than the rubies of the kings. Therefore, my son, think not any more of this matter, for it is a sin that may not be for- given. And as for the Sea-folk, they are lost, and they who would traffic with them are lost also. They are as the beasts of the field that know not good from evil, and for them the Lord has not died."

The young Fisherman's eyes filled with tears when he heard the bitter words of the Priest, and he rose up from his knees and said to him, "Father, the Fauns live in the forest and are glad, and on the rocks sit the Mermen with their harps of red gold. Let me be as they are, I beseech thee, for their days are as the days of flowers. And as for my soul, what doth my soul profit me, if it stand between me and the thing that I love?"

"The love of the body is vile," cried the Priest, knitting his brows, "and vile and evil are the pagan things God suffers to wander through His world. Accursed be the Fauns of the woodland, and ac- cursed be the singers of the sea! I have heard them at night-time, and they have sought to lure me from my beads. They tap at the window, and laugh. They whisper into my ears the tale of their perilous joys. They tempt me with temptations, and when I would pray they make mouths at me. They are lost, I tell thee, they are lost. For them there is no

heaven nor hell, and in neither shall they praise
God's name."

"Father," cried the young Fisherman, "thou
knowest not what thou sayest. Once in my net I
snared the daughter of a King. She is fairer than
the morning star, and whiter than the moon. For
her body I would give my soul, and for her love I
would surrender heaven. Tell me what I ask of
thee, and let me go in peace."

"Away! Away!" cried the Priest: "thy leman
is lost, and thou shalt be lost with her." And he
gave him no blessing, but drove him from his door.

And the young Fisherman went down into the
market-place, and he walked slowly, and with bowed
head, as one who is in sorrow.

And when the merchants saw him coming, they
began to whisper to each other, and one of them
came forth to meet him, and called him by name,
and said to him, "What hast thou to sell?"

"I will sell thee my soul," he answered: "I pray
thee buy it off me, for I am weary of it. Of what
use is my soul to me? I cannot see it. I may not
touch it. I do not know it."

But the merchants mocked at him, and said, "Of
what use is a man's soul to us? It is not worth a
clipped piece of silver. Sell us thy body for a slave,
and we will clothe thee in sea-purple, and put a ring
upon thy finger, and make thee the minion of the
great Queen. But talk not of the soul, for to us it
is nought, nor has it any value for our service."

And the young Fisherman said to himself:

"How strange a thing this is! The priest telleth me that the soul is worth all the gold in the world, and the merchants say that it is not worth a clipped piece of silver." And he passed out of the market-place, and went down to the shore of the sea, and began to ponder on what he should do.

And at noon he remembered how one of his companions, who was a gatherer of samphire, had told him of a certain young Witch who dwelt in a cave at the head of the bay and was very cunning in her witcheries. And he set to and ran, so eager was he to get rid of his soul, and a cloud of dust followed him as he sped round the sand of the shore. By the itching of her palm the young Witch knew his coming, and she laughed and let down her red hair. With her red hair falling around her, she stood at the opening of the cave, and in her hand she had a spray of wild hemlock that was blossoming.

"What d'ye lack? What d'ye lack?" she cried, as he came panting up the steep, and bent down before her. "Fish for thy net, when the wind is foul? I have a little reed-pipe, and when I blow on it the mullet come sailing into the bay. But it has a price, pretty boy, it has a price. What d'ye lack? What d'ye lack? A storm to wreck the ships, and wash the chests of rich treasure ashore? I have more storms than the wind has, for I serve one who is stronger than the wind, and with a sieve and a pail of water I can send the great galleys to the bottom of the sea. But I have a price, pretty boy, I have a price. What d'ye lack? What d'ye lack? I know a flower that grows in the valley, none know it but I. It has purple leaves, and a star in its heart, and its juice is as white as milk. Should'st thou touch with this flower the hard lips of the Queen, she would follow thee all over the world. Out of the bed of the King she would rise, and over the whole world she would follow thee. And it has a price, pretty boy, it has a price. What d'ye lack? What d'ye lack? I can pound a toad in a mortar, and make broth of it, and stir the broth with a dead man's hand. Sprinkle it on thine enemy while he sleeps, and he will turn into a black viper, and his own mother will slay him. With a wheel I can draw the Moon from heaven, and in a crystal I can show thee Death. What d'ye lack? What d'ye lack? Tell me thy desire, and I will give it thee, and thou shalt pay me a price, pretty boy, thou shalt pay me a price."

"My desire is but for a little thing," said the young Fisherman, "yet hath the priest been wroth with me, and driven me forth. It is but for a little thing, and the merchants have mocked at me, and denied me. Therefore am I come to thee, though men call thee evil, and whatever be thy price I shall pay it."

"What would'st thou?" asked the Witch, coming near to him.

"I would send my soul away from me," answered the young Fisherman.

The Witch grew pale, and shuddered, and hid her face in her blue mantle. "Pretty boy, pretty boy," she muttered, "that is a terrible thing to do."

He tossed his brown curls and laughed. "My soul is nought to me," he answered. "I cannot see it. I may not touch it. I do not know it."

"What wilt thou give me if I tell thee?" asked the Witch, looking down at him with her beautiful eyes.

"Five pieces of gold," he said, "and my nets, and the wattled house where I live, and the painted boat in which I sail. Only tell me how to get rid of my soul, and I will give thee all that I possess."

She laughed mockingly at him, and struck him with the spray of hemlock. "I can turn the autumn leaves into gold," she answered, "and I can weave the pale moonbeams into silver if I will it. He whom I serve is richer than all the kings of this world and has their dominions."

"What then shall I give thee," he cried, "if thy price be neither gold nor silver?"

The Witch stroked his hair with her thin white hand. "Thou must dance with me, pretty boy," she murmured, and she smiled at him as she spoke.

"Nought but that?" cried the young Fisherman in wonder, and he rose to his feet.

"Nought but that," she answered, and she smiled at him again.

"Then at sunset in some secret place we shall dance together," he said, "and after that we have danced thou shalt tell me the thing which I desire to know."

She shook her head. "When the moon is full, when the moon is full," she muttered. Then she peered all round, and listened. A blue bird rose screaming from its nest and circled over the dunes, and three spotted birds rustled through the coarse grey grass and whistled to each other. There was no other sound save the sound of a wave fretting the smooth pebbles below. So she reached out her hand, and drew him near to her and put her dry lips close to his ear.

"To-night thou must come to the top of the mountain," she whispered. "It is a Sabbath and He will be there."

The young Fisherman started and looked at her, and she showed her white teeth and laughed. "Who is He of whom thou speakest?" he asked.

"It matters not," she answered. "Go thou to-night and stand under the branches of the hornbeam, and wait for my coming. If a black dog run towards thee, strike it with a rod of willow, and it will go away. If an owl speak to thee, make it no answer. When the moon is full I shall be with thee, and we will dance together on the grass."

"But wilt thou swear to me to tell me how I may send my soul from me?" he made question.

She moved out into the sunlight, and through

her red hair rippled the wind. "By the hoofs of the goat I swear it," she made answer.

"Thou art the best of the witches," cried the young Fisherman, "and I will surely dance with thee to-night on the top of the mountain. I would indeed that thou hadst asked of me either gold or silver. But such as thy price is thou shalt have it, for it is but a little thing." And he doffed his cap to her, and bent his head low, and ran back to the town filled with a great joy.

And the Witch watched him as he went, and when he had passed from her sight she entered her cave, and having taken a mirror from a box of carved cedarwood, she set it up on a frame, and burned vervain on lighted charcoal before it, and peered through the coils of the smoke. And after a time she clenched her hands in anger. "He should have been mine," she muttered, "I am as fair as she is."

And that evening. when the moon had risen, the young Fisherman climbed up to the top of the mountain, and stood under the branches of the hornbeam. Like a targe of polished metal the round sea lay at his feet, and the shadows of the fishing boats moved in the little bay. A great owl, with yellow sulphurous eyes, called to him by his name, but he made it no answer. A black dog ran towards him and snarled. He struck it with a rod of willow, and it went away whining.

At midnight the witches came flying through the

air like bats. "Phew!" they cried, as they lit upon the ground, "there is someone here we know not!" and they sniffed about, and chattered to each other, and made signs. Last of all came the young Witch, with her red hair streaming in the wind. She wore a dress of gold tissue embroidered with peacocks' eyes, and a little cap of green velvet was on her head.

"Where is he, where is he?" shrieked the witches when they saw her, but she only laughed and ran to the hornbeam, and taking the Fisherman by the hand she led him out into the moonlight and began to dance.

Round and round they whirled, and the young Witch jumped so high that he could see the scarlet heels of her shoes. Then right across the dancers came the sound of the galloping of a horse, but no horse was to be seen, and he felt afraid.

"Faster," cried the Witch, and she threw her arms about his neck, and her breath was hot upon his face. "Faster, faster!" she cried, and the earth seemed to spin beneath his feet, and his brain grew troubled, and a great terror fell on him, as of some evil thing that was watching him, and at last he became aware that under the shadow of a rock there was a figure that had not been there before.

It was a man dressed in a suit of black velvet, cut in Spanish fashion. His face was strangely pale, but his lips were like a proud red flower. He seemed weary, and was leaning back toying in a listless manner with the pommel of his dagger. On the grass beside him lay a plumed hat, and a pair of riding gloves gauntleted with gilt lace, and sewn with seed-pearls wrought into a curious device. A short cloak lined with sables hung from his shoulder, and his delicate white hands were gemmed with rings. Heavy eyelids drooped over his eyes.

The young Fisherman watched him, as one snared in a spell. At last their eyes met, and wherever he danced it seemed to him that the eyes of the man were upon him. He heard the Witch laugh, and caught her by the waist, and whirled her madly round and round.

Suddenly a dog bayed in the wood, and the dancers stopped, and going up two by two, knelt down, and kissed the man's hands. As they did so, a little smile touched his proud lips, as a bird's wing touches the water and makes it laugh. But there was disdain in it. He kept looking at the young Fisherman.

"Come! let us worship," whispered the Witch, and she led him up, and a great desire to do as she besought him seized on him, and he followed her. But when he came close, and without knowing why he did it, he made on his breast the sign of the Cross, and called upon the holy name.

No sooner had he done so than the witches screamed like hawks and flew away, and the pallid face that had been watching him twitched with a spasm of pain. The man went over to a little wood, and whistled. A jennet with silver trappings came running to meet him. As he leapt upon the saddle he turned round, and looked at the young Fisherman sadly.

And the Witch with the red hair tried to fly away also, but the Fisherman caught her by her wrists, and held her fast.

"Loose me," she cried, "and let me go. For thou hast named what should not be named, and shown the sign that may not be looked at."

"Nay," he answered, "but I will not let thee go till thou hast told me the secret."

"What secret?" said the Witch, wrestling with him like a wildcat, and biting her foam-flecked lips.

"Thou knowest," he made answer.

Her grass-green eyes grew dim with tears, and she said to the Fisherman, "Ask me anything but that!"

He laughed, and held her all the more tightly.

And when she saw that she could not free herself, she whispered to him, "Surely I am as fair as the daughters of the sea, and as comely as those that dwell in the blue waters," and she fawned on him and put her face close to his.

But he thrust her back frowning, and said to her, "If thou keepest not the promise that thou madest to me I will slay thee for a false witch."

She grew grey as a blossom of the Judas tree, and shuddered. "Be it so," she muttered. "It is thy soul and not mine. Do with it as thou wilt."

And she took from her girdle a little knife that had a handle of green viper's skin, and gave it to him.

"What shall this serve me?" he asked of her, wondering.

She was silent for a few moments, and a look of terror came over her face. Then she brushed her hair back from her forehead, and smiling strangely she said to him, "What men call the shadow of the body is not the shadow of the body, but is the body of the soul. Stand on the sea-shore with thy back to the moon, and cut away from around thy feet thy shadow, which is thy soul's body, and bid thy soul leave thee, and it will do so."

The young Fisherman trembled. "Is this true?" he murmured.

"It is true, and I would that I had not told thee of it," she cried, and she clung to his knees weeping.

He put her from him and left her in the rank grass, and going to the edge of the mountains he placed the knife in his belt, and began to climb down.

And his Soul that was within him called out to him and said, "Lo! I have dwelt with thee for all these years, and have been thy servant. Send me not away from thee now, for what evil have I done thee?"

And the young Fisherman laughed. "Thou hast done me no evil, but I have no need of thee," he answered. "The world is wide and there is Heaven also, and Hell, and that dim twilight house that

lies between. Go wherever thou wilt, but trouble
me not, for my love is calling to me."

And his Soul besought him piteously, but he
heeded it not, but leapt from crag to 'crag, being
sure-footed as a wild goat, and at last he reached
the level ground and the level shore of the sea.

Bronze-limbed and well-knit, like a statue wrought
by a Grecian, he stood on the sand with his back to
the moon, and out of the foam came white arms
that beckoned to him, and out of the waves rose dim
forms that did him homage. Before him lay his
shadow, which was the body of his soul, and behind him hung the moon in the honey-coloured air.

And his Soul said to him, "If indeed thou must
drive me from thee, send me not forth without a
heart. The world is cruel, give me thy heart to take
with me."

He tossed his head and smiled. "With what
should I love my love if I gave thee my heart?" he
cried.

"Nay, but be merciful," said his Soul: "give me
thy heart, for the world is very cruel, and I am
afraid."

"My heart is my love's," he answered, "therefore
tarry not, but get thee gone."

"Should I not love also?" asked his Soul.

"Get thee gone, for I have no need of thee," cried
the young Fisherman, and he took the little knife
with its handle of green viper's skin, and cut away
his shadow from around his feet, and it rose up

and stood before him, and looked at him, and it was even as himself.

He crept back, and thrust the knife into his belt, and a feeling of awe came over him. "Get thee gone," he murmured, "and let me see thy face no more."

"Nay, but we must meet again," said the Soul. Its voice was low and flute-like, and its lips hardly moved while it spake.

"How shall we meet?" cried the young Fisherman. "Thou wilt not follow me into the depths of the sea?"

"Once every year I will come to this place, and call to thee," said the Soul. "It may be that thou wilt have need of me."

"What need should I have of thee?" cried the young Fisherman, "but be it as thou wilt," and he plunged into the water, and the Tritons blew their horns, and the little Mermaid rose up to meet him, and put her arms around his neck and kissed him on the mouth.

And the Soul stood on the lonely beach and watched them. And when they had sunk down into the sea, it went weeping away over the marshes.

And after a year was over the Soul came down to the shore of the sea and called to the young Fisherman, and he rose out of the deep, and said, "Why dost thou call to me?"

And the Soul answered, "Come nearer, that I

may speak with thee, for I have seen marvellous things."

So he came nearer, and couched in the shallow water, and leaned his head upon his hand and listened.

And the Soul said to him, "When I left thee I turned my face to the East and journeyed. From the East cometh everything that is wise. Six days I journeyed, and on the morning of the seventh day I came to a hill that is in the country of the Tartars. I sat down under the shade of a tamarisk tree to shelter myself from the sun. The land was dry, and burnt up with the heat. The people went to and fro over the plain like flies crawling upon a disk of polished copper.

"When it was noon a cloud of red dust rose up from the flat rim of the land. When the Tartars saw it, they strung their painted bows, and having leapt upon their little horses they galloped to meet it. The women fled screaming to the waggons, and hid themselves behind the felt curtains.

"At twilight the Tartars returned, but five of them were missing, and of those that came back not a few had been wounded. They harnessed their horses to the waggons and drove hastily away. Three jackals came out of a cave and peered after them. Then they sniffed up the air with their nostrils, and trotted off in the opposite direction.

"When the moon rose I saw a camp-fire burning on the plain, and went towards it. A company of merchants were seated round it on carpets. Their camels were picketed behind them, and the negroes who were their servants were pitching tents of tanned skin upon the sand, and making a high wall of the prickly pear.

"As I came near them, the chief of the merchants rose up and drew his sword, and asked me my business.

"I answered that I was a Prince in my own land, and that I had escaped from the Tartars, who had sought to make me their slave. The chief smiled, and showed me five heads fixed upon long reeds of bamboo.

"Then he asked me who was the prophet of God, and I answered him Mohammed.

"When he heard the name of the false prophet, he bowed and took me by the hand, and placed me by his side. A negro brought me some mare's milk in a wooden dish, and a piece of lamb's flesh roasted.

"At daybreak we started on our journey. I rode on a red-haired camel by the side of the chief, and a runner ran before us carrying a spear. The men of war were on either hand, and the mules followed with the merchandise. There were forty camels in the caravan, and the mules were twice forty in number.

"We went from the country of the Tartars into the country of those who curse the Moon. We saw the Gryphons guarding their gold on the white

rocks, and the scaled Dragons sleeping in their
caves. As we passed over the mountains we held
our breath lest the snows might fall on us, and
each man tied a veil of gauze before his eyes. As
we passed through the valleys the Pygmies shot
arrows at us from the hollows of the trees, and at
night time we heard the wild men beating on their
drums. When we came to the Tower of Apes we
set fruits before them, and they did not harm us.
When we came to the Tower of Serpents we gave
them warm milk in bowls of brass, and they let us
go by. Three times in our journey we came to the
banks of the Oxus. We crossed it on rafts of wood
with great bladders of blown hide. The river-
horses raged against us and sought to slay us.
When the camels saw them they trembled.

"The kings of each city levied tolls on us, but
would not suffer us to enter their gates. They
threw us bread over the walls, little maize-cakes
baked in honey and cakes of fine flour filled with
dates. For every hundred baskets we gave them a
bead of amber.

"When the dwellers in the villages saw us coming, they poisoned the wells and fled to the hill-
summits. We fought with the Magadae who are
born old, and grow younger and younger every
year, and die when they are little children; and
with the Laktroi who say that they are the sons of
tigers, and paint themselves yellow and black; and
with the Aurantes who bury their dead on the tops

of trees, and themselves live in dark caverns lest
the Sun, who is their god, should slay them; and
with the Krimnians who worship a crocodile, and
give it earrings of green glass, and feed it with
butter and fresh fowls; and with the Agazonbae,
who are dog-faced; and with the Sibans, who have
horses' feet, and run more swiftly than horses. A
third of our company died in battle, and a third
died of want. The rest murmured against me, and
said that I had brought them an evil fortune. I
took a horned adder from beneath a stone and let it
sting me. When they saw that I did not sicken they
grew afraid.

"In the fourth month we reached the city of Illel.
It was night time when we came to the grove that
is outside the walls, and the air was sultry, for
the Moon was travelling in Scorpion. We too : the
ripe pomegranates from the trees, and brake them
and drank their sweet juices. Then we lay down
on our carpets and waited for the dawn.

"And at dawn we rose and knocked at the gate
of the city. It was wrought out of red bronze, and
carved with sea-dragons and dragons that have
wings. The guards looked down from the battle-
ments and asked us our business. The interpreter
of the caravan answered that we had come from
the island of Syria with much merchandise. They
took hostages, and told us that they would
open the gate to us at noon, and bade us tarry till
then.

"When it was noon they opened the gate, and as we entered in the people came crowding out of the houses to look at us, and a crier went round the city crying through a shell. We stood in the market-place, and the negroes uncorded the bales of figured cloths and opened the carved chests of sycamore. And when they had ended their task, the merchants set forth their strange wares, the waxed linen from Egypt and the painted linen from the country of the Ethiops, the purple sponges from Tyre and the blue hangings from Sidon, the cups of cold amber and the fine vessels of glass and the curious vessels of burnt clay. From the roof of a house a company of women watched us. One of them wore a mask of gilded leather.

"And on the first day the priests came and bartered with us, and on the second day came the nobles, and on the third day came the craftsmen and the slaves. And this is their custom with all merchants as long as they tarry in the city.

"And we tarried for a moon, and when the moon was waning, I wearied and wandered away through the streets of the city and came to the garden of its god. The priests in their yellow robes moved silently through the green trees, and on a pavement of black marble stood the rose-red house in which the god had his dwelling. Its doors were of powdered lacquer, and bulls and peacocks were wrought on them in raised and polished gold. The tiled roof was of sea-green porcelain, and the jutting eaves were festooned with little bells. When the white doves flew past, they struck the bells with their wings and made them tinkle.

"In front of the temple was a pool of clear water paved with veined onyx. I lay down beside it, and with my pale fingers I touched the broad leaves. One of the priests came towards me and stood behind me. He had sandals on his feet, one of soft serpent-skin and the other of birds' plumage. On his head was a mitre of black felt decorated with silver crescents. Seven yellows were woven into his robe, and his frizzed hair was stained with antimony.

"After a little while he spake to me, and asked me my desire.

"I told him that my desire was to see the god.

" 'The god is hunting,' said the priest, looking strangely at me with his small slanting eyes.

" 'Tell me in what forest, and I will ride with him,' I answered.

"He combed out the soft fringes of his tunic with his long pointed nails. 'The god is asleep,' he murmured.

" 'Tell me on what couch, and I will watch by him,' I answered.

" 'The god is at the feast,' he cried.

" 'If the wine be sweet I will drink it with him, and if it be bitter I will drink it with him also,' was my answer.

"He bowed his head in wonder, and, taking me

by the hand, he raised me up, and led me into the temple.

"And in the first chamber I saw an idol seated on a throne of jasper bordered with great orient pearls. It was carved out of ebony, and in stature was of the stature of a man. On its forehead was a ruby and thick oil dripped from its hair on to its thighs. Its feet were red with the blood of a newly-slain kid, and its loins girt with a copper belt that was studded with seven beryls.

"And I said to the priest, 'Is this the god?' And he answered me, 'This is the god.'

"'Show me the god,' I cried, 'or I will surely slay thee.' And I touched his hand, and it became withered.

"And the priest besought me, saying, 'Let my lord heal his servant, and I will show him the god.'

"So I breathed with my breath upon his hand, and it became whole again, and he trembled and led me into the second chamber, and I saw an idol standing on a lotus of jade hung with great emeralds. It was carved out of ivory, and in stature was twice the stature of a man. On its forehead was a chrysolite, and its breasts were smeared with myrrh and cinnamon. In one hand it held a crooked sceptre of jade, and in the other a round crystal. It ware buskins of brass, and its thick neck was circled with a circle of selenites.

"And I said to the priest, 'Is this the god?' And he answered me, 'This is the god.'

" 'Show me the god,' I cried, 'or I will surely slay thee.' And I touched his eyes, and they became blind.

"And the priest besought me, saying, 'Let my lord heal his servant, and I will show him the god.'

"So I breathed with my breath upon his eyes, and the sight came back to them, and he trembled again, and let me into the third chamber, and lo! there was no idol in it, nor image of any kind, but only a mirror of round metal set on an altar of stone.

"And I said to the priest, 'Where is the god?'

"And he answered me: 'There is no god but the mirror that thou seest, for this is the Mirror of Wisdom. And it reflecteth all things that are in heaven and on earth, save only the face of him who looketh into it. This it reflecteth not, so that he who looketh into it may be wise. Many other mirrors are there, but they are mirrors of Opinion. This only is the Mirror of Wisdom. And they who possess this mirror know everything, nor is there anything hidden from them. And they who possess it not have not Wisdom. Therefore is it the god, and we worship it.' And I looked into the mirror, and it was even as he had said to me.

"And I did a strange thing, but what I did matters not, for in a valley that is but a day's journey from this place have I hidden the Mirror of Wisdom. Do but suffer me to enter into thee again and be thy servant, and thou shalt be wiser than all the wise men, and Wisdom shall be thine. Suffer me to enter into thee, and none will be as wise as thou."

But the young Fisherman laughed. "Love is better than Wisdom," he cried, "and the little Mermaid loves me."

"Nay, but there is nothing better than Wisdom," said the Soul.

"Love is better," answered the young Fisherman, and he plunged into the deep, and the Soul went weeping away over the marshes.

And after the second year was over the Soul came down to the shore of the sea, and called to the young Fisherman, and he rose out of the deep and said, "Why dost thou call to me?"

And the Soul answered, "Come nearer that I may speak with thee, for I have seen marvellous things."

So he came nearer, and couched in the shallow water, and leaned his head upon his hand and listened.

And the Soul said to him, "When I left thee, I turned my face to the South and journeyed. From the South cometh everything that is precious. Six days I journeyed along the highways that lead to the city of Ashter, along the dusty red-dyed highways by which the pilgrims are wont to go did I journey, and on the morning of the seventh day I lifted up my eyes, and lo! the city lay at my feet, for it is in a valley.

"There are nine gates to this city, and in front of each gate stands a bronze horse that neighs when the Bedouins come down from the mountains. The walls are cased with copper, and the watch-towers on the walls are roofed with brass. In every tower stands an archer with a bow in his hand. At sunrise he strikes with an arrow on a gong, and at sunset he blows through a horn of horn.

"When I sought to enter, the guards stopped me and asked of me who I was. I made answer that I was a Dervish and on my way to the city of Mecca, where there was a green veil on which the Koran was embroidered in silver letters by the hands of the angels. They were filled with wonder, and entreated me to pass in.

"Inside it is even as a bazaar. Surely thou should'st have been with me. Across the narrow streets the gay lanterns of paper flutter like large butterflies. When the wind blows over the roofs they rise and fall as painted bubbles do. In front of their booths sit the merchants on silken carpets. They have straight black beards, and their turbans are covered with golden sequins, and long strings of amber and carved peach-stones glide through their cool fingers. Some of them sell galbanum and nard, and curious perfumes from the islands of the Indian Sea, and the thick oil of red roses, and myrrh and little nail-shaped cloves. When one stops to speak to them, they throw pinches of frankincense upon a charcoal brazier and make the air sweet. I saw a Syrian who held in his hands a thin rod like a reed. Grey threads of smoke came from it, and its odour as it burned was as the odour of the pink almond in spring. Others sell silver bracelets embossed all over with creamy blue turquoise stones, and anklets of brass wire fringed with little pearls, and tiger's claws set in gold, and the claws of that gilt cat, the leopard, set in gold also, and ear-rings of pierced emerald, and finger-rings of hollowed jade. From the tea-houses comes the sound of the guitar and the opium-smokers with their white smiling faces look out at the passers-by.

"Of a truth thou should'st have been with me. The wine-sellers elbow their way through the crowd with great black skins on their shoulders. Most of them sell the wine of Schiraz, which is as sweet as honey. They serve it in little metal cups and strew rose leaves upon it. In the market-place stand the fruitsellers, who sell all kinds of fruit: ripe figs, with their bruised purple flesh, melons, smelling of musk and yellow as topazes, citrons and rose-apples and clusters of white grapes, round red-gold oranges, and oval lemons of green gold. Once I saw an elephant go by. Its trunk was painted with vermilion and turmeric, and over its ears it had a net of crimson silk cord. It stopped opposite one of the booths and began eating the oranges, and the man only laughed. Thou canst not think how strange a people they are. When they are glad they go to the bird-sellers and buy them a caged bird, and set it free that their joy may be greater, and when they are sad they scourge themselves with thorns that their sorrows may not grow less.

"One evening I met some negroes carrying a heavy palanquin through the bazaar. It was made of gilded bamboo, and the poles were of vermilion lacquer studded with brass peacocks. Across the windows hung thin curtains of muslin embroidered with beetles' wings and with tiny seed-pearls, and as it passed by a pale-faced Circassian looked out and smiled at me. I followed behind, and the ne-groes hurried their steps and scowled. But I did not care. I felt a great curiosity come over me.

"At last they stopped at a square white house. There were no windows to it, only a little door like the door of a tomb. They set down the palanquin and knocked three times with a copper hammer. An Armenian in a caftan of green leather peered through the wicket, and when he saw them he opened, and spread a carpet on the ground, and the woman stepped out. As she went in, she turned round and smiled at me again. I had never seen anyone so pale.

"When the moon rose I returned to the same place and sought for the house, but it was no longer there. When I saw that, I knew who the woman was, and wherefore she had smiled at me.

"Certainly thou should'st have been with me. On

the feast of the New Moon the young Emperor
came forth from his palace and went into the
mosque to pray. His hair and beard were dyed
with rose leaves and his cheeks were powdered
with a fine gold dust. The palms of his feet and
hands were yellow with saffron.

"At sunrise he went forth from his palace in a
robe of silver, and at sunset he returned to it again
in a robe of gold. The people flung themselves
on the ground and hid their faces, but I would
not do so. I stood by the stall of a seller of dates
and waited. When the Emperor saw me, he raised
his painted eyebrows and stopped. I stood quite
still, and made him no obeisance. The people marvelled at my boldness, and counselled me to flee from
the city. I paid no heed to them, but went and sat
with the sellers of strange gods, who by reason of
their craft are abominated. When I told them what
I had done, each of them gave me a god and prayed
me to leave them.

"That night, as I lay on a cushion in the tea-
house that is in the Street of Pomegranates, the
guards of the Emperor entered and led me to the
palace. As I went in they closed each door behind me, and put a chain across it. Inside was a
great court with an arcade running all round. The
walls were of white alabaster, set here and there
with blue and green tiles. The pillars were of green
marble, and the pavement of a kind of peach-blossom
marble. I had never seen anything like it before.

"As I passed across the court two veiled women looked down from a balcony and cursed me. The guards hastened on, and the butts of the lances rang out upon the polished floor. They opened a gate of wrought ivory, and I found myself in a watered garden of seven terraces. It was planted with tulip-cups and moonflowers, and silver-studded aloes. Like a slim reed of crystal a fountain hung in the dusky air. The cypress-trees were like burnt-out torches. From one of them a nightingale was singing.

"At the end of the garden stood a little pavilion. As we approached it two eunuchs came out to meet us. Their fat bodies swayed as they walked, and they glanced curiously at me with their yellow-lidded eyes. One of them drew aside the captain of the guard, and in a low voice whispered to him. The other kept munching scented pastilles, which he took with an affected gesture out of an oval box of lilac enamel.

"After a few moments the captain of the guard dismissed the soldiers. They went back to the palace, the eunuchs following slowly behind and plucking the sweet mulberries from the trees as they passed. Once the elder of the two turned round, and smiled at me with an evil smile.

"Then the captain of the guard motioned me towards the entrance of the pavilion. I walked on without trembling, and drawing the heavy curtain aside I entered in.

"The young Emperor was stretched on a couch of dyed lion skins, and a ger-falcon perched upon his wrist. Behind him stood a brass-turbaned Nubian, naked down to the waist, and with heavy earrings in his split ears. On a table by the side of the couch lay a mighty scimitar of steel.

"When the Emperor saw me he frowned, and said to me, 'What is thy name? Knowest thou not that I am Emperor of this city?' But I made him no answer.

"He pointed with his finger at the scimitar, and the Nubian seized it, and rushing forward struck at me with great violence. The blade whizzed through me, and did me no hurt. The man fell sprawling on the floor, and, when he rose up, his teeth chattered with terror and he hid himself behind the couch.

"The Emperor leaped to his feet, and taking a lance from a stand of arms, he threw it at me. I caught it in its flight, and brake the shaft into two pieces. He shot at me with an arrow, but I held up my hands and it stopped in mid-air. Then he drew a dagger from a belt of white leather, and stabbed the Nubian in the throat lest the slave should tell of his dishonour. The man writhed like a trampled snake, and a red foam bubbled from his lips.

"As soon as he was dead the Emperor turned to me, and when he had wiped away the bright sweat from his brow with a little napkin of purfled and purple silk, he said to me, 'Art thou a prophet that I may not harm thee, or the son of a prophet that I can do thee no hurt? I pray thee leave my city to-night, for while thou art in it I am no longer its lord.'

"And I answered him, 'I will go for half of thy treasure. Give me half of thy treasure, and I will go away.'

"He took me by the hand, and led me out into the garden. When the captain of the guard saw me, he wondered. When the eunuchs saw me, their knees shook and they fell upon the ground in fear.

"There is a chamber in the palace that has eight walls of red porphyry, and a brass-scaled ceiling hung with lamps. The Emperor touched one of the walls and it opened, and we passed down a corridor that was lit with many torches. In niches upon each side stood great wine-jars filled to the brim with silver pieces. When we reached the centre of the corridor the Emperor spake the word that may not be spoken, and a granite door swung back on a secret spring, and he put his hands before his face lest his eyes should be dazzled.

"Thou could'st not believe how marvellous a place it was. There were huge tortoise-shells full of pearls, and hollowed moonstones of great size piled up with red rubies. The gold was stored in coffers of elephant-hide, and the gold-dust in leather bottles. There were opals and sapphires, the former in cups of crystal, and the latter in cups of jade.

Round green emeralds were ranged in order upon
thin plates of ivory, and in one corner were silk
bags filled, some with turquoise-stones, and others
with beryls.   The ivory horns were heaped with
purple amethysts, and the horns of brass with chal-
cedonies and sards.   The pillars, which were of
cedar, were hung with strings of yellow lynx stones.
In the flat oval shields there were carbuncles, both
wine-coloured and coloured like grass.   And yet I
have told thee but a tithe of what was there.

"And when the Emperor had taken away his
hands from before his face he said to me: 'This is
my house of treasure, and half that is in it is thine,
even as I promised to thee.   And I will give thee
camels and camel drivers, and they shall do thy
bidding and take thy share of the treasure to whatever part of the world thou desirest to go.   And
the thing shall be done to-night, for I would not
that the Sun, who is my father, should see that
there is in my city a man whom I cannot slay.'

"But I answered him, 'The gold that is here is
thine, and the silver also is thine, and thine are the
precious jewels and the things of price.   As for me,
I have no need of these.   Nor shall I take aught
from thee but that little ring that thou wearest on
the finger of thy hand.'

"And the Emperor frowned.   'It is but a ring
of lead,' he cried, 'nor has it any value.   Therefore
take thy half of the treasure and go from my city.'

"'Nay,' I answered, 'but I will take nought but

that leaden ring, for I know what is written within it, and for what purpose.'

"And the Emperor trembled, and besought me and said: 'Take all the treasure and go from my city. The half that is mine shall be thine also.'

"And I did a strange thing, but what I did matters not, for in a cave that is but a day's journey from this place have I hidden the Ring of Riches. It is but a day's journey from this place, and it waits for thy coming. He who has this Ring is richer than all the kings of the world. Come therefore and take it, and the world's riches shall be thine."

But the young Fisherman laughed. "Love is better than Riches," he cried, "and the little Mermaid loves me."

"Nay, but there is nothing better than Riches," said the Soul.

"Love is better," answered the young Fisherman, and he plunged into the deep, and the Soul went weeping away over the marshes.

And after the third year was over the Soul came down to the shore of the sea, and called to the young Fisherman, and he rose out of the deep and said, "Why dost thou call to me?"

And the Soul answered, "Come nearer, that I may speak with thee, for I have seen marvellous things."

So he came nearer and couched in the shallow

water, and leaned his head upon his hand and listened.

And the Soul said to him, "In a city that I know of there is an inn that standeth by a river. I sat there with sailors who drank of two different coloured wines, and ate bread made of barley, and little salt fish served in bay leaves with vinegar. And as we sat and made merry, there entered to us an old man bearing a leathern carpet and a lute that had two horns of amber. And when he had laid out the carpet on the floor, he struck with a quill on the wire strings of his lute, and a girl whose face was veiled ran in and began to dance before us. Her face was veiled with a veil of gauze, but her feet were naked. Naked were her feet, and they moved over the carpet like little white pigeons. Never have I seen anything so marvellous, and the city in which she dances is but a day's journey from this place."

Now when the young Fisherman heard the words of his Soul, he remembered that the little Mermaid had no feet and could not dance. And a great desire came over him, and he said to himself, "It is but a day's journey, and I can return to my love," and he laughed, and stood up in the shallow water, and strode towards the shore.

And when he had reached the dry shore he laughed again and held out his arms to his Soul. And his Soul gave a great cry of joy and ran to meet him, and entered into him, and the young

Fisherman saw stretched before him upon the sand that shadow of the body that is the body of the Soul.

And his Soul said to him, "Let us not tarry, but get hence, for the Sea-gods are jealous, and have monsters that do their bidding."

So they made haste, and all that night they journeyed beneath the moon, and all the next day they journeyed beneath the sun, and on the evening of the second day they came to a city.

And the young Fisherman said to his Soul, "Is this the city in which she dances of whom thou did'st speak to me?"

And his Soul answered him, "It is not this city, but another. Nevertheless let us enter in."

So they entered in and passed through the streets, and as they passed through the Street of the Jewellers the young Fisherman saw a fair silver cup set forth in a booth. And his Soul said to him, "Take that silver cup and hide it."

So he took the cup and hid it in the fold of his tunic, and they went hurriedly out of the city.

And after that they had gone a league from the city, the young Fisherman frowned, and flung the cup away, and said to his Soul, "Why did'st thou tell me to take this cup and hide it, for it was an evil thing to do?"

But his Soul answered him, "Be at peace, be at peace."

And on the evening of the second day they came
to a city, and the young Fisherman said to his Soul,
"Is this the city in which she dances of whom thou
did'st speak to me?"

And his Soul answered him, "It is not this city,
but another. Nevertheless let us enter in."

So they entered in and passed through the streets,
and as they passed through the Street of the Sellers
of Sandals, the young Fisherman saw a child standing by a jar of water. And his Soul said to him,
"Smite that child." So he smote the child till it
wept, and when he had done this they went hurriedly
out of the city.

And after that they had gone a league from the
city the young Fisherman grew wrath, and said to
his Soul, "Why did'st thou tell me to smite the child,
for it was an evil thing to do?"

But his Soul answered him, "Be at peace, be at
peace."

And on the evening of the third day they came
to a city, and the young Fisherman said to his
Soul, "Is this the city in which she dances of whom
thou did'st speak to me?"

And his Soul answered him, "It may be that it
is this city, therefore let us enter in."

So they entered in and passed through the streets,
but nowhere could the young Fisherman find the
river or the inn that stood by its side. And the
people of the city looked curiously at him, and he
grew afraid and said to his Soul, "Let us go hence,

for she who dances with white feet is not here."

But his Soul answered, "Nay, but let us tarry, for the night is dark and there will be robbers on the way."

So he sat him down in the market-place and rested, and after a time there went by a hooded merchant who had a cloak of cloth of Tartary, and bare a lantern of pierced horn at the end of a jointed reed. And the merchant said to him, "Why dost thou sit in the market-place, seeing that the booths are closed and the bales corded?"

And the young Fisherman answered him, "I can find no inn in this city, nor have I any kinsman who might give me shelter."

"Are we not all kinsmen?" said the merchant. "And did not one God make us? Therefore come with me, for I have a guest-chamber."

So the young Fisherman rose up and followed the merchant to his house. And when he had passed through a garden of pomegranates and entered into the house, the merchant brought him rose-water in a copper dish that he might wash his hands, and ripe melons that he might quench his thirst, and set a bowl of rice and a piece of roasted kid before him.

And after that he had finished, the merchant led him to the guest-chamber, and bade him sleep and be at rest. And the young Fisherman gave him thanks, and kissed the ring that was on his hand, and flung himself down on the carpets of dyed goat's hair. And when he had covered himself with a covering of black lamb's wool he fell asleep.

And three hours before dawn, and while it was still night, his Soul waked him, and said to him, "Rise up and go to the room of the merchant, even to the room in which he sleepeth, and slay him, and take from him his gold, for we have need of it."

And the young Fisherman rose up and crept towards the room of the merchant and over the feet of the merchant there was lying a curved sword, and the tray by the side of the merchant held nine purses of gold. And he reached out his hand and touched the sword, and when he touched it the merchant started and awoke, and leaping up seized himself the sword and cried to the young Fisherman, "Dost thou return evil for good, and pay with the shedding of blood for the kindness that I have shown thee?"

And his Soul said to the young Fisherman, "Strike him," and he struck him so that he swooned, and he seized then the nine purses of gold, and fled hastily through the garden of pomegranates, and set his face to the star that is the star of morning.

And when they had gone a league from the city, the young Fisherman beat his breast, and said to his Soul, "Why didst thou bid me slay the merchant and take his gold? Surely thou art evil."

But his Soul answered him, "Be at peace, be at peace."

"Nay," cried the young Fisherman, "I may not

be at peace, for all that thou hast made me to do I hate. Thee also I hate, and I bid thee tell me wherefore thou hast wrought with me in this wise."

And his Soul answered him, "When thou didst send me forth into the world thou gavest me no heart, so I learned to do all these things and love them."

"What sayest thou?" murmured the young Fisherman.

"Thou knowest," answered his Soul, "thou knowest it well. Hast thou forgotten that thou gavest me no heart? I trow not. And so trouble not thyself nor me, but be at peace, for there is no pain that thou shalt not give away, nor any pleasure that thou shalt not receive."

And when the young Fisherman heard these words he trembled and said to his Soul, "Nay, but thou art evil, and hast made me forget my love, and hast tempted me with temptations, and hast set my feet in the ways of sin."

And his Soul answered him, "Thou hast not forgotten that when thou didst send me forth into the world thou gavest me no heart. Come, let us go to another city, and make merry, for we have nine purses of gold."

But the young Fisherman took the nine purses of gold, and flung them down, and trampled on them.

"Nay," he cried, "but I will have nought to do with thee, nor will I journey with thee anywhere, but even as I sent thee away before, so will I send thee away now, for thou hast wrought me no good." And he turned his back to the moon, and with the little knife that had the handle of green viper's skin he strove to cut from his feet that shadow of the body which is the body of the Soul.

Yet his Soul stirred not from him, nor paid heed to his command, but said to him, "The spell that the Witch told thee avails thee no more, for I may not leave thee, nor mayest thou drive me forth. Once in his life may a man send his Soul away, but he who receiveth back his Soul must keep it with him for ever, and this is his punishment and his reward."

And the young Fisherman grew pale and clenched his hands and cried, "She was a false Witch in that she told me not that."

"Nay," answered his Soul, "but she was true to Him she worships, and whose servant she will be ever."

And when the young Fisherman knew that he could no longer get rid of his Soul, and that it was an evil Soul and would abide with him always, he fell upon the ground weeping bitterly.

And when it was day the young Fisherman rose up and said to his Soul, "I will bind my hands that I may not do thy bidding, and close my lips that I may not speak thy words, and I will return to the place where she whom I love has her dwelling.

Even to the sea will I return, and to the little bay where she is wont to sing, and I will call to her and tell her the evil I have done and the evil thou hast wrought on me."

And his Soul tempted him and said, "Who is thy love that thou should'st return to her? The world has many fairer than she is. There are the dancing-girls of Samaris who dance in the manner of all kinds of birds and beasts. Their feet are painted with henna, and in their hands they have little copper bells. They laugh while they dance, and their laughter is as clear as the laughter of water. Come with me and I will show them to thee. For what is this trouble of thine about the things of sin? Is that which is pleasant to eat not made for the eater? Is there poison in that which is sweet to drink? Trouble not thyself, but come with me to another city. There is a little city hard by in which there is a garden of tulip-trees. And there dwell in this comely garden white peacocks and peacocks that have blue breasts. Their tails when they spread them to the sun are like disks of ivory and like gilt disks. And she who feeds them dances for their pleasure, and sometimes she dances on her hands and at other times she dances with her feet. Her eyes are coloured with stibium, and her nostrils are shaped like the wings of a swallow. From a hook in one of her nostrils hangs a flower that is carved out of pearl. She laughs while she dances, and the silver rings that are about her ankles

tinkle like bells of silver. And so trouble not thyself any more, but come with me to this city."

But the young Fisherman answered not his Soul,
but closed his lips with the seal of silence and with
a tight cord bound his hands, and journeyed back to
the place from which he had come, even to the
little bay where his love had been wont to sing.
And ever did his Soul tempt him by the way, but
he made it no answer, nor would he do any of the
wickedness that it sought to make him do, so great
was the power of the love that was within him.

And when he had reached the shore of the sea,
he loosed the cord from his hands, and took the
seal of silence from his lips, and called to the little
Mermaid. But she came not to his call, though he
called to her all day long and besought her.

And his Soul mocked him and said, "Surely thou
hast but little joy out of thy love. Thou art as one
who in time of dearth pours water into a broken
vessel. Thou givest away what thou hast, and
nought is given to thee in return. It were better
for thee to come with me, for I know where the
Valley of Pleasure lies, and what things are wrought
there."

But the young Fisherman answered not his Soul,
but in a cleft of the rock he built himself a house of
wattles, and abode there for the space of a year.
And every morning he called to the Mermaid, and
every noon he called to her again, and at night-
time he spake her name. Yet never did she rise

out of the sea to meet him, nor in any place of the sea could he find her, though he sought for her in the caves and in the green water, in the pools of the tide and in the wells that are at the bottom of the deep.

And ever did his Soul tempt him with evil, and whisper of terrible things. Yet did it not prevail against him, so great was the power of his love.

And after the year was over, the Soul thought within himself, "I have tempted my master with evil, and his love is stronger than I am. I will tempt him now with good, and it may be that he will come with me."

So he spake to the young Fisherman and said, "I have told thee of the joy of the world, and thou hast turned a deaf ear to me. Suffer me now to tell thee of the world's pain, and it may be that thou wilt hearken. For of a truth, pain is the Lord of this world, nor is there anyone who escapes from its net. There be some who lack raiment, and others who lack bread. There be widows who sit in purple, and widows who sit in rags. To and fro over the fens go the lepers, and they are cruel to each other. The beggars go up and down on the highways, and their wallets are empty. Through the streets of the cities walks Famine, and the Plague sits at their gates. Come, let us go forth and mend these things, and make them not to be. Wherefore should'st thou tarry here calling to thy love, seeing she comes

not to thy call? And what is love, that thou
should'st set this high store upon it?"

But the young Fisherman answered it nought, so
great was the power of his love. And every morning he called to the Mermaid, and every noon he
called to her again, and at night-time he spake her
name. Yet never did she rise out of the sea to meet
him, nor in any place of the sea could he find her,
though he sought for her in the rivers of the sea,
and in the valleys that are under the waves, in the
sea that the night makes purple, and in the sea that
the dawn leaves grey.

And after the second year was over, the Soul
said to the young Fisherman at night-time, and as
he sat in the wattled house alone, "Lo! now I have
tempted thee with evil, and I have tempted thee
with good, and thy love is stronger than I am.
Wherefore will I tempt thee no longer, but I pray
thee to suffer me to enter thy heart, that I may be
one with thee even as before."

"Surely thou mayest enter," said the young Fisherman, "for in the days when with no heart thou
didst go through the world thou must have much
suffered."

"Alas!" cried his Soul, "I can find no place of
entrance, so compassed about with love is this heart
of thine."

"Yet I would that I could help thee," said the
young Fisherman.

And as he spake there came a great cry of mourning from the sea, even the cry that men hear when one of the Sea-folk is dead. And the young Fisherman leapt up, and left his wattled house, and ran down to the shore. And the black waves came hurrying to the shore, bearing with them a burden that was whiter than silver. White as the surf it was, and like a flower it tossed on the waves. And the surf took it from the waves, and the foam took it from the surf, and the shore received it, and lying at his feet the young Fisherman saw the body of the little Mermaid. Dead at his feet it was lying.

Weeping as one smitten with pain he flung himself down beside it, and he kissed the cold red of the mouth, and toyed with the wet amber of the hair. He flung himself down beside it on the sand, weeping as one trembling with joy, and in his brown arms he held it to his breast. Cold were the lips, yet he kissed them. Salt was the honey of the hair, yet he tasted it with a bitter joy. He kissed the closed eyelids, and the wild spray that lay upon their cups was less salt than his tears.

And to the dead thing he made confession. Into the shells of its ears he poured the harsh wine of his tale. He put the little hands round his neck, and with his fingers he touched the thin reed of the throat. Bitter, bitter was his joy, and full of strange gladness was his pain.

The black sea came nearer, and the white foam moaned like a leper. With white claws of foam the sea grabbled at the shore. From the palace of

the Sea-King came the cry of mourning again, and
far out upon the sea the great Tritons blew hoarsely
upon their horns.

"Flee away," said his Soul, "for ever doth the
sea come nigher, and if thou tarriest it will slay
thee. Flee away, for I am afraid, seeing that thy
heart is closed against me by reason of the greatness of thy love. Flee away to a place of safety.
Surely thou wilt not send me without a heart into
another world?"

But the young Fisherman listened not to his Soul,
but called on the little Mermaid and said, "Love is
better than wisdom, and more precious than riches,
and fairer than the feet of the daughters of men.
The fires cannot destroy it, nor can the waters
quench it. I called on thee at dawn, and thou didst
not come to my call. The moon heard thy name,
yet hadst thou no heed of me. For evilly had I left
thee, and to my own hurt had I wandered away.
Yet ever did thy love abide with me, and ever was
it strong, nor did aught prevail against it, though I
have looked upon evil and looked upon good. And
now that thou art dead, surely I will die with thee
also."

And his Soul besought him to depart, but he
would not, so great was his love. And the sea came
nearer, and sought to cover him with its waves, and
when he knew that the end was at hand he kissed
with mad lips, the cold lips of the Mermaid, and

the heart that was within him brake. And as through the fulness of his love his heart did break, the Soul found an entrance and entered in, and was one with him even as before. And the sea covered the young Fisherman with its waves.

And in the morning the Priest went forth to bless the sea, for it had been troubled. And with him went the monks and the musicians, and the candle-bearers, and the swingers of censers, and a great company.

And when the Priest reached the shore he saw the young Fisherman lying drowned in the surf, and clasped in his arms was the body of the little Mermaid. And he drew back frowning, and having made the sign of the cross, he cried aloud and said, "I will not bless the sea nor anything that is in it. Accursed be the Sea-folk, and accursed be all they who traffic with them. And as for him who for love's sake forsook God, and so lieth here with his leman slain by God's judgment, take up his body and the body of his leman, and bury them in the corner of the Field of the Fullers, and set no mark above them, nor sign of any kind, that none may know the place of their resting. For accursed were they in their lives, and accursed shall they be in their deaths also."

And the people did as he commanded them, and in the corner of the Field of the Fullers, where so sweet herbs grew, they dug a deep pit, and laid the dead things within it.

And when the third year was over, and on a day that was a holy day, the Priest went up to the chapel, that he might show to the people the wounds of the Lord, and speak to them about the wrath of God.

And when he had robed himself with his robes, and entered in and bowed himself before the altar, he saw that the altar was covered with strange flowers that never had he seen before. Strange were they to look at, and of curious beauty, and their beauty troubled him, and their odour was sweet in his nostrils. And he felt glad, and understood not why he was glad.

And after that he had opened the tabernacle, and incensed the monstrance that was in it, and shown the fair wafer to the people, and hid it again behind the veil of veils, he began to speak to the people, desiring to speak to them of the wrath of God. But the beauty of the white flowers troubled him, and their odour was sweet in his nostrils, and there came another word into his lips, and he spake not of the wrath of God, but of the God whose name is Love. And why he so spake, he knew not.

And when he had finished his word the people wept, and the Priest went back to the sacristy, and his eyes were full of tears. And the deacons came in and began to unrobe him, and took from him the alb and the girdle, the maniple and the stole. And he stood as one in a dream.

And after that they had unrobed him, he looked at them and said, "What are the flowers that stand on the altar, and whence do they come?"

And they answered him, "What flowers they are we cannot tell, but they come from the corner of the Fuller's Field." And the Priest trembled, and returned to his own house and prayed.

And in the morning, while it was still dawn, he went forth with the monks and the musicians, and the candle-bearers and the swingers of censers, and a great company, and came to the shore of the sea, and blessed the sea, and all the wild things that are in it. The Fauns also he blessed, and the little things that dance in the woodland, and the bright-eyed things that peer through the leaves. All the things in God's world he blessed, and the people were filled with joy and wonder. Yet never again in the corner of the Fuller's Field grew flowers of any kind, but the field remained barren even as before. Nor came the Sea-folk into the bay as they had been wont to do, for they went to another part of the sea.

THE STAR-CHILD

ONCE upon a time two poor Woodcutters were making their way home through a great pine-forest. It was winter, and a night of bitter cold. The snow lay thick upon the ground, and upon the branches of the trees: the frost kept snapping the little twigs on either side of them, as they passed: and when they came to the Mountain-Torrent she was hanging motionless in air, for the Ice-King had kissed her.

So cold was it that even the animals and the birds did not know what to make of it.

"Ugh!" snarled the Wolf, as he limped through the brushwood with his tail between his legs, "this is perfectly monstrous weather. Why doesn't the Government look to it?"

"Weet! weet! weet!" twittered the green Linnets, "the old Earth is dead, and they have laid her out in her white shroud."

"The Earth is going to be married, and this is her bridal dress," whispered the Turtle-doves to each other. Their little pink feet were quite frost-bitten, but they felt that it was their duty to take a romantic view of the situation.

"Nonsense!" growled the Wolf. "I tell you that it is all the fault of the Government, and if you don't believe me I shall eat you." The Wolf had a thoroughly practical mind, and was never at a loss for a good argument.

"Well, for my own part," said the Woodpecker, who was a born philosopher, "I don't care an atomic theory for explanations. If a thing is so, it is so, and at present it is terribly cold."

Terribly cold it certainly was. The little Squirrels, who lived inside the tall fir-tree, kept rubbing each other's noses to keep themselves warm, and the Rabbits curled themselves up in their holes, and did not venture even to look out of doors. The only people who seemed to enjoy it were the great horned Owls. Their feathers were quite stiff with rime, but they did not mind, and they rolled their large yellow eyes, and called out to each other across the forest, "Tu-whit! Tu-whoo! Tu-whit! Tu-whoo! what delightful weather we are having!"

On and on went the two Woodcutters, blowing lustily upon their fingers, and stamping with their huge iron-shod boots upon the caked snow. Once they sank into a deep drift, and came out as white as millers are, when the stones are grinding; and once they slipped on the hard smooth ice where the marsh-water was frozen, and their faggots fell out of their bundles, and they had to pick them up and bind them together again; and once they thought that they had lost their way, and a great terror seized on them, for they knew that the Snow is cruel to those who sleep in her arms. But they put their trust in the good Saint Martin, who watches over all travellers, and retraced their steps, and went warily, and at last they reached the outskirts of the forest, and saw, far down in the valley beneath them, the lights of the village in which they dwelt.

So overjoyed were they at their deliverance that they laughed aloud, and the Earth seemed to them like a flower of silver, and the Moon like a flower of gold.

Yet, after that they had laughed they became sad, for they remembered their poverty, and one of them said to the other, "Why did we make merry, seeing that life is for the rich, and not for such as we are? Better that we had died of cold in the forest, or that some wild beast had fallen upon us and slain us."

"Truly," answered his companion, "much is given to some, and little is given to others. Injustice has parcelled out the world, nor is there equal division of aught save sorrow."

But as they were bewailing their misery to each other this strange thing happened. There fell from heaven a very bright and beautiful star. It slipped down the side of the sky, passing by the other stars in its course, and, as they watched it wondering, it seemed to them to sink behind a clump of willow-trees that stood hard by a little sheepfold no more than a stone's throw away.

"Why! there is a pot of gold for whoever finds it," they cried, and they set to and ran, so eager were they for the gold.

And one of them ran faster than his mate, and outstripped him, and forced his way through the willows, and came out on the other side, and lo! there was indeed a thing of gold lying on the white snow. So he hastened towards it, and stooping down placed his hands upon it, and it was a cloak of golden tissue, curiously wrought with stars, and wrapped in many folds. And he cried out to his comrade that he had found the treasure that had fallen from the sky, and when his comrade had come up, they sat them down in the snow, and loosened the folds of the cloak that they might divide the pieces of gold. But, alas! no gold was in it, nor silver, nor, indeed, treasure of any kind but only a little child who was asleep.

And one of them said to the other: "This is a bitter ending to our hope, nor have we any good fortune, for what doth a child profit to a man? Let us leave it here, and go our way, seeing that we are poor men, and have children of our own whose bread we may not give to another."

But his companion answered him: "Nay, but it were an evil thing to leave the child to perish here in the snow, and though I am as poor as thou art, and have many mouths to feed, and but little in the pot, yet will I bring it home with me, and my wife shall have care of it."

So very tenderly he took up the child, and wrapped

the cloak around it to shield it from the harsh cold, and made his way down the hill to the village, his comrade marvelling much at his foolishness and softness of heart.

And when they came to the village, his comrade said to him, "Thou hast the child, therefore give me the cloak, for it is meet that we should share."

But he answered him: "Nay, for the cloak is neither mine nor thine, but the child's only," and he bade him Godspeed, and went to his own house and knocked.

And when his wife opened the door and saw that her husband had returned safe to her, she put her arms round his neck and kissed him, and took from his back the bundle of faggots, and brushed the snow off his boots, and bade him come in.

But he said to her, "I have found something in the forest, and I have brought it to thee to have care of it," and he stirred not from the threshold.

"What is it?" she cried. "Show it to me, for the house is bare, and we have need of many things." And he drew the cloak back, and showed her the sleeping child.

"Alack, goodman!" she murmured, "have we not children enough of our own, that thou must needs bring a changeling to sit by the hearth? And who knows if it will not bring us bad fortune? And how shall we tend it?" And she was wroth against him.

"Nay, but it is a Star-Child," he answered; and

he told her the strange manner of the finding of it.

But she would not be appeased, but mocked at him, and spoke angrily, and cried: "Our children lack bread, and shall we feed the child of another? Who is there who careth for us? And who giveth us food?"

"Nay, but God careth for the sparrows even, and feedeth them," he answered.

"Do not the sparows die of hunger in the winter?" she asked. "And is it not winter now?" And the man answered nothing, but stirred not from the threshold.

And a bitter wind from the forest came in through the open door, and made her tremble, and she shivered, and said to him: "Wilt thou not close the door? There cometh a bitter wind into the house, and I am cold."

"Into a house where a heart is hard cometh there not always a bitter wind?" he asked. And the woman answered him nothing, but crept closer to the fire.

And after a time she turned round and looked at him, and her eyes were full of tears. And he came in swiftly, and placed the child in her arms, and she kissed it, and laid it in a little bed where the youngest of their own children was lying. And on the morrow the Woodcutter took the curious cloak of gold and placed it in a great chest, and a chain of amber that was round the child's neck his wife took and set it in the chest also.

So the Star-Child was brought up with the children of the Woodcutter, and sat at the same board with them, and was their playmate. And every year he became more beautiful to look at, so that all those who dwelt in the village were filled with wonder, for while they were swarthy and black-haired, he was white and delicate as sawn ivory, and his curls were like the rings of the daffodil. His lips, also were like the petals of red flower and his eyes were like violets by a river of pure water, and his body like the narcissus of a field where the mower comes not.

Yet did his beauty work him evil. For he grew proud, and cruel, and selfish. The chilren of the Woodcutter, and the other children of the village, he despised, saying that they were of mean parentage, while he was noble, being sprung from a Star, and he made himself master over them, and called them his servants. No pity had he for the poor, or for those who were blind or maimed or in any way afflicted, but would cast stones at them and drive them forth on to the highway, and bid them beg their bread elsewhere, so that none save the outlaws came twice to that village to ask for alms. Indeed, he was one enamoured of beauty, and would mock at the weakly and ill-favoured, and make jest of them; and himself he loved, and in summer, when the winds were still, he would lie by the well in the priest's orchard and look down at the marvel of his own face, and laugh for the pleasure he had in his fairness.

Often did the Woodcutter and his wife chide him, and say: "We did not deal with thee as thou dealest with those who are left desolate, and have none to succour them. Wherefore art thou so cruel to all who need pity?"

Often did the old priest send for him, and seek to teach him the love of living things, saying to him: "The fly is thy brother. Do it no harm. The wild birds that roam through the forest have their freedom. Snare them not for thy pleasure. God made the blind-worm and the mole, and each has its place. Who art thou to bring pain into God's world? Even the cattle of the field praise Him."

But the Star-Child heeded not their words, but would frown and flout, and go back to his companions, and lead them. And his companions followed him, for he was fair, and fleet of foot, and could dance, and pipe, and make music. And wherever the Star-Child led them they followed, and whatever the Star-Child bade them do, that did they. And when he pierced with a sharp reed the dim eyes of the mole, they laughed, and when he cast stones at the leper they laughed also. And in all things he ruled them, and they became hard of heart, even as he was.

Now there passed one day through the village a poor beggar-woman. Her garments were torn and ragged, and her feet were bleeding from the rough road on which she had travelled, and she was in very evil plight. And being weary she sat her down under a chestnut-tree to rest.

But when the Star-Child saw her, he said to his companions, "See! There sitteth a foul beggar-woman under that fair and green-leaved tree. Come, let us drive her hence, for she is ugly and ill-favoured."

So he came near and threw stones at her, and mocked her, and she looked at him with terror in her eyes, nor did she move her gaze from him. And when the Woodcutter, who was cleaving logs in a haggard hard by, saw what the Star-Child was doing, he ran up and rebuked him, and said to him: "Surely thou art hard at heart and knowest not mercy, for what evil has this poor woman done to thee that thou should'st treat her in this wise?"

And the Star-Child grew red with anger, and stamped his foot upon the ground, and said, "Who art thou to question me what I do? I am no son of thine to do thy bidding."

"Thou speakest truly," answered the Woodcutter, "yet did I show thee pity when I found thee in the forest."

And when the woman heard these words she gave a loud cry, and fell into a swoon. And the Wood-cutter carried her to his own house, and his wife had care of her, and when she rose up from the swoon into which she had fallen, they set meat and drink before her, and bade her have comfort.

But she would neither eat nor drink, but said to the Woodcutter, "Didst thou not say that the child was found in the forest? And was it not ten years from this day?"

And the Woodcutter answered, "Yea, it was in the forest that I found him, and it is ten years from this day."

"And what signs didst thou find with him?" she cried. "Bare he not upon his neck a chain of amber? Was not round him a cloak of gold tissue broidered with stars?"

"Truly," answered the Woodcutter, "it was even as thou sayest." And he took the cloak and the amber chain from the chest where they lay, and showed them to her.

And when she saw them she wept for joy, and said, "He is my little son whom I lost in the forest. I pray thee send for him quickly, for in search of him have I wandered over the whole world."

So the Woodcutter and his wife went out and called to the Star-Child, and said to him, "Go into the house, and there shalt thou find thy mother, who is waiting for thee."

So he ran in, filled with wonder and great gladness. But when he saw her who was waiting there, he laughed scornfully and said, "Why, where is my mother? For I see none here but this vile beggar-woman."

And the woman answered him, "I am thy mother."

"Thou art mad to say so," cried the Star-Child angrily. "I am no son of thine, for thou art a beggar, and ugly, and in rags. Therefore get thee hence, and let me see thy foul face no more."

"Nay, but thou art indeed my little son, whom I bare in the forest," she cried, and she fell on her knees, and held out her arms to him. "The robbers stole thee from me, and left thee to die," she murmured, "but I recognized thee when I saw thee, and the signs also have I recognized, the cloak of golden tissue and the amber-chain. Therefore I pray thee come with me, for over the whole world have I wandered in search of thee. Come with me, my son, for I have need of thy love."

But the Star-Child stirred not from his place, but shut the doors of his heart against her, nor was there any sound heard save the sound of the woman weeping for pain.

And at last he spoke to her, and his voice was hard and bitter. "If in very truth thou art my mother," he said, "it had been better hadst thou stayed away, and not come here to bring me to shame, seeing that I thought I was the child of some Star, and not a beggar's child, as thou tellest me that I am. Therefore get thee hence, and let me see thee no more."

"Alas! my son," she cried, "wilt thou not kiss me before I go? For I have suffered much to find thee."

"Nay," said the Star-Child, "but thou art too foul to look at, and rather would I kiss the adder or the toad than thee."

So the woman rose up, and went away into the forest weeping bitterly, and when the Star-Child saw that she had gone, he was glad, and ran back to his playmates that he might play with them.

But when they beheld him coming, they mocked him and said, "Why, thou art as foul as the toad, and as loathsome as the adder. Get thee hence, for we will not suffer thee to play with us," and they drove him out of the garden.

And the Star-Child frowned and said to himself, "What is this that they say to me? I will go to the well of water and look into it, and it shall tell me of my beauty."

So he went to the well of water and looked into it, and lo! his face was as the face of a toad, and his body was scaled like an adder. And he flung himself down on the grass and wept, and said to himself, "Surely this has come upon me by reason of my sin. For I have denied my mother, and driven her away, and been proud and cruel to her. Wherefore I will go and seek her through the whole world, nor will I rest till I have found her."

And there came to him the little daughter of the Woodcutter, and she put her hand upon his shoulder and said, "What doth it matter if thou hast lost thy comeliness? Stay with us, and I will not mock at thee."

And he said to her, "Nay, but I have been cruel to my mother, and as a punishment has this evil been sent to me. Wherefore I must go hence, and wander through the world till I find her, and she give me her forgiveness."

So he ran away into the forest and called out to his mother to come to him, but there was no answer. All day long he called to her, and when the sun set he lay down to sleep on a bed of leaves, and the birds and the animals fled from him, for they remembered his cruelty, and he was alone save for the toad that watched him, and the slow adder that crawled past.

And in the morning he rose up, and plucked some bitter berries from the trees and ate them, and took his way through the great wood, weeping sorely. And of everything that he met he made enquiry if perchance they had seen his mother.

He said to the Mole, "Thou canst go beneath the earth. Tell me, is my mother there?"

And the Mole answered, "Thou hast blinded mine eyes. How should I know?"

He said to the Linnet, "Thou canst fly over the tops of the tall trees, and canst see the whole world. Tell me, canst thou see my mother?"

And the Linnet answered, "Thou hast clipt my wings for thy pleasure. How should I fly?"

And to the little Squirrel who lived in the fire-tree, and was lonely, he said, "Where is my mother?"

And the Squirrel answered, "Thou hast slain mine. Dost thou seek to slay thine also?"

And the Star-Child wept and bowed his head, and

prayed forgiveness of God's things, and went on through the forest, seeking for the beggar-woman. And on the third day he came to the other side of the forest and went down into the plain.

And when he passed through the villages the children mocked him, and threw stones at him, and the carlots would not suffer him even to sleep in the byres, lest he might bring mildew on the stored corn, so foul was he to look at, and their hired man drave him away, and there was none who had pity on him. Nor could he hear anywhere of the beggar-woman who was his mother, though for the space of three years he wandered over the world, and often seemed to see her on the road in front of him, and would call to her, and run after her till the sharp flints made his feet to bleed. But overtake her he could not, and those who dwelt by the way did ever deny that they had seen her, or any like to her, and they made sport of his sorrow.

For the space of three years he wandered over the world, and in the world there was neither love nor loving-kindness nor charity for him, but it was even such a world as he had made for himself in the days of his great pride.

And one evening he came to the gate of a strong-walled city that stood by a river, and, weary and footsore though he was, he made to enter in. But the soldiers who stood on guard dropped their hal-

—

berts across the entrance, and said roughly to him, "What is thy business in the city?"

"I am seeking my mother," he answered, "and I pray ye to suffer me to pass, for it may be that she is in this city."

But they mocked at him, and one of them wagged a black beard, and set down his shield and cried, "Of a truth, thy mother will not be merry when she sees thee, for thou art more ill-favoured than the toad of the marsh, or the adder that crawls in the fen. Get thee gone. Get thee gone. Thy mother dwells not in this city."

And another, who held a yellow banner in his hand, said to him, "Who is thy mother, and wherefore art thou seeking for her?"

And he answered, "My mother is a beggar even as I am, and I have treated her evilly, and I pray ye to suffer me to pass that she may give me her forgiveness, if it be that she tarrieth in this city." But they would not, and pricked him with their spears.

And, as he turned away weeping, one whose armour was inlaid with gilt flowers, and on whose helmet couched a lion that had wings, came up and made enquiry of the soldiers who it was who had sought entrance. And they said to him, "It is a beggar and the child of a beggar, and we have driven him away."

"Nay," he cried, laughing, "but we will sell the foul thing for a slave, and his price shall be the price of a bowl of sweet wine."

And an old and evil-visaged man who was passing by called out, and said, "I will buy him for that
price," and, when he had paid the price, he took the
Star-Child by the hand and led him into the city.

And after that they had gone through many
streets they came to a little door that was set in a
wall that was covered with a pomegranate tree. And
the old man touched the door with a ring of graved
jasper and it opened, and they went down five steps
of brass into a garden filled with black poppies and
green jars of burnt clay. And the old man took
then from his turban a scarf of figured silk, and
bound with it the eyes of the Star-Child, and drove
him in front of him. And when the scarf was taken
off his eyes, the Star-Child found himself in a dungeon, that was lit by a lantern of horn.

And the old man set before him some mouldy
bread on a trencher and said, "Eat," and some brackish water in a cup and said, "Drink," and when he
had eaten and drunk, the old man went out, locking
the door behind him and fastening it with an iron
chain.

And on the morrow the old man, who was indeed
the subtlest of the magicians of Libya and had
learned his art from one who dwelt in the tombs of
the Nile, came in to him and frowned at him, and
said, "In a wood that is nigh to the gate of this city
of Giaours there are three pieces of gold. One is of
white gold, and another is of yellow gold, and the

gold of the third one is red. To-day thou shalt
bring me the piece of white gold, and if thou bringest it not back, I will beat thee with a hundred
stripes. Get thee away quickly, and at sunset I will
be waiting for thee at the door of the garden. See
that thou bringest the white gold, or it shall go ill
with thee, for thou art my slave, and I have bought
thee for the price of a bowl of sweet wine." And
he bound the eyes of the Star-Child with the scarf
of figured silk, and led him through the house, and
through the garden of poppies, and up the five steps
of brass. And having opened the little door with
his ring he set him in the street.

And the Star-Child went out of the gate of the
city, and came to the wood of which the Magician
had spoken to him.

Now this wood was very fair to look at from
without, and seemed full of singing birds and of
sweet-scented flowers, and the Star-Child entered it
gladly. Yet did its beauty profit him little, for wherever he went harsh briars and thorns shot up from
the ground and encompassed him, and evil nettles
stung him, and the thistle pierced him with her daggers, so that he was in sore distress. Nor could
he anywhere find the piece of white gold of which
the Magician had spoken, though he sought for it
from morn to noon, and from noon to sunset. And
at sunset he set his face towards home, weeping bitterly, for he knew what fate was in store for him.

But when he had reached the outskirts of the wood, he heard from a thicket a cry as of someone in pain. And forgetting his own sorrow he ran back to the place, and saw there a little Hare caught in a trap that some hunter had set for it.

And the Star-Child had pity on it, and released it, and said to it, "I am myself but a slave, yet may I give thee thy fredom."

And the Hare answered him, and said: "Surely thou hast given me freedom, and what shall I give thee in return?"

And the Star-Child said to it, "I am seeking for a piece of white gold, nor can I anywhere find it, and if I bring it not to my master he will beat me."

"Come thou with me," said the Hare, "and I will lead thee to it, for I know where it is hidden, and for what purpose."

So the Star-Child went with the Hare, and lo! in the cleft of a great oak-tree he saw the piece of white gold that he was seeking. And he was filled with joy, and seized it, and said to the Hare, "The service that I did to thee thou hast rendered back again many times over, and the kindness that I showed thee thou hast repaid a hundred fold."

"Nay," answered the Hare, "but as thou dealt with me, so I did deal with thee," and it ran away swiftly, and the Star-Child went towards the city.

Now at the gate of the city there was seated one who was a leper. Over his face hung a cowl of grey linen and through the eyelets his eyes gleamed like red coals. And when he saw the Star-Child coming, he struck upon a wooden bowl, and clattered his bell, and called out to him, and said, "Give me a piece of money, or I must die of hunger. For they have thrust me out of the city, and there is no one who has pity on me."

"Alas!" cried the Star-Child, "I have but one piece of money in my wallet, and if I bring it not to my master he will beat me, for I am his slave."

But the leper entreated him, and prayed of him. till the Star-Child had pity, and gave him the piece of white gold.

And when he came to the Magician's house, the Magician opened to him, and brought him in, and said to him, "Hast thou the piece of white gold?" And the Star-Child answered, "I have it not." So the Magician fell upon him, and beat him, and set before him an empty trencher, and said, "Eat," and an empty cup, and said, "Drink," and flung him again into the dungeon.

And on the morrow the Magician came to him, and said, "If to-day thou bringest me not the piece of yellow gold, I will surely keep thee as my slave, and give thee three hundred stripes."

So the Star-Child went to the wood, and all day long he searched for the piece of yellow gold, but nowhere could he find it. And at sunset he sat him down and began to weep, and as he was weeping there came to him the little Hare that he had rescued from the trap.

And the Hare said to him, "Why art thou weep-ing? And what dost thou seek in the wood?"

And the Star-Child answered, "I am seeking for a piece of yellow gold that is hidden here, and if I find it not my master will beat me, and keep me as a slave."

"Follow me," cried the Hare, and it ran through the wood till it came to a pool of water. And at the bottom of the pool the piece of yellow gold was lying.

"How shall I thank thee?" said the Star-Child, "for lo! this is the second time that you have suc-coured me."

"Nay, but thou hadst pity on me first," said the Hare, and it ran away swiftly.

And the Star-Child took the piece of yellow gold, and put it in his wallet, and hurried to the city. But the leper saw him coming, and ran to meet him, and knelt down and cried, "Give me a piece of money or I shall die of hunger."

And the Star-Child said to him, "I have in my wallet but one piece of yellow gold, and if I bring it not to my master he will beat me and keep me as his slave."

But the leper entreated him sore, so that the Star-Child had pity on him, and gave him the piece of yellow gold.

And when he came to the Magician's house, the Magician opened to him, and brought him in, and said to him, "Hast thou the piece of yellow gold?"

And the Star-Child said to him, "I have it not." So the Magician fell upon him, and beat him, and loaded him with chains, and cast him again into the dungeon.

And on the morrow the Magician came to him, and said, "If to-day thou bringest me the piece of red gold I will set thee free, but if thou bringest it not I will surely slay thee."

So the Star-Child went to the wood, and all day long he searched for the piece of red gold, but nowhere could he find it. And at evening he sat him down, and wept, and as he was weeping there came to him the little Hare.

And the Hare said to him, "The piece of red gold that thou seekest is in the cavern that is behind thee. Therefore weep no more but be glad."

"How shall I reward thee?" cried the Star-Child, "for lo! this is the third time thou hast succoured me."

"Nay, but thou hadst pity on me first," said the Hare, and it ran away swiftly.

And the Star-Child entered the cavern, and in its farthest corner he found the piece of red gold. So he put it in his wallet, and hurried to the city. And the leper seeing him coming, stood in the centre of the road, and cried out, and said to him, "Give me the piece of red money, or I must die," and the Star-Child had pity on him again, and gave him the piece of red gold, saying, "Thy need is greater than mine." Yet was his heart heavy, for he knew what evil fate awaited him.

But lo! as he passed through the gate of the city, the guards bowed down and made obeisance to him, saying, "How beautiful is our lord!" and a crowd of citizens followed him, and cried out, "Surely there is none so beautiful in the whole world!" so that the Star-Child wept, and said to himself, "They are mocking me, and making light of my misery." And so large was the concourse of the people, that he lost the threads of his way, and found himself at last in a great square, in which there was a palace of a King.

And the gate of the palace opened, and the priests and the high officers of the city ran forth to meet him, and they abased themselves before him, and said, "Thou art our lord for whom we have been waiting, and the son of our King."

And the Star-Child answered them and said, "I am no king's son, but the child of a poor beggar woman. And how say ye that I am beautiful, for I know that I am evil to look at?"

Then he, whose armour was inlaid with gilt flowers, and on whose helmet couched a lion that had wings, held up a shield, and cried, "How saith my lord that he is not beautiful?"

And the Star-Child looked, and lo! his face was even as it had been, and his comeliness had come back to him, and he saw that in his eyes which he had not seen there before.

And the priests and the high officers knelt down and said to him, "It was prophesied of old that on this day should come he who was to rule over us. Therefore, let our lord take this crown and this sceptre, and be in his justice and mercy our King over us."

But he said to them, "I am not worthy, for I have denied the mother who bare me, nor may I rest till I have found her, and known her forgiveness. Therefore, let me go, for I must wander again over the world, and may not tarry here, though ye bring me the crown and the sceptre." And as he spake he turned his face from them towards the street that led to the gate of the city, and lo! amongst the crowd that pressed round the soldiers, he saw the beggar-woman who was his mother, and at her side stood the leper, who had sat by the road.

And a cry of joy broke from his lips, and he ran over, and kneeling down he kissed the wounds on his mother's feet, and wet them with his tears. He bowed his head in the dust, and sobbing, as one whose heart might break, he said to her: "Mother, I denied thee in the hour of my pride. Accept me in the hour of my humility. Mother, I gave thee hatred. Do thou give me love. Mother, I rejected thee. Receive thy child now." But the beggar-woman answered him not a word.

And he reached out his hands, and clasped the white feet of the leper, and said to him: "Thrice did I give thee of my mercy. Bid my mother speak to me once." But the leper answered him not a word.

And he sobbed again, and said: "Mother, my suffering is greater than I can bear. Give me thy forgiveness, and let me go back to the forest." And the beggar-woman put her hand on his head, and said to him, "Rise," and the leper put his hand on his head, and said to him "Rise," also.

And he rose up from his feet, and looked at them, and lo! they were a King and a Queen.

And the Queen said to him, "This is thy father whom thou hast succoured."

And the King said, "This is thy mother, whose feet thou hast washed with thy tears."

And they fell on his neck and kissed him, and brought him into the palace, and clothed him in fair raiment, and set the crown upon his head, and the sceptre in his hand, and over the city that stood by the river he ruled, and was its lord. Much justice and mercy did he show to all, and the evil Magician he banished, and to the Woodcutter and his wife he sent many rich gifts, and to their children he gave high honour. Nor would he suffer any to be cruel to bird or beast, but taught love and loving-kindness and charity, and to the poor he gave bread, and to the naked he gave raiment, and there was peace and plenty in the land.

Yet ruled he not long, so great had been his suffering, and so bitter the fire of his testing, for after the space of three years he died. And he who came after him ruled evilly.

THE HAPPY PRINCE.

HIGH above the city, on a tall column, stood the statue of the Happy Prince. He was gilded all over with thin leaves of fine gold, for eyes he had two bright sapphires, and a large red ruby glowed on his sword-hilt.

He was very much admired, indeed. "He is as beautiful as a weathercock," remarked one of the Town Councillors who wished to gain a reputation for having artistic tastes; "only not quite so useful," he added, fearing lest people should think him unpractical, which he really was not.

"Why can't you be like the Happy Prince?" asked a sensible mother of her little boy who was crying for the moon. "The Happy Prince never dreams of crying for anything."

"I am glad there is some one in the world who is quite happy," muttered a disappointed man as he gazed at the wonderful statue.

"He looks just like an angel," said the Charity Children as they came out of the cathedral in their bright scarlet cloaks, and their clean white pinafores.

"How do you know?" said the Mathematical Master, "you have never seen one."

"Ah! but we have, in our dreams," answered the children; and the Mathematical Master frowned and looked very severe, for he did not approve of children dreaming.

One night there flew over the city a little Swallow. His friends had gone away to Egypt six weeks before, but he had stayed behind, for he was in love with the most beautiful Reed. He had met her early in the spring as he was flying down the river after a big yellow moth, and had been so attracted by her slender waist that he had stopped to talk to her.

"Shall I love you?" said the Swallow, who liked to come to the point at once, and the Reed made him a low bow. So he flew round and round her, touching the water with his wings, and making silver ripples. This was his courtship, and it lasted all through the summer.

"It is a ridiculous attachment," twittered the other Swallows, "she has no money, and far too many relations;" and, indeed, the river was quite full of Reeds. Then, when the autumn came, they all flew away.

After they had gone he felt lonely, and began to tire of his lady-love. "She has no conversation," he said, "and I am afraid that she is a coquette, for she is always flirting with the wind." And certainly, whenever the wind blew, the Reed made the most graceful curtsies. "I admit that she is domestic," he continued, "but I love travelling, and my wife, consequently, should love travelling also."

"Will you come away with me?" he said finally to her; but the Reed shook her head, she was so attached to her home.

"You have been trifling with me," he cried. "I am off to the Pyramids. Good-bye!" and he flew away.

All day long he flew, and at night-time he arrived at the city. "Where shall I put up?" he said; "I hope the town has made preparations."

Then he saw the statue on the tall column. "I will put up there," he cried; "it is a fine position with plenty of fresh air." So he alighted just between the feet of the Happy Prince.

"I have a golden bedroom," he said softly to himself as he looked round, and he prepared to go to sleep; but just as he was putting his head under his wing a large drop of water fell on him. "What a curious thing!" he cried, "there is not a single cloud in the sky, the stars are quite clear and bright, and yet it is raining. The climate in the north of Europe is really dreadful. The Reed used to like the rain, but that was merely her selfishness."

Then another drop fell.

"What is the use of a statue if it cannot keep the rain off?" he said; "I must look for a good chimney-pot," and he determined to fly away.

But before he had opened his wings, a third drop

fell, and he looked up, and saw—Ah! what did he see?

The eyes of the Happy Prince were filled with tears, and tears were running down his golden cheeks. His face was so beautiful in the moonlight that the little Swallow was filled with pity.

"Who are you?" he said.

"I am the Happy Prince."

"Why are you weeping then?" asked the Swallow; "you have quite drenched me."

"When I was alive and had a human heart," answered the statue, "I did not know what tears were, for I lived in the Palace of Sans Souci, where sorrow is not allowed to enter. In the daytime I played with my companions in the garden, and in the evening I led the dance in the Great Hall. Round the garden ran a very lofty wall, but I never cared to ask what lay beyond it, everything about me was so beautiful. My courtiers called me the Happy Prince, and happy indeed I was, if pleasure be happiness. So I lived, and so I died. And now that I am dead they have set me up here so high that I can see all the ugliness and all the misery of my city, and though my heart is made of lead yet I cannot choose but weep."

"What, is he not solid gold?" said the Swallow to himself. He was too polite to make any personal remarks out loud.

"Far away," continued the statue in a low, musical voice, "far away in a little street there is a poor

house. One of the windows is open, and through it
I can see a woman seated at a table. Her face is
thin and worn, and she has coarse red hands, all
pricked by the needle, for she is a seamstress. She
is embroidering passion-flowers on a satin gown for
the loveliest of the Queen's maids-of-honour to
wear at the next Court-ball. In a bed in the corner
of the room her little boy is lying ill. He has a
fever, and is asking for oranges. His mother has
nothing to give him but river water, so he is crying.
Swallow, Swallow, little Swallow, will you not
bring her the ruby out of my sword-hilt? My feet
are fastened to this pedestal and I cannot move."

"I am waited for in Egypt," said the Swallow.
"My friends are flying up and down the Nile, and
talking to the large lotus-flowers. Soon they will
be going to sleep in the tomb of the great King.
The King is there himself in his painted coffin. He
is wrapped in yellow linen, and embalmed with
spices. Round his neck is a chain of pale green jade,
and his hands are like withered leaves."

"Swallow, Swallow, little Swallow," said the
Prince, "will you not stay with me for one night,
and be my messenger? The boy is so thirsty, and
the mother so sad."

"I don't think I like boys," answered the Swallow. "Last summer, when I was staying on the
river, there were two rude boys, the miller's sons,
who were always throwing stones at me. They
r !ver hit me, of course; we swallows fly far too well

for that, and besides, I come of a family famous for
its agility; but still, it was a mark of disrespect."

But the Happy Prince looked so sad that the little
Swallow was sorry. "It is very cold here," he said;
"but I will stay with you for one night, and be your
messenger."

"Thank you, little Swallow," said the Prince.

So the Swallow picked out the great ruby from
the Prince's sword, and flew away with it in his
beak over the roofs of the town.

He passed by the cathedral tower, where the white
marble angels were sculptured. He passed by the
palace and heard the sound of dancing. A beautiful
girl came out on the balcony with her lover. "How
wonderful the stars are," he said to her, "and how
wonderful is the power of love!" "I hope my dress
will be ready in time for the State-ball," she answered; "I have ordered passion-flowers to be embroidered on it; but the seamstresses are so lazy."

He passed over the river, and saw the lanterns
hanging to the masts of the ships. He passed over
the Ghetto, and saw the old Jews bargaining with
each other, and weighing out money in copper scales.
At last he came to the poor house and looked in.
The boy was tossing feverishly on his bed, and the
mother had fallen asleep, she was so tired. In he
hopped, and laid the great ruby on the table beside
the woman's thimble. Then he flew gently round
the bed, fanning the boy's forehead with his wings.
"How cool I feel," said the boy, "I must be getting

better;" and he sank into a delicious slumber.

Then the Swallow flew back to the Happy Prince and told him what he had done. "It is curious," he remarked, "but I feel quite warm now, although it is so cold."

"That is because you have done a good action," said the Prince. And the little Swallow began to think, and then he fell asleep. Thinking always made him sleepy.

When day broke he flew down to the river and had a bath. "What a remarkable phenomenon," said the Professor of Ornithology as he was passing over the bridge. "A swallow in winter!" And he wrote a long letter about it to the local newspaper. Every one quoted it, it was full of so many words that they could not understand.

"To-night I go to Egypt," said the Swallow, and he was in high spirits at the prospect. He visited all the public monuments, and sat a long time on top of the church steeple. Wherever he went the sparrows chirruped, and said to each other, "What a distinguished stranger!" so he enjoyed himself very much.

When the moon rose he flew back to the Happy Prince. "Have you any commissions for Egypt?" he cried. "I am just starting."

"Swallow, Swallow, little Swallow," said the Prince, "will you not stay with me one night longer?"

"I am waited for in Egypt," answered the Swallow. "To-morrow my friends will fly up to the Second Cataract. The river-horse couches there among the bulrushes, and on a great granite throne sits the God Memmon. All night long he watches the stars, and when the morning star shines he utters one cry of joy, and then he is silent. At noon the yellow lions come down to the water's edge to drink. They have eyes like green beryls, and their roar is louder than the roar of the cataract."

"Swallow, Swallow, little Swallow," said the Prince, "far away across the city I see a young man in a garret. He is leaning over a desk covered with papers, and in a tumbler by his side there is a bunch of withered violets. His hair is brown and crisp, and his lips are red as a pomegranate, and he has large and dreamy eyes. He is trying to finish a play for the Director of the Theatre, but he is too cold to write any more. There is no fire in the grate, and hunger has made him faint."

"I will wait with you one night longer," said the Swallow, who really had a good heart. "Shall I take him another ruby?"

"Alas! I have no ruby now," said the Prince; "my eyes are all that I have left. They are made of rare sapphires, which were brought out of India a thousand years ago. Pluck out one of them and take it to him. He will sell it to the jeweller, and buy food and firewood, and finish his play."

"Dear Prince," said the Swallow, "I cannot do that;" and he began to weep.

"Swallow, Swallow, little Swallow," said the Prince, "do as I command you."

So the Swallow plucked out the Prince's eye, and flew away to the student's garret. It was easy enough to get in, as there was a hole in the roof. Through this he darted, and came into the room. The young man had his head buried in his hands, so he did not hear the flutter of the bird's wings, and when he looked up he found the beautiful sapphire lying on the withered violets.

"I am beginning to be appreciated," he cried; "this is from some great admirer. Now I can finish my play," and he looked quite happy.

The next day the Swallow flew down to the harbour. He sat on the mast of a large vessel and watched the sailors hauling big chests out of the hold with ropes. "Heave a-hoy!" they shouted as each chest came up. "I am going to Egypt!" cried the Swallow, but nobody minded, and when the moon rose he flew back to the Happy Prince.

"I am come to bid you good-bye," he cried.

"Swallow, Swallow, little Swallow," said the Prince, "will you not stay with me one night longer?"

"It is winter," answered the Swallow, "and the chill snow will soon be here. In Egypt the sun is warm on the green palm-trees, and the crocodiles lie in the mud and look lazily about them. My companions are building a nest in the Temple of Baalbec, and the pink and white doves are watching them, and cooing to each other. Dear Prince, I must leave you, but I will never forget you, and next spring I will bring you back two beautiful jewels in place of those you have given away. The ruby shall be redder than a red rose, and the sapphire shall be as blue as the great sea."

"In the square below," said the Happy Prince, "there stands a little match-girl. She has let her matches fall in the gutter, and they are all spoiled. Her father will beat her if she does not bring home some money, and she is crying. She has no shoes or stockings, and her little head is bare. Pluck out my other eye, and give it to her, and her father will not beat her."

"I will stay with you one night longer," said the Swallow, "but I cannot pluck out your eye. You would be quite blind then."

"Swallow, Swallow, little Swallow," said the Prince, "do as I command you."

So he plucked out the Prince's other eye, and darted down with it. He swooped past the match-girl, and slipped the jewel into the palm of her hand. "What a lovely bit of glass," cried the little girl; and she ran home, laughing.

Then the Swallow came back to the Prince. "You are blind now," he said, "so I will stay with you always."

"No, little Swallow," said the poor Prince, "you must go away to Egypt."

"I will stay with you always," said the Swallow, and he slept at the Prince's feet.

All the next day he sat on the Prince's shoulder, and told him stories of what he had seen in strange lands. He told him of the red ibises, who stand in long rows on the banks of the Nile, and catch gold fish in their beaks; of the Sphinx, who is as old as the world itself, and lives in the desert, and knows everything; of the merchants, who walk slowly by the side of their camels, and carry amber beads in their hands; of the King of the Mountains of the Moon, who is as black as ebony, and worships a large crystal; of the great green snake that sleeps in a palm-tree, and has twenty priests to feed it with honey-cakes; and of the pygmies who sail over a big lake on large flat leaves, and are always at war with the butterflies.

"Dear little Swallow," said the Prince, "you tell me of marvellous things, but more marvellous than anything is the suffering of men and of women. There is no Mystery so great as Misery. Fly over my city, little Swallow, and tell me what you see there."

So the Swallow flew over the great city, and saw the rich making merry in their beautiful houses, while the beggars were sitting at the gates. He flew into dark lanes, and saw the white faces of starving children looking out listlessly at the black streets. Under the archway of a bridge two little boys were lying in one another's arms to try and keep themselves warm. "How hungry we are!" they said. "You must not lie here," shouted the Watchman, and they wandered out into the rain.

Then he flew back and told the Prince what he had seen.

"I am covered with fine gold," said the Prince, "you must take it off, leaf by leaf, and give it to my poor; the living always think that gold can make them happy."

Leaf after leaf of the fine gold the Swallow picked off, till the Happy Prince looked quite dull and grey. Leaf after leaf of the fine gold he brought to the poor, and the children's faces grew rosier, and they laughed and played games in the street. "We have bread now!" they cried.

Then the snow came, and after the snow came the frost. The streets looked as if they were made of silver, they were so bright and glistening; long icicles like crystal daggers hung down from the eaves of the houses, everybody went about in furs, and the little boys wore scarlet caps and skated on the ice.

The poor little Swallow grew colder and colder, but he would not leave the Prince, he loved him too well. He picked up crumbs outside the baker's door when the baker was not looking, and tried to keep himself warm by flapping his wings.

But at last he knew that he was going to die. He had just strength to fly up to the Prince's shoulder once more. "Good-bye, dear Prince!" he murmured, "will you let me kiss your hand?"

"I am glad that you are going to Egypt at last, little Swallow," said the Prince, "you have stayed too long here; but you must kiss me on the lips, for I love you."

"It is not to Egypt that I am going," said the Swallow. "I am going to the House of Death. Death is the brother of Sleep, is he not?"

And he kissed the Happy Prince on the lips, and fell down dead at his feet.

At that moment a curious crack sounded inside the statue, as if something had broken. The fact is that the leaden heart had snapped right in two. It certainly was a dreadfully hard frost.

Early the next morning the Mayor was walking in the square below in company with the Town Councillors. As they passed the column he looked up at the statue: "Dear me! how shabby the Happy Prince looks!" he said.

"How shabby indeed!" cried the Town Councillors, who always agreed with the Mayor, and they went up to look at it.

"The ruby has fallen out of his sword, his eyes are gone, and he is golden no longer," said the Mayor; "in fact, he is little better than a beggar!"

"Little better than a beggar," said the Town Councillors.

"And here is actually a dead bird at his feet!" continued the Mayor. "We must really issue a proclamation that birds are not to be allowed to die here." And the Town Clerk made a note of the suggestion.

So they pulled down the statue of the Happy Prince. "As he is no longer beautiful he is no longer useful," said the Art Professor at the University.

Then they melted the statue in a furnace, and the Mayor held a meeting of the Corporation to decide what was to be done with the metal. "We must have another statue, of course," he said, "and it shall be a statue of myself."

"Of myself," said each of the Town Councillors, and they quarrelled. When I last heard of them they were quarrelling still.

"What a strange thing," said the overseer of the workmen at the foundry. "This broken lead heart will not melt in the furnace. We must throw it away." So they threw it on a dust heap where the dead Swallow was also lying.

"Bring me the two most precious things in the city," said God to one of His Angels; and the Angel brought Him the leaden heart and the dead bird.

"You have rightly chosen," said God, "for in my garden of Paradise this little bird shall sing for evermore, and in my city of gold the Happy Prince shall praise me."

THE NIGHTINGALE AND THE ROSE

"SHE said that she would dance with me if I brought her red roses," cried the young Student; "but in all my garden there is no red rose."

From her nest in the holm-oak tree the Nightingale heard him, and she looked out through the leaves, and wondered.

"No red rose in all my garden!" he cried, and his beautiful eyes filled with tears. "Ah, on what little things does happiness depend! I have read all that the wise men have written, and all the secrets of philosophy are mine, yet for want of a red rose is my life made wretched."

"Here at last is a true lover," said the Nightingale. "Night after night have I sung of him, though I knew him not: night after night have I told his story to the stars, and now I see him. His hair is dark as the hyacinth-blossom, and his lips are red as the rose of his desire; but passion has made his face like pale ivory, and sorrow has set her seal upon his brow."

"The Prince gives a ball to-morrow night," murmured the young Student, "and my love will be of the company. If I bring her a red rose she will dance with me till dawn. If I bring her a red rose, I shall hold her in my arms, and she will lean her head upon my shoulder, and her hand will be clasped in mine. But there is no red rose in my garden, so I shall sit lonely, and she will pass me by. She will have no heed of me, and my heart will break."

"Here indeed is the true lover," said the Nightingale. "What I sing of, he suffers: what is joy to me, to him is pain. Surely Love is a wonderful thing. It is more precious than emeralds, and dearer than fine opals. Pearls and pomegranates cannot buy it, nor is it set forth in the market-place. It may not be purchased of the merchants, nor can it be weighed out in the balance for gold."

"The musicians will sit in their gallery," said the young Student, "and play upon their stringed instruments, and my love will dance to the sound of the harp and the violin. She will dance so lightly that her feet will not touch the floor, and the courtiers in their gay dresses will throng round her. But with me she will not dance, for I have no red rose to give her;" and he flung himself down on the grass, and buried his face in his hands, and wept.

"Why is he weeping?" asked a little Green Lizard, as he ran past him with his tail in the air.

"Why, indeed?" said a Butterfly, who was fluttering about after a sunbeam.

"Why, indeed?" whispered a Daisy to his neighbour, in a soft, low voice.

"He is weeping for a red rose," said the Nightingale.

"For a red rose!" they cried; "how very ridiculous!" and the little Lizard, who was something of a cynic, laughed outright.

But the Nightingale understood the secret of the Student's sorrow, and she sat silent in the oak-tree, and thought about the mystery of Love.

Suddenly she spread her brown wings for flight, and soared into the air. She passed through the grove like a shadow, and like a shadow she sailed across the garden.

In the centre of the grass-plot was standing a beautiful Rose-tree, and when she saw it, she flew over to it, and lit upon a spray.

"Give me a red rose," she cried, "and I will sing you my sweetest song."

But the Tree shook its head.

"My roses are white," it answered; "as white as the foam of the sea, and whiter than the snow upon the mountain. But go to my brother who grows round the old sun-dial, and perhaps he will give you what you want."

So the Nightingale flew over to the Rose-tree that was growing round the old sun-dial.

"Give me a red rose," she cried, "and I will sing you my sweetest song."

But the Tree shook its head.

"My roses are yellow," it answered; "as yellow as the hair of the mermaiden who sits upon an amber throne, and yellower than the daffodil that blooms in the meadow before the mower comes with his scythe. But go to my brother who grows beneath the Student's window, and perhaps he will give you what you want."

So the Nightingale flew over to the Rose-tree that was growing beneath the Student's window.

"Give me a red rose," she cried, "and I will sing you my sweetest song."

But the Tree shook its head.

"My roses are red," it answered; "as red as the feet of the dove, and redder than the great fans of coral that wave and wave in the ocean cavern. But the winter has chilled my veins, and the frost has nipped my buds, and the storm has broken my branches, and I shall have no roses at all this year."

"One red rose is all I want," cried the Nightingale. "Only one red rose! Is there any way by which I can get it?"

"There is a way," answered the Tree; "but it is so terrible that I dare not tell it to you."

"Tell it to me," said the Nightingale, "I am not afraid."

"If you want a red rose," said the Tree, "you must build it out of music by moonlight, and stain it with your own heart's-blood. You must sing to me with your breast against a thorn. All night long you must sing to me, and the thorn must pierce your heart, and your life-blood must flow into my veins, and become mine."

"Death is a great price to pay for a red rose," cried the Nightingale, "and Life is very dear to all. It is pleasant to sit in the green wood, and to watch the Sun in his chariot of gold, and the Moon in her chariot of pearl. Sweet is the scent of the hawthorn, and sweet are the bluebells that hide in the valley, and the heather that blows on the hill. Yet Love is better than Life, and what is the heart of a bird compared to the heart of a man?"

So she spread her brown wings for flight, and soared into the air. She swept over the garden like a shadow, and like a shadow she sailed through the grove.

The young Student was still lying on the grass, where she had left him, and the tears were not yet dry in his beautiful eyes.

"Be happy," cried the Nightingale, "be happy; you shall have your red rose. I will build it out of music by moonlight, and stain it with my own heart's-blood. All that I ask of you in return is that you will be a true lover, for Love is wiser than Philosophy, though she is wise, and mightier than Power, though he is mighty. Flame-coloured are his wings, and coloured like flame is his body. His lips are sweet as honey, and his breath is like frankincense."

The Student looked up from the grass, and listened, but he could not understand what the Nightingale was saying to him, for he only knew the things that are written down in books.

But the Oak-tree understood, and felt sad, for he was very fond of the little Nightingale who had built her nest in his branches.

"Sing me one last song," he whispered; "I shall feel very lonely when you are gone."

So the Nightingale sang to the Oak-tree, and her voice was like water bubbling from a silver jar.

When she had finished her song the Student got up, and pulled a note-book and a lead-pencil out of his pocket.

"She has form," he said to himself, as he walked away through the grove—"that cannot be denied her; but has she got feeling? I am afraid not. In fact, she is like most artists; she is all style, without any sincerity. She would not sacrifice herself for others. She thinks merely of music, and everybody knows that the arts are selfish. Still, it must be admitted that she has some beautiful notes in her voice. What a pity it is that they do not mean anything, or do any practical good." And he went into his room, and lay down on his little pallet-bed, and began to think of his love; and, after a time, he fell asleep.

And when the Moon shone in the heavens the Nightingale flew to the Rose-tree, and set her breast against the thorn. All night long she sang with her breast against the thorn, and the cold crystal Moon leaned down and listened. All night long she sang, and the thorn went deeper and deeper into her breast, and her life-blood ebbed away from her.

.

She sang first of the birth of love in the heart of a boy and a girl. And on the topmost spray of the Rose-tree there blossomed a marvellous rose, petal followed petal, as song followed song. Pale was it, at first, as the mist that hangs over the river—pale as the feet of the morning, and silver as the wings of the dawn. As the shadow of a rose in a mirror of silver, as the shadow of a rose in a water-pool, so was the rose that blossomed on the topmost spray of the Tree.

But the Tree cried to the Nightingale to press closer against the thorn. "Press closer, little Nightingale," cried the Tree, "or the Day will come before the rose is finished."

So the Nightingale pressed closer against the thorn, and louder and louder grew her song, for she sang of the birth of passion in the soul of a man and a maid.

And a delicate flush of pink came into the leaves of the rose, like the flush in the face of the bridegroom when he kisses the lips of the bride. But the thorn had not yet reached her heart, so the rose's heart remained white, for only a Nightingale's heart's-blood can crimson the heart of a rose.

And the Tree cried to the Nightingale to press closer against the thorn. "Press closer, little Nightingale," cried the Tree, "or the Day will come before the rose is finished."

So the Nightingale pressed closer against the

thorn, and the thorn touched her heart, and a fierce pang of pain shot through her. Bitter, bitter was the pain, and wilder and wilder grew her song, for she sang of the Love that is perfected by Death, of the Love that dies not in the tomb.

And the marvellous rose became crimson, like the rose of the eastern sky. Crimson was the girdle of petals, and crimson as a ruby was the heart.

But the Nightingale's voice grew fainter, and her little wings began to beat, and a film came over her eyes. Fainter and fainter grew her song, and she felt something choking her in her throat.

Then she gave one last burst of music. The white Moon heard it, and she forgot the dawn, and lingered on in the sky. The red rose heard it, and it trembled all over with ecstasy, and opened its petals to the cold morning air. Echo bore it to her purple cavern in the hills, and woke the sleeping shepherds from their dreams. It floated through the reeds of the river, and they carried its message to the sea.

"Look, look!" cried the Tree, "the rose is finished now;" but the Nightingale made no answer, for she was lying dead in the long grass, with the thorn in her heart.

And at noon the Student opened his window and looked out.

"Why, what a wonderful piece of luck!" he cried; "here is a red rose! I have never seen any rose like it in all my life. It is so beautiful that I am sure it has a long Latin name;" and he leaned down and plucked it.

Then he put on his hat, and ran up to the Professor's house with the rose in his hand.

The daughter of the Professor was sitting in the doorway winding blue silk on a reel, and her little dog was lying at her feet.

"You said that you would dance with me if I brought you a red rose," cried the Student. "Here is the reddest rose in all the world. You will wear it to-night next your heart, and as we dance together it will tell you how I love you."

But the girl frowned.

"I am afraid it will not go with my dress," she answered; "and, besides, the Chamberlain's nephew has sent me some real jewels, and everybody knows that jewels cost far more than flowers."

"Well, upon my word, you are very ungrateful," said the Student angrily; and he threw the rose into the street, where it fell into the gutter, and a cart-wheel went over it.

"Ungrateful!" said the girl. "I tell you what, you are very rude; and, after all, who are you? Only a Student. Why, I don't believe you have even got silver buckles to your shoes as the Chamlain's nephew has;" and she got up from her chair and went into the house.

"What a silly thing Love is," said the Student as he walked away. "It is not half as useful as Logic, for it does not prove anything, and it is always telling one of things that are not going to happen, and making one believe things that are not true. In fact, it is quite unpractical, and, as in this age to be practical is everything, I shall go back to Philosophy and study Metaphysics."

So he returned to his room and pulled out a great dusty book, and began to read.

THE SELFISH GIANT

EVERY afternoon, as they were coming from school, the children used to go and play in the Giant's garden.

It was a large lovely garden, with soft green grass. Here and there over the grass stood beautiful flowers like stars, and there were twelve peach-trees that in the spring-time broke out into delicate blossoms of pink and pearl, and in the autumn bore rich fruit. The birds sat on the trees and sang so sweetly that the children used to stop their games in order to listen to them. "How happy we are here!" they cried to each other.

One day the Giant came back. He had been to visit his friend the Cornish ogre, and had stayed with him for seven years. After the seven years were over he had said all that he had to say, for his conversation was limited, and he determined to return to his own castle. When he arrived he saw the children playing in the garden.

"What are you doing there?" he cried in a very gruff voice, and the children ran away.

"My own garden is my own garden," said the Giant; "any one can understand that, and I will allow nobody to play in it but myself." So he built a high wall all around it, and put up a notice-board.

TRESPASSERS
WILL BE
PROSECUTED

He was a very selfish Giant.

The poor children had now nowhere to play. They tried to play on the road, but the road was very dusty and full of hard stones, and they did not like it. They used to wander round the high wall when their lessons were over, and talk about the beautiful garden inside. "How happy we were there," they said to each other.

Then the Spring came, and all over the country there were little blossoms and little birds. Only in the garden of the Selfish Giant it was still winter. The birds did not care to sing in it as there were no children, and the trees forgot to blossom. Once a beautiful flower put its head out from the grass, but when it saw the notice-board it was so sorry for the children that it slipped back into the ground again, and went off to sleep The only people who were pleased were the Snow and the Frost. "Spring has forgotten this garden," they cried, "so we will live here all the year round." The Snow covered up the grass with her great white cloak, and the Frost painted all the trees silver. Then they invited the North Wind to stay with them, and he came. He was wrapped in furs, and he roared all day about the garden, and blew the chimney-pots down. "This is a delightful spot," he said, "we must ask the Hail on a visit." So the Hail came. Every day for three hours he rattled on the roof of the castle till he broke most of the slates, and then he ran round and round the garden as fast he could go. He was dressed in grey, and his breath was like ice.

"I cannot understand why the Spring is so late in coming," said the Selfish Giant, as he sat at the window and looked out at his cold white garden; "I hope there will be a change in the weather."

But the Spring never came, nor the Summer. The Autumn gave golden fruit to every garden, but to the Giant's garden she gave none. "He is too selfish," she said. So it was always Winter there, and the North Wind, and the Hail, and the Frost, and the Snow danced about through the trees.

One morning the Giant was lying awake in bed when he heard some lovely music. It sounded so sweet to his ears that he thought it must be the King's musicians passing by. It was really only a little linnet singing outside his window, but it was so long since he had heard a bird sing in his garden that it seemed to him to be the most beautiful music in the world. Then the Hail stopped dancing over his head, and the North Wind ceased roaring, and a delicious perfume came to him through the open casement. "I believe the Spring has come at last," said the Giant; and he jumped out of bed and looked out.

What did he see?

He saw a most wonderful sight. Through a little hole in the wall the children had crept in, and they were sitting in the branches of the trees. In every tree that he could see there was a little child. And the trees were so glad to have the children back again that they had covered themselves with blossoms, and were waving their arms gently above the children's heads. The birds were flying about and twittering with delight, and the flowers were looking up through the green grass and laughing. It was a lovely scene, only in one corner it was still winter. It was the farthest corner of the garden, and in it was standing a little boy. He was so small that he could not reach up to the branches of the tree, and he was wandering all round it, crying bitterly. The poor tree was still quite covered with frost and snow, and the North Wind was blowing and roaring above it. "Climb up! little boy," said the Tree, and it bent its branches down as low as it could; but the boy was too tiny.

And the Giant's heart melted as he looked out. "How selfish I have been!" he said; "now I know why the Spring would not come here. I will put that poor little boy on the top of the tree, and then I will knock down the wall, and my garden shall be the children's playground for ever and ever." He was really very sorry for what he had done.

So he crept downstairs and opened the front door quite softly, and went out into the garden. But when the children saw him they were so frightened that they all ran away, and the garden became winter again. Only the little boy did not run, for his eyes were so full of tears that he did not see the Giant coming. And the Giant stole up behind him and took him gently in his hand, and put him up into the tree. And the tree broke at once into blossom, and the birds came and sang on it, and the little boy stretched out his two arms and flung them round the Giant's neck, and kissed him. And the other children, when they saw that the Giant was not wicked any longer, came running back, and with them came the Spring. "It is your garden now, little children," said the Giant, and he took a great axe and knocked down the wall. And when the people were going to market at twelve o'clock they found the Giant playing with the children in the most beautiful garden they had ever seen.

All day long they played, and in the evening they came to the Giant to bid him good-bye.

"But where is your little companion?" he said: "the boy I put into the tree." The Giant loved him the best because he had kissed him.

"We don't know," answered the children; "he has gone away."

"You must tell him to be sure and come here to-morrow," said the Giant. But the children said that they did not know where he lived, and had never seen him before; and the Giant felt very sad.

Every afternoon, when school was over, the children came and played with the Giant. But the little boy whom the Giant loved was never seen again. The Giant was very kind to all the children, yet he longed for his first little friend, and often spoke of him. "How I would like to see him!" he used to say.

Years went over, and the Giant grew very old and feeble. He could not play about any more, so he sat in a huge armchair, and watched the children at their games, and admired his garden. "I have many beautiful flowers," he said; "but the children are the most beautiful flowers of all."

One winter morning he looked out of his window as he was dressing. He did not hate the Winter now, for he knew that it was merely the Spring asleep, and that the flowers were resting.

Suddenly he rubbed his eyes in wonder, and looked and looked. It certainly was a marvellous sight. In the farthest corner of the garden was a tree quite covered with lovely white blossoms. Its branches were all golden, and silver fruit hung down from them, and underneath it stood the little boy he had loved.

Downstairs ran the Giant in great joy, and out into the garden. He hastened across the grass, and came near to the child. And when he came quite close his face grew red with anger, and he said, "Who hath dared to wound thee?" For on the palms of the child's hands were the prints of two nails, and the prints of two nails were on the little feet.

"Who hath dared to wound thee?" cried the Giant; "tell me, that I may take my sword and slay him."

"Nay!" answered the child; "but these are the wounds of Love."

"Who art thou?" said the Giant, and a strange awe fell on him, and he knelt before the little child.

And the child smiled on the Giant, and said to him, "You let me play once in your garden, to-day you shall come with me to my garden, which is Paradise."

And when the children ran in that afternoon, they found the Giant lying dead under the tree, all covered with white blossoms.

THE DEVOTED FRIEND

ONE morning the old Water-rat put his head out of his hole. He had bright beady eyes and stiff grey whiskers, and his tail was like a long bit of black india-rubber. The little ducks were swimming about in the pond, looking just like a lot of yellow canaries, and their mother, who was pure white with real red legs, was trying to teach them how to stand on their heads in the water.

"You will never be in the best society unless you can stand on your heads," she kept saying to them; and every now and then she showed them how it was done. But the little ducks paid no attention to her. They were so young that they did not know what an advantage it is to be in society at all.

"What disobedient children!" cried the old Water-rat; "they really deserve to be drowned."

"Nothing of the kind," answered the Duck; "every one must make a beginning, and parents cannot be too patient."

"Ah! I know nothing about the feelings of parents," said the Water-rat; "I am not a family man. In fact, I have never been married, and I never intend to be. Love is all very well in its way, but friendship is much higher.   Indeed, I know of nothing in the world that is either nobler or rarer than a devoted friendship."

"And what, pray, is your idea of the duties of a devoted friend?" asked a Green Linnet, who was sitting in a willow-tree hard by, and had overheard the conversation.

"Yes, that is just what I want to know," said the Duck, and she swam away to the end of the pond, and stood upon her head, in order to give her children a good example.

"What a silly question!" cried the Water-rat.   "I should expect my devoted friend to be devoted to me, of course."

"And what would you do in return?" said the little bird, swinging upon a silver spray, and flapping his tiny wings.

"I don't understand you," answered the Water-rat.

"Let me tell you a story on the subject," said the Linnet.

"Is the story about me?" asked the Water-rat. "If so, I will listen to it, for I am extremely fond of fiction."

"It is applicable to you," answered the Linnet: and he flew down, and alighting upon the bank, he told the story of The Devoted Friend.

"Once upon a time," said the Linnet, "there was an honest little fellow named Hans."

"Was he very distinguished?" asked the Water-rat.

"No," answered the Linnet, "I don't think he was distinguished at all, except for his kind heart, and his funny round good-humoured face. He lived in a tiny cottage all by himself, and every day he worked in his garden. In all the country-side there was no garden so lovely as his. Sweet-william grew there, and Gilly-flowers, and Shepherd's-purses, and Fair-maids of France. There were damask Roses, and yellow Roses, lilac Crocuses, and gold, purple Violets and white. Columbine and Ladysmock, Marjoram and Wild Basil, the Cowslip and the Flower-de-luce, the Daffodil and the Clove-Pink bloomed or blossomed in their proper order as the months went by, one flower taking another flower's place, so that there were always beautiful things to look at, and pleasant odours to smell.

"Little Hans had a great many friends, but the most devoted friend of all was big Hugh the Miller. Indeed, so devoted was the rich Miller to little Hans, that he would never go by his garden without leaning over the wall and plucking a large nosegay, or a handful of sweet herbs, or filling his pockets with plums and cherries if it was the fruit season.

" 'Real friends should have everything in common,' the Miller used to say, and little Hans nodded and smiled, and felt very proud of having a friend with such noble ideas.

"Sometimes, indeed, the neighbours thought it strange that the rich Miller never gave little Hans anything in return, though he had a hundred sacks of flour stored away in his mill, and six milch cows, and a large flock of woolly sheep; but Hans never troubled his head about these things, and nothing gave him greater pleasure than to listen to all the wonderful things the Miller used to say about the unselfishness of true friendship.

"So little Hans worked away in his garden. During the spring, the summer, and the autumn he was very happy, but when winter came, and he had no fruit or flowers to bring to the market, he suffered a good deal from cold and hunger, and often had to go to bed without any supper but a few dried pears or some hard nuts. In the winter, also, he was extremely lonely, as the Miller never came to see him then.

" 'There is no good in my going to see little Hans as long as the snow lasts,' the Miller used to say to his wife, 'for when people are in trouble they should be left alone, and not be bothered by visitors. That at least is my idea about friendship, and I am sure I am right. So I shall wait till the spring comes, and then I shall pay him a visit, and he will be able to give me a large basket of primroses, and that will make him so happy.'

" 'You are certainly very thoughtful about others,' answered the Wife, as she sat in her comfortable armchair by the big pinewood fire; 'very thoughtful indeed. It is quite a treat to hear you talk about friendship. I am sure the clergyman himself could not say such beautiful things as you do, though he does live in a three-storied house, and wear a gold ring on his little finger.'

" 'But could we not ask little Hans up here?' said the Miller's youngest son. 'If poor Hans is in trouble I will give him half my porridge, and show him my white rabbits.'

" 'What a silly boy you are!' cried the Miller; 'I really don't know what is the use of sending you to school. You seem not to learn anything. Why, if little Hans came up here, and saw our warm fire, and our good supper, and our great cask of red wine, he might get envious, and envy is a most terrible thing, and would spoil anybody's nature. I certainly will not allow Hans's nature to be spoiled. I am his best friend, and I will always watch over him, and see that he is not led into any temptations. Besides, if Hans came here, he might ask me to let him have some flour on credit, and that I could not do. Flour is one thing, and friendship is another, and they should not be confused. Why, the words are spelt differently, and mean quite different things. Everybody can see that.'

" 'How well you talk!' said the Miller's Wife, pouring herself out a large glass of warm ale; 'really I feel quite drowsy. It is just like being in church.'

" 'Lots of people act well,' answered the Miller; 'but very few people talk well, which shows that talking is much the more difficult thing of the two, and much the finer thing also;' and he looked sternly across the table at his little son, who felt so ashamed of himself that he hung his head down, and grew quite scarlet, and began to cry into his tea. However, he was so young that you must excuse him."

"Is that the end of the story?" asked the Water-rat.

"Certainly not," answered the Linnet, "that is the beginning."

"Then you are quite behind the age," said the Water-rat. "Every good story-teller nowadays starts with the end, and then goes on to the beginning, and concludes with the middle. That is the new method. I heard all about it the other day from a critic who was walking round the pond with a young man. He spoke of the matter at great length, and I am sure he must have been right, for he had blue spectacles and a bald head, and whenever the young man made any remark, he always answered 'Pooh!' But pray go on with your story. I like the Miller immensely. I have all kinds of beautiful sentiments myself, so there is a great sympathy between us."

"Well," said the Linnet, hopping now on one leg and now on the other, "as soon as the winter was over, and the primroses began to open their pale yellow stars, the Miller said to his wife that he would go down and see little Hans.

" 'Why, what a good heart you have!' cried his

Wife; 'you are always thinking of others. And mind you take the big basket with you for the flowers.'

"So the Miller tied the sails of the windmill together with a strong iron chain, and went down the hill with the basket on his arm.

" 'Good morning, little Hans,' said the Miller.

" 'Good morning,' said Hans, leaning on his spade, and smiling from ear to ear.

" 'And how have you been all the winter?' said the Miller.

" 'Well, really,' cried Hans, 'it is very good of you to ask, very good indeed. I am afraid I had rather a hard time of it, but now the spring has come, and I am quite happy, and all my flowers are doing well.'

" 'We often talked of you during the winter, Hans,' said the Miller, 'and wondered how you were getting on.'

" 'That was kind of you,' said Hans; 'I was half afraid you had forgotten me.'

" 'Hans, I am surprised at you,' said the Miller; 'friendship never forgets. That is the wonderful thing about it, but I am afraid you don't understand the poetry of life. How lovely your primroses are looking, by-the-bye!'

" 'They are certainly very lovely,' said Hans, 'and it is a most lucky thing for me that I have so many. I am going to bring them into the market and sell

them to the Burgomaster's daughter, and buy back
my wheelbarrow with the money.'

" 'Buy back your wheelbarrow? You don't
mean to say you have sold it? What a very stupid
thing to do!'

" 'Well, the fact is,' said Hans, 'that I was obliged
to. You see the winter was a very bad time for me,
and I really had no money at all to buy bread with.
So I first sold the silver buttons off my Sunday
coat, and then I sold my silver chain, and then I
sold my big pipe, and at last I sold my wheelbarrow.
But I am going to buy them all back again now.'

" 'Hans,' said the Miller, 'I will give you my
wheelbarrow. It is not in very good repair; indeed,
one side is gone, and there is something wrong with
the wheel-spokes; but in spite of that I will give it
to you. I know it is very generous of me, and a
great many people would think me extremely foolish
for parting with it, but I am not like the rest of
the world. I think that generosity is the essence of
friendship, and, besides, I have got a new wheelbarrow for myself. Yes, you may set your mind
at ease, I will give you my wheelbarrow.'

" 'Well, really, that is generous of you,' said little
Hans, and his funny round face glowed all over with
pleasure. 'I can easily put it in repair, as I have a
plank of wood in the house.'

" 'A plank of wood!' said the Miller; 'why, that
is just what I want for the roof of my barn. There
is a very large hole in it, and the corn will all get

damp if I don't stop it up. How lucky you men-
tioned it! It is remarkable how one good action
always breeds another. I have given you my
wheelbarrow, and now you are going to give me
your plank. Of course, the wheelbarrow is worth
far more than the plank, but true friendship never
notices things like that. Pray get it at once, and I
will set to work at my barn this very day.'

" 'Certainly,' cried little Hans, and he ran into
the shed and dragged the plank out.

" 'It is not a very big plank,' said the Miller,
looking at it, 'and I am afraid that after I have
mended my barn-roof there won't be any left for
you to mend the wheelbarrow with; but, of course,
that is not my fault. And now, as I have given you
my wheelbarrow, I am sure you would like to give
me some flowers in return. Here is the basket, and
mind you fill it quite full.'

" 'Quite full?' said little Hans, rather sorrow-
fully, for it was really a very big basket, and he
knew that if he filled it he would have no flowers
left for the market, and he was very anxious to
get his silver buttons back.

" 'Well, really,' answered the Miller, 'as I have
given you my wheelbarrow, I don't think that it is
much to ask you for a few flowers. I may be
wrong, but I should have thought that friendship,
true friendship, was quite free from selfishness of
any kind.'

" 'My dear friend, my best friend,' cried little

Hans, 'you are welcome to all the flowers in my garden. I would much sooner have your good opinion than my silver buttons, any day,' and he ran and plucked all his pretty primroses, and filled the Miller's basket.

" 'Good-bye, little Hans,' said the Miller, as he went up the hill with the plank on his shoulder, and the big basket in his hand.

" 'Good-bye,' said little Hans, and he began to dig away quite merrily, he was so pleased about the wheelbarrow.

"The next day he was nailing up some honeysuckle against the porch, when he heard the Miller's voice calling to him from the road. So he jumped off the ladder, and ran down the garden, and looked over the wall.

"There was the Miller with a large sack of flour on his back.

" 'Dear little Hans,' said the Miller, 'would you mind carrying this sack of flour for me to market?'

" 'Oh, I am so sorry,' said Hans, 'but I am really very busy to-day. I have got all my creepers to nail up, and all my flowers to water, and all my grass to roll.'

" 'Well, really,' said the Miller, 'I think that, considering that I am going to give you my wheelbarrow, it is rather unfriendly of you to refuse.'

" 'Oh, don't say that,' cried little Hans, 'I wouldn't be unfriendly for the whole world;' and he ran

in for his cap, and trudged off with the big sack
on his shoulders.

"It was a very hot day, and the road was terribly
dusty, and before Hans had reached the sixth mile-
stone he was so tired that he had to sit down and
rest. However, he went on bravely, and at last he
reached the market. After he had waited there
some time, he sold the sack of flour for a very good
price, and then he returned home at once, for he
was afraid that if he stopped too late he might
meet some robbers on the way.

" 'It has certainly been a hard day,' said little
Hans to himself as he was going to bed, 'but I am
glad I did not refuse the Miller, for he is my best
friend, and, besides, he is going to give me his
wheelbarrow.'

"Early the next morning the Miller came down
to get the money for his sack of flour, but little
Hans was so tired that he was still in bed.

" 'Upon my word,' said the Miller, 'you are very
lazy. Really, considering that I am going to give
you my wheelbarrow, I think you might work
harder. Idleness is a great sin, and I certainly don't
like any of my friends to be idle or sluggish. You
must not mind my speaking quite plainly to you.
Of course I should not dream of doing so if I were
not your friend. But what is the good of friendship if one cannot say exactly what one means?
Anybody can say charming things and try to please
and to flatter, but a true friend always says un-

pleasant things, and does not mind giving pain.
Indeed, if he is a really true friend he prefers it,
for he knows that then he is doing good.'

" 'I am very sorry,' said little Hans, rubbing his
eyes and pulling off his nightcap, 'but I was so
tired that I thought I would lie in bed for a little
time, and listen to the birds singing. Do you know
that I always work better after hearing the birds
sing?'

" 'Well, I am glad of that,' said the Miller, clap-
ping little Hans on the back, 'for I want you to
come up to the mill as soon as you are dressed, and
mend my barn-roof for me.'

"Poor little Hans was very anxious to go and
work in his garden, for his flowers had not been
watered for two days, but he did not like to refuse
the Miller, as he was such a good friend to him.

" 'Do you think it would be unfriendly of me
if I said I was busy?' he inquired in a shy and timid
voice.

" 'Well, really,' answered the Miller, 'I do not
think it is much to ask of you, considering that I
am going to give you my wheelbarrow; but of
course if you refuse I will go and do it myself.'

" 'Oh! on no account,' cried little Hans; and he
jumped out of bed, and dressed himself, and went
up to the barn.

"He worked there all day long, till sunset, and
at sunset the Miller came to see how he was getting
on.

" 'Have you mended the hole in the roof yet, little Hans?' cried the Miller in a cheery voice.

" 'It is quite mended,' answered little Hans, coming down the ladder.

" 'Ah!' said the Miller, 'there is no work so delightful as the work one does for others.'

" 'It is certainly a great privilege to hear you talk,' answered little Hans, sitting down and wiping his forehead, 'a very great privilege. But I am afraid I shall never have such beautiful ideas as you have.'

" 'Oh! they will come to you,' said the Miller, 'but you must take more pains. At present you have only the practice of friendship; some day you will have the theory also.'

" 'Do you really think I shall?' asked little Hans.

" 'I have no doubt of it,' answered the Miller: 'but now that you have mended the roof, you had better go home and rest, for I want you to drive my sheep to the mountain to-morrow.'

"Poor little Hans was afraid to say anything to this, and early the next morning the Miller brought his sheep round to the cottage, and Hans started off with them to the mountain. It took him the whole day to get there and back; and when he returned he was so tired that he went off to sleep in his chair, and did not wake up till it was broad daylight.

" 'What a delightful time I shall have in my garden,' he said, and he went to work at once.

"But somehow he was never able to look after his flowers at all, for his friend the Miller was always coming round and sending him off on long errands, or getting him to help at the mill. Little Hans was very much distressed at times, as he was afraid his flowers would think he had forgotten them, but he consoled himself by the reflection that the Miller was his best friend. 'Besides,' he used to say, 'he is going to give me his wheelbarrow, and that is an act of pure generosity.'

"So little Hans worked away for the Miller, and the Miller said all kinds of beautiful things about friendship, which Hans took down in a note-book, and used to read over at night, for he was a very good scholar.

"Now it happened that one evening little Hans was sitting by his fireside when a loud rap came at the door. It was a very wild night, and the wind was blowing and roaring round the house so terribly that at first he thought it was merely the storm. But a second rap came, and then a third, louder than either of the others.

" 'It is some poor traveller,' said little Hans to himself, and he ran to the door.

"There stood the Miller with a lantern in one hand and a big stick in the other.

" 'Dear little Hans,' cried the Miller, 'I am in great trouble. My little boy has fallen off a ladder and hurt himself, and I am going for the Doctor. But he lives so far away, and it is such a bad night, that it has just occurred to me that it would be much better if you went instead of me. You know I am going to give you my wheelbarrow, and so it is only fair that you should do something for me in return.'

" 'Certainly,' cried little Hans, 'I take it quite as a compliment your coming to me, and I will start off at once. But you must lend me your lantern, as the night is so dark that I am afraid I might fall into the ditch.'

" 'I am very sorry,' answered the Miller, 'but it is my new lantern, and it would be a great loss to me if anything happened to it.'

" 'Well, never mind, I will do without it,' cried little Hans, and he took down his great fur coat, and his warm scarlet cap, and tied a muffler round his throat, and started off.

"What a dreadful night it was! The night was so black that little Hans could hardly see, and the wind was so strong that he could scarcely stand. However, he was very courageous, and after he had been walking about three hours, he arrived at the Doctor's house, and knocked at the door.

" 'Who is there?' cried the Doctor, putting his head out of his bedroom window.

" 'Little Hans, Doctor.'

" 'What do you want, little Hans?'

" 'The Miller's son has fallen from a ladder, and

has hurt himself, and the Miller wants you to come at once.'

" 'All right !' said the Doctor; and he ordered his horse, and his big boots, and his lantern, and came downstairs, and rode off in the direction of the Miller's house, little Hans trudging behind him.

"But the storm grew worse and worse, and the rain fell in torrents, and little Hans could not see where he was going, or keep up with the horse. At last he lost his way, and wandered off on the moor, which was a very dangerous place, as it was full of deep holes, and there poor little Hans was drowned. His body was found the next day by some goat-herds, floating in a great pool of water, and was brought back by them to the cottage.

"Everybody went to little Hans's funeral, as he was so popular, and the Miller was the chief mourner.

" 'As I was his best friend,' said the Miller, 'it is only fair that I should have the best place;' so he walked at the head of the procession in a long black cloak, and every now and then he wiped his eyes with a big pocket-handkerchief.

" 'Little Hans is certainly a great loss to every one,' said the Blacksmith, when the funeral was over, and they were all seated comfortably in the inn, drinking spiced wine and eating sweet cakes.

" 'A great loss to me at any rate,' answered the Miller: 'why, I had as good as given him my wheel-barrow, and now I really don't know what to do

with it. It is very much in my way at home, and
it is in such bad repair that I could not get anything
for it if I sold it. I will certainly take care not to
give away anything again. One always suffers for
being generous.' "

"Well?" said the Water-rat, after a long pause.

"Well, that is the end," said the Linnet.

"But what became of the Miller?" asked the
Water-rat.

"Oh! I really don't know," replied the Linnet;
"and I am sure that I don't care."

"It is quite evident then that you have no sympathy in your nature," said the Water-rat.

"I am afraid you don't quite see the moral of
the story," remarked the Linnet.

"The what?" screamed the Water-rat.

"The moral."

"Do you mean to say that the story has a
moral?"

"Certainly," said the Linnet.

"Well, really," said the Water-rat, in a very angry
manner, "I think you should have told me that
before you began. If you had done so, I certainly
would not have listened to you; in fact, I should
have said 'Pooh,' like the critic. However, I can
say it now;" so he shouted out "Pooh" at the top
of his voice, gave a whisk with his tail, and went
back into his hole.

"And how do you like the Water-rat?" asked
the Duck, who came paddling up some minutes

afterwards. "He has a great many good points, but for my own part I have a mother's feelings, and I can never look at a confirmed bachelor without the tears coming into my eyes."

"I am rather afraid that I have annoyed him," said the Linnet. "The fact is, that I told him a story with a moral."

"Ah! that is always a very dangerous thing to do," said the Duck.

And I quite agree with her.

THE REMARKABLE ROCKET

THE King's son was going to be married, so there were general rejoicings. He had waited a whole year for his bride, and at last she had arrived. She was a Russian Princess, and had driven all the way from Finland in a sledge drawn by six reindeer. The sledge was shaped like a great golden swan, and between the swan's wings lay the little Princess herself. Her long ermine cloak reached right down to her feet, on her head was a tiny cap of silver tissue, and she was as pale as the Snow Palace in which she had always lived. So pale was she that as she drove through the streets all the people wondered. "She is like a white rose!" they cried, and they threw down flowers on her from the balconies.

At the gate of the Castle the Prince was waiting to receive her. He had dreamy violet eyes, and his hair was like fine gold. When he saw her he sank upon one knee, and kissed her hand.

"Your picture was beautiful," he murmured, "but you are more beautiful than your picture;" and the little Princess blushed.

"She was like a white rose before," said a young

page to his neighbour, "but she is like a red rose now;" and the whole Court was delighted.

For the next three days everybody went about saying, "White rose, Red rose, Red rose, White rose;" and the King gave orders that the Page's salary was to be doubled. As he received no salary at all this was not of much use to him, but it was considered a great honour, and was duly published in the Court Gazette.

When the three days were over the marriage was celebrated. It was a magnificent ceremony, and the bride and bridegroom walked hand in hand under a canopy of purple velvet embroidered with little pearls. Then there was a State Banquet, which lasted for five hours. The Prince and Princess sat at the top of the Great Hall and drank out of a cup of clear crystal. Only true lovers could drink out of this cup, for if false lips touched it, it grew grey and dull and cloudy.

"It is quite clear that they love each other," said the little Page, "as clear as crystal!" and the King doubled his salary a second time. "What an honour!" cried all the courtiers.

After the banquet there was to be a Ball. The bride and bridegroom were to dance the Rose-dance together, and the King had promised to play the flute. He played very badly, but no one had ever dared to tell him so, because he was the King. Indeed, he only knew two airs, and was never quite certain which one he was playing; but it made no matter, for, whatever he did, everybody cried out, "Charming! charming!"

The last item on the programme was a grand display of fireworks, to be let off exactly at midnight. The little Princess had never seen a firework in her life, so the King had given orders that the Royal Pyrotechnist should be in attendance on the day of her marriage.

"What are fireworks like?" she had asked the Prince, one morning, as she was walking on the terrace.

"They are like the Aurora Borealis," said the King, who always answered questions that were addressed to other people, "only much more natural. I prefer them to stars myself, as you always know when they are going to appear, and they are as delightful as my own flute-playing. You must certainly see them."

So at the end of the King's garden a great stand had been set up, and as soon as the Royal Pyrotechnist had put everything in its proper place, the fireworks began to talk to each other.

"The world is certainly very beautiful," cried a little Squib. "Just look at those yellow tulips. Why! if they were real crackers they could not be lovelier. I am very glad I have travelled. Travel improves the mind wonderfully, and does away with all one's prejudices."

"The King's garden is not the world, you foolish

squib," said a big Roman Candle; "the world is an enormous place, and it would take you three days to see it thoroughly."

"Any place you love is the world to you," exclaimed a pensive Catharine Wheel, who had been attached to an old deal box in early life, and prided herself on her broken heart; "but love is not fashionable any more, the poets have killed it. They wrote so much about it that nobody believed them, and I am not surprised. True love suffers, and is silent. I remember myself once——. But it is no matter now. Romance is a thing of the past."

"Nonsense!" said the Roman Candle, "Romance never dies. It is like the moon, and lives for ever. The bride and bridegroom, for instance, love each other very dearly. I heard all about them this morning from a brown-paper cartridge, who happened to be staying in the same drawer as myself, and knew the latest Court news."

But the Catharine Wheel shook her head. "Romance is dead, Romance is dead, Romance is dead," she murmured. She was one of those people who think that, if you say the same thing over and over a great many times, it becomes true in the end.

Suddenly, a sharp, dry cough was heard, and they all looked round.

It came from a tall, supercilious-looking Rocket, who was tied to the end of a long stick. He always coughed before he made any observation, so as to attract attention.

"Ahem! ahem!" he said, and everybody listened except the poor Catharine Wheel, who was still shaking her head, and murmuring, "Romance is dead."

"Order! order!" cried out a Cracker. He was something of a politician, and had always taken a prominent part in the local elections, so he knew the proper Parliamentary expressions to use.

"Quite dead," whispered the Catharine Wheel, and she went off to sleep.

As soon as there was perfect silence, the Rocket coughed a third time and began. He spoke with a very slow, distinct voice, as if he was dictating his memoirs, and always looked over the shoulder of the person to whom he was talking. In fact, he had a most distinguished manner.

"How fortunate it is for the King's son," he remarked, "that he is to be married on the very day on which I am to be let off. Really, if it had been arranged beforehand, it could not have turned out better for him; but Princes are always lucky."

"Dear me!" said the little Squib, "I thought it was quite the other way, and that we were to be let off in the Prince's honour."

"It may be so with you," he answered, "indeed, I have no doubt that it is, but with me it is different. I am a very remarkable Rocket, and come of remarkable parents. My mother was the most celebrated Catharine Wheel of her day, and was renowned for her graceful dancing. When she made her great public appearance she spun around nineteen times before she went out, and each time that she did so she threw into the air seven pink stars. She was three feet and a half in diameter, and made of the very best gunpowder. My father was a Rocket like myself, and of French extraction. He flew so high that the people were afraid that he would never come down again. He did, though, for he was of a kindly disposition, and he made a most brilliant descent in a shower of golden rain. The newspapers wrote about his performance in very flattering terms. Indeed, the Court Gazette called him a triumph of Pylotechnic art."

"Pyrotechnic, Pyrotechnic, you mean," said a Bengal Light; "I know it is Pyrotechnic, for I saw it written on my own canister."

"Well, I said Pylotechnic," answered the Rocket, in a severe tone of voice, and the Bengal Light felt so crushed that he began at once to bully the little squibs, in order to show that he was still a person of some importance.

"I was saying," continued the Rocket, "I was saying—— What was I saying?"

"You were talking about yourself," replied the Roman Candle.

"Of course; I knew I was discussing some interesting subject when I was so rudely interrupted. I hate rudeness and bad manners of every kind, for I am extremely sensitive. No one in the whole world is so sensitive as I am, I am quite sure of that."

"What is a sensitive person?" said the Cracker to the Roman Candle.

"A person who, because he has corns himself, always treads on other people's toes," answered the Roman Candle in a low whisper; and the Cracker nearly exploded with laughter.

"Pray, what are you laughing at?" inquired the Rocket; "I am not laughing."

"I am laughing because I am happy," replied the Cracker.

"That is a very selfish reason," said the Rocket angrily. "What right have you to be happy? You should be thinking about others. In fact, you should be thinking about me. I am always thinking about myself, and I expect everybody else to do the same. That is what is called sympathy. It is a beautiful virtue, and I possess it in a high degree. Suppose, for instance, anything happened to me to-night, what a misfortune that would be for every one! The Prince and Princess would never be happy again, their whole married life would be spoiled; and as for the King, I know he would not get over it. Really, when I begin to reflect on the importance of my position, I am almost moved to tears."

"If you want to give pleasure to others," cried the Roman Candle, "you had better keep yourself dry."

"Certainly," exclaimed the Bengal Light, who

was now in better spirits; "that is only common sense."

"Common sense, indeed!" said the Rocket indignantly; "you forget that I am very uncommon, and very remarkable. Why, anybody can have common sense, provided that they have no imagination. But I have imagination, for I never think of things as they really are; I always think of them as being quite different. As for keeping myself dry, there is evidently no one here who can at all appreciate an emotional nature. Fortunately for myself, I don't care. The only thing that sustains one through life is the consciousness of the immense inferiority of everybody else, and this is a feeling that I have always cultivated. But none of you have any hearts. Here you are laughing and making merry just as if the Prince and Princess had not just been married."

"Well, really," exclaimed a small Fire-balloon, "why not? It is a most joyful occasion, and when I soar up into the air I intend to tell the stars all about it. You will see them twinkle when I talk to them about the pretty bride."

"Ah! what a trivial view of life!" said the Rocket; "but it is only what I expected. There is nothing in you; you are hollow and empty. Why, perhaps the Prince and Princess may go to live in a country where there is a deep river, and perhaps they may have one only son, a little fair-haired boy with violet eyes like the Prince himself; and perhaps some day he may go out to walk with his nurse; and perhaps the nurse may go to sleep under a great elder-tree; and perhaps the little boy may fall into the deep river and be drowned. What a terrible misfortune! Poor people, to lose their only son! It is really too dreadful! I shall never get over it."

"But they have not lost their only son," said the Roman Candle; "no misfortune has happened to them at all."

"I never said that they had," replied the Rocket; "I said that they might. If they had lost their only son there would be no use in saying anything more about the matter. I hate people who cry over spilt milk. But when I think that they might lose their only son, I certainly am very much affected."

"You certainly are!" cried the Bengal Light. "In fact, you are the most affected person I ever met."

"You are the rudest person I ever met," said the Rocket, "and you cannot understand my friendship for the Prince."

"Why, you don't even know him," growled the Roman Candle.

"I never said I knew him," answered the Rocket. "I dare say if I knew him I should not be his friend at all. It is a very dangerous thing to know one's friends."

"You had really better keep yourself dry," said the Fire-balloon. "That is the important thing."

"Very important for you, I have no doubt," an-

swered the Rocket, "but I shall weep if I choose;"
and he actually burst into real tears, which flowed
down his stick like rain-drops, and nearly drowned
two little beetles, who were just thinking of setting
up house together, and were looking for a nice dry
spot to live in.

"He must have a truly romantic nature," said
the Catharine Wheel, "for he weeps when there is
nothing at all to weep about;" and she heaved a
deep sigh, and thought about the deal box.

But the Roman Candle and the Bengal Light were
quite indignant, and kept saying, "Humbug! humbug!" at the top of their voices. They were extremely practical, and whenever they objected to
anything they called it humbug.

Then the moon rose like a wonderful silver
shield; and the stars began to shine, and a sound
of music came from the palace.

The Prince and Princess were leading the dance.
They danced so beautifully that the tall white lilies
peeped in at the window and watched them, and
the great red poppies nodded their heads and beat
time.

Then ten o'clock struck, and then eleven, and
then twelve, and at the last stroke of midnight every
one came out on the terrace, and the King sent for
the Royal Pyrotechnist.

"Let the fireworks begin," said the King; and the
Royal Pyrotechnist made a low bow, and marched
down to the end of the garden. He had six attend-

ants with him, each of whom carried a lighted torch at the end of a long pole.

It was certainly a magnificent display.

Whizz! Whizz! went the Catharine Wheel, as she spun round and round. Boom! Boom! went the Roman Candle. Then the Squibs danced all over the place, and the Bengal Lights made everything look scarlet. "Good-bye," cried the Fire-balloon, as he soared away dropping tiny blue sparks. Bang! Bang! answered the Crackers, who were enjoying themselves immensely. Every one was a great success except the Remarkable Rocket. He was so damp with crying that he could not go off at all. The best thing in him was the gunpowder, and that was so wet with tears that it was of no use. All his poor relations, to whom he would never speak, except with a sneer, shot up into the sky like wonderful golden flowers with blossoms of fire. "Huzza! Huzza!" cried the Court; and the little Princess laughed with pleasure.

"I suppose they are reserving me for some grand occasion," said the Rocket; "no doubt that is what it means," and he looked more supercilious than ever.

The next day the workmen came to put everything tidy. "This is evidently a deputation," said the Rocket; "I will receive them with becoming dignity;" so he put his nose in the air, and began to frown severely as if he were thinking about some very important subject. But they took no notice of him at all till they were just going away. Then one of them caught sight of him. "Hallo!" he cried, "what a bad rocket!" and he threw him over the wall into the ditch.

"BAD Rocket; BAD Rocket?" he said as he whirled through the air; "impossible! GRAND Rocket, that is what the man said. BAD and GRAND sound very much the same, indeed they often are the same;" and he fell into the mud.

"It is not comfortable here," he remarked, "but no doubt it is some fashionable watering-place, and they have sent me away to recruit my health. My nerves are certainly very much shattered, and I require rest."

Then a little Frog, with bright jewelled eyes, and a green mottled coat, swam up to him.

"A new arrival, I see!" said the Frog. "Well, after all there is nothing like mud. Give me rainy weather and a ditch, and I am quite happy. Do you think it will be a wet afternoon? I am sure I hope so, but the sky is quite blue and cloudless. What a pity!"

"Ahem! ahem!" said the Rocket, and he began to cough.

"What a delightful voice you have!" cried the Frog. "Really it is quite like a croak, and croaking is of course the most musical sound in the world. You will hear our glee-club this evening. We sit in the old duck-pond close by the farmer's house, and as soon as the moon rises we begin. It is so

entrancing that everybody lies awake to listen to us.
In fact, it was only yesterday that I heard the
farmer's wife say to her mother that she could not
get a wink of sleep at night on account of us. It
is most gratifying to find oneself so popular."

"Ahem! ahem!" said the Rocket angrily. He was
very much annoyed that he could not get a word in.

"A delightful voice, certainly," continued the
Frog; "I hope you will come over to the duck-pond.
I am off to look for my daughters. I have six
beautiful daughters, and I am so afraid the Pike
may meet them. He is a perfect monster, and
would have no hesitation in breakfasting off them.
Well, good-bye: I have enjoyed our conversation
very much, I assure you."

"Conversation, indeed!" said the Rocket. "You
have talked the whole time yourself. That is not
conversation."

"Somebody must listen," answered the Frog,
"and I like to do all the talking myself. It saves
time, and prevents arguments."

"But I like arguments," said the Rocket.

"I hope not," said the Frog complacently. "Arguments are extremely vulgar, for everybody in
good society holds exactly the same opinions.
Good-bye a second time; I see my daughters in the
distance;" and the little Frog swam away.

"You are a very irritating person," said the
Rocket, "and very ill-bred. I hate people who talk
about themselves, as you do, when one wants to

talk about oneself, as I do.   It is what I call selfishness, and selfishness is a most detestable thing, espe-
cially to any one of my temperament, for I am well
known for my sympathetic nature.   In fact, you
should take example by me, you could not possibly
have a better model.   Now that you have the chance
you had better avail yourself of it, for I am going
back to Court almost immediately.   I am a great
favourite at Court; in fact, the Prince and Princess
were married yesterday in my honour.   Of course
you know nothing of these matters, for you are a
provincial."

"There is no good talking to him," said a Dragon-
fly, who was sitting on the top of a large brown
bulrush; "no good at all, for he has gone away."

"Well, that is his loss, not mine," answered the
Rocket.   "I am not going to stop talking to him
merely because he pays no attention.   I like hearing
myself talk.   It is one of my greatest pleasures.   I
often have long conversations all by myself, and I
am so clever that sometimes I don't understand a
single word of what I am saying."

"Then you should certainly lecture on Philosophy," said the Dragon-fly; and he spread a pair of
lovely gauze wings and soared away into the sky.

"How very silly of him not to stay here!" said
the Rocket.   "I am sure that he has not often got
such a chance of improving his mind.   However, I
don't care a bit.   Genius like mine is sure to be

appreciated some day;" and he sank down a little deeper into the mud.

After some time a large White Duck swam up to him. She had yellow legs, and webbed feet, and was considered a great beauty on account of her waddle.

"Quack, quack, quack," she said. "What a curious shape you are! May I ask were you born like that, or is it the result of an accident?"

"It is quite evident that you have always lived in the country," answered the Rocket, "otherwise you would know who I am. However, I excuse your ignorance. It would be unfair to expect other people to be as remarkable as oneself. You will no doubt be surprised to hear that I can fly up into the sky, and come down in a shower of golden rain."

"I don't think much of that," said the Duck, "as I cannot see what use it is to any one. Now, if you could plough the fields like the ox, or draw a cart like the horse, or look after the sheep like the collie-dog, that would be something."

"My good creature," cried the Rocket in a very haughty tone of voice, "I see that you belong to the lower orders. A person of my position is never useful. We have certain accomplishments, and that is more than sufficient. I have no sympathy myself with industry of any kind, least of all with such industries as you seem to recommend. Indeed, I have always been of opinion that hard work is simply the refuge of people who have nothing whatever to do."

"Well, well," said the Duck, who was of a very peaceable disposition, and never quarrelled with any one, "everybody has different tastes. I hope, at any rate, that you are going to take up your residence here."

"Oh! dear no," cried the Rocket. "I am merely a visitor, a distinguished visitor. The fact is that I find this place rather tedious. There is neither society here, nor solitude. In fact, it is essentially suburban. I shall probably go back to Court, for I know that I am destined to make a sensation in the world."

"I had thoughts of entering public life once myself," remarked the Duck; "there are so many things that need reforming. Indeed, I took the chair at a meeting some time ago, and we passed resolutions condemning everything that we did not like. However, they did not seem to have much effect. Now I go in for domesticity, and look after my family."

"I am made for public life," said the Rocket, "and so are all my relations, even the humblest of them. Whenever we appear we excite great attention. I have not actually appeared myself, but when I do so it will be a magnificent sight. As for domesticity, it ages one rapidly, and distracts one's mind from higher things."

"Ah! the higher things of life, how fine they are!"

said the Duck; "and that reminds me how hungry I feel:" and she swam away down the stream, saying, "Quack, quack, quack."

"Come back! come back!" screamed the Rocket, "I have a great deal to say to you;" but the Duck paid no attention to him. "I am glad that she has gone," he said to himself, "she has a decidedly middle-class mind;" and he sank a little deeper still into the mud, and began to think about the loneliness of genius, when suddenly two little boys in white smocks came running down the bank, with a kettle and some faggots.

"This must be the deputation," said the Rocket, and he tried to look very dignified.

"Hallo!" cried one of the boys, "look at this old stick! I wonder how it came here;" and he picked the rocket out of the ditch.

"OLD Stick!" said the Rocket, "impossible! GOLD Stick, that is what he said, Gold Stick is very complimentary. In fact, he mistakes me for one of the Court dignitaries!"

"Let us put it into the fire!" said the other boy, "it will help to boil the kettle."

So they piled the faggots together, and put the Rocket on top, and lit the fire.

"This is magnificent," cried the Rocket, "they are going to let me off in broad daylight, so that every one can see me."

"We will go to sleep now," they said, "and when

we wake up the kettle will be boiled;" and they lay
down on the grass, and shut their eyes.

The Rocket was very damp, so he took a long
time to burn. At last, however, the fire caught him.

"Now I am going off!" he cried, and he made
himself very stiff and straight. "I know I shall
go much higher than the stars, much higher than
the moon, much higher than the sun. In fact, I
shall go so high that——"

Fizz! Fizz! Fizz! and he went straight up into
the air.

"Delightful!" he cried, "I shall go on like this
for ever. What a success I am!"

But nobody saw him.

Then he began to feel a curious tingling sensation
all over him.

"Now I am going to explode," he cried. "I shall
set the whole world on fire, and make such a noise,
that nobody will talk about anything else for a whole
year." And he certainly did explode. Bang! Bang!
Bang! went the gunpowder. There was no doubt
about it.

But nobody heard him, not even the two little
boys, for they were sound asleep.

Then all that was left of him was the stick, and
this fell down on the back of a Goose who was
taking a walk by the side of the ditch.

"Good heavens!" cried the Goose. "It is going
to rain sticks;" and she rushed into the water.

"I knew I should create a great sensation," gasped
the Rocket, and he went out.

POEMS IN PROSE

THE ARTIST.

ONE evening there came into his soul the desire to fashion an image of "The Pleasure that Abideth for a Moment." And he went forth into the world to look for bronze. For he could only think in bronze.

But all the bronze of the whole world had disappeared; nor anywhere in the whole world was there any bronze to be found, save only the bronze of the image of "The Sorrow that Endureth for Ever."

Now this image he had himself, and with his own hands, fashioned, and had set on the tomb of the one thing he had loved in life. On the tomb of the dead thing he had most loved had he set this image of his own fashioning, that it might serve as a sign of the love of a man that dieth not, and a symbol of the sorrow of man that 'endureth for ever. And in the whole world there was no other bronze save the bronze of this image.

And he took the image he had fashioned, and set it in a great furnace, and gave it to the fire.

And out of the bronze of the image of "The Sorrow that Endureth for Ever" he fashioned an image of "The Pleasure that Abideth for a Moment."

THE DOER OF GOOD.

It was night-time, and He was alone.

And He saw afar off the walls of a round city, and went towards the city.

And when He came near He heard within the city the tread of the feet of joy, and the laughter of the mouth of gladness, and the loud noise of many lutes. And He knocked at the gate and certain of the gate-keepers opened to Him.

And He beheld a house that was of marble, and had fair pillars of marble before it. The pillars were hung with garlands, and within and without there were torches of cedar. And He entered the house.

And when He had passed through the hall of chalcedony and the hall of jasper, and reached the long hall of feasting, He saw lying on a couch of sea-purple one whose hair was crowned with red roses and whose lips were red with wine.

And He went behind him and touched him on the shoulder, and said to him:

"Why do you live like this?"

And the young man turned round and recognised Him, and made answer, and said: "But I was a leper once, and you healed me. How else should I live?"

And He passed out of the house and went again into the street.

And after a little while He saw one whose face and raiment were painted and whose feet were shod with pearls. And behind her came slowly, as a hunter, a young man who wore a cloak of two colours. Now the face of the woman was as the fair face of an idol, and the eyes of the young man were bright with lust.

And He followed swiftly, and touched the hand of the young man, and said to him: "Why do you look at this woman and in such wise?"

And the young man turned round and recognised Him, and said: "But I was blind once, and you gave me sight. At what else should I look?"

And He ran forward and touched the painted raiment of the woman, and said to her: "Is there no other way in which to walk save the way of sin?"

And the woman turned round and recognised Him, and laughed, and said: "But you forgave me my sins, and the way is a pleasant way."

And He passed out of the city.

And when He had passed out of the city, He saw, seated by the roadside, a young man who was weeping.

And He went towards him and touched the long locks of his hair, and said to him: "Why are you weeping?"

And the young man looked up and recognised Him, and made answer: "But I was dead once, and you raised me from the dead. What else should I do but weep?"

THE DISCIPLE.

WHEN Narcissus died, the pool of his pleasure changed from a cup of sweet waters into a cup of salt tears, and the Oreads came weeping through the woodland that they might sing to the pool and give it comfort.

And when they saw that the pool had changed from a cup of sweet waters into a cup of salt tears, they loosened the green tresses of their hair, and cried to the pool, and said: "We do not wonder that you should mourn in this manner for Narcissus, so beautiful was he."

"But was Narcissus beautiful?" said the pool.

"Who should know better than you?" answered the Oreads. "Us did he ever pass by, but you he sought for, and would lie on your banks and look down at you, and in the mirror of your waters he would mirror his own beauty."

And the pool answered: "But I loved Narcissus because, as he lay on my banks and looked down at me, in the mirror of his eyes I saw my own beauty mirrored."

202

THE MASTER.

AND when the darkness came over the earth, Joseph of Arimathea, having lighted a torch of pinewood, passed down from the hill into the valley. For he had business in his own home.

And kneeling on the flint stones of the Valley of Desolation he saw a young man who was naked and weeping. His hair was the colour of honey, and his body was as a white flower; but he had wounded his body with thorns, and on his hair he had set ashes as a crown.

And he who had great possessions said to the young man who was naked: "I do not wonder that your sorrow is so great, for surely He was a just man."

And the young man answered: "It is not for Him that I am weeping, but for myself. I, too, have changed water into wine, and I have healed the leper and given sight to the blind. I have walked upon the waters, and from the dwellers in the tombs I have cast out devils. I have fed the hungry in the desert where there was no food, and I have raised the dead from their narrow houses; and at my bidding, and before a great multitude of people, a barren fig-tree withered away. All things that this man has done I have done also. And yet they have not crucified me."

THE HOUSE OF JUDGMENT.

AND there was silence in the House of Judgment. And the Man came naked before God.

And God opened the Book of the Life of the Man.

And God said to the Man: "Thy life hath been evil, and thou hast shewn cruelty to those who were in need of succour; and to those who lacked help thou hast been bitter and hard of heart. The poor called to thee and thou didst not hearken, and thine ears were closed to the cry of My afflicted. The inheritance thou didst take unto thyself, and thou didst send the foxes into the vineyard of thy neighbour's field. Thou didst take the bread of the children and give it to the dogs to eat, and My lepers, who lived in the marshes and were at peace and praised Me, thou didst drive forth on to the highways; and on Mine earth, out of which I made thee, thou didst spill innocent blood."

And the Man made answer and said: "Even so did I."

And again God opened the Book of the Life of the Man.

And God said to the Man: "Thy life hath been

evil: and the Beauty I have shewn thou hast sought for, and the Good I have hidden thou didst pass by. The walls of thy chamber were painted with images and from the bed of thy abominations thou didst rise up to the sound of flutes. Thou didst build seven altars to the sins I have suffered and didst eat of the thing that may not be eaten, and the purple of thy raiment was broidered with the three signs of shame. Thine idols were neither of gold nor of silver that endure, but of flesh that dieth. Thou didst stain their hair with perfumes and put pomegranates in their hands. Thou didst stain their feet with saffron and spread carpets before them. With antimony thou didst stain their eyelids, and their bodies thou didst smear with myrrh. Thou didst bow thyself to the ground before them, and the thrones of thine idols were set in the sun. Thou didst shew to the sun thy shame and to the moon thy madness."

And the Man made answer and said: "Even so did I."

And a third time God opened the Book of the Life of the Man.

And God said to the Man: "Evil hath been thy life, and with evil didst thou requite good, and with wrong-doing kindness. The hands that fed thee thou didst wound, and the breasts that gave thee suck thou didst despise. He who came to thee for water went away thirsting, and the outlawed men who hid thee in their tents at night thou didst betray before dawn. Thine enemy who spared thee thou didst snare in an ambush, and the friend who walked with thee thou didst sell for a price, and to those who brought thee Love thou didst ever give Lust in thy turn."

And the Man made answer and said: "Even so did I."

And God closed the Book of the Life of the Man, and said: "Surely I will send thee into Hell. Even unto Hell will I send thee."

And the Man cried out: "Thou canst not."

And God said to the Man: "Wherefore can I not send thee to Hell, and for what reason?"

"Because in Hell have I always lived," answered the Man.

And there was silence in the House of Judgment.

And after a space God spake, and said to the Man: "Seeing that I may not send thee into Hell, surely I will send thee unto Heaven. Even unto Heaven will I send thee."

And the Man cried out: "Thou canst not."

And God said to the Man: "Wherefore can I not send thee unto Heaven, and for what reason?"

"Because never, and in no place, have I been able to imagine it," answered the Man.

And there was silence in the House of Judgment.

THE TEACHER OF WISDOM.

From his childhood he had been as one filled with the perfect knowledge of God, and even while he was yet but a lad many of the saints, as well as certain holy women who dwelt in the free city of his birth, had been stirred to much wonder by the grave wisdom of his answers.

And when his parents had given him the robe and the ring of manhood he kissed them, and left them, and went out into the world, that he might speak to the world about God. For there were at that time many in the world who either knew not God at all, or had but an incomplete knowledge of Him, or worshipped the false gods who dwell in groves and have no care of their worshippers.

And he set his face to the sun and journeyed, walking without sandals, as he had seen the saints walk, and carrying at his girdle a leathern wallet and a little water-bottle of burnt clay.

And as he walked along the highway he was full of joy that comes from the perfect knowledge of God, and he sang praises unto God without ceasing: and after a time he reached a strange land in which there were many cities.

And he passed through eleven cities. And some of these cities were in valleys, and others were by the banks of great rivers, and others were set on hills. And in each city he found a disciple who loved him and followed him, and a great multitude of people also followed him from each city, and the knowledge of God spread in the whole land, and many of the rulers were converted, and the priests of the temples in which there were idols found that half of their gain was gone, and when they beat upon their drums at noon, none, or but a few, came with peacocks or with offerings of flesh, as had been the custom of the land before his coming.

Yet the more the people followed him, and the greater the number of his disciples, the greater became his sorrow. And he knew not why his sorrow was so great. For he spoke ever about God, and out of the fulness of that perfect knowledge of God which God had Himself given to him.

And one evening he passed out of the eleventh city, which was a city of Armenia, and his disciples and a great crowd followed after him: and he went up on to a mountain, and sat down on a rock that was on the mountain, and his disciples stood round him, and the multitude knelt in the valley.

And he bowed his head on his hands and wept, and said to his soul: "Why is it that I am full of sorrow and fear, and that each of my disciples is as an enemy that walks in the noonday?"

And his soul answered him and said: "God filled

thee with the perfect knowledge of Himself, and thou hast given this knowledge away to others. The pearl of great price thou hast divided, and the vesture without seam thou hast parted asunder. He who giveth away wisdom robbeth himself. He is as one who giveth his treasure to a robber. Is not God wiser than thou art? Who are thou to give away the secret that God hath told thee? I was rich once, and thou hast made me poor. Once I saw God, and now thou hast hidden Him from me."

And he wept again, for he knew that his soul spake truth to him, and that he had given to others the perfect knowledge of God, and that he was as one clinging to the skirts of God, and that his faith was leaving him by reason of the number of those who believed in him.

And he said to himself: "I will talk no more about God. He who giveth away wisdom robbeth himself."

And after the space of some hours his disciples came near him and bowed themselves to the ground and said: "Master, talk to us about God, for thou hast the perfect knowledge of God, and no man save thee hath this knowledge."

And he answered them and said: "I will talk to you about all other things that are in Heaven and on earth, but about God I will not talk to you. Neither now, nor at any time, will I talk to you about God."

And they were wroth with him, and said to him:

"Thou hast led us into the desert that we might hearken to thee. Wilt thou send us away hungry, and the great multitude that thou hast made to follow thee?"

And he answered them and said: "I will not talk to you about God."

And the multitude murmured against him, and said to him: "Thou hast led us into the desert and hast given us no food to eat. Talk to us about God and it will suffice us."

But he answered them not a word. For he knew that if he spake to them about God he would give away his treasure.

And his disciples went away sadly, and the multitude of people returned to their own homes. And many died on the way.

And when he was alone he rose up and set his face to the moon, and journeyed for seven moons, speaking to no man nor making any answer. And when the seventh moon had waned he reached that desert which is the desert of the Great River. And having found a cavern in which a centaur had once dwelt, he took it for his place of dwelling, and made himself a mat of reeds on which to lie, and became a Hermit. And every hour the Hermit praised God that He had suffered him to keep some knowledge of Him and of His wonderful greatness.

Now one evening as the Hermit was seated before the cavern in which he had made his place of dwelling, he beheld a young man of evil and beautiful

face who passed by in mean apparel and with empty
hands.   Every evening with empty hands the young
man passed by, and every morning he returned with
his hands full of purple and pearls.   He was a robber, and robbed the caravans of the merchants.

And the Hermit looked at him and pitied him.
But he spoke not a word.   For he knew that he who
speaks a word loses his faith.

And one morning, as the young man returned
with his hands full of purple and pearls, he stopped
and frowned and stamped his foot upon the sand,
and said to the Hermit: "Why do you look at me
ever in this manner as I pass by?   What is it that
I see in your eyes?   For no man has looked at me
before in this manner.   And the thing is a thorn and
a trouble to me."

And the Hermit answered him and said: "What
you see in my eyes is pity.   Pity is what looks out
at you from my eyes."

And the young man laughed with scorn, and cried
to the Hermit in a bitter voice, and said to him: "I
have purple and pearls in my hands, and you have
but a mat of reeds on which to lie.   What pity
should you have for me?   And for what reason
have you this pity?"

"I have pity for you," said the Hermit, "because
you have no knowledge of God."

"Is this knowledge of God a precious thing?"
asked the young man, and he came close to the
mouth of the cavern.

"It is more precious than all the purple and pearls of the whole world," answered the Hermit.

"And have you got it?" said the young Robber, and he came closer still.

"Once indeed," answered the Hermit, "I possessed the perfect knowledge of God. But in my foolishness I parted with it, and divided it amongst others. Yet even now is such knowledge as remains to me more precious than purple or pearls."

And when the young Robber heard this he threw away the purple and the pearls that he was bearing in his hands, and drawing a sharp sword of curved steel, he said to the Hermit: "Give me, forthwith, this knowledge of God that you possess, or I will surely slay you. Wherefore should I not slay him who has a treasure greater than my treasure?"

And the Hermit spread out his arms and said: "Were it not better for me to go unto the uttermost courts of God and praise Him, than to live in the world and have no knowledge of Him? Slay me if that be your desire. But I will not give away my knowledge of God."

And the young Robber knelt down, and besought him, but the Hermit would not talk to him about God, nor give him his treasure, and the young Robber rose up and said to the Hermit: "Be it as you will. As for myself, I will go to the City of the Seven Sins, that is but three days' journey from this place, and for my purple they will give me pleasure, and for my pearls they will sell me joy." And he took up the purple and the pearls and went swiftly away.

And the Hermit cried out and followed him and besought him. For the space of three days he followed the young Robber on the road and entreated him to return, nor to enter the City of the Seven Sins.

And ever and anon the young Robber looked back at the Hermit and called to him, and said : "Will you give me this knowledge of God which is more precious than purple and pearls? If you will give me that, I will not enter the City."

And ever did the Hermit answer: "All things that I have, I will give thee, save that one thing only. For that thing it is not lawful for me to give away."

And in the twilight of the third day they came nigh to the great scarlet gates of the City of the Seven Sins. And from the City there came the sound of much laughter.

And the young robber laughed in answer, and sought to knock at the gate. And as he did so, the Hermit ran forward and caught him by the skirts of his raiment, and said to him: "Stretch forth your hands, and set your arms around my neck, and put your ear close to my lips, and I will give you what remains to me of the knowledge of God."

And the young Robber stopped.

And when the Hermit had given away his knowledge of God he fell upon the ground and wept, and a great darkness hid him from the City and the young robber, so that he saw them no more.

And as he lay there weeping he was aware of One who was standing beside him; and He who was standing beside him had feet of brass and hair like fine wool. And he raised the Hermit up, and said to him: "Before this time thou hadst the perfect knowledge of God. Now thou shalt have the perfect love of God. Wherefore art thou weeping?"

And He kissed him.